PRAISE FOR *THE* COMMITTED

"The funny, excoriating voice delivering these observations has lost none of its energy since *The Sympathizer*."
—SAM SACKS, *Wall Street Journal*

"Made me think of *Midnight's Children* . . . [Nguyen] gently seduces the reader."—RUMAAN ALAM, *New York Review of Books*

"One of the more irresistible characters in recent fiction . . . an even wilder book than *The Sympathizer*."
—CHRISTIAN LORENTZEN, *London Review of Books*

"Sumptuous . . . Captures, with grace and restraint, the foibles of two young men caught in a duel between East and West."—*O Magazine*

"Fierce in tone, capacious, witty, sharp."—OCEAN VUONG

"Rich and exhilarating . . . A deep, compelling, and humorous portrait of how we are shaped by fictions others have for us."—LAILA LALAMI

"Full of breathtaking and luminous insights and a pure joy to read."—EDWARD P. JONES

## Praise for *The Committed*

An Instant *New York Times* Bestseller
A *New York Times Book Review* Editors' Choice
An Amazon Best Book of the Month

"An invitation to the reader to think, not just to feel: to think deeply about political systems and ideologies, whose interests they serve and what, if any, answers they can provide . . . A powerful challenge to an enduring narrative of colonialism and neocolonialism. One waits to see what Nguyen, and the man of two faces, will do next."          —Aminatta Forna, *The Guardian*

"Powerfully influenced by the equally anonymous narrator of Ralph Ellison's *Invisible Man* . . . In *The Committed*, [the Captain] is mostly a cynic, and he has been ever since *The Sympathizer*. This is the heart of his charm, which in this reader's opinion is more potent than that of the French . . . He is free to let his sardonic flag fly. He's at his funniest when pointing out the absurdities around him."          —Laura Miller, *Slate*

"Nguyen is a perceptive, scathing, and genuinely funny writer . . . [He] is a maximalist par excellence, and the furious pace of this novel rarely lets up . . . The moments of pause, when they do come, testify powerfully to this reverberating violence, and to Nguyen's considerable skills as a novelist."          —Piper French, *Los Angeles Review of Books*

"The funny, excoriating voice delivering these observations has lost none of its energy since *The Sympathizer* . . . The biting back and forth of this double-edged novel remains a thrill and a provocation."          —Sam Sacks, *Wall Street Journal*

"Hinges on questions about individual and collective identity and memory, how wars are memorialized, whose war stories get told and what happens when abstract political ideologies are clumsily deployed in the real world."          —Alexandra Alter, *New York Times*

"Action-packed with sex, drugs and violence, but those events don't characterize the essence of the book. The strength of this novel is the same as that of its predecessor—the probing, sensitive, educated and droll mind of its narrator, who perceives power dynamics that few examine."

—Jenny Shank, *Minneapolis Star Tribune*

"One of the many strengths of Nguyen's writing is that nothing is spared from his clear-eyed analysis: not France, the United States, or Vietnam, not communism or capitalism, not his characters and most importantly, not his own work."

—Agatha French, *Los Angeles Times*

"Sumptuous . . . The Pulitzer Prize-winning novelist captures, with grace and restraint, the foibles of two young men caught in a duel between East and West."

—*O Magazine*, "20 of the Best Books to Pick Up This Month"

"The vibrant self-centeredness of 1980s Paris is perfectly captured in Nguyen's observant prose . . . Readers who found new ways to think about race and the refugee experience in *The Sympathizer* will find plenty more to explore." —Eliot Schrefer, *USA Today*

"Nguyen once more trades in genre staples—crime fiction and gangster drama get particularly juicy play here—but he's more dedicated than ever to the ideas behind them, the psychological experience of a life lived as haunted by war, colonization, disenfranchisement, and lies . . . Another exceptionally rendered treatise on identity and trauma."

—David Canfield, *Entertainment Weekly*

"Fortunately for us, this tormented double agent is back for another serving of ghostcolonial discontent in Nguyen's showstopper sequel . . . If this incandescent novel teaches us anything, it is that forgiveness is a joy of the living, not the burden of the dead."

—Junot Díaz, *New York Times Book Review* (cover review)

"A voice that shakes the walls of the old literary comfort zone wherein the narratives of nonwhite 'immigrants' were tasked with proving their shared humanity to a white audience . . . May that voice keep running like a purifying venom through the mainstream of our self-regard—through the American dream of distancing ourselves from what we continue to show ourselves to be."

—Jonathan Dee, *New Yorker*

"With smoke-and-mirrors panache, *The Committed* continues the travails of our Eurasian Ulysses, now relocated to France and self-identified as Vo Danh . . . From a satirical James Bond-esque spy story in *The Sympathizer*, the author shifts to James Baldwin's intersectional politics in *The Committed* to address greed, prejudice, and violence . . . *The Committed*'s revolutionary core is its plasticity—a novel of ideas that continuously shapeshifts to question its raison d'être."

—Thúy Đinh, NPR

"*The Sympathizer* and *The Committed* are, to borrow James Wood's phrase for such novels, perpetual-motion machines, their exuberance perhaps a suitable method given how vast a subject he aims to tackle . . . Nguyen does Salman Rushdie one better by deploying the conventions of genre fiction; he gently seduces the reader into two rambling, discursive works passionately interested in war and violence, race and identity, colonialism and history."

—Rumaan Alam, *New York Review of Books*

"The tension between the Tarantinoesque thriller elements and the more high-minded cultural critique mirrors the duality in the narrator, whose entire character is informed by a collision of Eastern and Western influences."     —Steven W. Beattie, *Toronto Star*

"If you made a coq au vin of John le Carré, Ralph Ellison, Amy Tan and Kurt Vonnegut, and threw in a significant amount of Red Bull and gave the potion to Edgar Wright to put on screen against a soundtrack of Eurotrash disco music, you may begin to come

close to describing *The Committed* . . . A powerhouse of a novel."
—Jana Siciliano, *Book Reporter*

"Wildly inventive . . . A wickedly lethal mix of black humor and the crueler truths of war and historical plunder. Elements of the shadowy intrigue of John le Carré and Graham Greene jostle with the revolutionary theories of Jean-Paul Sartre, *The Wretched of the Earth* author Frantz Fanon, and Aimé Césaire."
—Anderson Tepper, *Air Mail*

"Nguyen playfully subverts the tropes of crime novels, their stylized sex and violence . . . Trenchant."
—Vanessa Hua, *Journal of Alta California*

"Viet Thanh Nguyen is an American literary treasure . . . *The Committed* is another triumph of storytelling and the imagination."
—*Vietnam Veterans of America Magazine*

"A brilliant rollercoaster of ideas and action."   —*Daily Mail* (UK)

"That Nguyen can pull off this audacious marriage between gang violence and novel of ideas is down to the brilliance of his nameless narrator, a spy and a killer, the orphan son of a French priest (sacré bleu!) and a Vietnamese mother. He is strident, self-pitying, contradictory, perceptive, sentimental, unashamedly intellectual and furiously funny, a kind of post-colonial Portnoy."
—Duncan White, *Daily Telegraph* (UK)

"Excoriating . . . Savage humour keeps the reader wincing yet entertained."                           —*The Economist*

"An exhilarating roller-coaster ride . . . Pleasures abound, such as the narrator's hair-raising escapes, descriptions of the Boss's hokey bar, and thoughtful references to Fanon and Césaire. Nguyen continues to delight."        —*Publishers Weekly* (starred review)

"A quirky intellectual crime story that highlights the Vietnam War's complex legacy."        —*Kirkus Reviews* (starred review)

"Undeniably erudite and culturally fluent as ever—interweaving history, philosophy, political treatise, theology, even literary criticism—Nguyen effortlessly enhances the story with snarky commentary, sly judgments, and plenty of wink-wink-nod-nod posturing to entertain committed readers." —Terry Hong, *Booklist*

"Call *The Committed* many things. A white hot literary thriller disguised as a searing novel of ideas. An unflinching look at redemption and damnation. An unblinking examination of the dangers of belief, and the need to believe. A sequel that goes toe to toe with the original then surpasses it. A masterwork."
—Marlon James, author of *Black Leopard, Red Wolf*

"Nothing short of revelatory. As it haunts, bifurcates, and envelops us in its illumination of all that we have failed to notice about the far reaches of colonization, we are also thrilled by its many turns and charms. This book is fierce, and unrelentingly good. Hilarious and subversive, philosophical and hallucinatory, it is much more than a sequel, more like a necessary appendage in a brilliant and expansive anti-colonial body of work, from the twisted and playful mind of the one and only Viet Thanh Nguyen. Bravo."
—Tommy Orange, *New York Times*–bestselling
author of *There There*

"This follow-up to his seminal *The Sympathizer* is Nguyen at his most ambitious and bold. Fierce in tone, capacious, witty, sharp, and deeply researched, *The Committed* marks not just a sequel to its groundbreaking predecessor but a sum total accumulation of a life devoted to Vietnamese American history and scholarship. This novel, like all daring novels, is a Trojan Horse, whose hidden power is a treatise of global futurity in the aftermath of colonial conquest. It asks questions central both to Vietnamese everywhere—and to our very species: How do we live in the wake of seismic loss and betrayal? And, perhaps even more critically, How do we laugh?"
—Ocean Vuong, *New York Times*–bestselling
author of *On Earth We're Briefly Gorgeous*

"Part gangster-thriller, part searing cultural analysis of the post-colonial predicament, seen through the eyes of a Vietnamese-French mixed race bastard double agent. Paris of forty years ago swirls to life around him, from intellectual salons to filthy toilets—with glimpses of everyone from Johnny Hallyday to Frantz Fanon to Julia Kristeva. Like Ellison's *Invisible Man*, these novels will surely become classics."       —Claire Messud

"An elegy to idealism, Orientalism, and existentialism in all its tragic forms, Nguyen's novel doesn't so much inhabit early eighties Paris as it pulls the plug on the City of Light. Think of *The Committed* as the declaration of the 20th ½ Arrondissement. A squatter's paradise for those with one foot in the grave and the other shoved halfway up Western civilization's ass."       —Paul Beatty

"A splendid tapestry of a novel, full of dubious but richly realized characters. It solidifies what we already know—Viet Thanh Nguyen is a gifted storyteller. It is difficult to know where to start with the praise. The characters have a sad and often tragic complexity, and the language offers a terrific ride for the reader. This is a grand novel full of breathtaking and luminous insights and a pure joy to read. Anticipation is why we come to a book, and joy is why we keep turning page after page. *The Committed* offers both, and so very much more."       —Edward P. Jones, Pulitzer Prize–winning
author of *The Known World*

"A rich and exhilarating story of friendship, loyalty, and greed . . . Viet Thanh Nguyen gives us an unsparing look at the poisonous effects of ideology—whether colonialism, communism, or capitalism—even as he explores the deep-seated need we all have to believe in something. A deep, compelling, and humorous portrait of how we are shaped by fictions others have for us."
—Laila Lalami, author of *The Other Americans*,
finalist for the National Book Award

# THE
# COMMITTED

## Also by Viet Thanh Nguyen

### Fiction

*The Refugees*

*The Sympathizer*

### Nonfiction

*The Displaced:*
*Refugee Writers on Refugee Lives* (editor)

*Nothing Ever Dies:*
*Vietnam and the Memory of War*

*Transpacific Studies:*
*Framing an Emerging Field* (coedited with Janet Hoskins)

*Race and Resistance:*
*Literature and Politics in Asian America*

### Children's Literature

*Chicken of the Sea*
(with Ellison Nguyen, Thi Bui, and Hien Bui-Stafford)

# THE
# COMMITTED

## VIET THANH NGUYEN

Grove Press
*New York*

*Published simultaneously in Canada*
*Printed in the United States of America*

First Grove Atlantic hardcover edition: March 2021
First Grove Atlantic paperback edition: March 2022

This book was set in 12-pt. Arno Pro by Alpha Design & Composition
of Pittsfield, NH.

Library of Congress Cataloging-in-Publication data is available for this title.

ISBN 978-0-8021-5707-2
eISBN 978-0-8021-5708-9

Grove Press
an imprint of Grove Atlantic
154 West 14th Street
New York, NY 10011

Distributed by Publishers Group West

groveatlantic.com

22 23 24 25   10 9 8 7 6 5 4 3 2 1

For Simone

Nothing's more real than nothing.

  —Rithy Panh with Christophe Bataille, *The Elimination:*
  *A Survivor of the Khmer Rouge Confronts His Past and the*
  *Commandant of the Killing Fields*

# PROLOGUE

## *We*

We were the unwanted, the unneeded, and the unseen, invisible to all but ourselves. Less than nothing, we also saw nothing as we crouched blindly in the unlit belly of our ark, 150 of us sweating in a space not meant for us mammals but for the fish of the sea. With the waves driving us from side to side, we spoke in our native tongues. For some, this meant prayer; for others, curses. When a change in the motion of the waves shuttled our vessel more forcefully, one of the few sailors among us whispered, *We're on the ocean now*. After hours winding through river, estuary, and canal, we had departed our motherland.

The navigator opened the hatch and called us onto the deck of our ark, which the uncaring world denigrated as merely a boat. By the lopsided smile of the crescent moon, we saw ourselves alone on the surface of this watery world. For a moment we were giddy with delight, until the rippling ocean made us giddy in another way. All over the deck, and all over one another, we turned ourselves inside out, and even after nothing remained we continued to heave and gasp, wretched in our retching. In this manner we passed our first night on the sea, shivering with the ocean breezes.

Dawn broke, and in every direction we saw only the infinitely receding horizon. The day was hot, with no shade and no respite, with nothing to eat but a mouthful and nothing to drink but a spoonful, the length of our journey unknown and our rations limited. But even eating so little, we still left our human traces all over the deck and in the hold, and were by evening awash in our own filth. When we spotted a ship near the horizon at twilight, we screamed ourselves hoarse. But the ship kept its distance.

On the third day, we came across a freighter breaking through the vast desert of the sea, a dromedary with its bridge rising over its stern, sailors on deck. We screamed, waved, jumped up and down. But the freighter sailed on, touching us only with its wake. On the fourth and fifth days, two more cargo ships appeared, each closer than the one before, each under a different flag. The sailors pointed at us, but no matter how much we begged, pleaded, and held up our children, the ships neither swerved nor slowed.

On the fifth day, the first of the children died, and before we offered her body to the sea, the priest said a prayer. On the sixth day, a boy died. Some prayed even more fervently to God; some began doubting His existence; some who did not believe in Him began to; and some who did not believe disbelieved all the more strongly. The father of one of the dead children cried, My God, why are You doing this to us?

And it struck us all then, the answer to humanity's eternal question of *Why?*

It was, and is, simply this: *Why not?*

Strangers to one another before we clambered aboard our ark, we were now more intimate than lovers, wallowing in our own waste, our faces green, our skin blistered by salt and baked into the same shade by the sun. Most of us had fled our motherland because the communists in charge had labeled us puppets, or pseudo-pacifists,

or bourgeois nationalists, or decadent reactionaries, or intellectuals of the false conscience, or because we were related to one of these. There was also a fortune teller, a geomancer, a monk, the priest, and at least one prostitute, whose Chinese neighbor spat on her and said, Why is this whore with us?

Even among the unwanted there were unwanted, and at that some of us could only laugh.

The prostitute scowled at us and said, What do *you* want?

We, the unwanted, wanted so much. We wanted food, water, and parasols, although umbrellas would be fine. We wanted clean clothes, baths, and toilets, even of the squatting kind, since squatting on land was safer and less embarrassing than clinging to the bulwark of a rolling boat with one's posterior hanging over the edge. We wanted rain, clouds, and dolphins. We wanted it to be cooler during the hot day and warmer during the freezing night. We wanted an estimated time of arrival. We wanted not to be dead on arrival. We wanted to be rescued from being barbecued by the unrelenting sun. We wanted television, movies, music, anything with which to pass the time. We wanted love, peace, and justice, except for our enemies, whom we wanted to burn in Hell, preferably for eternity. We wanted independence and freedom, except for the communists, who should all be sent to reeducation, preferably for life. We wanted benevolent leaders who represented the people, by which we meant us and not them, whoever they were. We wanted to live in a society of equality, although if we had to settle for owning more than our neighbor, that would be fine. We wanted a revolution that would overturn the revolution we had just lived through. In sum, we wanted to want for nothing!

What we most certainly did not want was a storm, and yet that was what we got on the seventh day. The faithful once more cried out, *God, help us!* The nonfaithful cried out, *God, You bastard!*

Faithful or unfaithful, there was no way to avoid the storm, dominating the horizon and surging closer and closer. Whipped into a frenzy, the wind gained momentum, and as the waves grew, our ark gained speed and altitude. Lightning illuminated the dark furrows of the storm clouds, and thunder overwhelmed our collective groan. A torrent of rain exploded on us, and as the waves propelled our vessel ever higher the faithful prayed and the unfaithful cursed, but both wept. Then our ark reached its peak and, for an eternal moment, perched on the snow-capped crest of a watery precipice. Looking down on that deep, wine-colored valley awaiting us, we were certain of two things. The first was that we were absolutely going to die! And the second was that we would almost certainly live!

Yes, we were sure of it. *We—will—live!*

And then we plunged, howling, into the abyss.

# Part One
## *Me*

# CHAPTER 1

I may no longer be a spy or a sleeper, but I am most definitely a spook. How can I not be, with two holes in my head from which leaks the black ink in which I am writing these words. What a peculiar condition, being dead yet penning these lines in my little room in Paradise. This must make me a ghostwriter, and as such, it is a simple, if spooky, matter to dip my pen into the ink flowing from my twin holes, one drilled by myself, the other by Bon, my best friend and blood brother. Put your gun down, Bon. You can only kill me once.

Or maybe not. I am also still a man of two faces and two minds, one of which might perhaps yet still be intact. With two minds, I am able to see any issue from both sides, and while I once flattered myself that this was a talent, now I understand it to be a curse. What was a man with two minds except a mutant? Perhaps even a monster. Yes, I admit it! I am not just one but two. Not just I but you. Not just me but we.

You ask me what we should be called, having been nameless for so long. I hesitate to give you a straight answer, as that has never been my habit. I am a man of bad habits, and every time I have been

broken of one—never having given up such a thing willingly—I have always gone back to it, whimpering and dewy-eyed.

Take these words, for example. I am writing them, and writing is the worst of habits. While most people squeeze what they can from their lives, suffering for their paychecks, absorbing vitamin D as they enjoy the sunshine, hunting for another member of the species with whom to procreate or just to rut, and refusing to think about death, I pass my time with pen and paper in my corner of Paradise, growing ever whiter and thinner, frustration steaming from my head, the sweat of sorrow sticking to me.

I could tell you the name I have in my passport, VO DANH. I assumed this name in anticipation of coming here to Paris, or, as our French masters taught us to call it, the City of Light. We, Bon and I, arrived in the airport at night on a flight from Jakarta. Stepping out of the airplane, we were gripped by a sense of relief, for we had reached asylum, the fever dream of all refugees, especially those rendered refugees not just once or twice but three times: 1954, nine years after I was born; 1975, when I was young and reasonably handsome; and 1979, just two years ago. Was the third time the charm, as the Americans liked to say? Bon sighed before he pulled his airline-provided sleeping mask over his eyes. Let's just hope France is better than America.

That hope was ill-advised if one judged countries by their border officials. The one who inspected my passport wore the blank mask of all security guards as he studied my photograph and then me. His pale face seemed displeased that someone had granted me access to his beloved country, this man who lacked both an upper lip and a mustache to disguise his lack. You're Vietnamese, this white man said, the first words ever uttered to me on visiting my father's homeland for the first time.

Yes! I am Vo Danh! Along with my best French accent, I gave the border policeman my most fawning smile, ingratiating to the point of being grating. But my father is French. Maybe I am also French?

His bureaucratic brain processed this statement, and when he finally smiled, I thought, *Ah! I have made my first joke in French!* But what he said was: No . . . you . . . are . . . definitely . . . not . . . French. Not . . . with . . . a . . . name . . . like . . . this. Then he stamped my passport with my date of entry, 18/07/81, and flicked it across the counter, already looking over my shoulder at the next supplicant.

I met Bon on the other side of passport control. We had at last stepped foot on *la Gaule*, as my father had taught me to call France in his parish school. It was fitting, then, that the airport was named after Charles de Gaulle, the greatest of great Frenchmen in recent memory. The hero who had liberated France from the Nazis while continuing to enslave us Vietnamese. Ah, contradiction! The perpetual body odor of humanity! No one was spared, not even the Americans or the Vietnamese, who bathed daily, or the French, who bathed less than daily. No matter our nationality, we all become accustomed to the aroma of our own contradictions.

What's wrong? he said. Are you crying again?

I'm not crying, I sobbed. I'm just so overcome to be home at last.

By now Bon was used to my unpredictable bursts of tears. He sighed and took me by the hand. In his other hand, he carried only one bag, a cheap cloth duffel, a gift of the United Nations. His bag was nowhere near as fashionable as my leather one, presented to me by my old mentor Claude when I graduated from Occidental College in Southern California. My old man gave me one just like it

when I left Phillips Exeter and went to Yale, Claude had told me, his eyes misting. Although he was a CIA agent who saw interrogation and assassination as his trade, he could be sentimental about some things, such as our friendship and high-quality men's furnishings. I held on to the leather bag for this same nostalgic reason. Even though it was not very large, the bag, like Bon's, was not full. Like most refugees we barely had any material belongings, even if our bags were packed with dreams and fantasies, trauma and pain, sorrow and loss, and, of course, ghosts. Since ghosts were weightless, we could carry an infinite number of them.

Passing the baggage carousels, we were the only passengers not pulling suitcases or pushing trolleys burdened with luggage and touristic expectation. We were not tourists, or expatriates, or returnees, or diplomats, or businessmen, or any class of dignified traveler. No, we were refugees, and our experience in a time machine called an international jetliner was not enough to dispel the year we had languished in a reeducation camp or the two years we had passed in a refugee camp on an Indonesian island called Galang. The stainless steel and glass and tile and bright lighting of the airport disoriented us after the bamboo and thatch and mud and candles of the camps, and we walked slowly and haphazardly, bumping against other passengers as we sought the exit. Eventually we came to it and the doors slid open, and we emerged under the vast ceiling of the international arrivals area, where a crowd of expectant faces inspected us.

A woman called out my name. It was my aunt, or, to put it more accurately, the woman who I pretended was my aunt. During my years in the United States as a communist spy inserted into the shabby ranks of the exiled South Vietnamese army, I had written her periodic letters, ostensibly regarding my personal travails as a refugee, but really encoded with secret messages in invisible ink about the machinations of some elements of this army who hoped

to take back our homeland from communist rule. We had used Richard Hedd's *Asian Communism and the Oriental Mode of Destruction* as our common cipher, and it was her task to pass on my messages to Man, blood brother to me and to Bon. I greeted her with relief and trepidation, for she knew what Bon did not and could not ever know, that Man was a spy, as I had been. He was my handler, and if eventually he became my torturer in that reeducation camp, didn't that suit me, a man with two minds? And if my aunt was not really my aunt, wasn't that perfect for a man with two faces?

She was really Man's aunt, and she looked exactly as she had described herself in her last letter: tall, thin, with jet-black hair. There ended the resemblance to what I had imagined of her: someone middle-aged with a back permanently bent from working as a seamstress, humbled by her devotion to the revolution. Instead, this woman's closest relative was a cigarette, judging from the shape of her body and what she held in one hand. She exuded smoke and confidence, and with her aggressive high heels she equaled me in height, although she looked taller, given her slimness, her formfitting gray knit dress, and her hair styled into a peak, a uniform that she would wear every day. Although I knew she was likely in her fifties, she could have passed for someone in her late thirties, blessed as she was by both French style and a half share of Asian genes that rendered her ageless.

My God! She seized me by the shoulders and made kissing sounds as she touched first one cheek and then the other to mine in that charming French manner of greeting, which had never been extended to me by the French in my homeland, including my French father. You two need new clothes. And haircuts!

Yes, she was definitely French.

I introduced her to Bon in French, but he responded in Vietnamese. He had a lycée education, like me, but he hated the

French and was here only for my sake. It was true that the French had given him a scholarship, but he had otherwise never benefitted from them in any way, except for traveling on the roads that they had designed, which were hard to be grateful for given that the slave labor of peasants like Bon's family had built them. My aunt switched to Vietnamese as she led us to the taxi queue, inquiring about our travels and our travails in the purest, most classical version of our language, spoken by Hanoi's intellectuals. Bon was silent. His own dialect blended the rural north, where our families originated from, and the rural south outside of Saigon. His parents had settled there after our Catholic exodus from the north in '54, the first of our three refugee experiences. It was either shame for his dialect that kept him quiet or, more likely, seething rage. Anything from Hanoi might be communist, and anything that *might* be communist was *undoubtedly* communist, at least to someone as maniacally anticommunist as he was. He wasn't even thankful for the only gift our communist captors ever gave him, the lesson that what does not kill you makes you stronger. That must mean Bon and I were now supermen.

What do you do? he finally said once we were in the taxi, my aunt between us in the back seat.

My aunt looked at me with great reproach and said, I see my nephew has said nothing about me. I'm an editor.

*Editor?* I almost said it out loud but stopped myself, for I was supposed to know who my aunt was. In seeking a sponsor for our departure from the refugee camp, I had written to her—not in code this time—because she was the only one I knew who was not an American. She would likely inform Man of my arrival, but I preferred that certainty over returning to America, where I had committed crimes of which I had never been convicted but of which I was not proud.

She named a publishing house I had not heard of. I make my living in books, she said. Mostly fiction and philosophy.

The noise in Bon's throat indicated how he was not the kind that read, except for the army field manual, tabloid newspapers, and the notes that I stuck on the refrigerator door. He would have been more comfortable with my aunt if she were actually a seamstress, and I was thankful that I had told Bon nothing about her.

I want to hear about everything you've been through, my aunt said. The reeducation and then the refugee camp. You are the first ones I've met who went through reeducation!

Perhaps not tonight, dear aunt, I said. I did not tell her of the confession I had written under great duress in reeducation, hidden in my leather duffel's false bottom, along with a disintegrating copy of Hedd's book, its pages yellowing. I was not even sure why I bothered to hide my confession, for the last person who should read it, Bon, showed no interest in its existence at all. Like me, he had been tortured into writing his own confession many times in the reeducation camp; unlike me, he did not know that it was Man, his blood brother, who was the commissar of the camp. How could he, when the commissar did not have a face? What Bon did know, he said, was that a confession extracted under torture was nothing but lies. Like most people, he believed that lies, no matter how often you told them, never became truth. Like my father, the priest, I was the kind who believed quite the opposite.

My aunt's apartment was in the 11th arrondissement, abutting the Bastille, where the French Revolution started. A spire that we drove by in the darkness marked the Bastille's place in history. If I was once a communist and a revolutionary, then I, too, was a descendant of this event that decapitated aristocracy with the finality of

a guillotine. Off the highway and into the city, I now felt truly in France, or, even better, Paris, with its narrow streets and its buildings of uniform height and design, not to mention the charming lettering over the storefronts, instantly recognizable from postcards and movies like *Irma la Douce*, which I had seen in an American movie theater soon after I arrived in Los Angeles as a foreign student. Everything about Paris was charming, as I would eventually discover, even its prostitutes and even on Sundays, in the early morning, after lunch, and in August, when everything was closed.

Over the next few weeks, I would never exhaust myself of that word: "charming"! Neither my homeland nor America could ever be described as charming. It was too moderate of an adjective for a country and a people as hot and hot-blooded as mine. We repulsed or seduced, but we never charmed. As for America, just think of Coca-Cola. That elixir is really *something*, embodying as it does the addictive, teeth-decaying sweetness of a capitalism that was no good for you no matter how it fizzled on the tongue. But it is not charming, not like freshly brewed dark coffee served in a thimble-sized cup on a miniature plate with a doll's spoon, delivered by a waiter as assured in the value of his profession as a banker or an art collector.

The Americans owned Hollywood with its loudness and swagger, its generous brassieres and cowboy hats, but the French waged the charm campaign. It was evident in the details, as if Yves Saint-Laurent had designed all of France, from how our taxi driver actually wore a beret, to the name of my aunt's street, rue Richard Lenoir, to the peeling blue paint on the steel door of my aunt's apartment building, no. 37, to the echoing darkness of the hallway with its malfunctioning light, to the narrow wooden steps that led, four stories up, to my aunt's apartment.

The fact that none of this besides the beret was intrinsically charming indicates how the French had an enormously unfair

advantage in their charm offensive, at least for those like me who had been, despite our best efforts, nearly completely colonized. I say nearly because even as I was charmed huffing up those stairs, some small, reptilian part of my brain—the savage native in me—resisted the charm long enough to recognize it for what it was: the seduction of subjugation. It was that feeling that made me all but swoon at the shapely baguette that graced my aunt's dining table. Oh, baguette! Symbol of France, and hence symbol of French colonization! So spoke one side of me. But the other side said, at the same time, Ah, baguette! Symbol of how we Vietnamese have made French culture our own! For we were good bakers of the baguette, and the banh mi we created with baguettes were far tastier and more imaginative than the sandwiches the French fashioned from them. That dialectical baguette, along with a cucumber salad in a rice wine vinaigrette, a pot of chicken curry with potatoes and carrots, a bottle of red wine, and, eventually, a caramel flan in a dark brown puddle of caramelized sugar, was the repast prepared by my aunt. How I had longed for these dishes or anything like them! Fantasies of food had beckoned to me during the endless months spent in the reeducation camp, located somewhere in Hell's inner circle, and then in the refugee camp in Hell's outer fringes, where the best that could be said about our diet was that it was insufficient and the worst that it was rancid.

My father taught me how to cook Vietnamese food, my aunt said as she spooned the curry into our bowls. My father was a soldier like the two of you, but a forgotten one.

The very mention of a father caused my heart to pause. I was in the land of my father, the patriarch who had rejected me. Would my life have been different if he had recognized me as his son and claimed my mother as his mistress, if not his wife? Part of me yearned for his love, and the other part of me hated myself for feeling anything for him besides scorn.

The French drafted my father to fight in the Great War, my aunt went on. Both Bon and I sat on the edges of our chairs, waiting for her to pick up her spoon or tear into the baguette, the signal to attack the meal lying so provocatively before us. Eighteen years old and swept from tropical Indochina to the metropole, along with tens of thousands of others. Not that he saw Paris until well after war's end. And he never returned home. His ashes sit in my bedroom, on top of my bureau.

There's nothing sadder than exile, poor Bon said, fingers trembling on the tablecloth. For most of his life, he would never have said anything remotely philosophical, but his own exile and the tragic loss of his wife and son had made him increasingly ruminative. Bring the ashes home, he continued. Only then will your father's spirit truly know peace.

You would think such talk might blunt our appetites, but Bon and I were desperate to eat anything besides the subsistence rations of a nongovernmental organization tasked with keeping refugees alive but nothing more. Besides, the French and the Vietnamese shared a love for melancholy and philosophy that the manically optimistic Americans could never understand. The typical American preferred the canned version of philosophy found in how-to manuals, but even average Frenchmen and Vietnamese cherished a love of knowledge.

So we talked and ate, but just as important, we drank and smoked and thought freely, indulging three of my bad habits, all of which reeducation had denied me. To satisfy those habits, my aunt not only opened successive bottles of red wine but also uncapped a Moroccan canister on her dining table that held two kinds of cigarettes, with and without hashish. Even "hashish" sounds charming, or at least exotic, in comparison to "marijuana," America's drug of choice, despite how both come from the same plant. Marijuana

was what hippies and teenagers smoked, its symbol the terminally unfashionable band called the Grateful Dead, whom Yves Saint-Laurent would have lined up and shot for popularizing tie-dyed T-shirts. Hashish evoked the Levant and the souk, the strange and the exciting, the decadent and the aristocratic. One might try marijuana in Asia, but in the Orient, one smoked hashish.

Even Bon shared one of the potent cigarettes, and it was then, hunger sated, bodies and minds relaxed, feeling more than a touch French in our smug post-supper bliss, which was for refugees nearly as pleasurable as postcoital bliss, that Bon noticed one of the framed pictures on the mantel.

Is that—he stood up abruptly, staggered, caught his balance, and then walked across the fringes of a Persian rug to the fireplace. It's—he pointed a finger at the face—it's *him*.

When I said to my aunt that it seemed that they knew someone in common, she said, I can't imagine who.

Bon turned from the mantel, red with rage. I'll tell you who. The *devil*.

I leaped to my feet. If the devil was here, I wanted to meet him! But on closer inspection . . . That's not the devil, I said, looking at a colorized photo of a man in his prime, white-haired and goateed, a halo of soft light around his head. It's Ho Chi Minh.

Once I had been a dedicated communist like him, my mission continuing even in America, where I had worked to support the revolution at home by doing my best to scupper the counter-revolution abroad. I had kept this secret from nearly everyone, especially Bon. The only ones who knew my communist sympathies were my aunt and her nephew, Man. He, Bon, and I were blood brothers, the Three Musketeers, or perhaps, as history may judge us, the Three Stooges. Man and I were spies, secretly working against the anticommunist cause that Bon held so dear, the

subterfuge squeezing us into all manner of difficult situations, our method of escape usually involving someone's death. Even now Bon believed Man to be dead and me to be as anticommunist as he was, for he had seen how the communists had scarred me in reeducation, something he thought they would only do unto their enemies. I was not an enemy to communism, merely someone with a near-fatal weakness in being able to sympathize with communism's actual enemies, including Americans. What reeducation had taught me was that dedicated communists were like dedicated capitalists, incapable of nuance. Sympathy for the enemy might as well be sympathy for the devil, tantamount to betrayal. Bon, devout Catholic, fervent anticommunist, certainly believed this. He had killed more communists than anyone I knew, and while he realized that some of those he had killed were perhaps only mistaken for communists, he had faith that both History and God would forgive him.

Now he aimed his finger at my aunt and said, You're a communist, aren't you? I grabbed his hand out of reflex, knowing that if his finger were on a trigger, then my aunt might be dead in a moment. Bon slapped my hand away, and my aunt raised an eyebrow and lit a cigarette of the unlaced kind.

I'm a fellow traveler rather than a communist, she said. I have enough humility to know that I'm not a real revolutionary. Just a sympathizer. She was as nonchalant about her politics as only the French could be, a people so cool that they had almost no use for the air-conditioning that Americans demanded. Like my father, I'm more Trotskyist than Stalinist. I believe in power for the people and international revolution, not a party running the show for its own country. I believe in the rights of man and equality for all, not collectivism and the revolution of the proletariat.

Then why have a picture of the devil in your home?

Because he's not the devil but the greatest of patriots. When he lived in Paris he even called himself Nguyen the Patriot. He believed in the independence of our homeland, as do you and I, as did my father. Shouldn't we celebrate what we have in common?

She spoke calmly and with reason. She might as well have been speaking a foreign language to Bon. You're a communist, Bon said conclusively. When he turned to me, he had the wild and frantic look of a wounded tomcat backed into a corner. I can't stay here.

I knew then that my aunt's life was safe. In Bon's rigid honor code, repaying hospitality with murder was immoral. But it was nearly midnight and we had nowhere else to go.

Sleep here tonight, I said. Tomorrow we'll find the Boss. His address was in my wallet, written down in the Pulau Galang camp before the magicians in charge of the camp's departures had teleported the Boss to Paris a year ago. The mention of the Boss calmed Bon down, for the Boss owed him his life and had promised to take care of us if we ever made it here.

All right, he said, hashish, wine, and exhaustion blunting his murderous instincts. He looked again at my aunt with something like regret, the closest he might ever come to actual regret. It's not personal.

Politics is always personal, my dear, she said. That's what makes it deadly.

My aunt retired to her bedroom, leaving us in the living room with a sofa and a pile of bedding on the Persian rug.

You never told me she was a communist, Bon said from the sofa, his eyes bloodshot.

Because you never would have agreed to stay here, I said, sitting down next to him. And blood's more important than belief, isn't it?

I raised my hand to him, the one with the red scar on the palm, the mark of our blood brotherhood, sworn back in Saigon one night in a grove on the grounds of our lycée. We had sliced our palms and gripped each other's hands, mingling our blood then and forever.

Now, a century or two after our adolescence—or so it felt after all we had suffered—in the land of our Gallic ancestors, Bon raised his scarred hand and said, So who's sleeping on the sofa?

While lying on the floor I heard Bon on the sofa whispering the prayers he uttered every night, addressed to God and to Linh and Duc, his dead wife and son. They had died on the tarmac of the Saigon airport as we sprinted to board the last airplane out of the city in April 1975, the second of our refugee experiences. An uncaring bullet lanced them both, fired by an unknown gunman in the chaos. Sometimes he heard their mournful ghosts calling, occasionally pleading with him to join them, other times urging him to stay alive. But his hands, so adept at killing others, would not turn against himself, for committing suicide was a sin against God. Taking another's life, however, was sometimes permissible, for God oftentimes needed the faithful to be His instrument of justice, or so Bon explained to me. He was at peace with being a devout Catholic and a calm killer, but what worried me more than how Bon contradicted himself, and how I surely contradicted myself, was that one day we might contradict each other. On that day when he learned of my secret, Bon would render justice on me, regardless of the blood we shared.

Before we left the next morning, we presented my aunt with a gift from Indonesia, a package of *kopi luwak*, one of four in Bon's duffel. We had been inspired by one of the Boss's henchmen, who had approached us the day before our departure with three packages

of *kopi luwak* as gifts for his patron. The Boss loves this coffee, the henchman said. His quivering nose, scraggly whiskers, and black pupils made him resemble the weasellike creature on the packages, or so I had thought at the time. Boss asked for it special, the henchman said. Bon and I scraped together our money at the airport and bought the fourth package of *kopi luwak* my aunt now held, choosing the same brand. When I explained that the *luwak*, the civet cat, ate the raw beans and excreted them, its intestines supposedly fermenting the beans in a gastronomic way, she burst out laughing, which rather hurt. *Kopi luwak* was very expensive, especially for refugees like us, and if there was anything that the French should love, it should have been civet-percolated coffee. Given their gastronomic peculiarities for eating brains, guts, snails, and the like, the French were honorary Asians in their heroic determination to eat every kind and part of an animal.

Oh, the poor farmer! she said, wrinkling her nose. What a way to make a living. But aware now of her faux pas, she quickly added, I'm sure this is delicious. Tomorrow morning I'll brew us a cup—or at least, I'll make one for you and me.

She nodded toward me, as by tomorrow morning, Bon should be with the Boss. Sober in the morning light, Bon made no mention of the devil that had divided them, a sign that the City of Light might already have enlightened him just a touch. Neither did she, instead offering directions to the metro station Voltaire, a block away, from where we made our way to the 13th arrondissement. This was the Asiatic Quarter, or Little Asia, of which we had heard many rumors and tales in the refugee camp.

Stop crying, Bon said. My God, you're more emotional than a woman.

I could not help myself. These faces! The people around us reminded me of home. There were a good number of them, but

nowhere near as many as one would find in the Chinatowns of San Francisco or Los Angeles, where almost everyone was Asian. But as I soon came to learn, more than a handful of people who were not white made the French nervous. Hence, Little Asia offered a notable if not overwhelming number of Asian faces, most of them ugly or unremarkable, but nevertheless reassuring to me. The average person of any race was not good-looking, but while the ugliness of others only confirmed prejudices, the homeliness of one's own people was always comforting.

I wiped the tears from my eyes, the better to see our customs and practices, which might have been out of place here but nevertheless raised the temperature of our hearts. I speak of the shuffle that Asians preferred to longer steps, and how the men typically walked ahead of their long-suffering women, who carried all the shopping bags, and how one of these same examples of chivalry cleared his nose by closing one nostril with a finger and forcibly ejecting its contents through the other, the missile narrowly missing my two feet by a foot or two. Disgusting, perhaps, but easily washed away by the rain, which is more than can be said for a balled-up tissue.

Our destination was an import-export store that announced its intentions in French, Chinese, and Vietnamese, its services including the dispatch to our homeland of parcels, letters, and telegrams, which is to say the delivery of hope to a starving country. The clerk looked at us from where he was sitting on a stool behind the counter and grunted by way of greeting. I told him I was looking for the Boss.

He's not in, the clerk said, just as the henchman told us he would say.

We're the ones from Pulau Galang, Bon replied. He's expecting us.

The clerk grunted again, eased himself off his stool with hemorrhoidal care, and disappeared down an aisle. A minute later he reappeared and said, He's waiting for you.

Behind the counter, down an aisle, and through a door was the Boss's office, scented with lavender air freshener, decked in linoleum, and adorned with pinup calendars featuring nubile Hong Kong models in exuberant poses and a wooden clock whose type I had seen before in the Los Angeles restaurant of my old commander of the Special Branch, the General, the man I had betrayed and who betrayed me in return. Admittedly I had fallen in love with his daughter, but who wouldn't fall in love with Lana? I still longed for her the way we refugees longed for our homeland, which was the shape into which the clock was carved. Now our homeland was irrevocably altered, and so was the Boss. We almost did not recognize him when he stood up from behind his steel desk. In the refugee camp, he had been as emaciated and ragged as everyone else, hair shoddy, his one shirt stained brown under the pits and between the shoulder blades, his only footwear a pair of thin flip-flops.

Now he was clad in loafers, creased slacks, and a polo shirt, the casual wear of the urban, Western branch of *Homo sapiens*, his trimmed hair parted so neatly one could have laid a pencil in the groove. In our homeland, he had owned considerable interests in rice, soda pop, and petrochemicals, not to mention certain black-market commodities. After the revolution, the communists had relieved him of his excessive wealth, but these overeager plastic surgeons had sucked away too much fat from this cat. Threatened with death by starvation, he had fled here, needing only one year to become a businessman again and reassume the padded appearance of affluent humanity.

So, he said. You brought the goods.

We commenced our masculine social grooming ritual by embracing and slapping each other on the back, followed by Bon and myself assuming the position of the socially inferior simians by offering the alpha male our tribute: the three packages of *kopi luwak*. Then the fun began, which involved smoking French cigarettes and drinking Rémy Martin VSOP from snifters that fit in our hands like the most perfectly shaped breasts. For the last couple of years, I had drunk nothing more refined than moonshine rice whiskey, which could blind a man, and the reunion of my tongue with one of its truest loves, cognac, made me weepy. The Boss said nothing. He, like Bon, had seen me cry many times in the refugee camp. While some of the others had suffered from malaria, I had been shaken by unexpected bouts of blubbering, a fever from which I still had not fully recovered.

When my tongue had recovered from contact with the voluptuous copper body of the cognac, I sniffed and said that I had never taken him for the type to appreciate coffee brewed from the beans defecated by a civet. He gave his best imitation of a smile, picked up a letter opener, slit open one of the packages, and shook out a gleaming brown bean onto his palm, where it glistened under the desk lamp.

I don't drink coffee, he said. Tea, yeah, but coffee's too strong.

We looked at the poor bean, the tip of the letter opener pressed against its belly. The Boss rolled the bean with his fingers until it ended up between his thumb and index, and then scraped it gently with the blade. The brown flaked off, revealing whiteness underneath.

It's just vegetable dye, he said. Won't hurt you, even when you snort it.

He opened the second bag, shook out another bean, and scratched off a portion of the coloring again to reveal the whiteness beneath.

Got to check the product, he said. Can't always trust the henchmen. Matter of fact, rule of thumb: Never trust the henchmen.

He opened a drawer and casually took out a hammer, as if hammers were always to be found in drawers, and gently tapped the bean until it crumbled into a fine powder. He dabbed a finger in the white powder, tinged with the brown coloring, and licked it. The brief glimpse of his pink tongue made my big toe twitch.

Sniffing's the best test. But I got people for that. Or you could do it. Want a try?

We shook our heads. He offered another facsimile of a smile and said, Good boys. This is a great remedy, but you don't want to need the cure.

Then he slit open the third bag, shook out another bean, laid it on the desk, and tapped it with the hammer—once, twice, a third time. The bean did not crumble. He frowned and tapped it again a little harder. Then he smashed the bean with a blow that made the desk lamp jump in surprise, and when he lifted the head of the hammer from the table, we saw not fine white powder but a circle of debris, brown to the core.

Shit, Bon muttered.

No, coffee, the Boss said, gently laying the hammer down. He reclined in his chair, the corners of his lips crinkling just a little, an amused auditor discovering a cheat's fatal error. Time must have frozen because I could see that the hands on the clock had not moved at all since we had come into the Boss's office. Hey, guys, he said. I think we've got a problem.

And by "we," he of course meant "you," or "us."

No one knew what the Boss's name was, or if he did, no one dared utter it aloud. His passport had a name, but no one knew if it was

real, and only the authorities had seen it. Presumably his father and mother knew his name, but he was an orphan, and perhaps they had not even given him a name before leaving him at the orphanage. An orphan was akin to a bastard, and this made me feel a certain amount of sympathy for the Boss, who had run away from his orphanage at twelve, no longer willing to tolerate the Catholic instruction, the repetitive diet of porridge with a few flakes of dried pork, the abuse from other orphans for being Chinese, the unending rejection of never being adopted. His experience among children meant that he had no desire to have children. The Boss had no need for a legacy outside of the one he made for himself, the only kind worth possessing. He focused on the two men before him—one of whom was me—and decided they were not a threat to his legacy, not dumb enough to risk their profitable relationship with him for half a kilogram of this remedy of the finest kind.

Tell you what. Come back tomorrow with the other *kopi luwak*. No big deal, right?

In chorus, they said yes. People who knew him always said yes, if that was what he wanted, or no, if that was what he wanted. As for people who did not know him, it was his task to let them know who he was and how they should respond. These two knew him and understood that if he could not trust them with half a kilo he could not trust them with anything. He drew a smile on his face and said, Honest mistake, I'm sure. Sorry to put you through the trouble. You say your aunt likes hashish? I'll give her some. On me. Free of charge.

Then he wrote two addresses down for Bon on a piece of paper and said, Drop off your stuff, then get to the restaurant. You don't want to be late for your first job.

They finished their cognac, shook his hand, and left him alone with the bottle of Rémy Martin, the packet of cigarettes, a dirty

ashtray, three empty snifters, the coffee beans, and the hammer. He brushed off the white powder and brown coffee smeared on the hammer's head and, holding it in his hand, admired its weight, balance, and elegance. He had bought it in a hardware store soon after arriving in Paris, along with a box of nails. Wherever he went, one of the first things he liked to buy, if he didn't already have it, was a hammer. A hammer was a simple tool, but it was the only thing he had ever needed, besides his mind, to change the world.

# CHAPTER 2

Although I feared the Boss for good reason, I feared Bon a little bit less. This was a mistake, in retrospect, given that Bon has shot me in the head. I had known Bon for more than two decades, ever since we had met at the lycée. He had seen too much violence and death, and dealt them as well, to be afraid even of someone like the Boss. For most of his life, in a way that was completely unhealthy for everyone but him, Bon had been concerned with what it meant to die. If that was one aim of philosophy, then Bon was a fine philosopher. He had dwelt on death ever since the childhood moment when a Viet Cong cadre aimed the accusatory finger of a revolver at the back of his father's head, puncturing the fragile shell, revealing what no son should ever see, and awakening a homicidal urge in Bon, one that knew no restraint until his time in reeducation. It was there that Death woke him every morning, holding the broken shard of a mirror close enough for him to see the fog of his breath clouding his image.

In the years before reeducation, hunting and killing had not bothered Bon in the least. After reeducation, he took more care with the offer of employment the Boss gave him in the refugee camp.

Having witnessed Bon's handiwork in saving his life, the Boss had said, I could use a man like you to do things like that.

I don't hurt innocent people, Bon said.

They studied the man crumpled at their feet, unconscious or perhaps expired, the elements of his face rearranged by Bon in a cubist manner. The Boss shrugged and agreed, since the price of entry into the Boss's profession entailed a loss of innocence. But the Boss hesitated about Bon's other stipulation, that he provide a job for me as well.

I don't employ people like this crazy bastard, he said at last. He could see that I had a screw loose, the trusty screw that had, for years, held together my two minds. Sometimes I did not even notice that I had two minds, since that was my natural condition, even if it was unnatural. Now the threads of the screw were stripped, having been placed under a great degree of stress from my years of being a spy, a sleeper, and a spook. As long as the screw had remained tightly screwed, my two minds had worked together reasonably well. Now I was no longer screwed—humanity's universal condition—but was instead unscrewed.

It's either both of us, Bon said, or neither of us.

That's the problem with loyalty. The Boss sighed. It's great until it's a pain in the ass.

Outside the Boss's import-export store, we were faced with a dilemma. The Boss wanted us to get to work right away. The Boss also wanted the return of his *kopi luwak*, which my aunt possessed and might open at any moment. What was to be done?

She did say she'd make the coffee tomorrow, I said. And she didn't seem enthusiastic, so I don't think there's much chance of her drinking it by herself.

All right, Bon said, looking at the sun to determine the time. His watch had been taken from him by our guards in reeducation in order to . . . in order to . . . well, there was no justification for it. Let's get this done as quickly as we can.

The housing was a short walk away, through an area whose pedestrian architecture was charmless. Unlike the Paris of Maurice Chevalier and Catherine Deneuve, most of the 13th arrondissement was deficient in charm, although it was unclear whether the authorities permitted Asians to live in this quarter because of its ill-favored qualities or whether the presence of Asians added to the unloveliness. Regardless, Bon was satisfied when the weary concierge with the deflated perm showed us his lodgings, the stacks of bunk beds recalling for Bon the military barracks he had loved with true ardor. The atmosphere was nostalgic, too, tangy with masculine sweat that evoked honesty and camaraderie. Otherwise the room was lived in by civilians, judging from the blankets huddled in shame on the mattresses, the rumpled reed mats on the parquet floor, and what passed for a kitchen: a folding table on which sat a rice cooker and a greasy two-burner plug-in stove.

Everyone's at work, the concierge said. This bunk's yours.

What's the rent?

The Boss takes care of that. Good deal, huh?

A good deal for Bon meant an even better deal for the Boss. But with no other recourse than my aunt's apartment, Bon dropped his duffel on the mattress and said, I'll take it.

That, as reeducation had taught him, was his unique talent. He could take anything.

Our next stop was Delights of Asia, located on rue de Belleville, where Bon would work as a line cook. Cook? Bon had said. I don't

know how to cook. Don't worry about it, the Boss had said. The place isn't known for its food.

In this restaurant not known for its food, the white tiles of the floor throbbed with varicose veins of brown grease, the yellow walls were stained with what I hoped were sticky fingerprints, and the surly waiters and cursing chefs could be heard shouting and cackling whenever the kitchen doors swung open. Next to the register, a stereo played cassettes of high-pitched Chinese and Vietnamese opera. Behind the register was the maître d' and musical curator, Le Cao Boi, who, from looks to manners, was the typical romantic Vietnamese man: part poet, part playboy, and part gangster.

I love seeing their bodies tense after I hit the play button, he said with a laugh, watching the lone customer leave behind a plate still swarming with worms, which on closer inspection turned out to be greasy and gelatinous noodles. He ejected the cassette and inserted another. Led Zeppelin, "Stairway to Heaven," he said. That's better. So! The Boss told me all about you two bad boys.

Le Cao Boi was the Boss's field marshal. He introduced the restaurant's employees: the two waiters, the three chefs, the busboy, and the janitor, or, as Le Cao Boi called them, the Seven Dwarfs. Unlike the Seven Dwarfs of *Snow White*, they were not cute and not even that dwarfish, being merely nasty, brutish, and short. Most notable, as I pointed out to Le Cao Boi, was that seven of them seemed excessive for a restaurant empty at noon on a weekend. He grinned and said, Makes you wonder why the Boss would send me two more employees, doesn't it?

As must be obvious even to a tourist or stranger, the restaurant was not surviving on its culinary output, being instead an outpost for the Boss's ambitions to expand from the ghetto of Little Asia to inner Paris, the heart of whiteness, even with its shadows of darkness. This outpost was a front for Le Cao Boi and the Seven

Dwarfs, who, besides being short, were angry and ambidextrous. Their favored weapons were cleavers, functional in the kitchen and on assignment, when they would each carry two of the big blades sheathed under their armpits in custom leather holsters.

They're angry because they're short, Le Cao Boi said. And they're hard to beat because they're short. Someone takes a swing at where they think their heads should be and they hit air. You don't want all seven coming at you at once, but that's how they do their job. One cuts off your manhood, another slices your kneecaps, a third hamstrings you, all at the same time. He exhaled a cloud of smoke. But they're not great on nuance. "Nuance" is not in their vocabulary. Hell, "vocabulary" is not in their vocabulary. That's what *you're* here for.

Le Cao Boi adjusted his aviator sunglasses, which he never removed, not even during lovemaking, or so it was said, especially by him. He was proud of their name-brand status as authentic American Ray-Bans, not, as he liked to point out, cheap imitations. Le Cao Boi was fashion-conscious, from designer socks to hair so streamlined with pomade that not a strand moved regardless of whether he was declaiming poetry (his own), making love (energetically), or swinging his favored weapon, a baseball bat gifted by an American cousin. It was Le Cao Boi's bitter experience to come as a refugee to France instead of America, the country for which he pined during his youth in Cholon. Le Cao Boi, like the Boss, was ethnic Chinese, son of a Cholon gangster and grandson of a Guangdong merchant who had settled in Saigon at century's turn. The grandfather sold silk and opium, the father sold only opium, and the grandson sold nothing except his violent services, a great decline over which he ruminated often in his poetry, which was so unspeakably bad that none of it will be quoted here.

Just think of me as Baudelaire with a baseball bat, he said, showing us his prized Louisville Slugger. What a name, he added, rolling the baseball bat on the counter where the depressed cash register stood, its sole purpose in life—to have its keys punched—hardly ever achieved. So, what should we call you? You're Killer, that's obvious. I wouldn't want to see your face when I open the door. But you! Le Cao Boi turned his reflective gaze to me. The Boss said you already had a name. Know what it is?

He offered a smile, the kind that the Americans he admired so much called a "shit-eating grin," a phrase whose meaning was the exact opposite of what one would suppose. Hello, Crazy Bastard, Le Cao Boi said. I've heard a lot about you.

Once, I would have taken offense. But after all I had suffered and seen, perhaps I actually was a crazy bastard. Perhaps that was just another name for a man with two faces and two minds. If so, at least I knew who I was, and that was more than could be said for most. The dual images of myself floating in his lenses reminded me that I was not one but two, not only me or *moi* but also, on occasion, we or us. We might have been two people in one body, two minds in one shell, but if this was a weakness, to be divided against oneself, it was also a strength, to be one's own twin. We were not half of anything. As my mother had told me time and again, You are twice of everything!

Okay, enough chitchat, Le Cao Boi said. Small talk kills me. Let's get to work.

Hey, chief, said one of the dwarfs, emerging from the back of the restaurant. He had droopy eyelids. Grumpy did it again.

Du ma! Le Cao Boi said. Well, why don't you do something about it?

Du ma! Sleepy said, pointing at me. He's the new guy.

Good point. Le Cao Boi nodded at me. Follow Sleepy. He'll show you what to do. After that, we get to the real work.

I followed Sleepy to the back of the restaurant. He paused before a grimy door and said, with a grin, Got to start from the bottom and work your way up, right?

Sleepy laughed mightily at his joke and seemed somewhat resentful when I did not laugh in turn. Grumbling, he kicked open the door and said, Got to keep your hands clean. Clean hands, clean food, am I right? When Sleepy noticed me gagging, tears coming to my eyes, he stood on his tiptoes outside the open door to look down into the toilet and said, Jesus Christ. Ugh. I mean . . . good luck, new guy.

I saw no sign of rubber gloves, not that the interior of such gloves would have been sanitary. The only tools for the excavation of the clogged orifice were a plunger with a short handle and a woefully small rubber cup, as well as a soiled toothbrush of a toilet scrub. If either the plunger or the scrub could speak, they would undoubtedly scream eternally, as I was already doing internally.

I emerged from the toilet some twenty minutes later, trembling and trying not to think of the fine droplets of water that had sprayed all over my clothes and possibly even misted my arms and face. I had seen worse in the refugee camp, but this was supposed to be the City of Light!

All done? Le Cao Boi said. I keep telling Grumpy not to eat the food here. Fair warning. Okay, let's go. There's a debt to be collected.

Our destination was in the Marais, popular with Jews and faggots, according to Le Cao Boi, although our target was neither. What he was, Le Cao Boi said, was a client who liked to beat the

girls, which could be acceptable, depending on the payment. What was not acceptable was that he had accrued a debt for which he was now in arrears.

Never go into debt for a woman, said Le Cao Boi, pausing outside the door to a travel agency to let a Japanese tourist wander by, a zoom lens the length of his forearm attached to a camera around his neck. Inside, a young couple sat before the travel agent, whose only crime appeared to be combining a knit tie with a short-sleeved plaid shirt. His eyes twitched in fear at the sight of two and a half Asian men who did not appear to be respectable bourgeoisie seeking respite from the low-grade demands of 1980s French capitalism. Bon sat down in the chair next to the young couple and stared at the client. Le Cao Boi explained that we would wait, they should take their time, the Spanish coast was beautiful this time of year. The next few minutes passed awkwardly, at least for the travel agent, with Le Cao Boi meandering around the office, whistling "Stairway to Heaven" as he ran his finger along the posters of beaches and palm trees on the walls, the brochures on the counter, and the backs of the chairs on which the young couple sat.

Bon remained next to them, staring only at the travel agent but keeping the couple in his peripheral vision. They glanced at each other as the travel agent began stuttering, fingers trembling over the binder of travel packages. I watched them all while I stood silently with my back to the wall by the door, and when the young couple smiled nervously and promised to return, I opened the door for them. The travel agent waved his hands at Le Cao Boi and alternated between explaining and begging, but Le Cao Boi ignored him and said to Bon, He's a thief who beats girls. We couldn't give you a better job to begin with, could we?

No, you couldn't have. Bon stood up. This will be easy. At least for me.

* * *

As I watched the travel agent tremble and moan as he curled up on the spotless floor—Bon being careful not to extract blood—I understood with a sudden twist of shame that I shared something in common with this man, besides our plaintive desire to live. I also shared his manhood, his lust, his febrile brain that could not pass ten minutes without a sexual fantasy crossing its field of vision. Men were all the same, or at least 90 to 95 percent of them. Bon, perhaps, might be an exception, so pure of heart that even in the oceanic depths of his mind and soul he did not fantasize about the opposite sex. But most men will. And I—I was like most men.

I wept a little for the travel agent, but more for me and myself and my mother, who had to watch me in dismay from above. Le Cao Boi sniffed in disgust, not over the battered travel agent but over my tears. Pull yourself together, man, he said outside the door of the agency.

Bon, embarrassed, said, Get that *kopi luwak*, and we parted ways. While they returned to Delights of Asia, I made my way to my aunt's, wiping away my tears, seeing Bon twisting the travel agent's manhood until the pitiful fellow nearly blacked out and cried for his mama, which made me think of my mother. I had never lived with a woman other than my mother, and I had no idea what to do with a woman who was not my mother and who I was not pursuing. I opened the door to my aunt's apartment softly and found her at her desk, tucked into an alcove of the hallway. She was editing a manuscript while smoking, or perhaps smoking was the real activity and editing the distraction.

How was your day? She waved her cigarette at me and offered me one.

Nothing remarkable, I said, wondering if the *kopi luwak* was still intact. Just met my boss and did some work for him.

Freshen up and tell me about it. She pointed toward the bathroom, halfway down the hall. Some guests will be arriving soon and I have told them all about you, my accomplished nephew.

As I would discover over the coming months, my aunt's apartment hosted a veritable salon for writers, editors, and critics, a crowd of intellectuals so leftist that I was always surprised to see that almost all of them ate with their right hands. My aunt's career in editing, along with a penchant for socializing and a talent for the subtle stroking of masculine ego—though subtlety was rarely required—had led to an extensive network of friends, mostly male, who traded in words and ideas. At least two or three times a week, a visitor would come by, bearing a bottle of wine or a box of colorful macarons. My aunt consumed wine and macarons heedlessly and without any evident impact on her slim waistline. This talent was due to the fact that she barely ate real food, at least in my presence, filling herself instead with smoke, the aforementioned words and ideas, and those light, sweet macarons.

Can I make you some of the *kopi luwak*? I called from the kitchen, out of view from my aunt's nook. To my relief, the gift was untouched. When my aunt said yes, it was then a simple matter to switch the packages and return to the living room with a glass coffee press full of the dark brew. My aunt joined me, and I reported on my day's activities while we smoked Gauloises and sipped the civet coffee.

I can't say I taste the difference, she said. Not that it's not delicious. In fact, it's quite potent.

It's psychological. Knowing where it comes from affects the taste.

Just like knowing where this Boss and Le Cao Boi come from, she said. I imagine them as dark and potent, like this coffee. The gangster and the romantic. The violent and the lyrical. Doesn't that define our homeland's culture?

Isn't France our homeland? My father, when he was teaching me in school, would make us repeat after him: *la Gaule* is the land of our ancestors.

Your father was a colonizer and a pedophile, which go hand in hand. Colonization is pedophilia. The paternal country rapes and molests its unfortunate pupils, all in the holy and hypocritical name of the civilizing mission!

When you talk about me like that, I feel like a symbol.

Get used to it, my dear. We French love nothing more than symbols.

That was the nature of our conversation, the discourse refreshing after the reeducation camp's brute propaganda and the nuts-and-bolts pseudo-realism of the somewhat rusted American Dream. Americans loathed symbols, except for patriotic, sentimental ones like guns, flags, Mom, and apple pie, all of which the average American proclaimed he would defend to the death. One had to love such a practical, pragmatic people, impatient with interpretation, eager just to get the facts, ma'am. If one tried to interpret a movie's deeper significance with Americans, they would reflexively claim that it was just a story. To the French, nothing was ever just a story. As for facts, the French thought them rather boring.

Facts, my aunt said, are just the beginning, not the end.

Speaking of facts, I thought you were a seamstress.

And I thought you were a patriotic captain who became a refugee. You were given your cover and I was given mine.

By Man? I asked. When she nodded, I said, Have you told him that I am here?

34

Of course. No reply yet. She regarded me shrewdly. My first loyalty lies with him, my actual nephew, or not even really him, but the revolution you have abandoned.

I didn't abandon the revolution. It abandoned me.

Disappointments, abandonments, betrayals—unfortunately all typical of revolutions, as with all passionate love affairs. Something happened between you two?

Because I became a refugee again?

Yes. Or is that just another cover? To keep you safe from Bon? He would kill you if he knew you were a communist, wouldn't he?

My cup was empty except for a fine black silt of coffee ground. Yes.

When you wrote me and asked for help, I agreed—

And thank you for that—

—because of all that you have done for the revolution. And because I want to know what has happened to our revolution. I can recognize propaganda when I see it, and what is coming from our revolution is propaganda. But as imperfect as our revolution may be—and what revolution is perfect?—that does not mean I support counterrevolutionaries. So tell me, my former communist: Are you now a reactionary?

Are communist or reactionary my only choices?

What are your other choices?

You're an editor, I said. I have something for you to read.

I retrieved my confession from the false bottom of my leather duffel and gave it to her, all 367 pages of it. She had barely had a chance to look at the first page when a knock at the door announced our visitors, dressed well and yet casually, making me aware of my simple white long-sleeved shirt, rolled up to the elbows, and my boring black slacks, and my dusty shoes—an ensemble that made me look like a waiter, which was what I now was. They, too, wore shirts and slacks and had

arms, legs, and eyes as I did. But while we shared the same elements that made us human, they were clearly filet mignon, rare and perfectly seared, while I was boiled organ meat, most likely intestine. We were distantly related, in other words, but no one would ever mix us up. The fine quality of the cotton of their shirts, woven by a bedraggled child laborer somewhere in a dark, poor, hot country, was visible from a distance. As for their pants, they fit so well they needed no belts, while my pants were so loose they required a hideous strap of snake leather, provided by the refugee camp and donated, presumably, by somebody of typical American girth from Texas or Florida, which is to say it was long enough for two emaciated Vietnamese.

The first gentleman, whose rumpled black hair was speckled with gray, was a psychoanalyst. The other gentleman, whose sleekly coiffed gray hair was streaked with black, was a politician. He was a socialist, an honorable affiliation in France, and a very happy man, since a fellow socialist had won the presidency last week. The politician was well-known enough that he could be introduced just by his initials, which initially befuddled me.

BHV? I said.

BFD, my aunt repeated.

BFD and the psychoanalyst, who was also a Maoist and who had completed his PhD, regarded me with a curiosity that soon devolved into disdain, which the French have difficulty concealing, since they consider disdain a virtue. My aunt introduced me as a refugee from the communist revolution in my homeland, and these two were leftists for whom the Vietnamese revolutionaries were modern-day noble savages. If I was not one of these noble savages, then I must be an ignoble savage, a situation that was not helped by the fact that my schoolboy French was stiff from not having been used for many years after the lycée. After a few halting rounds of conversation where I rapidly proved that I could not swim in the

intellectual, cultural, and political currents of Paris or France or the French—I mentioned Sartre, for example, and did not know that the great existentialist had died two years previous—the Maoist PhD, BFD, and my aunt ignored me. I sat on a corner of the couch in the state of humiliation, a region I have visited quite often, most often when someone called me a bastard. I usually responded with rage, a good mask. But I was not myself, or rather I was both me and myself, my screw quite wobbly, taking comfort from the first and then the second bottle of wine that the visitors had brought, the conversational freight train rushing past me and revealing only glimpses through its windows. Smoking my aunt's cigarettes, gazing at the ceiling, the carpet, the polished toes of the men's shoes, I knew I was not just a clown but a dunce.

When my aunt offered hashish, I accepted with relief, unsure of how to exit gracefully from their ménage à trois. But under the spell of the hashish it was all perfectly normal that later in the evening, when the Maoist PhD said farewell, even to me, BFD stayed seated. My aunt closed the door behind the Maoist PhD and said, What a very nice evening. Until tomorrow . . .

She nodded at BFD, who rose, inclined his head to me somewhat mockingly, and followed her into her bedroom. I could hear them laughing behind the door, undoubtedly at me. I laughed with them. I was, after all, the refugee, not the revolutionary, the hick from the hinterlands, the nitwit nephew from the colony, the dumb bastard who was so provincial and prudish that even floating on hashish he was shocked at the idea of his aunt making love to a politician, or any man, even if he was a socialist.

Later that evening, a time bomb of a lesson finally exploded in my head as I lay on the sofa. I was trying to sleep when I suddenly recalled

a professor at the lycée who had earned his degree in Paris in the 1930s. We students worshipped and envied him. Indeed, worship and envy pervaded our steamy colony, as they do any colony. Colonizers imagined themselves as divine, and the native middlemen who served them, like my professor, fancied themselves as priests and disciples. Not surprisingly, the colonizers looked down on us as savages, infants, or sheep, while we looked up at them as demigods, masters, or brutes. The danger with worshipping human beings, of course, is that eventually they reveal their flawed humanity, at which point the believer has no choice but to kill the fallen idols or die trying.

Some of us loved the French, our patrons, and some hated the French, our colonizers, but all of us had been seduced by them. It is difficult to be loved by someone, as the French imagined their relationship with us, or to be abused by someone, though the French pretended otherwise, without being shaped by their hand and touched by their tongue. Thus we learned French literature and language under the tutelage of this professor who had actually stepped foot on the soil of *la Gaule*, our fatherland, as a scholarship student dispatched to absorb the best of French culture. He returned as a sopping wet sponge to us benighted natives, applying himself to foreheads that might be feverish with revolution.

Ah, the Champs-Élysées, the Sponge rhapsodized. Oh, the Eiffel Tower!

And we all swooned, just a little, and dreamed that one day we, too, could board a steamer ship for the metropole with nothing more than a suitcase, a scholarship, and an inferiority complex.

Ah, Voltaire! the Sponge effused. Oh, Descartes! Oh, Rousseau!

In truth, we delighted in reading these masters in the original French for the Sponge's classes, and we believed what the Sponge told us, that the greatest of literature and philosophy was universal, and that French literature and philosophy was the greatest of the

greatest, and by learning French literature and philosophy and language we, too, could one day be Frenchmen, although our lessons in the canon were complicated by our context of a colony. From Descartes, for example, I learned that because I think, therefore I am! But I also learned that in a world divided between the body and the mind, we Vietnamese were ruled by our bodies, which was why the French could rule us with their minds. From Voltaire, I learned that it was best to tend to my own garden, which might mean many things, but when taught to us by the French meant to mind our own business and be happy with our little plots, while the French took care of our entire colony and inflicted *Candide*-like horrors on us. As for Rousseau, perhaps I learned the most from him, for as I wrote my confession under Man's heavy-handed guidance in the reeducation camp, the beginning of Rousseau's own confession came back to me in a flash:

> I am resolved on an undertaking that has no model and will have no imitator. I want to show my fellow-men a man in all the truth of nature; and this man is to be myself ... As to whether nature did well or ill to break the mould in which I was cast, that is something no one can judge until after they have read me.

Thank you, Jean-Jacques! By you I was inspired to be true to myself, for even if myself was a rotten bastard, I was like no other rotten bastard in history, before or since. I learned to love confessing and have never stopped acknowledging my crimes of violence, torture, and betrayal, all of which our French masters had taught us through the violence and torture they had inflicted on us as they betrayed their own ideals.

These complicated lessons were only reinforced each time I left the hallowed grounds of the lycée and walked the streets of

Saigon with a French book under my arm, where, on occasion, I would be abused in the language of Dumas, or Stendhal, or Balzac. Any Frenchman or -woman or child, rich or poor, beautiful or plain, could call us anything he or she wanted and, occasionally, did. *Yellow-skinned bastard! Slanty-eyed chink!* The most perfectly formed lips and the whitest teeth, borne about by the nicest shoes and daintiest footwear, could spit these seeds at us, ones that would take fertile root underneath our tainted skin, as happened to Ho Chi Minh, who put it best when he wrote about how we, the colonized of Africa and Asia, were to our masters "only dirty niggers and dirty Annamese, good at the very most for pushing rickshaws and receiving the blows of our administrators."

Some of us ignored the insults, wanting only for our masters to love us.

Some of us could not forget the insults and wanted to slay our masters.

And some of us—me and myself most of all—loved and hated our masters at the same time.

Loving a master who kicks you is not a problem if that is all one feels, but loving *and* hating must be kept a dirty little secret, for loving the master one hates inevitably induces confusion and self-hatred. That was why I never threw myself as wholeheartedly into the study of French as I did with English and why, ever since leaving the lycée, I had hardly ever spoken a word of French. French was the language of our enslaver and rapist, whereas English was a novelty, heralding an American arrival that spelled the end of our French debasement. I mastered English without ambivalence because it had never mastered us.

Now, in Paris at last, the land of my father, in the company of the socialist BFD and the Maoist PhD, it suddenly struck me that I was not just seen as an other by white people. They also *heard* me as

other, for when I opened my mouth and broke the beautiful china of their French language, they heard what the poet, boy wonder, gun runner, and slave trader Rimbaud must have heard and then plagiarized from some nameless African or Oriental traveler: *I is an other.*

There was no need for the French to condemn us. So long as we spoke in their language, we condemned ourselves.

I, the other, woke from sleep, but it was as if me, or I, was still dreaming, for I could see through my eyes but I could also see me and myself through the eyes of my aunt and BFD. They walked out of the bedroom rumpled yet elegant, but they saw me as just rumpled. BFD was clad in a blue velvet robe, like a boxer after a victorious round in the ring, a postcoital costume kept for all my aunt's visitors. My aunt wore a gray satin robe with a turban of the same material wrapped around her hair, an outfit a movie star from the black-and-white era might wear between scenes. They chatted amiably as they smoked and drank civet coffee while skimming the newspapers. BFD had sniffed at the coffee before dipping his tongue in it and then laughing, which made me fantasize about strangling him. Never mock another culture's food or drink; it is a mortal sin. Brooding over my coffee and toast, I barely paid attention to their conversation, except to note the mentions of *le haschisch* and *les boat-people.*

The mention of the latter was prompted by an item in *L'Humanité,* my aunt's newspaper of choice (BFD preferred *Libération,* but *L'Humanité,* he said, would do). BFD held it up and pointed to the headline about *les boat-people* and a photograph of a trawler floating in the ocean, as crowded with my countrymen as a metro train at rush hour. But while a rider endures the train's conditions for only a number of minutes, my countrymen endured their conditions

for days and weeks, under full exposure to the sun, wind, and rain, pirates dropping in periodically to select the most succulent parts of the cargo and sharks swimming alongside to window-shop, gazing longingly at the fresh cuts of meat on display.

*Very sad,* BFD said, very deliberately and very loudly, his lips moving in exaggerated slow motion. *You, too. A boat person. Like them. Verrry saaad. They have nothing. We have everything. We must help them. We must help you.*

He aimed his finger at me as if his words were not quite enough. I forced myself to smile and swallowed my resentment, which tasted like blood—that is to say, not as bad as you might imagine, given how so many people apparently enjoy dining on rare, juicy meat. The heat of his pity was so strong that it did not make me feel warm. Instead, I boiled, the steam hissing from my ears as I kept my mouth closed after the few conciliatory words I could manage. How could I say that the so-called boat people had already helped themselves by getting on their boats in the first place? How could I say that I refused to be called a "boat person," a term so overpowering that even the Anglophobic French had simply borrowed and worn it on a regular basis, like *un jean* and *le week-end*?

I was not a boat person unless the English Pilgrims who fled religious persecution to come to America on the *Mayflower* were also boat people. Those refugees just happened to be fortunate that the soon-to-be-hapless natives did not have a camera to record them as the foul-smelling, half-starved, unshaven, and lice-ridden lot that they were. In contrast, our misery was forever recorded in *L'Humanité*, where we were seen as anything but human. No, the boat people were not human, they did not get the benefit of some romantic painter casting them in oils, standing boldly on the prow of their sinking ships, facing the monstrous elements with the nobility of Greek heroes, enshrined in the Louvre to be admired

by tourists and studied by art historians. No, boat people were victims, objects of pity fixed forever in newspaper photographs. Part of me, my mama's baby, wanted that pity. But the part of me that was a grown man neither wanted nor deserved pity, neither wanted to be called a victim nor deserved to be seen as such, not after all my deeds and misdeeds. If the price of being human was to be recognized through being pitiful, then to hell with humanity! I was a rotten bastard—recognize that!

But instead all I said was: Thank you. Yes, please help them.

BFD stood up to leave, satisfied that he had not only put me and my people in our pitiful place but that he had also gotten me to thank him for his condescension. It occurred to me that if my French was awkward and my Vietnamese was incomprehensible to him, my English was fluent, and nothing would make a Frenchman feel more inferior, and hence angry, than to hear English. Within a corner of every French soul slouched an American, coughing quietly now and again to remind the Frenchman of their shared history, beginning with how the French helped the pitiful upstart Americans in their revolution against the English, only to find themselves needing the aid of these same Americans twice in the World Wars. Then, finally, "Indochina," whatever that word meant, since we were neither Indian nor Chinese. It was this fantastic Indochina that the exhausted French handed off to the now very loud Americans. How it must hurt to be reminded of the decline of one's own empire by being confronted with the rise of a new one! Oh, yes, English in this case was an insult and a challenge, especially from one such as me, who was not even American but "Indochinese."

So, in perfect American English, I said, Did I hear you say hashish? Because I happen to have some, and of a very fine grade.

BFD hesitated, surprised by this yellow parrot. The sleek socialist could have dismissed me in French, but the temptation to prove

that he, too, could speak English was too much for him. Well, yes, in fact, I was saying to your aunt that our . . . purveyor . . . has gone missing.

Six months ago, without a word, my aunt added. Her fluent English, like BFD's, was inflected with a charming French accent, but it was nevertheless not as good as mine, for I could say that most American of things—*hee-haw!*—which most of the French could not say, except with a great degree of concentration as they tried not to drop their *h*'s. I suppose that can only mean bad news for the salesman, my aunt went on.

Unless he found religion, I said.

Doubtful, said my aunt. Saïd only cares about money. Speaking of which—if I could be so crass—

No, no, no, I said, knowing intuitively that someone like BFD, a politician, would not buy the goods, at least from me. I held up the sliver of aluminum between my fingers that the Boss had meant for me to pass on to my aunt. *This*—the glow of my aunt's lamp struck the aluminum so that it gleamed like distant lightning—*this* is a gift.

# CHAPTER 3

O h, what a migraine! And it was due not just to these holes in my head but to the long-lingering hangover from that morning and its ill-considered decision. Oh my God— or my Karl Marx, or my Ho Chi Minh—what had I done? As the General had once told me: Nothing is so expensive as what is given for free. How true, given that I had given him my loyalty freely, and yet I was also spying on him (not to mention seducing Lana). I was his aide-de-camp, Saigon was about to fall, and although he was an American ally, he was speaking of the dangers of American assistance, which Americans gave freely, even though their help always cost a great deal. In our southern Vietnamese case, we had fought the war against communism that the Americans wanted, only to see them abandon most of us in our time of greatest need. So who was paying for this gift, and how much? Was this the beginning of my downfall, when I had barely begun to rise from the downtrodden position that I occupied as a three-time refugee? My intention was to hook BFD for future sales, even if those sales must be conducted through my aunt. He has a reputation to protect, she had said after closing the door behind him. He's the mayor of the 13th arrondissement.

Even better. I could taste the salty flavor of revenge, which was what I wanted, even if it would leave me thirsty and with bad breath. But in seeking my revenge on the socialist, was I actually becoming that most horrid of criminals? No, not a drug dealer, which was a matter of bad taste. I mean was I becoming a *capitalist*, which was a matter of bad morals, especially as the capitalist, unlike the drug dealer, would never recognize his bad morality, or at least admit to it. A drug dealer was just a petty criminal who targeted individuals, and while he may or may not be ashamed of it, he usually recognized the illegality of his trade. But a capitalist was a legalized criminal who targeted thousands, if not millions, and felt no shame for his plunder. Perhaps only someone like the Maoist PhD would understand, and indeed he understood so well that he called my aunt later that afternoon and asked for some of the goods, having been informed by BFD of their quality. Unlike BFD, he apparently was not worried about his reputation. If anything, being a known hashish smoker probably enhanced the Maoist PhD's reputation.

It appears that your product is excellent, she said, hanging up the phone with a hint of reproach in her voice. I wouldn't have minded a sample of it myself.

I'll see what I can do, I said, a plan leaping into the waiting arms of my mind, which had not held such a thing for so long. As for my aunt, she had her own plans for me.

I have a friend who teaches French to immigrants, she went on. You need to polish your French. You're half French, and you should know the language of your father as well as you do English. And you can't work at that restaurant forever. Or shouldn't, anyway. Not that there's anything wrong with working in a restaurant. But you have greater talents.

I thought of my career as a spy, my plans and my manipulations, my ideals and my delusions, my decisions and my blunders. My

life as a revolutionary and a spy had been designed to answer one question, one inherited from that vanguard of revolution, Lenin, the one that drove me since my lycée years: WHAT IS TO BE DONE? In my case, I had killed two men, and they were innocent, or mostly innocent, and I was guilty, or mostly guilty. I had killed both of them at the behest of the General, who had committed the error of trusting me enough to make me an officer in the Special Branch, our task to root out communists and dissidents. The General had never suspected me of being a spy, not during our years in Saigon or the years afterward, when I fled with him and his family as refugees to Los Angeles. When Man had ordered me to go with the General to America, he was right: the General and his men would continue to fight the war from there, trying to take our homeland back and defeat the revolution. If best actor awards were given to spies, I deserved one, for I had been suave enough to convince the General that the real spy was my colleague in the secret police, the crapulent major. And when the General decided that the crapulent major should be given a one-way ticket to the afterlife, he chose me to deliver it. I had not pulled the trigger as the crapulent major smiled at me in his driveway—that was Bon—but I was the one responsible for his death.

As for the second man I killed, Sonny, I had known him when we were both foreign students in Southern California in the 1960s, when he was a left-wing activist and I was a communist pretending to be a member of the right wing. Sonny had wisely stayed in California and become a journalist, a perilous occupation in our own country. But our country caught up to him when we refugees came to America, including the General, who suspected Sonny of being a communist agent. Once more the General made me his delivery boy, and if I, his über-competent, super-anticommunist aide, refused, I would have been rightly suspect in his paranoid

imagination. I had shot Sonny at close range, and he and the crapulent major had haunted me intermittently ever since, their voices emerging clearly every now and again from the static-ridden channel of my unconscious.

Talents? My laugh sounded weird even to my own ears. What talents?

My aunt looked disconcerted, her *sang* no longer so *froid*. You can write, she said. I'm almost done reading your confession, just thirty or forty pages left to go.

I just gave it to you last night.

I'm an editor. I read fast and I don't sleep much.

What do you think so far?

I think you love your mother. I think you have a problem with women. I think you were treated a bit harshly by Man, who may have had no choice, and yet I think you were too seduced by American culture. You lived a dangerous life as a double agent and a spy, and you were, as you say, a man of two faces and two minds. I wonder what face I am looking at now. And whether you can be trusted.

I could say that you should trust me, but I don't even trust myself.

Now that is an honest answer. So, you who can sympathize with anyone, what do you think I should do in regards to you? I have welcomed you into my home because you were my revolutionary comrade. But you are not my comrade anymore, are you?

You read about what the revolution did to me!

I read what you said the revolution did to you. But do you not think that perhaps the revolution had reason to be suspicious of you? That you were, or are, in fact too Americanized? Even here in France we are in danger of being Americanized. The American Way of Life! Eat too much, work too much, buy too much, read too little, think even less, and die in poverty and insecurity. No, thank you. Don't you

see that's how the Americans take over the world? Not just through their army and their CIA and their World Bank, but through this infectious disease called the American Dream? You were infected and you barely even realized it! You were an addict, and Man had to cure you. Unfortunately the cure for addiction is always painful.

I was dumbfounded. She had read my confession and this is what she got out of it? So I am wrong, I said, and the revolution was right in punishing me?

From an editorial point of view, I cannot help but admire Man's methods. My aunt lit a cigarette and smiled. If only I could make all my writers produce this many pages this quickly. You have to respect his rigor, don't you?

I, who could sympathize with anyone, wanted more than anything for someone to sympathize with me. I had believed that surely my aunt would be gentler than the man for whom I had been spying in America, also the commissar of the camp in which I was later interned, the faceless man, also known as my best friend and blood brother Man, stripped of a great deal of his humanity by an errant napalm strike. Man was very sympathetic to me. He knew me very well, more so than any priest or analyst, but he had used that knowledge to interrogate me and torture me. Unlike Man, my aunt would most likely not torture me. But if she could not understand me, who could?

Maybe, I said, I should get some more of the hashish.

The hemorrhoidal clerk grunted painfully when he saw me at five that afternoon. He struck a match, and the flash of its flame and the hiss of its short, deep breath lit something within me at the moment he lit his cigarette—the fuse of a plot, the long trail of gunpowder in a children's cartoon that led to the explosive climax.

Could I see the Boss?

Does he want to see you?

Just tell him I have a proposition for him.

The Boss let me wait for an hour, just to show me exactly where I stood, or sat, in his waiting room. At least here, in France, one waited by sitting on a seat versus squatting on one's well-developed haunches, muscular from a lifelong scarcity of chairs. How many times had I seen my mother squatting on her haunches, her feet flat on the ground, her torso leaning slightly forward to maintain her balance, especially if I was draped on her back? She could squat for hours, forced to stay in a pose that most Westerners could not maintain for more than a minute. She would hum to me, rock me, sing me lullabies, and then, when I was older, tell me fairy tales and recite folk sayings and poems, all while a thin film of sweat glued us together. Every time I waited, I thought of her endless patience, borne not for the sake of whoever was making her wait but for me, who had to wait with her wherever she went. After I grew too heavy for her back, I squatted beside her and the rest of the masses. Then I went to the lycée, and there I became a part of the class that no longer squatted but assumed the right to sit on chairs.

When I was at last called into the office, my buttocks were slightly sore from the hard cup of the plastic chair, ergonomically designed for round Western buttocks rather than flat Eastern ones. I found the Boss sitting on a well-padded chair at a clean desk examining a ledger. Rumor had it that he had never gone to school but was taught on the streets, and anything that he had not learned there, he had taught himself. My heart softened for this poor, abandoned orphan when I imagined what he, with his talent and ambition, could have become with a proper education:

The manager of an investment fund!

The president of a bank!

The captain of an industry!

Or, to consult my Marxist thesaurus:

A vulture of capitalism!

A sucker of blood!

A launderer of profits distilled from the sweat of the people!

I was no longer a communist who believed in a party, but I was still a descendant of Marx who believed in a theory, and that theory offered the best critique of capitalism available. To expect capitalists to critique themselves was like asking the police to police themselves—

What's the matter? the Boss said. Snap out of it, you crazy bastard.

Sorry, I—or me, or maybe we—muttered.

Do you have the *kopi luwak*?

He nodded in satisfaction when I placed the package on his desk, and I watched him examine the bean's anatomy, his letter opener revealing a sliver of the white core. Satisfied, the Boss laid down the blade and said, Anything else?

The hashish . . .

He grinned and leaned back in his chair. Good stuff, right?

So I've heard. I haven't tried it myself.

Good. There are some things you should neither try nor buy.

I saw myself explaining, with the enthusiasm of a sales pitch, the situation with BFD and the Maoist PhD. I gave them a taste of the goods, I heard myself saying. My screw was quite loose at that moment, providing me with enough distance to see myself become what I swore I would never become: a capitalist.

Interesting, the Boss said, the fingers of his hands touching in a steeple. Not that it's a surprise. Not at all. Even those people would enjoy the things I can give them.

They're only human. So very human.

Exactly! He was greatly amused, if the smile on his face was any indication. Even the French are only human. The rich, too. Especially the rich.

I'm not sure that they're rich. They're intellectuals.

If they don't work with their hands, they're rich. And that politician is definitely rich. I know his name. He's the one in charge of this arrondissement. He's as bad as the rest of the politicians. They're all sleazy socialists and caviar communists.

I totally agree, I said, performing my best yes-man act.

But even if you're not a politician or an intellectual—he turned his palms to me so I could see the map of his toil, the scars and calluses of his personal geography—that doesn't mean you can't get rich by working with your hands.

This is a new opportunity. A new market.

Grow or die. That's my thinking.

It's a good philosophy.

He checked the symmetrical white cuticles of his fingernails, manicured at a nail salon that he owned, then looked at me again. If eyes were the windows to a soul, he had blackout curtains pulled shut behind his. What do you want?

What I wanted was revenge, but as I watched myself with that unfeeling sense that I was a stranger even to me, all I heard myself say was: You supply, I sell.

He named a price for the goods, per gram. I explained that I was a refugee working a menial job—not that there was anything wrong with the job he had given me, all refugees have to start somewhere, that somewhere being at the bottom, where we offered our bottom to be kicked, which provided endless merriment for the citizenry of our host countries. The point was that I did not have the capital to purchase the goods. Instead of investing my nonexistent financial capital in his goods, I offered to barter my social capital, my access

to my aunt's friends, for his goods. In exchange, I would expand
his market and deliver to him profits he would not otherwise have,
divided fifty-fifty between us, after deducting the cost of the goods.

Something behind the curtains twitched. Thirty percent.

Forty percent.

He was amused. Twenty-five percent.

It was difficult to negotiate with someone who could take a
hammer out of his desk drawer and break your knuckles or kneecaps
without compunction or hesitation. You're too generous, I said.
The Boss nodded toward the door and told me to see Le Cao Boi,
who would provide me with the goods. In parting he said, I'm not
sure whether you're less crazy or more crazy for wanting to do this.

I'm not crazy.

That's what the crazy ones always say.

Looking back, it is clear to me now, as it must be to you, that per-
haps the balance between my two minds, always precarious, had
suddenly tilted too far right, into a place where I could watch myself
becoming more and more about *me* and *me* alone, the best justi-
fication there was for capitalism. Did that make me crazy, as the
Boss and many others have claimed? Maybe I was crazy, or a little
bit crazy, or maybe I was simply flawed. Yes, I am flawed, we are all
flawed, even you, but I blame my flaws on the fact that all my life
I only ever aspired to one thing—*to be human.* That was my first
mistake, since I was already human, a fact not always recognized by
others. Perhaps Saïd wanted to be human, too, despite being a drug
dealer, or perhaps he was smarter than me and took his humanity for
granted, which allowed him to be a drug dealer, as he had nothing
to prove. Now he had disappeared and left an opportunity, a void in
the market. Someone would eventually fill that void. Why not me?

By the time I arrived at the restaurant, an answer was waiting for my rhetorical question, a square brown paper package the size of a croque monsieur, wrapped with string. Sliding the package across the countertop, Le Cao Boi said, Glad you've decided to join us. His face was statuesque in its impassivity, the faint ghosts of me and myself floating in the lenses of his sunglasses. I matched his impassivity as I accepted the package and slipped it into a jacket pocket, where it rested against my hip with a pistol's patience, utterly confident that it would, sooner or later, be used.

Bon watched the transaction from a table where he was refilling bottles of soy sauce with a chemist's precision, the only person sitting in the barren restaurant. I hope you know what you're doing, smart guy, he said.

Of course I don't, I said, implying in my lighthearted way that I indeed did know what I was doing, even if, in fact, I did not. And it will give me a chance to improve my French, I went on. Nothing makes people more talkative than mutual intoxication.

You could just go to school to refine your French.

Yes, but you always told me that not all the answers can be found in books.

I'll tell you what else you can't find in a book, Le Cao Boi said. The Boss expects at least a twenty percent return. He doesn't like to waste his time. Or his goods. In other words, you better make this little investment worthwhile.

Hey, new guy, Sleepy called out from the kitchen. The toilet needs cleaning!

I left the worst Asian restaurant in Paris with the sound of Sleepy's laughter in my ears, the scent of disinfectant on my hands, and the taste of bile on my tongue. Only a shot of revenge could wash that

taste away. I would not be the obsequious Asiatic object of pity, the pathetic or polite little refugee who would agree to begin from the beginning, as a student of my master's language—

Hey you!

—or as a waiter or a busboy or a dishwasher—

You!

—or a plumber—

# YOU!

I froze. The voice, loud and stern, seemed aimed at me, although I was not the only one on the street who turned. Everyone around me pivoted to see a pair of policemen striding toward us, the one in front pointing his finger at me. I knew exactly why. Something was transmitting a signal on the invisible airwaves. Although the packet in my pocket was silent, that did not mean it had nothing to say. No, it exuded a sense of confidence, perhaps even a touch of menace, as all valuable things did. It had power over me, as it was well aware. I could throw it away, of course, destroy it in any number of ways, and it could do nothing to stop me—except simply by existing.

# *YOU!*

The policemen suddenly broke into a run, and my body and mind became quite calm as they braced themselves. I had felt that same stillness on the boat as it soared into the sky, borne on the wave. *Hashish*, the packet in my pocket whispered, knowing only its own

name. *Hashish*. It knew that it was literally more valuable than me. It had a price that people were willing to pay, whereas my life had almost no value at all. Because no one would pay for me what one would for the goods in the packet, I was now in debt to it. I was about to raise my hands in surrender to it and to the policemen, but they charged right past me, one on either side, close enough that their sleeves brushed mine.

# YOU!

They were not shouting at *me* after all, but at a shambolic man whose hair was so unkempt and skin was so unwashed that he was of indeterminate race or ethnicity, which was the French ideal. Everyone could be French, including the homeless!

One policeman jerked a beer can from the bewildered bum's hand and shoved him against a wall. The other cop kicked him in the seat of his pants and sent him nearly tumbling to the ground, all while the rest of the upstanding citizens—and me, not to mention myself—stood watching. When the policeman with the beer can hurled it at the back of the bewildered bum, splashing him with its contents, which seemed to defeat the purpose of making him less hideous to Parisian eyes, I averted my own eyes and walked past the scene in silence.

That night, my aunt and I smoked the finest hashish and drank the finest Haut-Médoc and listened to the finest American jazz, that black-and-blue music so beloved by the French partially because every sweet note reminded them of American racism, which conveniently let them forget their own racism. Since I was also black and

blue all over, at least on the inside, Nina Simone singing "Mississippi Goddam" was a perfect accompaniment for me. And then there was my aunt, who had finished my confession and was feeling kind of blue herself. She remained unbothered by what had happened to me, imprisoned with a thousand fetid fellows for a year on starvation rations, forced to write and rewrite a confession, and then, for the coup de grâce, thrown into solitary confinement, naked, with sacks over my head, hands, and feet, periodically jolted by low-level electricity that kept me awake for an unknown amount of time, until I could no longer distinguish my body from its surroundings, time itself losing meaning as I was bombarded with an unrelenting sonic attack composed of an infant's recorded howling, until at last I could pass the final exam. It was this exam, which she had finally gotten to, that disturbed my aunt, leading her to mutter over and over again its only question:

WHAT IS MORE PRECIOUS THAN INDEPENDENCE AND FREEDOM?

Like every good revolutionary, my aunt already knew the answer, Ho Chi Minh's most famous slogan, a spell that mobilized millions to rise and die in order to evict the French and then the Americans, to unify our country and liberate it. After she muttered the question, she declaimed the answer, first as an incantation, which was how it was intended to be said:

NOTHING IS MORE PRECIOUS THAN INDEPENDENCE AND FREEDOM!

And then again with her voice rising, as a question:

NOTHING IS MORE PRECIOUS THAN INDEPENDENCE AND FREEDOM?

Exactly, I said sadly, shaking my head and giving her for free what had cost me so much to learn. *Nothing* is, in fact, more precious than independence and freedom.

No, no, no! Nothing *is* more precious than independence and freedom—I mean, independence and freedom are *more* precious than nothing, not the other way around!

You read my confession. I sighed, then inhaled so deeply from the laced cigarette that my lungs sizzled, the smoke that issued forth reminding me of how everything solid eventually melts into air. Have you learned nothing?

Shut up! she cried. Give me that cigarette.

Doesn't *nothing* make more sense after hashish?

No. Nothing makes sense at all after your confession.

Of course it does. You just refuse to make sense of nothing, as most people do. Now if you had gone through reeducation like I had, under the hands of a master revolutionary theorist like Man, you would understand that nothing is *contradictory*, like everything meaningful—love and hate, capitalism and communism, France and America. Leave it to the simple-minded to understand only one side of a contradiction. You're not simple-minded, are you?

I hate you, she groaned, eyes closed. Why did I invite you into my house?

It's all quite funny, if you think about it. Almost as funny as the funniest part of my confession, said by none other than Man himself, which should be engraved on the pedestal of Ho Chi Minh's statue, if he has a statue. Except that it is unprintable, as the truth too often is: "Now that we are the powerful, we don't need the French or the Americans to fuck us over—"

"We can fuck ourselves just fine," she said.

I howled with laughter, slapped my knee, felt tears moistening my cheeks. This hashish was really something else! Come on, I said after my laughter had subsided. Isn't that funny?

No. She stubbed out her cigarette. That's not funny.

A trumpet blared and my vision was hazy, and if I could have seen myself in a mirror, I surely would have seen double of me, or two of us, not so much black and blue but red and yellow.

You used to believe in the revolution, she said. What do you believe in now?

Nothing, I said. But isn't that something?

So you're going to sell drugs.

Well, I muttered. Even under a cloud of hashish, I could see that her contempt had a point. It's better than nothing.

My aunt drew herself up from where she had been reclining on the couch and turned off the stereo. So long as you were a revolutionary, I could have you living here for free as my service to the revolution and as an expression of my belief in solidarity, she said. She was remarkably eloquent after the hashish, or perhaps her passion had focused her. But if you're going to be dealing drugs—

You're making a moral judgment?

I make no moral judgment. I'm the one smoking hashish. And sometimes criminals make the best revolutionaries, or revolutionaries are condemned as criminals. But if you're no longer a revolutionary and you're going to be selling drugs, and sleeping on my couch, and asking me to protect you from Bon by keeping your communist past a secret, then you can afford to split the profits with me.

My mouth, already slightly agape under the influence of the hashish, fell completely open.

What's the matter? she said, lighting another hashish cigarette. Too contradictory for you?

* * *

Walking the next morning to the Maoist PhD's apartment from the metro, I experienced déjà vu for the second time in less than twelve hours (strange that even my psychic tics or malfunctions were named in the master's language). The first time was when I offered to split the profits with my aunt fifty-fifty, only to have her counter with sixty-forty, terms to which I had to agree once again. The second time was walking on the Maoist PhD's street, where I had the eerie sense that I had been there before, since his street evoked for me one of Saigon's boulevards, or rather, Saigon's boulevards evoked a street like his. The French had designed Saigon in the spirit of Haussmann's Paris, with wide thoroughfares and broad sidewalks lined with fetching trees and elegant apartment buildings of no more than six or seven stories, decorated with balconies and capped by garrets where, during the heat of August, one could roast artists or the poor, which we in Saigon could do year-round. Oh, Saigon, Pearl of the Orient! Or so it was called, presumably by the French, using a term of endearment that we ourselves had adapted, for there was nothing the people of a small country liked better than to be flattered, so rarely did it happen. But sometimes we were not just the Pearl of the Orient, and sometimes the Pearl of the Orient did not even refer to us. I had heard the Chinese of Hong Kong claim that their port was the Pearl of the Orient, and when I was in the Philippines, the Filipinos insisted that Manila was the Pearl of the Orient. Colonies were a pearl choker adorning the alabaster-white neck of the colonizer. And sometimes a Pearl of the Orient could be a Paris of the Orient as well. The Parisians and the French and just about everyone meant that as a compliment, but it was a backhanded compliment, the only kind a colonizer could

give to the colonized. After all, as the Paris of the Orient, Saigon was just a cheap imitation of haute couture.

I had worked myself into such a lather of resentment that I was practically frothing at the mouth when Paris suddenly gave me a sticky reminder of one way that Saigon was considerably superior. *Squish!* I stopped and looked with dread and then disgust at the sole of my shoe. Nowhere in Saigon would the unwitting pedestrian have a chance of stepping on canine excrement, because the statistical truth was that we preferred to consume canines rather than keep them as pets, and if we kept them, we never allowed them to wander the streets, for fear that they might be eaten. *Vive la différence!* Here in Paris, dogs roamed everywhere, liberated to do their business as they pleased. In this case, some degenerate Parisian dog owner, of whom thousands existed, had left the prize almost on the doorstep of the Maoist psychoanalyst's building. The imprint of my sole was on the thick brown smear, ready for a detective to study my shoe-print. No amount of scraping against the cement would get rid of the foul substance from the crevices of my shoe. I gave up, hesitated before buzzing the Maoist PhD's apartment, but then remembered the first lesson of capitalism, which was so hard for Vietnamese people to learn: Never be late. I pressed the button.

In the tiny elevator, which offered room for no more than three adults of average French build, or four Vietnamese of average Vietnamese build, or perhaps three and a half Eurasians like me, the odor from my shoe was evident. I kept my sole off the floor, and when the Maoist PhD let me into his apartment, I did my best to walk in that manner, limping, I said, because of a sore ankle. It was not my fault that the French were not as civilized as Asians, who believed, for very good reason, that one should take off one's shoes before entering a house. In this regard, the French were medieval.

You have a beautiful apartment, I said in rapid-fire English when he greeted me in his rapid-fire French. He hesitated, but in the end he replied in English. Like BFD, he could not pass up the chance to prove to someone like me that he could speak today's imperial lingua franca. Like BFD, the Maoist PhD's English was good but accented. He would know all too well how impeccable mine was, judging from the framed posters of *The Big Sleep*, *Vertigo*, *King Kong*, and *Frankenstein* hanging on the walls. His gilt-edged mirrors were door-sized, his furniture was varnished with age, his Turkish rug was intricate, and his parquet floorboards moaned underfoot. All were fitting decor for an eighteenth-century apartment with exposed beams and a ceiling tall enough to circulate the heated air of a hardworking brain.

I nearly forgave him for being a French intellectual when he poured me two fingers of a brand of fifteen-year-old scotch whose name was so Gaelic I could neither spell nor pronounce it. I closed my eyes in appreciation, shivering and swirling the magic potion in my mouth and over my deprived tongue, which had drunk more wine than spirits here in Paris. I happily offered the Maoist the goods, and the generous soul immediately rolled a cigarette with the product and offered to share it with me in communist fraternity.

Although I surmise that you hate the communists, the Maoist PhD added, lighting the cigarette. I was grateful for the aroma, its scent disguising how something was foul here, namely me. Your aunt told me about your experiences in the reeducation camp.

I was back in the role I could not escape, typecast as the anti-communist patriot of South Vietnam that had been my cover as a spy. How I wished to no longer play the role of the reactionary! I could not claim to be a communist, but did that mean I could not be a revolutionary? Just because one revolution failed, was revolution itself dead? I hadn't wanted to explain myself to my aunt. For her and

for most self-proclaimed revolutionaries like me, "revolution" was a magic word, like God, that foreclosed certain avenues of thinking. We believed in revolution, but what was it? Was it, in the end, really nothing? I wanted her to *understand* nothing, or help *me* understand nothing, because I did not yet fully understand what it meant, except that it was somehow revolutionary in its own way. For now, a revolutionary without a revolution, I had to create a new story. So, under the influence of a fine scotch and an equally fine hashish, a pairing that I recommend to all, I said, You might be surprised that I do not hate communists. Do I think they are mistaken? Yes. But their impulse toward revolution—well, that I can support.

I cannot tell you how disappointed I am in the outcome of your country's revolution, the Maoist PhD said. It is the same as what happened under Stalin. A corruption of communist ideals! The Party elevated itself and the state instead of the people. We of the Left, who opposed the American war in your country, hoped that your revolution would destroy the American empire. But the American empire persists and the genuinely communist society has not been created.

Perhaps something is wrong with the theory if it can't be put into practice, I said.

But it's never been put into real practice. Unfortunately, conditions are not yet in place for genuine communism. Capitalism has to win globally and become the worst version of itself before communism can subvert it. The workers of the world have to see that capitalism is only interested in profit, not them, and that it will inevitably reduce them to slave labor as it maximizes profit. See Marx, *Capital*, volume one.

When will this triumph of capitalism happen?

The Maoist PhD blew a cloud of smoke. Whole swathes of the world still have to fall completely to capitalism before we see a

genuine global uprising of the oppressed. Take Africa, for example. Capitalism looted Africa, first for slaves and then for resources. Capitalism will continue to exploit Africa with renewed cruelty. Someone must provide the cheap labor for cheap goods, and then those same workers have to buy the expensive goods imported into their country that have been made from the resources extracted from their country. Ah, the perpetual motion machine of capitalist fantasy! But once that happens, a proletariat is created and then a middle class, and even as some of the poorest are lifted out of absolute poverty, the gap in inequality widens and widens, as the wealthy become wealthier at a much faster rate than the very poor become a little less poor. This inevitable process is built into capitalism, which means that the conditions for revolution are inherent in capitalism itself.

Have you ever lived through a revolution? I said.

May 1968, the Maoist PhD said proudly. I will never forget how we students all over the world almost changed the world, until we encountered what Althusser—my teacher Louis Althusser—called the "Repressive State Apparatus." I was studying for my doctorate with him but I still manned the barricades here. I admit to throwing a cobblestone or two. Our friend, the future BFD—no one called him just by his initials then—did the same. The police—that is, one part of the Repressive State Apparatus—tear-gassed and beat us. Never will I forget the blow of that baton! That baton taught me as much as theory and philosophy have ever taught me. That baton made real what Benjamin—Walter Benjamin—argued in "Critique of Violence"—that what makes the state legitimate is not the law but *violence*. The state wants to monopolize violence, the monopoly of violence is named the law, and the law legitimizes itself. The police are not there to protect us, the citizens, but to protect the state and its rule of law. That is why one proper response to the blow of the baton

is revolution in the streets! And student revolutions in streets around the world, from Tokyo to Mexico City, only echoed the revolutions in Algeria and Vietnam, where the Algerians and the Vietnamese confronted not batons but bullets. The Vietnamese were revolting against the monopoly of violence that was colonization! And by doing so, they revealed how illegitimate colonization actually was. They fought against not only the Repressive State Apparatus but also what Althusser described as the Ideological State Apparatus, which gets us to believe in the laws that are written against our self-interest! Why else would workers believe that capitalism is for them? Why else would the colonized believe in the white man's superiority? The blow of that baton told me that what Che Guevara called for was true: we will need a hundred more Vietnams to flower across the world.

But at least three million people died during our war, I said slowly, my cloudy brain trying to perform basic mathematical functions. If you multiplied this by one hundred . . . it would equal . . .

At that point my cognitive abilities ended, as my math could not rise to that level of misery. I could not tell whether I wanted to laugh, to cry, to shout, or to commit myself to an asylum. I, too, believed in everything he said, but unlike the Maoist PhD, I had lived through a revolution and its consequences. And it was not just capitalism that created fantasies through these Ideological State Apparatuses and enforced them through Repressive State Apparatuses—so did communism. What was the reeducation camp but a Repressive State Apparatus designed to carry out the work of the Ideological State Apparatus? The reeducation camp's task was to turn the inmates into people who would swear that they were free even if they were enslaved, proclaim that they had been remade when they had only been broken. Che Guevara and the Maoist PhD saw the Vietnamese revolution only from afar, with all its glamorous makeup, whereas I had seen it up close, denuded. Three million people dead for a

Being neither Chinese nor Arab, I was not sure how this koan applied to me, and I turned it over in my mind for a second before I found the right response: And what does the West have?

The West? The Maoist PhD smiled. The West has woman, or so Malraux said.

I smiled back, and we smiled at each other for a moment.

Well, I said. I suppose I'm getting back to my European roots.

I always tell my students that they should strive to be the first of their kind.

I guess I'm a true original then, I said, rubbing the sole of my shoe into his Turkish rug. And I intend to be so very good at being bad.

# CHAPTER 4

**A**fter my aunt had gone to sleep, I sat on the sofa with my two new companions, the hashish and the money. The only way to make the hashish stop giggling and whispering at me was to smoke some of it, which made it, and me, relax. Under the dim light cast by the one lamp I kept on, an antique older than me, I surveyed the handful of bills that I had earned that day, with my aunt's 60 percent already deducted but with the Boss's 75 percent yet to be deducted. I had earned almost nothing, but did I truly deserve almost nothing? What I had done was exchange the hashish for the money, and before that, I had exchanged something for the hashish with the Boss. I had offered him a part of myself.

The more I stared at the francs, the more they seemed unreal. What made each of those leaves of paper nearly as powerful as a human being, and what made them, together, more valuable than a human being? After all, I would no more harm one of those bills than I would harm a human being.

Actually . . . the specter of Sonny said.

In fact . . . said the equally ghostly crapulent major.

And it was true. I had killed them both, and I had never done more to money than fold it. I had never ripped a corner off a bill, the way little boys tore the wings off captured flies. I had never lit even the smallest denomination just to see how it would burn, in the manner that I had once seen an American child use a plastic magnifying glass to incinerate an ant on the sidewalk. Collectively, money was invulnerable. And individually, a bill like the ones I now found in my possession was protected by that aura of invulnerability, the way an individual cop embodied the entire Repressive State Apparatus. That was how the almost weightless bills I picked up in my hand affected me with their magic.

Perhaps I felt anew the strange power of money because of my new occupation. I had only ever been paid for my work as a soldier, which was, in theory, if not always in practice, an honorable occupation. As a spy, I had never been paid, believing that not even my life was more precious than independence and freedom. But now I was selling hashish, and there was nothing noble or honorable in that, as one part of me understood and as another part of myself did not care. Why should I? For most of my life, I had constantly and desperately believed in *something*, only to discover that at the heart of that something was *nothing*. So why not give nothing a chance?

And yet—what would my mother think of my new career? I tried not to think about how much I would have disappointed her. How could I break her heart, when she had given it all to me? But when I thought about what my father might think, I was filled only with happiness. Here I was in the land of my father, infecting it with Eastern drugs, a small payback for how his country had infected mine with Western civilization.

My new job was made easier because my predecessor in supplying hashish, the mysterious Saïd, had built an impressive network of clients over the past decade, with the Maoist PhD being the oldest.

Saïd never could get a job with a name like Saïd, the Maoist PhD had told me in parting. A meaningful job, that is. And he wouldn't do something so simple as change his name.

The Maoist PhD thought of himself as not just Saïd's client but his patron, helping him become a financially self-reliant young man by introducing him to his many eager friends, colleagues, students, and former students. Now through the Maoist PhD and my aunt, the news of the quality of my goods and the speediness of my delivery circulated through the network. I was a novelty—a Eurasian pharmacologist of the black market, a half-Vietnamese dealer of partly beneficial, partly dangerous goods that were not so good but also not so bad. Over the next few weeks, I made my deliveries with the nonchalant air of the law-abiding citizen, assured in the knowledge that the police tended not to look twice at Asians, or so Le Cao Boi had reassured me. At the restaurant, he pointed to how the Arabs and the blacks did us the unintentional favor of being our racial decoys, drawing the attention of police who thought them to be as brown, sticky, and aromatic as hashish itself.

I looked out the window at the passersby and said, How can you tell who's Arab?

How do you tell? You tell by looking! It's obvious!

I wasn't trying to be dense. I had some understanding of the Arab situation in France: the war that the French had fought with the Algerians right after fighting a war with us; the Pieds-Noirs who had fled from Algeria to France, refugees like us; the hard feelings that always remained after this kind of forcible separation. But I had never met an Arab, and I had not been here long enough so that the differences within French society felt natural to me. To an outsider, another society's differences always looked odd, which was why the French had a very good understanding of the absurdities of American racism and the specter of THE BLACK, which to

Americans was simply the way the world was. But for me, here in France, THE ARAB was an abstraction. Just to provoke Le Cao Boi, I pointed at a man walking by and asked, Is he Arab?

No, Camus, he's French. (I was not certain that Le Cao Boi had ever read Camus, but in this and other conversations, whenever he got frustrated with me, he would call me Camus, perhaps the only philosopher he had heard of.) Look, there's an Arab now.

The man walking by wore a white sweatshirt, gray sweatpants, and white sneakers. Yes, I could see it! He could be an Arab! Or he could just be a very tan Frenchman with somewhat curly dark hair. I can't tell the difference, I said, still having fun at Le Cao Boi's expense. What are the signs?

The signs? Le Cao Boi wrinkled his forehead, a sure indication the mechanism behind it was working. It's—I mean—you just can, all right? The hair, the skin, the way they carry themselves, the way they talk. You just haven't been here long enough to read the signs. Just take my word for it. The police aren't going to be looking at you except as a harmless foreigner, so long as there's only one of you. Two of you, still acceptable. Three of you, or us, the French get a little uneasy. Four—forget about it. That's an invasion.

Since I was already me and myself, I felt already in danger of being too noticeable. So, to accentuate my disguise as an innocent, harmless Asian, I draped a Japanese camera around my neck, borrowed from my aunt. I also wore a small backpack in reverse, the straps around my back, the pack on my chest. With a fedora, a pair of horn-rimmed glasses that lent the illusion of a slant to my eyes that were not slanted, at least not to me, and a little bit of cotton wedged behind my upper lip, to imply something wrong with my teeth, my disguise was complete. I was not just a mostly harmless domestic Asian; I was a completely harmless and well-disciplined Japanese tourist. In this disguise, as an innocent visitor intent on

VIET THANH NGUYEN

taking photographs rather than an invader who might be taking
French jobs, I could go almost anywhere.

I confess that I thought I was pretty smart. I had not anticipated
that Bon might be even smarter. But he had changed, too, as a result
of reeducation, something I began to understand one day when
he waved me over to a table at the restaurant on a typically empty
afternoon and said, I have an idea.

You have an idea? I said. Bon did not have ideas; I had ideas.

Bon stared at me. There are communists here.

There are communists everywhere.

In our community.

You're talking about my aunt.

She's not a part of the community. She's turned French.

So have a lot of our countrymen here.

They don't like to get together very much, do they? But one
place where we could find them and begin doing some investiga-
tions is the Vietnamese Union.

I had heard about this Union. The restaurant had a few mimeo-
graphed flyers announcing the Union's various activities: promoting
the learning of the Vietnamese language, celebrating Vietnamese
culture, advocating for the Vietnamese community's interests in
France. Even in Vietnam we had not seen the word "Vietnamese"
deployed as often as at the Union, whose official name was the
Union for the Advancement of Vietnamese Culture. You think the
Union is communist? I said.

Not officially. But everybody knows they're commies. The Viet-
namese government recognizes them. The Vietnamese ambassador
comes to their events. And if they look like commies and smell like
commies, they're commies. But if it's a problem, it's an opportunity,
too. Every problem is an opportunity.

What's the opportunity?

You're the opportunity. We can make some money and corrupt some commies all at the same time with what you sell for the Boss. Beautiful, isn't it?

It was a plan. But Bon was not a planner, he was the action man. Did the Boss give you this idea?

No, but the Boss thinks it's a great idea.

You went to the Boss? I said. What do you get out of it?

I tag along. Maybe I'll have the chance to kill some commies.

Does that mean we'll have to play at being communists?

If I can do it, so can you, he said. There was a light in his eyes that I had seen only when he was with his wife and son and then, after their deaths, when he spoke of killing communists. Now you get a chance to hurt some commies, he said. You should thank me for that.

Thank you, I said.

Would our war never end? At least for Bon, it appeared that it never would, not until he was dead or incapable of continuing in his quest to kill all the communists in the world. Like many people, he saw the world in an either/or fashion, communist or anticommunist, evil or good. Whereas his vision of the world was a mirror image of how the communists saw things, I felt being forced to choose between communism and its opposite was a false choice, imposed by the Ideological State Apparatuses of both sides. The most difficult thing, when offered two false choices, was imagining a third choice, withheld deliberately or otherwise. This was the most basic lesson of the dialectic, the swing between thesis and antithesis that allowed one to reach a synthesis. Whether the thesis or the antithesis was communism or anticommunism, the point was that they composed the polar opposites of what the West unironically called the Cold War, as fought between the USA and USSR. But the synthesis was the

recognition that this war had been extremely hot for us Asians, and Africans, and Latin Americans. Seeing the failures of both communism and anticommunism, I chose nothing, a synthesis that neither capitalists nor communists could understand. You may think that I am being a nihilist, but you could not be more wrong. While nihilists thought life was meaningless and rejected all religious and moral principles, I still believed in the *principle* of revolution. I also believed that nothing was full of meaning—in short, that nothing was actually something. Wasn't that a kind of revolution in itself?

In this state of mind, I ventured forth with Bon two weeks later to the next meeting of the Union, whose membership appeared to consist entirely of respectable Vietnamese. In France, unlike in the United States, respectable people could include communists or communist sympathizers, and it was strange to think that some of them would likely be attending the meeting. This particular meeting's purpose was to plan the annual Tet show, the Chairman of the Tet committee explained to Bon and me, the only newcomers.

There will be traditional dancing and singing, the cheerful Chairman said. He was an ophthalmologist by trade, a slender, white-haired man with long fingers suitable for a pianist or a gynecologist. Both his Vietnamese and French were flawless, and I made up for my jealousy by pitying how he wore a tweed blazer at least a size too large for him, the cuffs brushing the bases of his thumbs. The Chairman did not believe, as I did, that every man should have a tailor, who was as important as a priest, for it made no sense to be good if one did not look good.

There will also be traditional costumes and foods, he went on. It's a way for us to present our authentic Vietnamese culture.

I nodded sympathetically, even vigorously, and said, Promoting our authentic culture is very important, to which the cheerful Chairman nodded even more vigorously.

Although I did not say so out loud, I wondered if perhaps authentic Vietnamese culture should also include gambling, which we taught to our children during Tet celebrations and then wondered why we had a predilection for gambling as adults; or smoking and drinking coffee in cafés, for which, if there were an Olympic competition for such a sport, we Vietnamese men would be gold medal contenders, for we treated these cafés, inherited from the French, as second homes away from abrasive wives and pesky children; or drinking beer, cognac, and wine (preferably of the native rice kind) until we reached the doorway to oblivion, whereon some of us beat the aforementioned wives and children or each other; or getting a good deal, even at the expense of our customers or our merchants or our principles, and then being outraged when we ourselves were cheated; or gossiping about our friends and relatives, whom we loved to backstab even more than stabbing our enemies, whose backs were harder to reach; or taking pride in the accomplishments of our neighbors and countrymen, until they accomplished too much, whereupon we resented them and waited for the sweet opportunity to gleefully witness their downfall; or making the women stay in the kitchen and serve the men, or expecting said women to reproduce at least six or seven times, and hopefully more, until their uteruses were as dusty as the Sahara—all aspects of our culture we performed much more frequently than a fan dance, or singing a snatch of opera or folk song, or wearing a silk gown, or reenacting a courtship ritual in the rice paddies, which only ever happened once in a lifetime, if at all, and if it did, likely involved scraping off the buffalo dung encrusted between our toes and swatting away the squadrons of dive-bombing mosquitoes.

But it seemed bad manners to bring up these issues when all the Chairman and his committee wanted was to enshrine the beauty of our culture and share it with others, even if staging a culture

show was really an acknowledgment of one's cultural inferiority. The truly powerful rarely needed to put on a show, since their culture was always everywhere. Americans knew their culture was ubiquitous, whether burgers or bombs. As for the French, they exported the Parisian Dream, a street show for tourists who went gaga over wine and cheese and accordion music. Mentioning none of this, I volunteered at the meeting's end for the song-and-dance routines, betting that any hashish-smoking bohemians would be found there. I volunteered Bon for the dancing and singing as well, even though he clearly did not look like a dancer, and he certainly could not be a singer, not after I spoke on his behalf and explained that he was mute. This, too, was Bon's idea.

*Ah bon?* the Chairman said, an expression I loved almost as much as *oh là là*.

A war wound, I said, my voice catching. I had not planned on any emotion for this fake story—where was it coming from?

The atmosphere was hushed, all the members of the Tet committee focusing their attention on us now.

No one knows the cause of his muteness, I said, tears once more coming to my eyes. I could feel Bon staring at me as I told the story that I had invented. A B-52 bomb landed almost on top of us. After that, he lost his voice. Perhaps the blast damaged something in his throat. Or perhaps it's all psychological.

I sobbed. My story had me, and I had them. I saw it in their eyes, their slightly parted lips, the holding of the collective breath.

You see, that B-52 attack caught us in the open. It wasn't meant for us. It was meant for the guerrillas. But the Americans bombed us, their own friends, I continued. Bon twitched but said nothing. The Americans vaporized almost an entire battalion of southern soldiers. The Americans call it "friendly fire." I just call it fire. The only thing you could hear were the bombs and, afterward, the screaming

76

of whoever was left. But there wasn't much left. All those voices gone forever . . . perhaps thinking of all our young comrades lost so tragically made my friend lose his own voice.

Oh my God, a matron said, hand to mouth.

And now to polish the wax on Bon's story:

I thought . . . I thought . . . if he could see the beauty of our culture, he could forget the war's horror. I hoped . . . hoped . . . if he could see our people sing and dance, even if he cannot sing and dance—I looked down, a salty tide of genuine emotion lapping against my toes—his voice might come back . . . and that we, former soldiers of the south, might be friends with you, many of whom, or so I've been told, sympathize with our former enemies. But we are enemies no longer. Now's the time to be friends. Don't you agree?

If I was the crazy bastard, then Bon was the lucky bastard, because after this story and the meeting was concluded, all the girls and women surrounded him, each hoping to be the princess who could return the hero's voice with a kiss (or more, if needed). Bon was grateful for the excuse of having lost his voice, since nothing frightened him more than speaking to women, including killing people, which he regarded mostly as a technical challenge and only occasionally a moral one. He was a very moral person who had joined his church choir in Saigon partly out of faith and partly out of hoping to meet his future wife, which he did. He and his future wife had sat across the aisle from each other on a bus trip to the Catholic shrine of La Vang, before the war's cross fire destroyed it. She almost tripped getting off the bus, accidentally or deliberately, and he had grabbed her elbow. That was the excuse Linh needed to say hello, initiating a conversation that would not end until she died on the tarmac of the Saigon airport without the chance to say goodbye. Even now he saw her dead face and the face of his dead

son, Duc, just a little boy. Ever since their deaths he had refused to think of another woman, much less speak to the few women to whom he had been attracted. The loneliness and sadness that resulted was the fate he thought he deserved for living.

Poor Bon! I didn't care if he was a killer. He was my blood brother, my best friend, and it pained me that ever since the death of his wife and son—my godson!—he had nobody to love him but me, which was a horrible fate. To then be unexpectedly encircled by a half dozen women, gazing at him as if he were an infant lying in a cradle, made him lose the voice he actually had. All he could do was smile, nod, and shrug, a mute pantomime that suited him perfectly. Muteness was a kind of freedom from the world for him, if not for those who wanted to speak to him. But since they could say only so much to a man who could not or would not talk back, they eventually rotated to me, the one who would benefit even more than Bon from his muteness.

But not all the women were looking at me. One of them, still turned toward Bon, was writing in a notepad with a fountain pen gripped in a most delicate, graceful hand. When she looked up and saw him watching her, she smiled and silently offered him the notepad and pen.

*My name is Loan,* she had written, as if he were not only mute but deaf. *Do you want to come watch us practice?*

Bon surprised himself by writing *yes.*

As we left the meeting, I was uncertain about who was more astonished, Bon or me. He bore with him a sheet of paper with Loan's name and phone number and the time, date, and location of the next practice for the dancers and singers. I was going to ask him if he was ready to kill any of the nice people whom we had met, including

the Chairman, who seemed to me like he could be a communist, when Bon, even though he was supposed to be mute, said, Look.

Fortunately, no one else was in the Union's foyer. He pointed to a bulletin board, on which was pinned a large poster with garish colors and bold lettering, the most significant word of which was FANTASIA. The next most significant words were EPISODE 7. Various singers and dancers, male and female, single or in duos, trios, or quartets, populated the poster. They wore suits and ties, or spandex and glitter, or modest ao dai and conical hats, or fishnet stockings and bras. I understood immediately that *Fantasia* the show was based on the nightclub in Los Angeles of the same name, a place where I had passed a night soaked in cognac and testosterone, my tongue hanging out at the sight of the one woman I should have kept my eyes, hands, and mind off of: Lana.

Oh, Lana! When the General had learned of my love affair with her in Los Angeles, he had dispatched me on a suicide mission to retake our country, the mission that had led to my capture and the reeducation camp. My reeducation had clearly taught me nothing, for the sight of Lana ignited the puddle of passion sloshing inside my gas tank. She posed by herself on the poster among the others, a headliner, barely wearing a slinky and kinky black dress that reached to the ankle but which overcompensated for that modesty by having a slit for her leg cut up to the pelvic bone, revealing her amazing leg in all its bare glory, a leg that ended in a foot harnessed into a high-heeled shoe that with its six-inch spike was both a heinous device of podiatric torture and also a potentially homicidal tool.

Don't even think of it, Bon said, but I already was.

If this forthcoming episode of *Fantasia* was the seventh, that meant six episodes had preceded it, all available on something called

videotape, a technology that had come into the world while I was in the dark ages of my reeducation. The machines used to play videocassettes were expensive, but even after earning almost nothing, my profits from selling the goods provided me with more disposable income than I had ever known. If I were sensible, I would have put my money in the bank and become even more capitalist, using money to conjure more money. But when was I ever sensible?

My aunt already owned a small Japanese television, and hooking up the videocassette recorder was a simple matter. Then I called Bon and told him to come over and watch.

She's a communist, he said.

Put it aside for a night, I said. You were already here one night. It didn't kill you. You didn't kill her. She's a civilian. And you do your best not to kill civilians, remember?

The pause on the line meant he was thinking. I'm not going to kill her. I just don't want to be in her apartment.

Why was it so important for me to get Bon to visit my aunt's apartment? Because I sensed he was changing, and I wanted to change him more. Something had shifted inside him despite himself. He was still ferocious and committed, but he was willing to meet Loan. He was admitting to being lonely. Perhaps that was my point of leverage in my effort to budge him, just a little, from the rock of his fanatical anticommunism, which would lead him to kill me if he found out about my communist past. Besides my self-interest, however, I just wanted him to be less lonely. To find, once again, a family.

You have to see *Fantasia* with your own eyes. And you have to see it with other Vietnamese people. Because it's a show about us, by us, and for us. We're the stars and the emcees, the singers and the dancers, the actors and the comedians, the performers and the spectators! We're doing what we do best—sing, dance, and have fun!

I heard him breathing over the line.

All right, I said, you don't sing or dance. But I know you love watching other people sing and dance. We did it all the time in the clubs in Saigon. We took it for granted back then that we would be entertained in our language, by people with our faces. Now here's our chance again. Come on, Bon!

When, after a moment, he agreed, I knew his loneliness was greater than his hatred. He came bearing a bottle of wine, albeit cheap wine. But the social grace was still a measure of how far he had come from the reeducation camp. Neither my aunt nor he mentioned their last, awkward meeting, and both settled down on the couch to an unspoken truce, with the aid of *Fantasia*. The show had been filmed live in Los Angeles, in a shadow Hollywood where our people had ascended to be the stars. The awesomeness of that feat was evident whenever the camera cut to the audience and showed ecstatic, smiling faces, the viewers absolutely delighted as they watched what our people of the south do best: make a spectacle of themselves. Leave it to the people of our north, where I was born, to dwell on ideology, politics, scholarship, and poetry. They saw the people of the south, where I had grown up, as decadent and indecent. Perhaps that was so, but while the northerners offered a utopia that could be found nowhere, the southerners had created a *Fantasia* that could be experienced everywhere there was a television, a dreamland where men fearlessly wore sequins and women fearlessly wore . . . almost nothing. These men and women did the cha-cha, the tango, and the rhumba. They sang classics as well as covers of Western pop songs. They performed original numbers, some so new I had not heard them before. They acted in vulgar comedic skits. The audience especially loved the bit featuring men dressed up as women, constantly tugging the hems of their skirts, complaining about the runs in their stockings caused by their hairy legs, cupping their unrealistically American-sized breasts in order to adjust them, and flaunting backsides so padded they could

have protected an American football player. Oh, how we howled at those scenes! We, as in the audience at the filming and as in Bon, my aunt, and me. Oh, *Fantasia*!

This was our Hollywood, but as was too often the case in Hollywood movies, the worst thing about the show was the ending. For the final number, the entire troupe of singers and dancers returned to the stage, the men respectably attired in Western suits and the women in Eastern ao dai, serenading the audience with an original song whose title said it all: "Thank You, America!" Additional memorable, if unimaginative, lines included:

> *Thank you, Germany!*
> *Thank you, Australia!*
> *Thank you, Canada!*
> *Thank you, France!*

The geography lesson continued, and I wondered what handful of bewildered souls had found themselves swept up by the whirlwind of war and deposited in, say, Israel, a lovely country, I am sure, but surely a very depressing one for people like us. Still, regardless of our exile, we apparently found at least some degree of gratitude for being taken in, leading to this appreciative, heartfelt ballad to all the countries that had welcomed us.

Unfortunately—though this was a strange trait for a Vietnamese—I hated nothing more than appreciative, heartfelt ballads. My aunt, being an intellectual, and a French intellectual in particular, likewise detested them. Bon, being a killer, should have hated or at least been unmoved by them, but he shocked me by weeping, or weeping as much as he could, which amounted to a few trickles of tears accompanied by some sniffling, the equivalent to an emotional breakdown in a normal person.

But you think America betrayed us, I said as the credits rolled.
That doesn't mean everyone betrayed us.

You think France raped our country.

Why do you have to ruin everything? he cried. Just enjoy the damn song!

And then it struck me that what he was crying about was not the endless, schmaltzy gratitude that host countries demanded of refugees who came from countries raped and bombed by the host countries. He was crying about the story of the song, enacted by an attractive duo playing a husband and wife separated by the war, the woman fleeing to America with their children, the man left behind as a prisoner of war. Eventually he escaped on a refugee boat—no, not a boat, a "vessel," a more dignified term, for his journey and those of thousands of refugees equaled the greatest boat journey of all, Homer's *Odyssey*. Surviving that odyssey, he made it to America. Here he was reunited with his wife, who wore a very flattering mini-skirt, and his boy and girl, who were impossibly cute and talented, playing the piano and violin, respectively, as their parents embraced. That was why Bon was so moved: he was remembering his dead wife and son, my godson, with whom he would never be reunited except, perhaps, in Heaven.

As for my aunt and me, being connoisseurs of criticism did not prevent us from being deeply gratified to see our people on-screen, even if dancing in a leotard or strutting in a miniskirt. For the first time since we lived in our homeland, we starred in our own show. For all its frivolity, *Fantasia* was political, as I had learned when I was released from reeducation and came to Ho Chi Minh City, a Saigon renamed for a new era. There I discovered that Uncle Ho's revolutionary nephews considered this kind of singing, dancing, and lovemaking to be reactionary and dangerous. Good communists listened to blood-stirring red music that hailed blood-soaked

revolution, while we who loved yellow music were sick cowards who refused class struggle and hard work. But somehow, despite my reeducation, or because of it, I still loved a good love song, while a red ode to the masses marching toward a glorious scarlet dawn only made the blood pool in my legs. *Fantasia* might have been mere entertainment, but so what? As the anarchist Emma Goldman said, "If I can't dance, I don't want to be in your revolution." How did our so, so serious revolutionary leaders not understand that to own the means of entertainment was also revolutionary! What was wrong with self-determination of this kind, given that entertainment was probably the fourth human priority after sustenance, shelter, and sex? I could hardly wait to watch episode two of *Fantasia*, and was just about to say so, when Bon finished wiping his tears away and said, I have another idea.

Another idea? my aunt said. What was the first?

I assumed Bon would say nothing, but instead he smiled and said, Sell hashish to the Union and kill communists.

My aunt raised an eyebrow. How interesting, she said. You know, in France, it's the communists who most support the Vietnamese.

The wrong kind of Vietnamese.

You'd be surprised who might be a communist, my aunt said, looking at me, which made Bon look at me, too. My blood went cold.

Nothing surprises me, Bon said. Communists are everywhere.

Indeed they are, my aunt said. Hypothetically speaking, what if you discovered that a friend was secretly a communist? Even your best friend here? Your blood brother?

Bon laughed at the impossibility of this scenario, but like a good philosopher, he played along. I'd kill him, of course, he said, smiling at me. It's a matter of principle.

I, too, laughed at the absurdity of this bad joke and stood up to turn off the TV. *Fantasia* was definitely over.

of French culture. I merged the two with the Walkman, which played cassettes that could fit in one's palm, forty-five minutes of music on each side. With my headphones on, I floated through Paris on my magic carpet of hashish, sunglasses cloaking my eyes. Unlike Le Cao Boi's authentic and expensive aviators, mine were inauthentic ones that did not have the Ray-Ban logo imprinted on a corner of the lens. Even though they tended to slide down my nose, I wore them day and night, above and underground, camera around my neck and backpack on my chest, the curious Japanese tourist ready to offer the simpering smile of the exotic Asiatic in an Occidental land. Invisible so long as I was also inaudible, I explored Paris in my free time or on my deliveries, the city a setting for a musical performed by my headphones. Having once visited the parts of the city that could have served as decorations on wedding cakes, from Notre-Dame to the Eiffel Tower, from the Louvre to Sacré-Coeur, I avoided them. I preferred the grimier quarters or the small parks where I could sit on a bench near the bums and drunks, my not-so-distant cousins, and watch the innocent pigeons. I wondered who was madder, me, the supposedly crazy bastard, or Bon, the martyr intent on throwing himself once more onto the pyre of a grand idea, a lost cause, a last gasp. Bon and I were mad enough to join the biweekly rehearsals for the culture show, where our limited talents turned us into background dancers, if "dancing" was the right word. One of our skits was about rural life, where our entire performance consisted of mimicking plowing, shoveling, hoeing, and heaving in highly stylized, possibly poetic ways that cast farming as a bucolic lifestyle and the backbone of our culture, whereas I am fairly sure that farming was a sweaty, hot mode of hellish, backbreaking survival that left little time for culture. No matter! The mission of the culture show was to compete with the charms of French life by showing the charms of Vietnamese life, which had become much more charming to the Vietnamese in France

after so many years spent away from Vietnam. They all needed their own kind of nostalgia, as the producers of *Fantasia* well understood. And the rehearsals provided me with the opportunity I thought they would, to smoke cigarettes with the other performers, have a few drinks afterward, drop a hint about the goods, give a few samples, and quietly build a new customer base of the young and cool, students and professionals, plus hardworking types who also needed some rest and relaxation and were quite surprised, as well as pleased, to discover that they could get the goods from someone somewhat like them. The only difficulty in gaining the confidence of the young and the cool was that most of them, French born, could speak French faster than me, and with the newest, hippest argot that I did not know.

Who's that friend of yours who teaches French? I asked my aunt.

You'll love him, she said, giving me the address. He's a communist.

So I began taking advanced morning classes, near the Gare du Nord, with adult students from every corner of the former French colonies, while also delivering my goods throughout Paris. I used my profits to buy an excellent pair of brown leather oxfords from Bruno Magli, recommended to me by BFD. They look good and you can walk or stand all day in them, he said. He had looked at my dusty, cracked, faux-leather slip-ons, bought from a street vendor on the way to the Jakarta airport. You can always judge a man by his shoes. BFD's judgment irritated me but I also could not forget it. I wore the Bruno Magli shoes with pride and polished them weekly, succumbing to the capitalist seduction that Marx warned about: loving a commodity, a thing, as if it were an actual living being, an affair that could only be short-lived at best.

A few months into this new episode of my life, I was leaving a small park on passage Dumas when a young man at the gate nodded at me, raised his eyebrow, and held his fingers to his lips in

the universal language of the brotherhood of smokers, unified in our death wish. Jean-Claude Brialy was singing a song with Anna Karina that I loved, "Ne dis rien," and I was humming along. In a good mood, I smiled, took out my packet of cigarettes, and offered him one, making sure it wasn't one laced with hashish. When he said something to me, I took off the headphones, continuing to smile mutely, a Japanese tourist, and was hence surprised when he, smiling back, said, We hear you have some terrific hashish?

*Domo arigato,* I said, pretending not to understand. It was not a good idea to sell to strangers, and I bowed and backed away for two steps before bumping into a hard, muscular body. The young man behind me was, like the one in front of me, wearing blue Levi's jeans, an unzipped jacket, and a T-shirt, except that one T-shirt featured the Beatles, the other the Rolling Stones. We were alone in the small park, a deliberate choice of these young men, who appeared to be the Arabs about whom Le Cao Boi had warned me. They had the careless lankness of youth, protected from knowing what they would look like in twenty years' time, a knowledge that we middle-aged men possessed, to our regret. The inertia of age and the easily accessible pleasures of French baked goods had helped me regain all the fat I had lost during reeducation, plus extra, giving me a small swell over my belt and another little bulge under my chin. I was a soft, round andouillette, my guts tightly packed inside me, and they were the serrated knives ready to slice me open.

Don't pretend you're Japanese, said Beatles. We know you're Vietnamese.

Vietnamese? Rolling Stones said. I thought you were a chink.

The word he actually used was *Chinois,* which only meant "Chinese," but inflected and emphasized the proper way—with a certain amount of spit—it was an epithet, one I had heard quite a few times from our French colonizers. It saddened me to hear this word said

88

by someone who should know better, but responding to his insult would only inflame the situation. Trying to calm the situation by expressing genuine curiosity about their origins or ancestry, I said, What are you?

Algerian, you rat's ass, Beatles said.

Rolling Stones scowled and said, We're butter.

Butter? I said. If anyone should be butter, it should be me, yellow, soft, and easily melted. Why are you butter?

Butter! Rolling Stones shouted. Butter!

Beatles sighed and said, Shit, we're French. Now give us the hashish.

Let's talk about this, I said. My Algerian brothers, have you never read Ho Chi Minh's case against French colonization? We should not be fighting each other, we should not be robbing each other, we should be working together against our abusive stepfather! Forget the "Marseillaise," whose lyrics are a little too murderous for me. Let's sing "The Internationale" instead! Come on, you wretched of the earth, with gusto! *Nous ne sommes rien, soyons tout!*

My little speech appeared to confound them, for they paused and frowned, and perhaps if just one of them had said, Maybe he has a point, we could have changed history itself—at least my history—but they were impulsive teenagers and Rolling Stones shook his head, refusing the dialectical thread of solidarity I had thrown at him, and said, Give us the hashish, you stupid bastard!

I had tried, hadn't I?

Sure you did, Sonny said.

If you say so, the crapulent major added.

Some hashish then, I muttered, making as if to unzip the backpack. They took a step toward me, but there was just enough distance between us that I could swing the backpack as hard as I could, waist up, toward the jaw of Beatles, where the two bricks at the

bottom of the backpack connected with a crack as loud as the battle cry unleashed from my gut, *BASTARD*, there never being a time when my belly was not full with that word, and while I thought that I had gotten used to it, I was only used to being called a crazy bastard, which had an element of truth to it, whereas the absolutely real truth here was that these two should have called me brother, or cousin, or maybe uncle, because we were related—were we not?—our mutual ancestors being the Gauls, who had the gall to call us their descendants, with Algerians the oldest sons, as my father had told our class, while we Indochinese were the gifted middle children, destined to be clerks, assistants, adjutants, and minor bureaucrats, unlike the Cambodians and the Laotians and so on down the empire's chain of being, each of us clinging to a link as we looked up toward the red cheeks of the slightly less oppressed simian above us, yearning for a benevolent white hand to help us claw past the undeserving creatures in our way and onto that beautiful battleship named *La Mission Civilisatrice*, which had shelled Haiphong and killed six thousand civilians, but who's counting? We were just natives, who did not count.

Bastard! screamed Rolling Stones, punching me before I could swing the backpack one more time. Fucking slope!

Rolling Stones punched me again and a bell rang in my head, and I felt almost nostalgic at hearing myself called *un bridé*, which I had not heard since the days of French colonialism in Saigon, and while the rest of my French might have faltered, my memory of being called a slant, a slope, or a chink, depending on one's interpretation, was as unforgettable as knowing how to say *merci* and *au revoir*, and whether my eyes actually slanted was really just a technicality. I was much more concerned with how, when I fell, I heard something crack in the expensive Japanese camera around my neck, which was not as alarming as Rolling Stones jumping on me and

choking me, which made my eyes bulge out and expanded my peripheral vision, so that I could see Beatles dripping blood and tears onto the park's packed earth and holding his nose, possibly broken by the bricks, a trick I had come up with on my own, although decades of socializing with Bon had undoubtedly led me to absorb some of his predisposition for violent anticipation, such as always having a means of self-defense and usually more than one, a strategy that counts in mounting an offensive as well, for in assaulting me Rolling Stones was not only choking me, leading my highly constricted larynx to gag in protest, but also wrenching my head up to pound it repeatedly against the packed earth, both strategies damaging my perception, now mottled and dappled with flares of light such as one might see when falling in love, or so I've been told, or when one is about to faint and perhaps die, as I knew from personal experience, and as it was absolutely necessary to prevent these latter outcomes, I let Rolling Stones progress in his attempt to murder me so as to distract him from seeing how I had pulled my legs up until my thighs were against his back as he straddled me, the hems of my pants riding up and exposing my socks, into one of which I had tucked a switchblade, a lesson Bon had taught me, and as I tugged the switchblade free something stiff pressed against my waist, for Rolling Stones was erect, a fact that meant he would certainly kill me then, his teeth bared now not just in fury and rage but hatred and self-hatred, and when I pushed the button that opened the switchblade the edge of the knife sliced into my palm, which barely registered given the red film descending over my vision and the roar of my blood rushing in my head, loud but not loud enough to prevent me from hearing Rolling Stones shouting, *Fucking yellow bastard chink slope,* slurs that made me flush with nostalgia for that more innocent time when colonialism was photographed in black and white, with no audio recordings so that one could hear the way

"Annamite" must have sounded on a French tongue and in a Vietnamese eardrum, a spit wad sodden with contempt and condescension, with what was visible of our oppression quite distant, perhaps charming, so that even rebels with their heads locked in cangues or peasants carrying white men on their backs appeared picturesque and quaint, as my own impending death was remote to me, my senses receding and my extremities numb except for the weight of the body on my belly and the cool handle of the switchblade in my slippery hand, which I had managed to reverse so that the six-inch blade could finally snap out, and with the last vestiges of my consciousness I drove the blade into the nearest part of the body on me, which elicited a scream and led to one hand falling away from my neck, an encouragement for me to stab once more, the result being another scream and Rolling Stones's other hand letting go as he wrenched away, and when I drove the blade into him again and again, he was fortunate that it only found his buttocks and the bone of his pelvis, the pain forcing him to fall off me, thrashing about and kicking me, who, now freed from his grasp, kicked back, rolled away, and staggered upright only to nearly trip over Beatles, on his hands and knees and shaking his head and turning his face toward me with such fire in his eyes that I slammed my knee into his face, and if his nose had not been broken before it was now, but as this one of my enemies fell down the other rose up, Rolling Stones howling and clutching at his bleeding ass but very much physically capable of damaging me, except that psychologically he was distracted by pain, marking him as an amateur, for if he were a professional, as Bon had told me many times, he would know that the mind was as important to survival as the body, a fact that I knew well because I had endured years of hardening as a spy followed by the finishing school of reeducation, which, not having killed me, had made me as unkillable as a cliché, and certainly stronger than this young man,

who had sufficient desire to kill me but not the wiliness, experience, and requisite fear of death that I had learned through the lifetime of bitterness and resentment that one knows as a bastard, me and myself, with me in pain and gagging while myself was clear-eyed and in control, closing on him quickly and stabbing him several more times in the region of his heart and vital organs, the sensation similar to inserting a knife into a whole, raw chicken, except that his rib cage and sternum deflected the blade twice, jarring my wrist, when all I wanted was for him to stop and lie down and leave me alone and promise not to kill me, but my French was only good enough to say, *Stop, stop, stop,* meaning that he should stop and that I should stop, but neither of us could stop until one of us was down, he, on his knees, on his side, on his face, not seeing me as I left the park quickly, scooping up my backpack with one hand as I snapped the switchblade shut with the other, not looking to see if Rolling Stones was dead or if Beatles was getting up, thankful that the empty park that was their advantage was now their disadvantage and grateful that I was wearing dark clothing, as Bon told me I should always do, not just to be fashionable, as was the mode in Paris, but because blood was less visible on dark clothing and I could keep my bleeding hand in the pocket of my pants while I pulled up the hood of my sweatshirt, which Bon had also told me I should wear on those occasions when I might need to hide my hideous appearance, as I did while walking rapidly to the Nation metro station, beginning to hear cries and shouts behind me when I was some distance away, so dazed that I did not realize until later that I should have gone to the rue des Boulets station right around the corner from the park, but still I managed to keep my pace steady, even on hearing the wail of a siren crying, *You're dead, you're dead,* as I neared the metro, the sound fading as I sprinted down the stairs, backpack around my chest again, and the camera, its lens cracked and its cap missing,

bouncing around my neck as I passed the gates and went down more stairs and through a tunnel before I made it to the nearest platform, not caring what the train or its direction was, just happy to finally stop, lean against a wall, and surreptitiously retrieve a handkerchief from my backpack, something a gentleman should always have, not only to wipe away the secretions of another's body or his own but to use as a tourniquet or a bandage, in this case for my right hand, which I thrust into my pocket again, the skin of my heart stretched tight from adrenaline and fear, its drumbeat drowned out only by the grumble of the train whose approach reminded me to focus my eyes enough so that I could enter without tripping and sit down next to a grizzled old man, one who was none too kempt and a little odorous, all the better for me, for we both appeared slightly degenerate together, which was better than appearing degenerate by oneself, especially if one were a battered Japanese tourist on a very bad trip, benefitting from the general callousness of the urban masses, especially those surviving metros and subways, their eyes occasionally turning to me before quickly flicking away, except for the one little pigtailed girl who pointed at me and said, rather loudly,

LOOK,

MAMA,

LOOK!

which indeed made everyone within earshot look at me, and I kept my monstrous self very still in the manner of a gecko on a wall who knows that it has been spotted, blending into the background while the mama did nothing to prevent her half-cute, half-creepy offspring

from staring at me with her adorable, buglike eyes, and eventually I ripped her gaze off me as I exited at the appropriate transfer at Belleville and walked through the crowds at a normal pace to the connecting line, altogether a thirty-minute journey in which no one said a word to me, who discouraged any words by putting on my headphones and listening to Jacques Brel singing "Ne me quitte pas" over and over until I finally understood that he wanted to be the shadow of a dog, whereupon I made it to the restaurant, where Le Cao Boi said, What the fuck happened to you? which I would have said to me as well, knowing that this was one of the more affectionate things that could be said between one man and another, an expression of care and concern that promised action, and when I attempted to sit down at a table he pulled me into the kitchen, where the Seven Dwarfs washed out my hand in a blue plastic bowl also used to clean fish, the clear water growing murky and red with my blood before they anointed me with iodine and eucalyptus oil, both of which made the skin of my palm and the bruises on my head and throat blaze, a fire that lent a hot halo to Bon when he loomed in my vision, saying, I'll kill the motherfuckers, the subtext of which was obviously that he loved me, but what really made me sentimental and bawl uncontrollably was when he said, I'm going to gut them and make them eat their own shit fresh from their bowels, a delightful culinary image that provoked the Seven Dwarfs into much laughter, a few of them drawing their cleavers and mock fighting each other as Le Cao Boi improvised a terrible ode to me, the weeping warrior returned from his journey, which there is no need to quote, and in fact it was so awful that I have forgotten the words, but Le Cao Boi was not offended by my lack of enthusiasm, ascribing it, I am sure, to my physical condition, the manly pain that the Seven Dwarfs could understand and the awful, embarrassing tears that they could not, and to cover up my

weakness Le Cao Boi brought me a bottle of Chinese liquor that looked like water, or vodka, the transparent fluid removing a layer of tender pink skin cells when poured down my throat, helping me for a brief moment to stanch my tears and forget my split palm, wrapped in a doughnut of bandages, and when I said, Give me some more, he said, I got something better than that, disappearing from my sight and then reappearing with a square of aluminum in his hand on which he had plated a single white lump of sugar, the morsel as a meal, the kind of presentation one might expect in a Michelin-starred restaurant, except it wasn't white sugar but, as Le Cao Boi proclaimed, *the remedy*, which would take too long to affect me if I swallowed it, whether whole or diluted, so he crushed it in a mortar and pestle and put it back on the aluminum square, holding it beneath my face with one hand while using his other hand to flick on a lighter beneath the square, the white powder dissolving into a sizzling, smoking puddle of liquid clarity as one of the Seven Dwarfs handed me a clear plastic tube, the barrel of a pen from which the ink cartridge had been removed, Le Cao Boi telling me to inhale through the tube, which I did, because if doctors and scientists are so daring and ethical as to always experiment on themselves then so should WE, a monstrous creation whose two-faced appearance was grotesque to all who beheld us, me and myself, and maybe *moi*, the two faces—or was it now three—that only a mother could love, our mother, who died today, or perhaps yesterday, and who will most likely die tomorrow, our mother dying every day and living every day in our memory, there never being a day when WE did not think of her and how WE were not there by her side when she passed, a crime as unforgivable as the crime of our birth in breaking out of our mother and beginning the lifelong process of our separation from her, the memory of it causing us to weep once more, which everyone thought was due to the beating

or the remedy, with Le Cao Boi saying, It's incredible, isn't it? to which WE could only close our eyes and moan, our faces coming together as one so that WE were completely in focus to ourselves, on the surface and underneath, all the thousand different layers of ourselves that stretched from the present to the past merging into the flaky, sweet, addictive, fattening mille-feuille of our histories and identities, all of us existing at the same moment, glued together by the perennial, sticky questions, such as what did this mean? who were WE? what were WE? where did WE come from? where were WE going? what have WE done? what will WE do?—unanswerable questions that barely let us breathe, so intensely did WE feel our body, our present, our past, and our future, until we could no longer feel our body at all, the border between it and the world dissolving completely so that every wave of light and sound and touch rippled through us and washed us away into a whirlpool of euphoric, even orgasmic, sensation that lasted for an unknown amount of time until the whirlpool was no longer bringing us ever deeper into the depths but reversed course and spiraled above us, turning into a staircase of light, where, at the top, Bon said, I might as well tell you what I've just heard, his words flowing right over our skin, the faceless man is at the embassy, which was the only thing that could ruin the pleasure of the remedy, for there could be only one faceless man, a frightful, fearful figure somehow conjured back into existence by the mere presence of Bon's idea, which was now clearly a sign of fate taking form, and somehow WE had always known that WE would not be apart from him for long, WE who were not just monstrous or grotesque but *awesome*, so amazing that at some point WE walked down the staircase of light to the bakery next door, refusing to eat at the worst Asian restaurant in Paris, weeping slightly at the many intriguing varieties of bread and pastries that collectively embodied centuries of good taste and culinary sophistication and technical

# Part Two

*Myself*

# CHAPTER 6

I have a dream! Martin Luther King Jr. said.

I was coming down from nearly having reached Heaven, or I was rising from nearly having descended into Hell. The soles of my feet were singed from the heat of Hell, and my nose was dripping from the chilliness of shivering in the clouds of Heaven, where I had stood at the gates. The revving of a two-stroke engine broke the reverential atmosphere, and a motorbike roared past the line of hopefuls and cut right in front of Martin Luther King Jr. That was my first clue that the rider was Vietnamese. Who was it? No, it couldn't be—it was!—Le Duan, general secretary of the Communist Party! Ho Chi Minh's successor! One of the founding fathers of our reunified country! A truly committed man! A revolutionary crazy enough to have voluntarily gone from the south to the north when everyone sensible, including my mother, was heading in the exact opposite direction! What the hell was he doing here?

Who are you? Martin Luther King Jr. said.

I am the man with the plan! Le Duan hopped off his motorbike, grinning and not at all offended about having to explain who he was. That was the fate of anyone from a small country, no matter how

accomplished. Even when we had names, hardly anyone besides our countrymen knew what they were or could pronounce them. It might be better to be nameless, since then no one could get our names wrong. Not that anyone in our country would get Le Duan's name wrong.

This very committed man continued: I am the magician who took the upper half of our country and sewed it back onto the lower half of our country! And then I gave it the iron backbone of our revolution, so that it could stand up for itself! And then I dug around in a graveyard and found a brain for our new creation! So what if the brain came from a foreigner, Karl Marx? Let's not be racist here. The Germans make very fine brains, just as good as their cars. See our country down below? It's wobbling a bit, sure, but what do you expect so soon after such a radical surgery on both the backbone and the brain? I'd like to see you try to walk, much less run, after having been abused for so long and after such an intense operation to rid our body of all its foreign bodies. The Chinese, the French, the Japanese, the Koreans, the Americans, they all took their turn with us. Now—and here Le Duan nudged Martin Luther King Jr.— you're not the only one with a dream, buddy! Grinning with glee, Le Duan pointed at his motorbike and crowed, *I have a dream, too!*

We all looked at the logo on his Honda motorbike, and it indeed said,

# *DREAM*

A Honda Dream? Was I dreaming? The Japanese, after proving that they could make transistor radios and tape cassette recorders, were now making dreams, too? I had never heard of such a dream until this dream, but now that I had heard of it, I wanted

that Japanese Dream, too! How dreamy! It must be so much better than an American Dream! The American Dream was so simple and so optimistic that it required no psychoanalysis, no deep-sea diving. It was as shallow, boring, and sentimental as a bad television show that had somehow become a hit. The Japanese Dream, however, must be really kinky. I longed for that dream with such hunger that I forgot that dreams could get you killed, which was the appropriate moment to wake from the dream to find myself with a clump of crusty bread in my mouth, sitting on the lowered seat of the toilet in the worst Asian restaurant in Paris, which, judging from the nauseating odor, I had apparently done a terrible job of cleaning. I can only blame someone else, which is to say me, a sane person who wanted no part of that disgusting bathroom. The air was fetid, the aroma somewhere between armpit, belly button, and the sweaty folds of the nether regions. The orifice of the toilet was the mirror of the anus, each one a portal into mysterious depths and twisting tunnels, which was why I had to lower the seat rather than gaze, gagging, into the chute.

*Pull yourself together!* I told myself. That was hard to do, as I was sobbing, partly out of pain, partly out of regret, and partly from the aftereffects of the remedy, one of which was similar to how I had sometimes felt after a fling with someone I barely knew: disgust. Mama! I moaned. Mama! What have I done?

Don't worry, the crapulent major said. They're not dead.

If they were, Sonny added, they'd already be here with us.

Get out of the bathroom, I said. The remedy had worn off, like love, leaving me with the pain in my hand and the desperate desire to fall in love again, even for one night, even knowing the shameful outcome. Give me some privacy!

But we haven't talked in so long, the crapulent major said, peering over my right shoulder into the mirror. Sonny nodded behind

my left shoulder, his face as pale and bloodless as the major's, even though the hole in the major's forehead, his third eye, was still leaking blood, as was the hole in Sonny's hand, one of several places where I had shot him. Did ghosts ever stop bleeding, stop weeping, stop returning? The fact that my mother had never appeared to me meant that she must be content in her afterlife. She had no reason to haunt me, for I was her good son, the one who always thought about her, who kept her picture in his wallet and spoke to it every night. In the black-and-white picture, taken shortly before I left for the lycée so that I would have a memento of her, she is wearing an ao dai borrowed from one of my aunts. She needed to borrow only the dress, not the pants, as she was being photographed from the shoulders up. Her hair had been styled professionally, in a salon, with a curling iron, so that it floats around her face in waves. For once, her face, usually so plain, has been adorned with blush and mascara and lipstick. I always knew my mother was beautiful, but I also knew it was hard to be beautiful when one was exhausted, which was her normal condition. Here in the photograph, her burdens—namely, her son and her life—had been magically erased, leaving only her beauty. I kept my mother's photograph to remind me of her, but also to make me remember that so many others among the wretched of the earth could look like angels, and vice versa, if history were different. I wanted to ask my ghosts if they had seen my mother, but I did not want them to see the child who still lived within me, the boy who screamed for his mama every morning.

So you haven't seen them on your side? I asked.

What, you think we know everybody here? Sonny pretended to be incredulous. Sarcasm was even more irritating when it came from a ghost. There's only about a hundred billion of us.

Give or take a few billion, the crapulent major said. Not exactly sure, since the afterlife doesn't have a census department. Contrary

104

to popular belief, this is not a gated enclave with someone check-
ing you in.

It's also a little dark and murky, Sonny added. Hard to get a
clear visual.

Which is a good thing. People in the afterlife are not the
best-looking.

On average. There are some exceptions.

Yes, but the die-young, leave-a-beautiful-corpse crowd is
unbearable.

The die-old-and-alone, leave-a-decaying-corpse crowd tends
to be humbler.

But they keep to themselves.

Even so, they stink. That's what nobody tells you about the
afterlife. It smells like rotten meat and putrid water and black mold.

You can't have everything, I said. The point is, if somebody
were dead, you may not see them there, but I would most likely
see them here.

If you killed them, Sonny said. As you did us.

That's generally how haunting works, the crapulent major
added.

You haven't been haunting me for a while.

What can we say? We've been sightseeing. Paris is a great city.
So much history! So many catacombs to explore! So many ghosts
to meet! Anybody who's anybody is at Père Lachaise!

I left them in the restaurant's bathroom, the sound of their
laughter coming through the closed door. Were they real or were
they side effects of the remedy? They must be real, as I had seen
them before. Their reappearance as a familiar comedy duo told
me that what I dreaded had not happened. Beatles and Rolling
Stones were alive, not doomed to be prehistoric amphibians drag-
ging themselves from the amniotic underworld by their fingernails.

And the communist agent must not be dead, either, for I had never seen her beside me, taunting me, as I had seen the crapulent major and Sonny.

Those guys aren't dead, Bon agreed. In the restaurant's kitchen, abandoned except for us, he poured me a large whiskey, my favorite kind. It's hard enough for you to kill somebody with a gun. Your conscience gets in the way. And killing with a knife takes something special. You don't have it in you to finish someone off at that close range. But don't tell the Boss that. With the Boss, you tell him those guys are dead.

They're kids, I said. The whiskey slid down my throat and coated my decaying insides with a fresh layer of paint. My hand throbbed where Grumpy had stitched the wound shut, whistling the entire time. More, I said. It was one of my favorite words, as long as I was the one saying it.

They're men. Bon refilled my glass. Young men, but old enough to go to war, to die in war. I've seen kids younger than that fight, kill, die. You think they planned to let you just walk away? No. It was going to be murder or serious harm, two versus one. You have every right in that situation to save your skin. Now, if it was me, they would be dead. Because that's the only guarantee that they don't come after you. Like with the faceless man.

Even mentioning him out loud brought a chill to the kitchen, where we crouched on low plastic stools that reminded us of home, our knees nearly level with our chests. The faceless man was our blood brother, the third Musketeer, though Bon did not know this, having seen him only from a distance in the reeducation camp. To Bon, the faceless man was simply the camp commissar, whereas to me the commissar was our blood brother, Man. What a fate it was, to be interrogated and then tortured by my best friend, the one who knew me better than I knew myself, the one who put his gun in my

hand and tried to get me to shoot him even as I was strapped down for my torture. He was in as much pain as I was. But I couldn't finish him, just as he couldn't finish me.

How did you find out about him?

You think it's going to stay a secret for long when someone without a face shows up? He's at the embassy. At least he's wearing a mask, or so they say. A war hero, they call him.

If he's wearing a mask, how do you know it's the faceless man?

How many people need to wear a mask? Only if they're faceless!

I sipped my whiskey and said, What's his name?

He said a name that was not Man's. Dung.

What I thought was that it was a nom de plume, an alias, for it meant "heroic" in our tongue, "shit" in English, and nothing at all in French. What I said was: How do you know he was the commissar? Even the camp guards just called him by his rank. And how many guys are walking around without a face after the war? You don't know it's him for sure.

You want evidence? Fine. We'll have to get close enough to him to see. And then we'll kill him. Or at least I'll kill him.

I drained my glass. Sometimes I preferred to sip my whiskey, to draw out the experience, because it was so good, and sometimes I needed to pour it down my throat as fast as possible, cranking up my liver to full throttle, because life was so bad.

How do you not feel guilty about all the men you've killed?

I only have to feel guilty if it's a crime. He refilled our glasses. Now drink up.

One hundred percent! I said, my sacred glass of spirits clinking against his. Spirits delivered us to another world, even if it was one often populated with angels, demons, ghosts, and figments. I hadn't told Bon about my ghosts, as that would only confirm my unsteadiness to him. But ghosts were as real and as invisible as termites,

nibbling away unseen at one's foundations. How did one fumigate the dead? The remedy was an easy answer, but it only salved the living, or whoever passed for the living, like me.

But I was afraid of the remedy. It felt so good that it reminded me of religion.

The Boss called later that night and summoned me for a visit to his apartment the next day, a sign of heightened respect. Bon went home and I spent the night lying on a cot in the restaurant, behind the counter, because I did not want my aunt to see me with a bruised face and lacerated hand. The throbbing pain kept me awake and transported me back to my cell at the reeducation camp, naked and strapped to the floor, the entire ceiling covered in lightbulbs, the room so bright that closing my eyes did nothing to hide the glare. Man had successfully managed to probe that most inaccessible part of me, my mind . . . even, perhaps, my soul, if such a thing existed. Maybe, if I met him again, he would reveal more of me that I still did not know. Maybe that was why my instinct had led me to seek shelter with my aunt, knowing she would tell Man all about me. Now he had come to the neutral ground of Paris, the city where the end of the war had been brokered. He had come for me. And Bon.

I shivered and listened for the rustle of the cockroaches and the scurrying of mice. For the first time I noticed, beneath the cash register, on an open shelf, a stash of pornographic magazines, their covers and pages sticky with what I hoped was grease. Despite the pain in my head and hand, something inside me twitched, the threads running from my eyes, through my two minds, and down to the other pair of orbs that made me a man. The glossy, pale bodies of these very sincere young women seemed carved from marzipan, breasts looming much larger than average. Their makeup was

applied as artfully as for a wedding, but while my eyes and my minds responded, the rest of me refused, distracted by the pain in my hand. Putting away the magazines, I wondered what the reason was for my actions, why the young men—boys, really—had assaulted me, why I had repaid them in kind. And, above all, besides my concern about failing to achieve the necessary structural rigidity for ejaculation even with the dirty magazines, I wondered what the reason was for my certainly dubious and perhaps unnecessary existence.

Perhaps the Boss would provide an answer one day. He was not my creator, but he was my re-creator, giving me a chance not through a gift but a loan. If God resided in Heaven, then the Boss's domain was a casino, heaven to some and hell to others. He ran his schemes from his home, located a few blocks from his import-export store, in a brutalist tower of thirty or so stories that I made my way to the next morning, dull from the pain and lack of sleep. The tower was so distinctly un-Parisian that the nearest major traffic marker was place d'Italie, as if the disastrous architecture could be blamed on Mussolini. The culmination of a presumably socialist vision, the architecture amounted to a stack of shoeboxes, with humans being the shoes. This efficient design was meant to house enormous numbers of people on limited amounts of earth, given the problem in central Paris of limited land and many people, or so the Boss told me as we sat on the hot rod of his scarlet leather sofa.

Look at the view, he said.

The Boss lived halfway up the tower and the sofa faced the living room window, with a matching sofa perpendicular to it. This other sofa faced a behemoth television set, approximately the weight of an adult gorilla and flanked by speakers the size of teenagers. Like all male refugees, the Boss was fascinated by gigantic audiovisual equipment, the better with which to see the videos and listen to the music that transported him home. The French, from what I

could see in the apartments of my aunt and the Maoist PhD, preferred smaller television sets, preserving the precious space of their small homes for books, mirrors, and mementos collected from their trips to flea markets and their four weeks of paid vacation per year. We, meanwhile, got no vacations, or at least no vacations to exotic locations, unless you counted the countries where we came from, which were not exotic to us. Coming from the ancient cultures of Asia, which were much more antique than the merely old culture of France, we desired the modern, the gleamingly new, with some exceptions, like the clock above the television, which was identical to the clock in the Boss's office, carved from wood in the shape of our country.

The view is spectacular, I said.

Here, try one of these, the Boss said, pointing to a tin of Danish butter cookies on his pseudo-marble coffee table, which could also function as the mortar against which a hard head could be pounded. I was averse to dairy but reluctantly plucked a butter cookie from its paper cradle out of politeness.

When those kids were attacking me, they said they were butter.

Butter? said the Boss.

Butter? said Le Cao Boi.

The secretary laughed. She sat on the other couch next to Le Cao Boi, both watching an episode of *Fantasia* on the behemoth television, its volume muted to the background hum of gossip. The luscious secretary was young, healthy, and slender, as well as tall, haughty, and skimpily dressed. Those elements multiplied, like three times three, to a total greater than their sum. Her taut skin glowed with the light rising from the furnace of her ovaries, her long black hair was as full and voluptuous as the rest of her, and her breasts appeared perfectly delectable, of such appropriate shape and tasteful size that I would have been happy to be reincarnated

as her brassiere. Yes, I looked, because there was no way a man can *not* look—is there?

They didn't say they were butter, she said with a slight sneer. They said they were butter.

What? I said.

*B-e-u-r-r-e* is "butter," she said very, very slowly, staring at me while the Boss and Le Cao Boi chuckled. *B-e-u-r* is slang for people born here whose parents are Arab.

I took a bite of my butter cookie and tried to hide my gag reflex at its taste. When the Boss poured me a cup of green tea and looked at me expectantly, I realized I was being given some extra-special hospitality. Before I could pick up the hot cup, the Boss said, You want coffee instead? He snapped his fingers before I could reply and his secretary turned her head. Get some coffee for everybody, the Boss said.

She pouted on cue and uncrossed her crossed legs, the maneuver making me swallow the burst of saliva in my throat. We all looked at her walk toward the kitchen, wordlessly admiring her perfect posterior. When she disappeared into the kitchen, the Boss reclined and said, The Eiffel Tower. Right there. Well, not right there. In the distance. But still, the Eiffel Tower, right? I have a pair of binoculars here if you want a closer look. People are paying stupid amounts of money to live close to the Eiffel Tower, and I'm paying barely anything and I can see it just fine! Who's smarter? No people sightseeing out here to bother me when I go downstairs. No cops worrying about tourists or rich residents. That's who they want to protect, tourists and bankers. This place? If it was full of white people, cops would be here like fruit flies on fruit. But white people don't want to live here. Not enough parks, not enough charm, not enough je ne sais quoi. But most important, not enough white people. A self-fulfilling prophecy. When there's

already a lot of white people, white people will come. When there's not enough white people, white people are nervous about moving in. So we had an opportunity.

We?

Asians! Chinese, Vietnamese. Your yellow brothers and sisters, or half brothers and half sisters. We took over. We always live where we have to, mostly because we have no choice. Well, actually, I could have gone to the United States. But I chose France. You know why? Less competition. There're already plenty of Asian entrepreneurs in the United States. The Asians in France are fewer, and the ones who are here are sheep. But this Asian community here will grow, and they will need my services.

By "entrepreneur," the Boss clearly meant "gangster," but I only said, I've been to the United States. Definitely a lot of entrepreneurs there.

Right. More opportunity here. And if I see an opportunity, I'm going to take it. Not taking an opportunity is like not taking food when you have the chance. And when it comes to food, we eat what we can, when we can. Right? Look. He pointed at the iridescent cherries on the coffee table, nestled in a white plastic bowl imprinted with a blue pattern invoking Ming vases. What do you see?

The black-haired heads of refugees in an unseaworthy vessel, jammed so tightly together that none could move. I could not help but whimper at the memory, but I suppressed it and said, Cherries?

Imperfect cherries, the Boss said, pretending not to notice my unmanly weakness.

While some of the cherries were spherical and quite perfect, so deep and darkly red that they verged on black, others bloomed in odd shapes and sizes. Several had twinned with fellow cherries, which, if the pairing was symmetrical, resembled a duality of

buttocks. In most cases, one cherry was bigger than the other, lending the fruit the appearance of a hunchback.

I get them from the Chinese market, because the French markets—the *white* markets—would never sell them. The Boss picked up a deformed twin and popped it in his mouth. But they're cheaper and taste exactly the same. Just as an ugly tit tastes the same as a good-looking one, so long as you close your eyes.

So you would take the ugly one over the good-looking one? asked Le Cao Boi.

The Boss smiled and said, What, you think I'm an idiot? Of course it's nice if things look pretty, but you can live when things don't. I can buy a place next to the Eiffel Tower, but why? People— *white* people—will think, *Who's the Asiatic guy?* Cops will think, *What's an Asiatic doing here?* My neighbors will think, *I can't believe someone yellow has moved in.* Funny thing about white people. They think we Asians stick together too much, but when white people come to our country, all they do is stick together.

Le Cao Boi laughed and so did the secretary. She had come back into the room with a silver tray, on which rested three glasses, each with a half inch of condensed milk at the bottom. On top of each glass stood an aluminum filter from which the black coffee dripped slowly onto the condensed milk, and all was quiet as the secretary bent over to put the tray onto the coffee table. Then she sat down and I swallowed again and the Boss looked at me expectantly. Where were we? Oh, yes, kissing the Boss's ass. I laughed, too, although only for a second, because the noise caused my skull to ring. He nodded and said, And here, white people tell us we shouldn't stick together, and then when we don't stick together, they say we've lost our culture.

You can't win, said Le Cao Boi.

Yes, you can, said the Boss. So long as you don't look at the world the way white people look at the world. Once you do that, you lose. For example, white people think we're sheep. And mostly, they aren't wrong. Our people think that by being sheep, by following the law, they'll be accepted and respected here. It's pathetic. I'm going to change that because I understand that white people will not respect us until they fear us, and they won't fear us until they think we can break their laws.

It's true that we have no gangsters here, I said.

Gangsters! That's one way to describe us. In the old country, they would call us pirates or bandits. We would have to hide in the ghettos or the marshes. But I prefer outlaws. And I prefer being here, not hiding somewhere. Here, I get my view and no one looks at me. I see everything and no one sees me.

You have a plan, I said.

Everyone should have a plan.

Since it would be stupid to admit that I did not have a plan, I nodded, but only once, as it hurt.

You don't look too good.

No, he doesn't, Le Cao Boi agreed.

Nothing that time or a plastic surgeon won't fix. I know a guy. A week or two for the face. The stitches in the hand will come out a little later.

███████████████████████████, the Boss said in Chinese.

████████████, Le Cao Boi agreed, laughing.

Don't worry, we're not talking about you.

Yes, we are.

Okay, yes, we are. If you don't want us to talk about you, you should learn Chinese. Easy enough, right? Just like I hired somebody to teach me some French. Here the Boss nodded at his French

teacher, who was also his secretary as well as his mistress. You did good, by the way. I didn't think you had it in you.

Maybe he just got lucky, Le Cao Boi said.

We all get lucky. An honest man admits that. The Boss paused at the irony. Bon says you need a place to stay.

My aunt won't be happy if I show up looking like this, I muttered.

She's a civilian, Le Cao Boi said.

Not involved, I confirmed. And wouldn't want to be.

She's your connection to your network, the Boss said. We wouldn't want to endanger that. All right, I've got a place for you. You'll love it.

Is it like this?

Trust me, the view's even better, the Boss said, grinning. He turned his gaze back to the windows spanning the width of the living room. What do you see?

The Eiffel Tower? I said.

Yes, yes, the Eiffel Tower. But what does it remind you of?

I hesitated. Even thinking hurt. A sundial?

A sundial? The Boss squinted. I guess so . . . but look again.

A finger?

Just one finger? Where are the other fingers?

I stared at the tower once more. A pipe?

Are you fucking blind? he cried. It's a gigantic dick!

Le Cao Boi and the luscious secretary both chuckled at my lack of imagination.

Of course I realize that, I said feebly. It's just a little . . . obvious.

If it was so obvious why didn't you say it? the luscious secretary said.

College boy, Le Cao Boi said. Looks like a few days of rest will do you good.

Seven days, to be exact, the Boss said. By then you might look human again.

And then . . .

Then we'll talk about plans.

I was in no condition to talk about plans or think about them, and yet an hour later there I was thinking as I sat in an RER train car rumbling toward a northern suburb. While I stared out at the grim prison blocks of apartment buildings and tried to hold myself together, I wondered if it was true, if the Eiffel Tower was just a Gallic erection thrusting forth from the supine French body, shooting off bursts of clouds, seen and invisible at the same time.

Was it so obvious that it was not obvious?

Was the French empire simply exposing itself for all to see?

Was the Eiffel Tower any different from the Washington Monument, the white missile erupting from the American capital, foreshadowing all the nuclear missiles buried in silos across the American landscape?

Had a giant vagina ever served as the emblem of a nation's sacrifice? I wondered. (Except, perhaps, for the Arc de Triomphe, the maternal thighs through which the French military passed every year on the fourteenth of July, or so I had seen in pictures from *Paris Match*, never having witnessed such a birth myself.) But besides that exception—

Had a womb ever become a monument?

Had a uterus ever been the model for a memorial?

Had a pair of breasts ever floated above a capitol?

*Why had I never thought of these things before?*

My neighbor got up and moved to another seat.

# CHAPTER 7

**D**izzy with my profundity, or just as likely dizzy with the ache in my head, I walked to my destination along a route where the houses and apartments were boring boxes two or three stories high, with cafés and brasseries few and far between. The depressed vegetables and disappointed fruits on display outside the two produce markets that I passed were the street's saddest occupants besides myself, all of us yearning to be handled by nonjudgmental hands. Instead of looking like the France of my colonized imagination, this lackluster quarter had no place worth walking to and nothing worth walking by, as if it had been designed by an American or a Vietnamese. At last I came to a bruised green door on a melancholic street, where I pushed the doorbell and waited.

*Allô?*

I sighed and said what Le Cao Boi had told me to say, what he himself had come up with: I'd like to go to Heaven.

Are you kidding me? I had said to him, but he only shrugged. The clients don't mind, so why should you? And what's wrong with a little aspiration?

The travel agent, I'm sure, had thought the same thing.

The green door to Heaven opened and a smiling woman with the hideous teeth of a Third World childhood waved me in. She was of retirement age, with a Filipina lilt to her accent. Hello, sir, she said in English. May I take your coat? May I untie your shoes? May I show you to the living room? May I get you a coffee? Tea? Wine? Whiskey?

Whiskey, I said with a catch in my throat, always touched by such an offer.

The obsequious housekeeper bowed and backed out of the waiting room. Metal shutters had been rolled down over the windows, leaving a chamber illuminated with cheap torchiere lamps and a television almost as big as the Boss's. The sofas had the sheen of stain resistance, and if they were not stain resistant, they should have been.

Have a seat, my friend, the only occupant said. Sitting near the television was Heaven's muscle, big and black, ankles crossed, cracking his knuckles and looking bored. The television was tuned to a talk show, and judging from the cover of Sartre's *Being and Nothingness* on the screen, the topic was existentialism, as discussed by a comedian and a football player whom I recognized from previous television exposure, as well as two well-fed, eyeglass-wearing men. It took me a moment to recognize one of these professional intellectuals as the Maoist PhD, who, from his sober, scholarly look, appeared to never so much as think of his body at all below his throat or lungs, and only because he needed those parts in order to speak and smoke. *I think, therefore I am* was the sentiment he exuded, or perhaps it was *I speak, therefore I am.*

First time, huh?

Yes, I said, focusing on the white Band-Aid stamped on the muscle's cheek. Then, fearing that I seemed inexperienced, I said, First time *here.*

The muscle brooded as he watched the television. On closer inspection, the Band-Aid wasn't exactly white but rather beige. It only appeared white against the blackness of his cheek, which wasn't really black but appeared more so against the Band-Aid.

Sartre, he's okay, the muscle said. I prefer Fanon and Césaire.

Me, too, I said.

The muscle continued watching the debate about Sartre, but his mention of Fanon and Césaire sent me back to the last time that I had encountered them, at Occidental College, where I had spent six years studying for my bachelor's and master's degrees in American studies. My mentor Professor Hammer had taught Fanon and Césaire in his seminar on Third World literature. It was 1964, Algerian independence from France was two years old, and anticolonialism was sweeping through the Third World. Understanding *the wretched of the earth* was crucial, Professor Hammer said, citing the title of Fanon's book of experiences in the Algerian war. They were rising, as "The Internationale" proclaimed. I took advantage of a commercial break during the talk show to say, I like Fanon and Césaire. *Discourse on Colonialism.* And when Fanon talks about violence. He speaks about Algeria. But he speaks of Vietnam, too.

I prefer *Black Skin, White Masks.*

I was embarrassed to admit that I had not read it, but the muscle merely shrugged.

I can lend it to you. And have you read Césaire's *A Tempest*? No? You have much to discover. They teach you about life and death. Most people only want to talk about life.

Well, I like to talk about death, too, I said.

Then we'll get along, he said. He was a self-proclaimed eschatologist, most interested in breaking down the meaning of eternal judgment and the afterlife, the very fate of humankind. This was heady stuff, and I was happy to see the housekeeper return with a

tumbler of whiskey. Short of the remedy, the only thing keeping me in the warm land of the living was this antifreeze, which ensured my blood did not stop moving. Oh, whiskey! How much I needed you, and the memory of my mother, who endured so much and yet never turned to whiskey or any other addiction. Perhaps I inherited my weaknesses from my father, a bastard in the moral sense, if not the racial one.

Where are you from? the eschatological muscle said.

If a white person had asked me that question, I would have said, From my mother. But because we shared a widespread subequatorial condition called "colonization," which only afflicted nonwhite people, I said, Vietnam. Although my father is French.

A fine gentleman, I'm sure, the eschatological muscle said, chuckling. Someone who probably visited a place like this.

He was a priest, I said. I wonder if he ever visited this type of place.

Not sure if we have seen such a man here. But it would not surprise me.

And you? I tried to shake off the sadness of my origins that had settled on me with the inevitability and persistence of dust, but even that little bit of shaking made my head protest. Where are you from?

Here, but my parents are from Senegal. He grinned. My father, he went to your country as a soldier. A lovely place, he said. Beautiful women. Beautiful children.

He fought for the French?

Yes. I don't know too much. My father, he didn't like to talk. But I know one thing. He grinned again and leaned over to open the drawer of a table on which stood a lamp with its tasseled lampshade askew. Here you go, compliments of the house.

A silver package arced toward me, reminding me of the chocolate bars that American soldiers hurled from their armored

personnel carriers at ragamuffins. Three little squares landed on my palm, but instead of being chocolate, they were condoms.

His job was to guard the rubber plantations. Funny, huh? To think that when you put those on, maybe the rubber came from your country. They will remind you of home!

Very funny, I said, already knowing I would never forget the thought now seeded in the soft soil of my vulnerable mind, that perhaps how most of the world had contact with our spunky little country—besides knowing of the war that was now our brand—was through a device used to limit the world's population and male pleasure.

The curtain of beads rattled again, parting to reveal the mistress of the house, a woman whose stark, expressionist makeup accentuated both her attractiveness and her avariciousness. A black silk jumpsuit clung to her curves, and stacks of jade bracelets rattled on her wrists. She walked with an acrobat's confidence on twin heels that added a half foot to her height, so her chin was level with my nose when I stood up.

She glanced at the condoms and said, Three? A little optimistic, aren't you?

A gentleman should always be ready, I said. And I am a realist, not an optimist.

The mistress smiled coldly and said, I'll show you to our guest room.

Ciao ciao, said the eschatological muscle, flexing his biceps in farewell.

We descended to the guest room, a small dwelling in the cellar dominated by a bed big enough for two. Pushed into a corner were a chair and a desk, as if a visitor to this erotic establishment might spend time writing. But the guest room was also, apparently, a hideout, so perhaps some visitors did need a place to reflect.

Madeleine will be with you soon, the mistress said. You'll like her. Everybody likes Madeleine. She knows the eight ways to please a man in bed. The first meeting is complimentary, courtesy of the Boss. After that, you get a twenty percent discount.

Usually the prospect of a beautiful woman or a discount excited me, but when the door closed behind her, I felt . . . *nothing*. What was wrong with me? Three or four ways were more than enough for me, much less eight! I blamed my anhedonia on that screw being loose, and my body being in pain, and feeling, for the first time in my life, old. I could not even pull myself together to haggle, a skill that was practically genetic, bred into me by centuries of our people's survival in the face of war, famine, poverty, and the precariousness of life without the welfare state.

I was trying to distract myself from my memory, my con-science, and my guilt, which I—along with a majority of the human species—excel at doing, when someone knocked on the door. Madeleine.

Oh, my poor boo-boo, she said. Her French was slow and breathy, perfectly paced for me and my mood. What happened to you?

Oh, the performance was about to start! At last, something inside of me fluttered with excitement. I was about to be both the spectator and the performer in the unofficial culture show that a great number of our men and some of our women were familiar with.

Don't worry, she murmured. Madeleine is the right medicine for you.

Madeleine was not, by conventional definitions, the most beau-tiful of women. Those gorgeous creatures should be seen only from afar, for they can be quite expensive as well as extraordinarily sensi-tive. Madeleine, in contrast, invited proximity. Unlike most in her

profession, she had not doused herself with so much cheap perfume that one might require a gas mask to handle her. Her features were cute and her body cuddly, with a slightly rounded tummy and even rounder breasts, hips, and eyes. She was as buxom as one of those goddesses carved into an Angkor Wat temple, and indeed Cambodia was her origin, as I eventually discovered. But instead of statuesque hardness, she radiated softness, warmness, tenderness, and, most of all, *desire*—for me! I was reduced to an infant who only wanted to be wanted, which Madeleine, as a professional, understood.

First, she said, we will get you clean all over. And I mean *all* over.

I nodded mutely.

That means you have to get out of those clothes, honey baby.

*Oh, yes,* I thought.

Why, hello, big boy. Poor you. So neglected. Don't worry. I'll take care of you.

*Oh, please, yes!*

Come to the shower, sweet darling. Let Mama scrub down every one of your nooks and crannies. Do you like it hot?

Uh-huh, I finally managed to say.

Careful now . . . wouldn't want to burn you, would we? Oh, no. Does this feel good? It does, doesn't it? I can tell by the look in your eye, my widdle cabbage. No one's loved you in a long time, have they? And you are someone who deserves a widdle wove, aren't you? I can't believe someone did that to your face. And your hand. Are you in pain? Oh, poor widdle baby. You won't be for much longer. Not if Mama Madeleine has anything to say about it. Let's make sure we get the soap in there . . . right there . . . Oh, yes, I'll be going there, don't you worry, my chicken. You smell wonderful, good enough to eat, if I can say so. This way, hold my hand. It's a

small bed, but it's big enough for what Mama wants to do to you. Sit down. Right there, my *doudou*. Now unwrap me, big boy.

Madeleine took my trembling hands and placed them on the sash keeping her mini-kimono closed. The last naked woman I had seen was Lana, three years ago. An eternity, given how the average man experiences a sexual fantasy every three minutes, or so I speculate, based on over two decades of personal experience. I tugged, the sash came undone, and what I saw almost made *me* pass out.

Ready, baby?

Madeleine did not wait for my consent, because I am certain that in her experience there was no such thing as a male who would not say, *Yes, yes, a thousand times yes!* I closed my eyes to try to prevent myself from seeing what I had just seen, while she proceeded to display a perverse biologist's encyclopedic knowledge of the male body, an effort that completely mapped all my erogenous zones, a probing hydraulic campaign that would have found water in a desert, a heroic labor of erotic integrity that established Madeleine as a worthy descendant of Mary Magdalene, a mistress of every technique and trick known since Eve first coaxed a snake to talk and then offered Adam the forbidden fruit, all of which left me gasping. And yet—

Huh, Madeleine said.

What? I whispered, eyes closed.

Hmm, she said, louder.

*What?* I opened my eyes.

Nothing's happening.

We both stared accusingly at the criminal committing this unspeakable crime, her finger propping up the guilty member. Nothing had never happened to me before! But—but—but— I sobbed, and Madeleine put her finger to my lips and said, Shhhh, big boy. Just close your eyes and *relax*. This happens all the time. I laid back, and as Madeleine valiantly continued, I thought desperately

of everything, from the Madonna to Marilyn Monroe, from come-hither centerfolds to the lascivious squid with whom I had lost my virginity, but nothing continued to happen. This strongest of medicine was not curing my illness, not even after she had worked through all eight ways of pleasing a man in bed.

At last Madeleine drew back, still smiling, this time out of pity as she closed the drapes of her mini-kimono. Anything I said would sound like a lie or an excuse, so I said nothing as I fumbled for my underwear while Madeleine suddenly became a different person, probably herself. As I clutched the loincloth of the bedsheet around my waist, she strapped back on her high-heeled shoes and then reapplied her lipstick. Inside every prostitute is an accountant, and this one said, Unfortunately, *that* was your free one.

Inside every client is a daydreamer, an optimist at best and a fool at worst. This one could only sputter, But—but—

It's okay. It happens to everyone.

So does death, I wanted to say. This was not premature ejaculation. This was premature emasculation! I was not scheduled for such deflation and humiliation for at least another thirty or forty years, by which time I should already be prematurely dead, indifferent to sex, or comatose from a decades-long affair with whiskey and cigarettes. But I had too much dignity to beg for a second chance and instead admitted to defeat with a mixture of humility and defiance: It's a war wound. I'll do better next time.

Yes, you will, she said with the tremendous conviction of a kindergarten teacher.

A war wound was not a lie. I had the worst kind of injury, a mental one, which was exacerbated by having two minds. The past that was contained in one mind was now leaking into the present of my other mind, so that what had made me almost pass out when Madeleine first disrobed was not her spectacular nudity but the

sight of the communist agent's face. She was taking her ghostly vengeance on me, and she was not even dead. Wait until she actually was! I could nevertheless see her face vividly, from chapped lips to bruised cheekbone to unkempt, unwashed, serpentine hair, the fully focused sight of her face floating on Madeleine's body cutting off my blood flow.

That face had been seeping into my consciousness ever since my interrogation sessions with Man in the reeducation camp, where he had begun unscrewing me. I had done my best to forget her until then, for her fate had been my greatest failure and my greatest shame, unless you count my own existence, which I had premised on answering the most important question of the twentieth century: WHAT IS TO BE DONE?

What is to be done about slavery?

What is to be done about colonialism?

What is to be done about occupation?

What is to be done about racial inequality?

What is to be done about class exploitation?

What is to be done about the decline of Western civilization?

What is to be done about the woman question and the male ego?

*WHAT IS TO BE DONE ABOUT WHAT NEEDS DOING?*

So many things to do! But I had known what to do with great conviction ever since I became a revolutionary, and I knew what must be done when the three policemen of the southern regime began their interrogation of the communist agent. She was my ally, except that I was undercover as a spy, working alongside Claude of the CIA, who had trained many of our secret and not-so-secret policemen, like these three. Before leaving the interrogation, he had merely said, I didn't teach them to do that. He left me as the only witness, besides my comrade of the Special Branch, the crapulent major—

Don't drag me into this, cried the ghost of the crapulent major.

—who sat beside me and also did nothing as we watched the three policemen do what men have undoubtedly been doing to women since Adam blamed Eve for listening to the serpent. It had not occurred to me until now, blind man that I was and surely still am, that the serpent was Adam's own uncontrollable penis, which the writer of the Book of Genesis had detached from Adam and flung into the grass. From there it could rear its head and talk Eve into eating the forbidden fruit, as if Adam had nothing to do with it. And how does one eat forbidden fruit? By asking permission? Or by taking it, which, for all we know, Adam might have done and then blamed Eve? If prostitution was the world's oldest profession, then rape was the world's original crime.

Instead of doing nothing, what I should have done was to stop the policemen, even at the cost of my cover and my life. I should have made the sacrifice the communist agent had made by refusing to talk or to confess. But instead of making a sacrifice, I made the one thing that only human beings can make: an excuse. Whoever said the road to Hell was paved with good intentions had gotten it all wrong. If you looked more closely, you could see that the road to Hell was paved with excuses.

On the last of my seven days in Heaven, when the pain in my hand and my head no longer required the remedy but just aspirin, and the puffiness of my bruised face had subsided to the point where I could bear looking at myself, and my periodic bouts of weeping had tapered off, the Ronin appeared. I envied him. He was never bothered by guilt, although his politics—not to mention his morality— were questionable. His breath was as clean as his conscience, and he had a mint in his mouth, a glint in his eye, and a gleam to his

teeth when we met in the waiting room. So you're him, he said in Vietnamese. The man himself, the one and only Crazy Bastard. The Boss told me you'd be here. I'm the Ronin.

That's what he called himself, as did everyone else. The next surprise was that he spoke in grammatically correct southern Vietnamese, mixed with a heavy, charming French accent. The third surprise was that he was the best-looking man I had seen for a long time, and he knew it. His suit was formfitting, his body was trim, his fingernails were manicured, his pocket square was a rakish puff, his blue silk tie was the width of my forearm, and his teeth were American teeth, or movie star teeth, which he exposed with the frequency and salacious enjoyment of a flasher. He had barely begun telling me about the business arrangement between him and the Boss when Crème Brûlée—nicknamed as such because of the color of her skin—parted the beaded curtains and cried out, Ah! My favorite Corsican!

The Ronin winked at me and said, Might as well be my nickname, I hear that so often. Come here, my Laotian love, it's been a long time.

They proceeded to give a long demonstration of French-kissing, which involved a lot of tongue, which made me wonder if the French themselves called it French-kissing. Done at last, the Ronin winked at me and showed how Vietnamese he was by beckoning to me the Vietnamese way, hand flat, palm downward. He had remarkably small hands, like those of a young boy's. Come on, he said.

What?

He snapped his fingers and pointed at his gold watch. I don't have much time. We can talk business while I take care of business. I've got appointments.

You want me to—

Sit there and watch. Unless you want to get in on it, too.

I glanced at the eschatological muscle, who shrugged as if he understood the gist of our conversation, even in Vietnamese. He had seen everything, and yet had seen nothing, during his time in Heaven. The Ronin's invitation, or demand, was nothing new. Since everyone else, including the Ronin's favored Crème Brûlée, was treating the matter with a Gallic shrug, I shrugged, too, and followed them through the curtain of beads to Crème Brûlée's room upstairs. Throwing herself on her bed, Crème Brûlée said, Sorry, Ronin, but he is extra. Even if he can't do it.

Can't do it? said the Ronin, astonished, assuming automatically and correctly what the unspeakable "it" was.

It's a war wound, I cried, collapsing into a chair. A war wound!

My outburst and subsequent tears startled Crème Brûlée, who froze in her come-hither position on the bed, but the Ronin did not seem disturbed.

There, there, he said, patting my shoulder, which was a bit awkward for me, since he had unbuckled his gold-buckled belt and his naked manhood was dangling uncomfortably close to my face. Now, now, this kind of war wound has happened to a few fellows I know, none of them is any less of a man for it. You have to be a man to get this kind of war wound, after all. It can't happen to a woman, right? Now just sit back and enjoy the show. It'll take your mind off—off—well, you know.

With that, he turned his attention back to Crème Brûlée. I sat on the armchair in the corner and longed for some whiskey in which to dissolve my discomfort and humiliation. I neither enjoyed being looked at while being intimate with a woman nor enjoyed looking at others, even if they were as good-looking a pair as Crème Brûlée and the Ronin. I settled for smoking cigarettes, which at least allowed me to do something with my hands. I crossed and uncrossed my legs, glanced at the ceiling and the floor and the prints of Degas and

Van Gogh on the wall, cupped my chin on my hand, rested my hand on the armchair, coughed discreetly, and tried not to see the face of the communist agent. Meanwhile the Ronin talked constantly while he worked his way through half the Kama Sutra in a display of truly astonishing endurance, all while providing a running commentary for me, as if I were watching a particularly competitive tennis match at Roland-Garros. In between descriptions of the strokes, the Ronin explained his interest in meeting me, of which I provide an edited version here, minus the repetitive moans, groans, and obscene accounts of his carnal exercises:

The Boss and I go way back, to the fifties in Saigon, when men were men and women were women and fucking was fucking, not like today with these so-called feminists. Now Madame Nhu, the Dragon Lady, she was a real feminist. She looked great in an ao dai and could shoot a gun, too. How many of these so-called feminists can do that? Gun battles in the streets, car bombs, grenades thrown in your courtyard—that's the stuff that makes you feel alive. Kings used to get killed in battle; that doesn't happen very much anymore, but it sure did in Saigon. Look at our president Ngo Dinh Diem—*bang*, dead, right there with Madame Nhu's husband in the back of an American armored personnel carrier. I heard the assassin castrated the poor son of a bitch and ate a piece of his liver. Real gangster stuff, and Diem did not like us gangsters, even if he was nasty to the commies. Yeah, I'm a gangster and proud of it. Why should it be a shame to be a gangster? That's one reason I like the Boss. He's not ashamed. I knew that when we were youngsters. Me, I was born in the Mekong Delta, where I met him. Don't you think that makes me Vietnamese? My father was a plantation overseer. He had to cut deals with the river pirates to keep the business going smoothly, not to mention the governor and the general and the French bureaucrats and all the Vietnamese ones who replaced them.

Corruption is a way of life. Corruption is the salt on our meat. Just don't oversalt. The fact of the matter is that everybody's corrupt everywhere. Everybody does business behind the scenes. You have wives, but also you have lovelies like this lady here. You have clean deals and dirty deals. You need both. That's how the world spins, gives us night and day. Here, people call corruption "connections." I prefer the corruption in Indochina and Corsica, because at least it's honest. Now I'm not in this because I'm Corsican, just like the Boss isn't in this because he's Chinese. We're in this because we're sincere. Gangsters are the most honest people in the world because we know how the world works. We're honest about being dishonest, and we're no more dishonest than a Swiss banker, which is, to be fair, pretty dishonest. The Nazis loved the Swiss so much they didn't invade them, and if the Nazis love you, you must be a piece of shit, not that there weren't some fine Nazis, like the ones I met in the Foreign Legion. Now you, so the Boss tells me, have found a nice little market among these intellectuals. We want you to grow that intellectual market. Then if all goes well, we can introduce some of these intellectuals to the angels of Heaven. Look at this little lady here. Laotian born and bred. God, I miss Laos! The most beautiful country in the world. The most spiritual people in the world, and they grew some damned good opium. To this day I cannot believe that the French lost Laos and all of Indochina. I am Corsican and French, but I am also Indochinese, or Vietnamese, whichever term you prefer. I never even set foot in France until I started coming here for business in the sixties. How do you think the Boss got established here so quickly? He was already investing through me. You got to diversify in a dangerous and unpredictable world, just in case your country goes nowhere one day. How I miss our old plantation! The tastiest bananas, the sweetest coconuts, the juiciest mangoes! We were happy, our workers were happy. Now what do

What would God say? I thought I had spoken my question to myself, but it must have been out loud, because the Ronin replied, What would God say? He'd say, Why not?

That's what I once thought, too, I said. But I have had a great deal of time to think about what God would say and now I know what the real answer is.

Oh, yeah? The Ronin lit a cigarette. What is it?

Why *the hell* not?

You crazy bastard, the Ronin said, grinning. I like you.

# CHAPTER 8

**W**hy the hell not? Was that also the question you asked yourself, Bon, before you pulled the trigger in front of my face? Well, yes, then, why the hell not, that is my motto, especially when it comes to whiskey, or cognac, or vodka, or gin, or sake, or wine, or beer, but not when it comes to pastis, because that tastes like shit. There was a bottle of Ricard in Heaven, but during my last night there, after the Ronin's departure, I wallowed in the more universal Johnnie Walker and fell asleep in a heart-shaped bed. Was my mother watching from above? Could she see my disgrace? Would she offer me her love and tenderness, her total understanding, her empathy that far surpassed sympathy? From the real Heaven, if it existed, gazing down on this earthly one, she would say, You are my son, and you are not half of anything, you are twice of everything! You will find a way to lift the curse that echoes in your ears—the words of the communist agent, defiant against the policemen about to rape her:

*My surname is Viet, and my given name is Nam!*

Oh, Mama . . . if only I believed in me as much as you do. I look at me all the time, and because I do not like what I see, I must turn to

whiskey, which is so much better at improving one's eyesight than any pair of glasses. To drink whiskey, in sufficient quantities, regardless of sufficient quality, is to polish the fuzzy mirror of one's self and to adjust, in the manner of an optometrist, the focus of one's lenses. But unfortunately, whiskey wears off, the hangover simply an adjustment to the reality of being oneself and another, where one is constantly looking at the other. This was my state of being when Bon phoned me the next morning.

So you had a good time? Bon said.

A pretty good time, I lied.

Great. Just wanted to let you know: Sleepy is dead.

For a man telling me about the violent demise of one of the Seven Dwarfs, Bon sounded rather cheerful. That was him. While he loved whiskey, too, what truly brought him into focus was love for his family and hatred of his enemies. All the enormous emotional force in the love that he could no longer give to his wife and child had been converted, in the strange dynamo of his soul, into potential violence he could direct at his enemies. Now he had an excuse: Sleepy was dead and his younger brother, Shorty (who was considered short even by other short people), was barely alive. The brothers had been assaulted near Tang Frères as they made their rounds collecting monthly membership dues for the Secret Society, as the Boss romantically called his insurance company. The dues were insurance against—who else?—the Boss himself. That could not be said out loud, of course. It was a great racket to be both the source of fear and the protection against that fear, not that the Boss was an original in this regard. Organized religion was the first and greatest protection racket, an economy of perpetual profit built on voluntary fear and coerced guilt. Donating money to churches, temples, mosques, synagogues, cults, et cetera, to help ensure a spot for one's soul in the express elevator to that penthouse in the sky

known as the afterlife was marketing genius! Had Sleepy paid his spiritual insurance? If so, had it done him any good?

According to Shorty, whose memory had been beaten into the consistency of oatmeal by a length of pipe, or so said Bon, a quartet of Arab youth had set on them. The ambush had occurred in a grimy residential passage, the youths punching, kicking, and stabbing Sleepy and Shorty with fists, feet, and knives before introducing some pipes and chains for variety. Afterward, they relieved Sleepy and Shorty of several thousand francs and a few promissory notes. A brave witness screaming from a window above them saved Shorty. The assailants had run off laughing, leaving Shorty to drag himself to the next stop on the collection tour a street away, where he demanded that the owner hide him in his storeroom and call Le Cao Boi. Shorty was hiding as much from the police as from the thieves, who were undoubtedly sending a signal. The moral of the story, Bon concluded, was not that there had been too much killing. Rather, there hadn't been enough (though Sleepy might disagree).

I told you those kids weren't dead, Bon said. When he said that I should have killed them when I had the chance, Sonny and the crapulent major snorted in my ears. Even if they didn't do this, Bon went on, they told their friends and their bosses, and this is what happens. When you stick a knife in somebody, you have to finish him off. Whoever did that to Shorty and didn't kill him will regret it.

Jesus Christ, I said sadly. It's war.

Oh, yes, he confirmed happily. It's war!

As with any war, the origins could be disputed. Was it their fault, whoever they were, because they had killed Sleepy? Was it my fault because I had nearly killed Beatles and Rolling Stones, who presumably belonged to the same gang as Sleepy's killers? Was it their fault

136

because they had attempted to rob me? Was it my fault because I had strayed out of my assigned place among the invisible Indochinese who never needed a visit from the Repressive State Apparatus, since we had learned to repress ourselves? Was it their fault because they had not sought an alliance or even just a chat with their colonized comrades? Who were they, anyway, the people with whom we were now at war?

I would have time to answer these questions now that my heavenly sabbatical was over. My face was somewhat healed, if still puffy and sensitive, and the pain in my head and hand had subsided to a persistent, uncomfortable itch. Even if I had wanted to stay further and prolong my humiliation, my wallet was spent. I went up to the waiting room and found that the eschatological muscle, knowing it to be my last day, had prepared a loan for me: his densely underlined copies of Fanon's *Black Skin, White Masks* and *The Wretched of the Earth*, as well as Césaire's *A Tempest*.

How should I return them to you? I said.

You'll be back, he said. Everyone comes back to Heaven.

I went to the kitchen to say goodbye and found the expressionist mistress, Crème Brûlée, and Madeleine in their nightgowns, consuming their breakfast of cigarettes and coffee. When I saw Madeleine wiping tears from her eyes, my first thought was that a client had hurt her in some way. A manly surge of outrage rippled through my breast, but when I asked her what was wrong, she did not name a man. Instead she pointed at the newspaper on the table. The headline said MASS GRAVES IN CAMBODIA.

My family, she said. Most of them are still there.

The picture beneath the headline showed stacks of grimy bones and heaps of accusatory skulls, freshly excavated and laid out on tarps. Seeing these haunting remnants reminded me that I was poorly equipped to deal with death, pain, sorrow, or depression,

whether experienced by others or myself. Witnessing the suffering of others left me in a panic, unsure of what gesture to make or what words to offer. It was all I could do just to put my hand on her shoulder, tentatively, and say, I'm sorry.

You Vietnamese. She closed her eyes, dismissing me with a wave of her hand. *You* invaded Cambodia.

The expressionist mistress looked at me and shrugged, as if to say she, like the Boss, was ethnic Chinese from Cholon, and therefore not responsible. Crème Brûlée glared at me as if to say she was Laotian, and also therefore not responsible for being Vietnamese. I wanted to say, I'm only half Vietnamese. And we are all Indochinese, aren't we? Courtesy of our Franco-Frankenstein, who killed us, cut us up, and stitched us together, christening us with this bastard name that we now all shared, "Indochina." Furthermore, I wished Madeleine knew that it was the communists who invaded Cambodia. I was in a reeducation camp when it happened, and I was not even a communist anymore.

But none of that mattered. If we believed in collective guilt for the French, the Americans, the Japanese, and the Chinese, who had all in one way or another flagellated our country—if we believed so fervently that *you* committed violence on *us*—then *we* had to believe in our own collective guilt as well. Guilt, indeed, was a bitch.

Well, goodbye, I said awkwardly. The mistress and Crème Brûlée bid me goodbye just as half-heartedly, reminding me that one should never leave a place like Heaven in the morning, only under the cover of night. Madeleine said nothing, lighting a hashish cigarette and keeping her eyes closed, behind which she was undoubtedly watching a movie only she could see, the rickety reel of memories in which everyone she knew was still alive.

\* \* \*

I read the newspaper on the RER back to Paris, with Sonny and the crapulent major reading over my shoulders. The article confirmed the news I had already heard in the refugee camp on Pulau Galang, relayed by the aid workers and my language teacher. He was an earnest, sweaty young man from Bordeaux who had come to the camp to help us refugees who were destined for our homeland, France. We learned about what the Khmer Rouge had done from one of his dictation lessons, which I attended out of boredom.

Repeat after me, he had said. Khmer Rouge.

Khmer Rouge, we said.

Year Zero, he said.

Year Zero, we said.

Pol Pot is evil, he said.

Pol Pot is evil, we said.

Very slowly, in basic French, he explained how the Khmer Rouge and their leader, Pol Pot, wanted to take Cambodia back to Year Zero, to cleanse their country of all foreign contamination, to start all over again from nothing. Nothing, we repeated, and the song that our French teacher had played for us before came back to me: *Non, je ne regrette rien.* Édith Piaf's voice was echoing in my mind when he gave us his final dictation for the day: The Khmer Rouge are communists. Once more we repeated his words, but after that I raised my hand and said, The Khmer Rouge leaders studied in Paris as students.

Pff! the sweaty French teacher said. Or maybe it was Pfffffff! He was very French, after all. They did not understand what they read, he said. They corrupted what they were taught. They took things too far.

*Too far?* I said it to myself, not wanting to debate the sweaty French teacher, whose approval might help me get out of the refugee camp. "Too far" implied that everything the French had done

in their colonies was not too far, although Toussaint Louverture and the Haitians might disagree. If the French had not gone too far in exploiting the Cambodians, would the Khmer Rouge even exist? And wasn't the student always supposed to go further than the teacher? Wasn't the student supposed to do what the teacher did, not just follow what the teacher said?

In our Indochinese case, the teacher extolled *liberté, égalité, fraternité,* while the teacher's people enslaved the student's people. The contradictions mounted when the student read about how the French revolutionaries had gone too far in using the guillotine to behead the French aristocracy, then saw the teacher using the guillotine to behead the native revolutionaries. It was all so confusing! No wonder the natives were so unruly. With the master's messages quite mixed, the native was inevitably mixed up.

Just like you, Sonny and the crapulent major whispered over my shoulder. It was uncanny how they always managed to be in unison. They were more harmonious than me and myself. And they were right. I was mixed and mixed up, and perhaps I had gone too far. But all that being said, the Khmer Rouge had definitively, indisputably gone too far. They hated us for having colonized them centuries ago and taking away their land, so they had attacked us in a series of bloody border incursions, and my outraged countrymen had responded with more communist fratricidal behavior by invading what was once Cambodia. The invasion had uncovered evidence of what had been mostly rumors: mass graves. They were all over the country, holding the remains of thousands who had died during the Khmer Rouge's three years of rule. Probably tens of thousands, the article said. Possibly hundreds of thousands. A picture in the newspaper article showed an open pit with hundreds of bones from disassembled skeletons, heads and rib cages no longer attached, femurs and shoulder blades thrown together, human

remains shattered and jumbled, along with the utopian dream of the Khmer Rouge. The pit of my stomach felt as hollow as that dream. Was my revolution the same as their revolution? Jean-Paul Sartre, in his introduction to Fanon's *The Wretched of the Earth*, had written this, which I had once underlined and memorized and which I found that the eschatological muscle had also marked: "In order to triumph, the national revolution must be socialist; if its career is cut short, if the native bourgeoisie takes over power, the new State, in spite of its formal sovereignty, remains in the hands of the imperialists." *Yes!* I had written in the margins. *Yes!* the eschatological muscle had likewise scribbled in his margins. Had the Khmer Rouge read this introduction, too? Or had they misread it? Or had they simply inhaled what was in the atmosphere of all revolutions, including the French one? Speaking of the Algerian revolution, Fanon wrote that "decolonization is always a violent phenomenon," and so far, my personal experience bore out his analysis. As for Pol Pot and his revolutionaries, wherever their ideas came from, they had simply pursued them to the logical end and eradicated the native bourgeoisie, including many people who were not native bourgeoisie. The Khmer Rouge had so much to prove to us, their colonizers, and to the French, the colonizers of their colonizers. They wanted to show that no one was more committed to revolution than they were, the reddest of the red. But in the end, Pol Pot may have just proven another of Fanon's points: "The colonized is a persecuted person whose permanent dream is to become the persecutor."

The Boss sent Shorty to recover in Heaven, where the semi-lucky son of a bitch would remain for several weeks, given the gravity of his injuries and the generosity of the Boss's disability allowance. Bon and I moved to the dim, charmless second-story apartment

that Sleepy and Shorty had shared in the 5th arrondissement near the Jardin des Plantes. Here we assumed their identities and Bon took up permanent residence, now that Sleepy was permanently asleep. When I mentioned to Le Cao Boi that neither Bon nor I looked anything like Sleepy and Shorty, he said, As someone who's lived here many years, let me assure you: the French won't be able to tell the difference.

They're short, Bon said. *Really* short.

And ugly, I said. *Really* ugly.

Don't flatter yourself, Camus, Le Cao Boi said. You two wouldn't win any beauty contests, either. In any case, Sleepy and Shorty took over that apartment from another couple of guys a few years ago and were living under their names. But those guys took over that apartment from another couple of guys and were living under *their* names. Who knows how far back this goes? That's why the apartment is so cheap. The lease is decades old. And that's why those first two guys, whoever they are, wherever they came from, will never die. They will live in that apartment forever.

No wonder why the French feared us. We were not just Invisible Indochinese. We were Immortal Orientals! We died by the ones or by the millions, but we were always reborn. As ugly as we were, we never aged, and we all looked the same, whether we were Chinese or Vietnamese or ethnic Chinese from Vietnam, or even Eurasians like me. Indeed, except for a couple of hesitant glances shot our way over the next few weeks, no one in the building even looked at us or spoke to us. Maybe we were strangers in the building—but maybe we weren't. The tenants had never looked at these Chinese, or Vietnamese, or Asians, very closely before, so now they could not be certain if we were who we claimed to be. Uncertain of their ability to identify what some Americans with their trademark good-natured humor would call Unidentifiable Fucking Orientals,

and what the French might call Ambiguous Asiatics, our neighbors decided to err on the side of their own prejudice, or politeness, and pretend that we did not exist, or that we had always existed.

But before moving to that apartment, I had returned to my aunt's to collect my things. I packed up my negligible belongings, hardly enough for a capitalist but not too bad for an ex-communist who was now watered down enough to pass for a socialist. These belongings were sufficient to fill out my leather duffel, with the hefty weight of my confession returned to its false bottom. I had not read it in months, but its mnemonic presence lent the duffel a demonic glow. I told my aunt about my apartment with Bon, and she did not insist that I stay, although she was polite enough to say that I could always come back. Our time together was coming to a slightly awkward end, and fiddling with my duffel, I said, Have you heard?

About what?

Man is in Paris.

She looked genuinely surprised. No, I hadn't known.

But you told him about me being here.

Of course. You knew I would, didn't you?

I nodded. You still believe in the revolution.

Unlike you I can't believe in nothing, she said. Or rather, like the part of you that the revolution abused, I have to believe in something, even if I also believe in what happened to you.

Those who believe in revolutions are the ones who haven't lived through one yet.

We learn from those mistakes. You yourself are making a mistake of judging the revolution too soon.

Too soon? I was flabbergasted. You read what they did to me—

I didn't say that was justified. What I'm saying is that all revolutions have excesses. It's in their nature. People are too exuberant, too passionate. They get carried away. Feelings run high. And sometimes

the wrong people are damaged. But you have to put yourself and what happened to you aside. You have to take the long view. Look at America. No one remembers now what happened to the Americans who chose to side with the British king. Should the American Revolution not have happened, or should we condemn it because all those people were exiled? Or look at the French Revolution. The Terror was unfortunate, but look where we are now. Revolutions need to be judged fifty years later, a hundred years later, when the passions have cooled and the revolution's accomplishments have had the time to take root and flourish.

I won't be alive by then. How convenient.

Don't be sarcastic. It doesn't become you.

On the contrary, I think it suits me very well.

She sighed. You know that revolutionaries have to sacrifice themselves. Think about all the communists that the French executed in our homeland. It's depressing to see that those young martyrs died in their teens, their twenties, their thirties. But they gave themselves up because they believed that the revolution would continue. They made the ultimate sacrifice. You haven't done that yet. I'm sorry to be harsh, but you need to stop pitying yourself—

If I don't pity myself, who will?

—and separate your subjective feelings about what was done to you from your objective understanding of how revolutions work. You are mistaking your personal experience for political knowledge. I'm sad to say that despite your proclamations of still believing in revolution, you look and sound like a counterrevolutionary. I was hesitant to say this before, but now I know for certain: you are a reactionary.

I was speechless. To be called a counterrevolutionary and a reactionary was the worst thing anyone could say to me, and even if part of me disagreed in anger, another part of me quailed in doubt.

The best response I could muster was to say, If I'm a reactionary, then you're just an armchair revolutionary.

That doesn't mean I may not be right. You believe in Marx, don't you?

I hesitated, sensing a trap. I believe in him more than I believe in his followers.

Exactly. He was a philosopher. Many of his followers aren't. They're men of action, and look at what they did to you. But doesn't everybody philosophize from an armchair? Marx, so far as I know, never used a gun. She was amused to see me speechless again. There's a bottle of Chablis on ice. Pour yourself a glass and one for me as well. You might as well stay for one last soiree. Friends are coming over.

My aunt mentioned BFD and the Maoist PhD, the most common visitors to her apartment. I had no desire to see them, but it was hard to turn down free Chablis. Returning from the kitchen with the glasses, I looked in the gigantic gilt-framed mirror hanging over her fireplace. I looked in mirrors often, because as a spy I had always needed to know what I looked like or what I should look like. Like an actor, I practiced my expressions and responses, especially to the questions that I had feared the most: Are you a communist? Are you a spy? Shock, disbelief, anger—that's what my face had to convey. Now my face had to be pleasant, and the face that stared back at my face was not unpleasant. After my recovery in Heaven, the face in the mirror at least looked vaguely human, which was surely a distortion of the antique glass. Nevertheless reassured, I handed my aunt a glass and took a sip of the Chablis, the chill of which soothed my soul, which was sore and aching even if my face was not.

Are you going to settle on one of them?

Settle? My aunt laughed as if I had told the funniest joke ever.

No husband? I was just making small talk, but small talk is drawn from a deep well. No children?

For someone who was once a revolutionary, she said with a sigh, you are so depressingly conventional.

Before BFD and the Maoist PhD came, I went into my aunt's bathroom, locked the door, and poured out a vial of the remedy onto the glass face of a hand mirror, rolled up a twenty-franc note, leaned close enough to the mirror to see my face, and inhaled the entire dose of white powder through one nostril and then the other. Then I waited, trembling. Hashish was not enough. I needed the power of the remedy to rescue me from the nausea of being—or just being called—a *reactionary*. By the time BFD and the Maoist PhD arrived, the remedy had calmed me down. I poured them some wine, having at last found a way to be socially useful.

My dear, BFD said to my aunt, you're as beautiful as a geisha tonight.

Not to be outdone, the Maoist PhD said, Darling, only a Gauguin would be worthy of painting you.

My aunt accepted their compliments gracefully and rolled some of my hashish into tight, slender cigarettes mixed with tobacco. I explained that I had gone away for a week to help at the second-worst Asian restaurant in Paris, this time near canal Saint-Martin, but I needn't have worried about offering an explanation. No one was curious, and that was fine with me, for I mostly just wanted to enjoy the tender and seductive hashish. I ignored the conversation as they raced through a variety of topics, although a few bits did penetrate my bliss: their approval of the fifth week of paid vacation that had been added to the four weeks of paid vacation under the new socialist regime, although they agreed that a sixth week was

needed; their scorn of a Far Right politician who had been making news with his attacks on immigrants and foreigners; their affirmation that France must continue to be a country of hospitality for immigrants and asylum for refugees, like those from Indochina . . .

Don't you agree? BFD said.

So unused was I to being spoken to that it took me a moment to realize he was speaking to me, which he was, because he spoke in English, which was not being polite but being condescending. What? I said, blinking my eyes.

Don't you agree that it's right that France should be a country of asylum?

Asylum? Why? Are we insane?

I thought I was being quite clever, but BFD grimaced and said, No, you know what I mean, a country of refuge.

Ah, I said. It was then, emboldened by the hashish, that I said, Even if they are fleeing from socialists and communists and utopia?

The Maoist PhD said, I don't agree with how these refugees are colonial compradors who participated in the colonization of their own country. But that doesn't mean that they're not human. They are quite human and so deserve our help, not least because we were the colonizers who ruined your country in the first place.

I don't disagree with you there, I said.

He hasn't changed, said BFD. He's too modest to tell you, but he led the Maoist committee against the American imperial war in your country in the sixties.

It was the right thing to do, the Maoist PhD said.

He was the most Maoist of all the Maoists, a Mao-Mao, so to speak, said BFD. In fact, he was so Maoist that our nickname for him was—

Chairman Mao, I said.

No, even better—Le Chinois!

147

They all burst out laughing and I smiled weakly, befuddled. Le Chinois? Was that a compliment, an insult, or both? But since he was the resident expert on Maoism, I asked, Can you still be a Maoist after the Cultural Revolution? Or the Great Leap Forward? You don't think that the deaths of all those Chinese on the wrong side of the Ideological State Apparatus and the Repressive State Apparatus should make you rethink Maoism? Or what about this—I retrieved the newspaper with the picture of the mass grave and the bones—in Cambodia? The Chinese are supporting the Khmer Rouge. Doesn't that make you at least queasy about communist revolution?

The Maoist PhD shook his head sadly over the picture. I saw that this morning, he said. Yes, of course, revolutions make mistakes and sometimes on the scale of the deaths of millions. Tragic? Yes. Wrong? Yes. But if you stop there, you've simply stepped into the trap of the capitalists. Ha! they'll say. Got you! Now your only choice is capitalism and its pseudo-democracy, its trickery of false choices. For if communism is bad, then capitalism must be good, yes? No! Capitalists love to point out how tens of millions have died under Stalin and Mao, all while conveniently forgetting how *hundreds* of millions have died under capitalism. What were colonialism and slavery but forms of capitalism? What was the genocide of the natives of the Americas but capitalism? But let's forget about those nasty contradictions of capitalism and focus on what the communists have done!

What did I tell you? BFD said, pouring himself another glass of wine. Le Chinois!

I know all that, I said. But that's all theory—

No, it's practice. You asked me about Mao and the Cultural Revolution. I am not convinced it was a mistake, for Mao was not on the side of the state. He was trying to purge the state of its reactionary elements and give power back to where it belonged—to the

people, to the masses. We will look back on the Cultural Revolution the way we look back at the Paris Commune—a defeat then, but a triumph eventually for the people! As for Mao, he was being infinitely dialectical, realizing, unlike Stalin, who the Vietnamese communists have followed, that you cannot allow the revolution to calcify into the state. Once that happens, the revolution will be corrupted by its own power, which is why you ended up in a reeducation camp. The revolution, like the dialectic, must be perpetual!

My aunt offered me another hashish cigarette. I accepted dumbly, unable to respond to the theoretical barrage, even in English. The Maoist PhD sipped his wine and took pity on me, saying, You have been through a great deal. I understand. You should understand that you can be forgiven for being on the wrong side of history, but have you really and truly engaged in the self-criticism to realize that?

Self-criticism? I cried. I am nothing if not self-critical! *My entire life is a self-criticism session between me, myself, and I!*

No need to raise your voice, said BFD.

If you are so self-critical, said the Maoist PhD, do you see where you deviate from the masses?

Why should I worry about deviating from the masses when I am also me and myself? Am I not a mass? Am I not already a collective? Do I not contain multitudes? Am I not a universe unto myself? Am I not always infinitely dialectical as I synthesize the thesis of me and the antithesis of myself?

That's the hashish talking, said BFD.

I don't think you should be so harsh on him, said my aunt, and my spirit lifted at this unexpected encouragement, until it plummeted when she said, He's actually not the absolute reactionary he seems to be. He was actually a communist spy working undercover among the reactionaries, only to be sent to reeducation for having

been perhaps too enthusiastic in his pretense to being a capitalist-loving American ally.

BFD and the Maoist PhD looked at me with new interest, or possibly because my jaw had followed my spirit and dropped to the floor in astonishment. You're not—that's not—why—

It's all right, you're among allies, my aunt said, waving her hand dismissively. The problem with you is that you live completely in your head. You have no one to talk to except me. Have you forgotten the importance of solidarity?

I never would have imagined him as a spy, BFD said.

Which is what makes him a good spy, the Maoist PhD said.

At least I'm good at something! I shouted. And I do have someone to talk to besides you—I talk to myself all the time!

And it shows, my aunt said.

They were all looking at me as if I had said something deeply problematic like "I love America," which one should never do among French intellectuals. One should confess to that only in private, as with a liking for pornography. I stood up so abruptly that I made myself dizzy, a vertigo that was compounded when I saw myself in the gilt-framed mirror hanging over my aunt's fireplace, a man of two faces. Which face was I showing to myself and to them? Was I a revolutionary or a reactionary? And if I was a revolutionary, what did I believe in? To what was I committed? And was I myself or another? I mumbled an excuse and went to the bathroom, where I locked the door, absorbed some more of the remedy, and waited, trembling, for my nausea to subside.

# CHAPTER 9

**W**e—me, myself, and I—were neither real nor unreal but surreal, a condition that the holes in my head have not helped at all, a condition that was even more pronounced when we dusted ourselves with the white powder of the remedy, which we knew we should not do but which it was too easy to do, given how good such a dusting felt, or when we donned the guise of the Japanese tourist to once again walk the streets of Paris. With our glasses on, we had four eyes instead of two. Even though the lenses were fake, everything seemed sharper, more focused, even if we were high on hashish, or maybe because we were high on hashish, and even more so when we were high on the remedy, or when we multiplied hashish with the remedy. We found we needed to take a dosage of the remedy more and more often, since the purpose of walking the streets of Paris was now to serve as bait, and being bait was frightening. Whoever had killed Sleepy and tried to kill Shorty and us would try it again, or so Le Cao Boi told us. That knowledge was somewhat taxing, and the remedy helped to soothe us, or delude us, as we tried to draw out our rival gangsters.

To say that we walked the streets of Paris, however, was inaccurate. We floated, we glided, but we did not walk as we participated in our rehearsals for the culture show and as we made our round of appointments, delivering our orders to the Vietnamese performers, the Maoist PhD, and to all their friends and acquaintances who preferred their goods delivered by a yellow Asiatic or a fellow Vietnamese rather than a brown Oriental—that is, an Arab. As Ho Chi Minh long ago recognized in his writings against colonialism, the Asiatic and the Arab (as well as the African) were all related as colonial stepchildren sharing the same abusive guardian, France. When it came to the Asiatic and the Arab, we were distant cousins who shared the vast regions that lay to the east of the West, or at least east of the Western mind. The brown Oriental was like the yellow Asiatic in that our once glorious civilizations lay in decayed ruin, only good now for our tea, our religions, our rugs, our trinkets, our tapestries, our textiles, our servitude, our solitude, our sex, and perhaps our rage. Or were our rages and our rants not as good as our goods?

This circular logic was the Easterner's way of thinking, versus the Westerner's linear logic. That linear logic aimed always toward the horizon of Enlightenment, whose perpetual dawn of knowledge was illuminated by the atomic bombs exploding on some poor tropical island of French Polynesia, just beyond the skyline. The closer we came to the source of that luminescence, the more that light hurt our four eyes. With our optical quartet, we preferred twilight. Twilight was the time of hashish, the dusky native, the swarthy subaltern, and the mellow yellow. Twilight was the best time to contemplate the truth, which was usually found in the shadows rather than in stark light. Twilight was also the best time to savor whiskey, make love, foment revolution, and go in circles. We made circles and circles through the neighborhoods of Paris, knowing

that somewhere in the vicinity roamed a Citroën CX driven by one of the Seven Dwarfs (for so we thought of them, even if they no longer numbered seven). Le Cao Boi sat in the front and Bon sat in the back with one or two dwarfs, armed with their cleavers as well as knives and pipes and chains and blackjacks and a couple of handguns in case things got really bad.

That's it? we had asked.

Le Cao Boi had shrugged. No need to escalate now, Camus, he said. Just keep talking if you get cornered. We'll be coming for you.

Americans in the good old US of A would have cradled shotguns and Tommy guns with the care that mothers reserved for babies. Vietnamese in Vietnam would have been armed with hand grenades and collapsible rocket launchers bought on the black market of American surplus and stolen firepower. But the French—and apparently the natives living in France—were too civilized for any of that. They still believed in starting with revolvers.

The Citroën trailed us at some distance, discreetly, we assumed, since we saw it only occasionally out of the corner of an eye as we turned into a building or left one. This routine continued for a week, with little result except that our feet got sore and our cash reserves got replenished. Intellectuals really liked hashish, as did some of the bohemians of the Union, who were not such good, law-abiding natives or children of natives that they did not like to get high. And some even bought the remedy, which seemed to them, in all its fine whiteness, rather chic.

Selling the goods doesn't offend you? we asked Bon late one night at our new apartment.

We were drinking cognac the way we sometimes did, using a teapot as our decanter and serving the cognac in thimble-sized

teacups. Poor Bon loved cognac and saw no contradiction between imbibing that glorious liquid and saying, The French got rich by stealing from us. Right?

Right.

And then they tried to turn us French. They were worse than the Americans. The Americans betrayed us, but at least they didn't try to turn us into Americans. They never stole anything from us. They just wanted to sell us things. So here, I'm happy to sell the French some things. They owe us.

We doubted that the French understood our mutual history in that manner, except for the part about turning us French. After all, even as we criticized the French, were we not drinking their cognac? Oh, *quelle contradiction!*

We continued to reacquaint ourselves with French perspectives at our morning language classes. We took dictation from the teacher with pleasure and felt once again the thrill of being called on in class, the chance of this little success or failure. On our own time, with the aid of a dictionary, we read Césaire's *A Tempest*, a rewriting of Shakespeare's *The Tempest* from Caliban's perspective. Césaire gave back to Caliban, "a black slave," the voice he always had, strong enough to say what every colonized person has wanted to say to his colonizer, in this case Prospero:

# I HATE YOU!

Prospero's response was self-serving: "I've tried to save you, above all from yourself." There, the civilizing mission! And then: "I shall set aside my indulgent nature and henceforth I will answer your violence with violence!" There, the cannons of civilization! And blaming the colonized for a situation the colonizer created. Césaire's vision was like Fanon's in *The Wretched of the Earth*, where

the violence of the colonizer begat the violence of the colonized. Perhaps that was the only way to get rid of the colonizer, but where did it leave the colonized, infected with the parting gift of the colonizer, the venereal disease of hatred? The triumphant among the formerly colonized would turn this hatred of the colonizer into a barely disguised self-hatred for letting themselves be colonized for so long. They would not take out the self-hatred on themselves; they would take it out on the rest of the formerly colonized who were not so violent as the victorious. The only solution to this revolution was therefore another revolution, one to which we were committed but whose shape we could not articulate, which was fitting, since our place in this allegory was that of Ariel, the "mulatto slave" of ambiguous loyalty, neither black nor white, a position of weakness that might yet be of some strength if Ariel could finally say something of substance, not having been given much to say by either Shakespeare or Césaire.

We took unknown words from Césaire, Fanon, and others, composed flash cards in French vocabulary, and turned learning into a drinking game, with Bon drilling us at night and us being forced to take a shot of cognac for every word we missed. "Forced," of course, is a euphemism with the exact opposite meaning, like "pacification," which usually involved a great degree of homicidal force on rambunctious natives. History was full of such examples, from the Chinese pacification of Vietnam, which we enjoyed so much that we let it last a thousand years; to the Vietnamese pacification of the Cham, which was so successful that there were barely any Cham left anymore; to the French pacification of Indochina through bringing that religion of peace, Catholicism, which the contemporary French here did not even seem to believe in; to the American pacification of the Mekong Delta, where thousands of "guerrillas" were killed by the Americans but only dozens of weapons were recovered. Where

had all their weapons gone? The vanishing was a tropical miracle! But pacification always was.

At the end of one such vocabulary session, triggered by the expression "coup de foudre," Bon mentioned seeing Loan a few times. The confession—for that was what it was—stunned us into momentary sobriety with its stroke of lightning. A few times? we demanded. Only a few weeks had passed since he met her at the Union. How do you two even talk?

I talk. I have things to say.

You're supposed to be mute, remember?

Psychologically mute. Not physically mute.

We cranked our hanging jaw to a close. You're saying—

I'm saying that I told Loan the truth. I was mute not because my vocal cords had been cut in some way, but because I could not bring myself to talk.

That's not the truth.

Spiritually it's the truth. Have I talked very much over the last few years?

We shook our head and felt its liquid contents shift and slosh.

Have I looked at a woman besides the photo of Linh?

We shook our head again, gently, our mind floating on a waterbed full of cognac.

It's been six years since Linh and Duc died. I've suffered with them and for them every day. I still suffer. But the night after I met Loan, I heard Linh's voice. He paused.

What did she say? we asked.

*It's time.* That's all. Not time to move on. I can never move on. But it's time . . .

We each flung two more shots of cognac down our throats, prefacing every round with a ritual toast that evoked our regular drinking games with Man so many years ago: *One hundred percent!* We took

pleasure in knowing that drinking 100 percent of each shot would have made the French choke on their own cognac. But swallowing whole shots of a noble French liquor in one heroic gesture was a Vietnamese masculine tradition, its origin unknown but most likely arising as a way of demonstrating two things: the first that we, too, could afford cognac, and the second that we were manly enough to drink it very quickly, unlike the French, who only sipped it.

Riddled by several shots of cognac, Bon then told us more: he had devised a plan for the faceless man, Dung, or whatever his name was.

What kind of a plan? we said, even though we knew that Bon only ever devised one type of plan.

The Union invites the entire staff from the communist embassy to come to the Tet show, Bon said. That includes the faceless man. When he shows up, that's our chance.

Our chance?

Or my chance, if you don't want to be a part of this.

He went to the closet and retrieved a round blue tin of Danish butter cookies. Was it the same tin offered to us by the Boss? He opened the tin to reveal the sweetest cookie of all, the ultimate male prosthesis, a perpetually hard gun capable of rapid-fire ejaculation. Not a civilized Gallic revolver that could only be fired in slow motion. No, this was a ruthless, Germanic, clip-fed, rapid-fire nine-millimeter Walther P38.

You're going to get caught, we said.

Bon merely smiled. I don't give a fuck.

*What does not kill you makes you stronger.*
*Why the hell not.*
*I don't give a fuck.*

So many eloquent philosophies to choose from! But what was ours? Once it was simply this: *Something must be done!* Doing something had been the great cause of our life, and we still felt its pressure. In the name of doing something, we had become revolutionary, which had landed us in a reeducation camp. In the name of doing something, we had followed Bon on his suicide mission to invade our homeland and rescue it from communism, just so we could save his life. We had succeeded, barely. And now we had to do something more: we had to stop Bon from killing Man. That was one thing I knew I was still committed to, our oath of blood brotherhood. Of course part of me blamed Man for torturing me, but another part of me saw that he had done what he thought was best for me, to make me see the truth of our revolution. He was locked into the broken world sketched by Fanon and Césaire, where the problem was violence and the solution was violence. We were bound together, not only as blood brothers, but also as revolutionaries who had to pursue our now divergent revolutions to our individual ends.

Walking the streets of Paris on our delivery routes gave us a great amount of time to puzzle over how to save the life of one blood brother from the hands of another blood brother, as well as to ponder our philosophy, or lack thereof, until the cosmic clock of karma rang. On the day our time came up, Le Cao Boi and Bon were being too discreet, or perhaps too tired and inattentive after days of trailing us. Maybe our circular patterns were too circular, because when Beatles finally appeared, the Citroën was nowhere to be seen.

Instead of the Citroën, a plain white van pulled up to the curb, passenger-side window rolled down. The driver was a low-browed fellow we had never seen before, but we recognized the passenger immediately, even if he wore a gray sweatshirt instead of a print of the Fab Four. Before we could run, the side door slid open to reveal

two more young men, one middle-browed and one high-browed. The high-browed one aimed a revolver at us and for some reason was smiling, perhaps just to offset the optical heat rays of hatred pulsating from Beatles's eyes. He spoke rapidly in a stream of French, of which we understood less than half, but this time our lack of comprehension mattered not. The gunman spoke a grammatically perfect English when he translated.

He said get in or we'll blow your brains out, the gunman said, still smiling, and it was odd how charming it sounded with its French inflections.

You speak very good English.

So do you, he said. He bore an uncanny resemblance to the *Mona Lisa*, except for his hair, which was short and curly. But his smile was as serene as her famous one, his nose just as elongated, and his eyes as enigmatic. You speak even better English than Bruce Lee.

That's quite a compliment, we said. He was amazing in *Fist of Fury*.

Even better in *Enter the Dragon*.

What the fuck are you talking about? Beatles yelled.

He's a little impatient, the Mona Lisa said, the black caterpillars of his eyebrows arching their backs. His expansive forehead gave them plenty of room. You should get in the car.

We looked at the small gun in his hand. A small gun implied confidence, accuracy, and grace, unlike a big gun, which in most cases was overkill. We raised our hands, but there was no one on the street to notice the gesture. Then we climbed into the van and squeezed into the middle row between the Mona Lisa and the middle-browed goon, who smelled of smoke and sweat. His muscular thigh, pressed against me, jiggled to the strange music playing on the van's radio, heavy with beats and a staccato black voice enunciating

forcefully in English. The van pulled away from the curb, Beatles turned to glare at us from the front seat, and his face was the last thing we saw.

We, or me, or myself, or I, woke with conversation and laughter echoing in the cracked bell of my head. My neck hurt from holding up the weight of that heavy bell. I was strapped to a wooden chair, hands behind my back, ankles affixed to the legs of the chair, in a cold cellar with gray stone walls lined with industrial-strength wooden shelves, as wide as small beds and stacked with wooden crates. A movie on low volume occupied the face of a television, in front of which a couple of ratty sofas ganged up on a coffee table. Beatles, the Mona Lisa, and the two goons, Ugly and Uglier, were playing cards and smoking cigarettes. My extremities were numb, but the fear clamped on to my spine more than made up for the lack of feeling in my arms and legs. This was not surreal. This was most definitely real. The best-case scenario was that while I might leave this cellar alive, it would only be on condition of having left behind various parts of myself, from fingers and toes to entire limbs, eyes, or ears. The worst-case scenario was that I would leave this cellar dead, although there were various gradations of this scenario, given that I could be dead in one piece, a few pieces, or many pieces.

Ugly noticed me first and nudged Beatles. Beatles glared at me and lobbed a volley of words that included "bastard," "asshole," and "chink." Each word that I understood and did not understand was a stroke of a hammer against my cracked bell. Echoing there were all the bad words that I had learned in French, including all the anti-Asian racial epithets directed at Le Cao Boi and the Seven Dwarfs over their years in Paris, which they had passed on to me. Beatles wanted to let me know that he knew these slurs, too, but

having endured a lifetime of racial abuse, I pretended not to be bothered and forced myself to laugh. I was the Crazy Bastard. No gangster was going to intimidate me, even if, in fact, he intimidated me. But it would not do to show any dread to this crew. Like all gangsters, lawyers, and priests, they enjoyed the fear of others.

Asshole? I said with as much bluster as I could. Chink? How about *Asiate. Chinetoque. Jaune. Tchong. Bridé!*

Beatles laughed. You forgot *niakoué.*

*Niakoué*? I haven't heard that one.

How about *FILS DE PUTE!*

Well, yes, I have heard that one.

From now on, I will no longer record all the instances where *fils de pute* or *sale fils de pute* were uttered, since they functioned thenceforth like commas or periods, invisible and inaudible. In this way, the gangsters in this grimy cellar differed little from the gangsters in the worst Asian restaurant in Paris, who overcompensated for their emasculated status on the lower rungs of the service industry by spitting out "motherfucker" like it was spit, which one should not do in a restaurant. Of course, for me and myself to embrace not just "motherfucker" and *fils de pute* but the very racist terms used against us was to step onto a slanted slope, but that was always the angle that I, or we, took, first in our dubious profession as a spy and now in our even more dubious apprenticeship as a gangster. But if I thought I was being menacing by stealing from these gangsters the words they might use against me, they seemed less than impressed. At least that was the case for Uglier, who sneered and said, Who's afraid of the Big Bad Chink?

I was going to die, wasn't I? But if I was going to die, then I would die to the best of my ability, at least until it was too painful to do so. I like that, I cried. That's even better than Crazy Bastard, you racists!

We're not racists, said Beatles. We just don't like you.

So why haven't you slit my throat? I said. On the one hand, it might not be a good idea to remind my captors of one of the nastiest options available to them. On the other hand, why not clear the air on the matter of most pressing concern?

Where's the fun in slaughtering you like a sheep? said Beatles. You're not even a proper sacrifice.

Ho ho! said the crapulent major with a chortle.

Ha ha! Sonny chimed in with a laugh.

Shut up! I said.

No, *you* shut up! Beatles shouted, leaping up from the sofa through a cloud of cigarette smoke. *Who the fuck do you think you are?*

Ah! me and myself both said at once. That is the question, is it not? The universal question. The question that has been with us since the beginning of time!

Let's not confuse him, said the Mona Lisa. I don't want him— *you*—to shut up. I want you to talk.

I imitated God and said nothing.

Are you hard of hearing, you crazy bastard? Tell us about Le Chinois.

Who?

*Le Chinois!* yelled Beatles.

The Maoist PhD?

Beatles jumped over the coffee table and slapped me twice across the face, first with the forehand and then with the backhand, as if he were Jean Gabin slapping an actress, something charmingly French, as a Vietnamese or an American would have just punched me in the nose. Le Chinois! Le Chinois! *Le Chinois!*

Your boss, said the Mona Lisa. Stop slapping him. I think he heard you.

He tossed a transparent plastic packet of the remedy onto the table. How innocuous the remedy looked! Nothing more than a white powder that could be flour or sugar.

I would like to find your boss, the one who is selling this and the one who is taking business from me.

I almost said, What do you want to know? Almost. If I had been sane, I would have said it. What loyalty did I owe the Boss? He was a gangster, a drug dealer, a pimp, and a killer, which is not to say that these are characteristics disqualifying one from sympathy. As a sympathizer par excellence, I could see not just any issue from both sides but any person from both sides. That was how I knew that many of our most important world leaders have also been gangsters, drug dealers, pimps, and killers, although they prefer to call themselves presidents, kings, diplomats, and statesmen. The only thing preventing the Boss from ascending to a more legitimate stage of existence, to become a pillar of society, was time. That much I owed him and could give him, not for his sake but for Bon's. If I turned the Boss over, I would almost surely be turning over Bon as well, and that I would never do.

Who is Saïd? I said instead.

Saïd? Beatles said, astounded.

Careful, said the crapulent major.

The mysterious Saïd, I said.

Not a good idea, added Sonny.

Beatles shook his head and looked at the Mona Lisa, who appeared, more and more, to be the leader. Saïd, the Mona Lisa said, drawing the name out. Saïd is my brother.

Of course, I muttered.

He has unfortunately gone on vacation. But just because he has gone on vacation does not mean that you get to take his business, which is my business. Now I advise you to tell us all you know about

this—he pointed at the remedy—and Le Chinois, or things will go very badly for you, as they did for your friend.

My friend?

The short one.

Sleepy.

Is that his name? He's sleeping for good now.

I did that, Beatles said. Just like you almost did Ahmed.

Ahmed?

My friend! The one you almost killed.

So Rolling Stones was still alive somewhere. I would have felt happy for him, and for me, if I didn't feel so bad at the moment. Are you going to torture me? I said.

Stop giving them ideas, said Sonny.

I laughed. You can't torture me. I've lived through a reeducation camp.

Now you've done it, said the crapulent major.

You think you're so tough because you went to a reeducation camp? said Beatles. Your war wasn't so bad! Our war was worse. The stories I've heard! You think you're tough, Crazy Bastard? Let's try a few things on you that the French did to us.

Aren't you French? I said.

Shut the fuck up.

They then proceeded to fuck me up. Part of me was in tremendous pain and did the requisite groaning, screaming, begging, and fearing for my life. But part of me was the professional who, in retrospect, could analyze and assess their performance. These guys were amateurs, but that did not mean that what ensued did not hurt. Amateurs can do a lot of damage, even if they damage without finesse. But finesse is key. One can get away with mass murder and wholesale looting of countries and continents if one handles oneself with a splash of élan, a dash of finesse, and gallons

of hypocrisy and selective amnesia. Just ask the French (or the English or the Dutch or the Portuguese or the Belgians or the Spanish or the Germans or the Americans or the Chinese or the Japanese or even us Vietnamese, but not the Italians, who were not very good at colonization, having forgotten what their Roman ancestors had done so well). And just as the French did everything with élan and finesse, both terms that they coined, so must those of us who are professionals in "intelligence" carry out our tasks with skill. The extraction of intelligence, like the extraction of a tooth, requires delicacy. The real question is this: Does the torturer understand this fundamental issue? The interrogator is much more likely to succeed in his task with the aid of cigarettes, sympathy, compassion, and an intuitive grasp of human psychology and cultural sensitivity. If the torturer does not understand this, he is a fool. If the torturer really does understand this and simply enjoys the torture, then he is a sadist. Not to say that one cannot be both a fool and a sadist at the same time. One can be just about anything and a fool at the same time.

As for me, perhaps I am a masochist, which is not to say that I am not also a fool. How else to explain why, in the midst of all the shouting and grunting (on the part of my torturers) and the screams and tears (on my part) I began to laugh? Tortured laughing, for sure. Strangled laughing, certainly. What with the electrodes to the nipples and the ropes and the wires used to hang me by the arms from the ceiling and the water poured down my throat—it was very difficult to laugh in a convivial, pleasant way. But it was laughter nonetheless, and the gurgling and snorting appeared to confuse my gangster torturers, who undoubtedly expected the more usual responses.

Is he laughing? said Ugly, grimacing because of his bruised knuckles.

I think he's laughing, said Uglier, leaning against the wall as he took a cigarette break, somewhat worn out from the chokehold he had placed me in, intermittently, for the last hour.

*What the fuck is wrong with you?* said Beatles. He had stripped off his shirt, as it was quite hot work to beat someone with a rubber hose.

I lay facedown on the cold cement floor, naked and shivering, my cheek resting in a puddle of liquid that may have come from me or may have come from one of them. I wondered whether my mother could see me now. How she and I both loved it when I lay like this, at four or five years old, naked on a bamboo mat with my head on her lap and purring with pleasure as she slowly scratched my dorsal side, beginning from the upper buttocks, proceeding up the back, and ending between the shoulder blades, before starting all over again with the excruciating pleasure.

And then it occurred to me with a sudden stab to my already wounded side that I was now a few years older than my mother was when she died at thirty-four, by herself, in that same ragged hut where she raised me, without anyone to care for her, or so I surmised when I finally returned to my village after my six years in America as a foreign student. I wore my uniform as a newly commissioned lieutenant in the army. No one in the village dared meet my gaze or call me "bastard" the way they used to when I was a boy, not when I now had an American-manufactured pistol on my hip. The hut was so barren that no one had bothered to loot it or steal any part of it, built as it was out of sticks, and mud, and straw, and scraps of canvas, and pieces of cardboard stripped from the packaging of American equipment and rations. Without anyone to tend to it, the hut had gradually collapsed in on itself until it was only an empty husk. I peered inside at the small wooden bed on which my mother and I had slept, its bamboo mat in shreds, and saw the small shelf

on which my mother kept a picture of Jesus Christ and a crucifix. She was an orphan and had no mother and father whom she could honor, so she was left only with Jesus Christ, his picture her most precious possession besides me.

From the door, with the carpet of sunlight it allowed into the dim recesses of the hut, I could see the red heart on the breast of a suspiciously Anglo Jesus, with his brown hair, brown goatee, brown eyes, and fair skin. Had my mother been saved, she who had saved me with all the love she had given me without complaint? Where had her love come from, she who had not been loved? From whom had she learned affection, and caresses, and the gentle words that she rubbed on me daily and unsparingly until I had absorbed the little dose of humanity that I now possessed?

Part of me, the recalcitrant communist, believed she had not been saved because there was no God and no afterlife. That part of me was bitter. But another part of me, the recalcitrant Catholic, half fearful and half faithful, shaken and not stirred, believed that she had been airlifted to Heaven along with all the other refugees from that day, which is to say everyone who had died. What were any of us, once dead, but refugees fleeing the wretched earth for the refuge of eternal life? What was the entire earth but a Third World compared with the Second World of purgatory and the First World of Heaven? That fearful and faithful part of me was ashamed at the thought that from her balcony in Paradise, that most exclusive of gated communities, she might be able to see me.

Lying on my face in that cellar, I could see myself on the trip back to my village and the cemetery where my mother was buried. I had knelt and touched her name. At least she had a name. My headstone, if I ever had a headstone, would most likely read VO DANH. Seeing her name and the dates of her birth and death etched in a vermilion ink that was fading like memory itself, I found myself

on a raft carried away by a torrent of my pent-up, dammed love. Eventually I stopped weeping. Leaning against a sturdy steel beam of homicidal rage, I dried my eyes and surveyed the desecration of my mother's memory. Her grave was located in a marshy margin of the cemetery, where she had been exiled in death as she was in life. She had borne the cross of being a single mother to me, scorned by relatives and villagers who did not know that my father was their priest. My mother protected him out of a misplaced Catholic belief in goodness and kindness, which that very same priest had instilled in her. For her faith in God and him, she was consigned in death to a plot distant from any other grave, far from the honorable dead and their honorable survivors, who could not bear to be near her, she who was the most honest one among them, given her utter lack of the hypocrisy that was fundamental to anyone with even a bit of respectability.

I returned to the hut where I had lived with my mother, the only home where I had known any love, and set fire to it with a Zippo lighter applied to its dry thatch. The neighbors emerged from their homes and watched along with me as the hut became a pyre for my memories, which I hoped would also turn to ashes. My neighbors said nothing, which was the right response. If they had said anything, I might have used my American-made pistol for the purpose for which it was intended when it was designed in the early twentieth century, the slaughter of natives, or so my mentor Claude had taught me. It had proven its worth first in the pacification of the Philippines but was now just as useful in our country. Claude had also given me the Zippo, personally inscribed to me. See this? he had said, his index finger underlining the words. Just between you and me, it's the CIA's unofficial motto:

## FUCK THEM BEFORE THEY FUCK US

I say this every night before I go to bed, Claude said, winking at me as he slipped the lighter into my palm.

Wise words, I said. Wise words.

After the hut was reduced to a campfire, I walked down the road to the small country church where my father was, miraculously, still the pastor. His survival was not a miracle because of his advanced age—he was now in his seventies—but because he was a white man, a Frenchman, and a Catholic, during a time when all those factors made him a highly attractive target for assassination by the local revolutionaries. He received me in his office, which I had never visited, since I had seen him only in three places: the classroom of the Catholic school, where he had taught me; the church, where I watched him only from a distance; and the confessional, where I saw only his silhouette behind the screen. That bowed shadow was also what his assassin would see the moment before she turned him into a shade.

You are quite the man now, my father said. He spoke in the slow, deliberate, patient French that he used with students and peasants. They were the first words he had spoken to me since I had left his classroom, his best student and his worst fear. We had communicated only once since then, when he had written to me in the United States to tell me of my mother's passing. He had not used my name in the letter, except to inscribe it above the address, just as he did not utter my name now. He had only ever said my name when taking attendance. Otherwise he called me nothing at all, except "you."

I've been to the cemetery, I replied in the slow, deliberate, patient Vietnamese that I used with the French and the Americans who thought they knew Vietnamese, which my father did after decades of living here. I've seen Mother's grave.

He said nothing from behind his desk, stacked with student exams.

Thank you for getting that headstone for her. It's the least you could do.

Silence. He would say not another word until the end of our conversation, which was really my monologue. Nor would he drop his gaze, keeping his eyes fixed on mine in a gesture of defiance, or contempt, or pride, or regret, or inarticulate love. Who knows?

Here's the money to pay for the headstone, I said, tossing an envelope onto the desk. I didn't have any money when I was a student. I have a little bit now. I should be the one to pay for her headstone, not you.

Still nothing. He was enacting for me the silence of his boss, the godfather of godfathers, the Man Himself, God. This was the silence my father encountered every day during his prayers, the silence that hundreds of millions of people heard every day as they beseeched God to say something, anything. He always said nothing, which hardly disabused His legions of fans. For someone who never said anything, God certainly spoke to a lot of people.

Why is my mother gone instead of you? I said, getting up to leave. And the fact that she is dead and you are alive—that's just proof there is no such thing as God.

Now he was provoked. Now he finally spoke, his eyes flashing with the inspiration for his next sermon. Your dear mother believed in God with all her soul, and she is alive now in Heaven because God saved her, he said. Is nothing sacred to you?

Is nothing sacred? I burst into laughter. Then I stopped and said, I wish you were dead instead of her.

My words echoed what I had written to Man from California on learning of my mother's death and burial from my father's letter: *I wish he were dead.* My words foreshadowed what would happen a month after my meeting with my father, when the assassin, posing as a penitent kneeling in my father's confessional, fired a bullet into

his temple, which might have been experienced by his dying brain as the flash of lightning and the boom of thunder that was, at long last, the actual Word of God, spoken by God Himself. Years later, during our tête-à-tête in the reeducation camp, when Man opened my skull with a can opener and fondled my brain, he told me that my fatal wish had been his command. After all, he was my best friend and blood brother. Taking me at my word, he had dispatched the communist agent to carry out my words, and she had found the assassin, a sixteen-year-old girl whose grandfather had been killed by the French and whose father had been killed by the Americans and whose brother had been killed by the Republicans. Who said words couldn't kill? But I had not known the power of my words, or so I had told myself. I knew their power now, although I also knew that the only thing more powerful than words was silence.

# CHAPTER 10

The ringing in my head reminded me of the ringing of the bell in my father's church. The sound of that bell, imported from France, boomeranged across all the years to return to me in this obscure, moist French cellar. It seemed to me that I heard my father speaking to me, too, the word he used for me coalescing from the echoing within my cracked bell: *You!* Somebody was ringing my bell, which is to say somebody was slapping me in the face. Each blow lit up the insides of my closed eyelids, showering them with yellow and red sparks.

## HEY!

# YOU!

The you that was me opened my eyes. I was not in my mother's hut. I was not in my village. I was not in my father's church. I was still on that wet cellar floor, and the hand slapping my face belonged not to God but one of the two goons. Ugly. Or maybe it was Uglier.

That got his attention, the Mona Lisa said, squatting by my side. He's awake now. Got some color in his cheeks.

Why don't you put up a fight? said the goon who had been slapping me. My eyes focused. It was definitely Ugly. Where's the fun if we don't get to torture you?

This is boring, Uglier said.

Can't we just kill him now? asked Ugly.

Shut up! Beatles said. He was pacing behind the Mona Lisa. You lazy-ass little shits. You can't even beat somebody up without complaining about it.

Okay, Ugly said. Fine. But my toes are hurting.

I guess kicking somebody with your sneakers wasn't a good idea, Beatles said. Get some boots.

Ugly sighed and stood up, presumably to kick me again, but just as he was drawing back his leg, the Mona Lisa raised his hand.

I have an idea, he said. The Mona Lisa knelt on one knee before me, and for the first time I noticed that he was wearing my Bruno Magli shoes. He noticed that I noticed and said, These very nice shoes are wasted on you. Now, are you ready to play a game?

I'd rather not, I said, but either I did not say it, or I said it so softly that only I heard, or I said it and no one cared, for everyone ignored me. The Mona Lisa drew a revolver from his waistband, aimed the gun at me, and slowly moved it closer and closer until the muzzle was pressed against my forehead. Then he drew the gun back, snapped open its cylinder, shook out six bullets, and cupped them in his palm.

Look at that, he said.

I could not look at anything else.

He dropped a bullet onto the cement floor and it bounced with a metallic *ping* in front of my nose.

Such a small thing, the crapulent major whispered in my ear. But it's big enough to smash through your skull. I should know, shouldn't I?

I'm sorry, I said to the crapulent major. I'm so sorry.

You should be sorry, said the Mona Lisa. He dropped a second bullet onto the floor, where it bounced in a different direction and ended up near my eye. But you're going to be sorrier still.

Where's my apology? whispered Sonny in my other ear as the third bullet hit the floor. In my case, you actually pulled the trigger. I would have appreciated it if you could have been a better shot and killed me with one bullet instead of the six bullets you actually used.

I'm sorry, I said to Sonny. I'm so sorry.

I heard you the first time, the Mona Lisa said, dropping the fourth bullet. Say it all you want, being sorry is not going to save you now.

He dropped the fifth bullet. It fell in slow motion and I was able to study it in all its splendor as it descended. This particular beauty was jacketed in a copper that reflected the light in such a way that the bullet appeared to wink at me as it fell, graceful as an Olympic diver. The tip of the bullet was a dull orange. I was sure it was a soft-nosed bullet, an ironic term, since the purpose of the bullet was not to be soft but to inflict great damage when the tip expanded on contact, namely with me and myself. When the fifth bullet finally hit the floor and bounced, I wondered why I had never apologized to these two men whom I had killed.

We wondered that, too, they said.

I didn't think you would want an apology from me, I said.

Of course we want an apology from you, the Mona Lisa said, holding the sixth bullet between his thumb and forefinger. Not that it's going to do you any good, but it's good form to apologize when you have fucked up. Especially when you have fucked up as much as you have. You do realize you are in deep shit now, right?

He placed the bullet above a chamber of the cylinder and let it hover there. Then he slowly inserted the shaft of the bullet into the chamber waiting to receive it. I had a great deal of time to study the bullet with my name on it. That was an expression I had learned from Claude. You can't dodge a bullet with your name on it, he would say. In this case, there was literally no name on the blank bullet, which for me, VO DANH, was perfect. Baptizing myself as ANONYMOUS was my little joke on French bureaucracy, because if one could not level a joke at the bureaucracy, one would keel over and die of ennui, which would be endlessly preferable to how I was about to die.

I had not blinked for the entire timeless time that the Mona Lisa had been dropping bullets on the floor, and now my dry eyes forced me to blink, and in the blink of an eye the Mona Lisa snapped the cylinder shut, sealing my fate. He spun the cylinder once, twice, three times.

You Vietnamese like to play Russian roulette, don't you? he said. I saw it in a movie once. Are you ready to show us how good you are at that game?

I'm sorry, I'm sorry, I'm sorry, I said, sobbing.

Too late now, said the Mona Lisa. Sit up.

Sit up, I told myself, but myself was nowhere to be found. I was immobilized, even after Beatles slapped me a few more times. Ugly and Uglier had to be called in to pull me up by my arms and prop me on a sofa.

I've been very patient with you, said the Mona Lisa. He put the gun into my hand. Now either you play the game or we'll make it even more painful for you if you don't play the game.

A lose-lose scenario was a fitting scenario for a man with two faces and two minds. No matter which way the coin landed, which face showed, the result would be bad. Theoretically that made the

choice easier than a win-or-lose scenario, since there was no way to change the outcome. Even so, nobody in his right mind would play Russian roulette.

*You!* Beatles slapped me in the face so hard that I saw double. *Hey, you!* Are you going to play the game?

I was not crazy enough to play the game! But YOU were, you crazy bastard. I saw you pick up the revolver with my hand, moving in slow motion. Ever so languorously, you raised the gun and you saw that Ugly and Uglier both had their guns aimed at you, which included me, just in case you were inspired to theatrical heroics. But you have never been a hero. You have just been a survivor and a believer who sincerely wanted to do what needed to be done. And what needed to be done now was to get things over with as soon as possible. In a lose-lose scenario, what was the point in dragging things out?

*Click!*

I can't believe it! YOU did it! YOU pulled the trigger! The whole world was silent after the click of the hammer. The Mona Lisa was saying something, but while his mouth was moving, we could not hear a thing, except for the turning of the gears in our head, grinding away uselessly since there was a screw missing. The odds were on your side, one out of six, or, looked at another way, five against one. Math was never your strong suit, ever since YOU were born as half of one whose other half was ME. History was the subject that caught your interest, and here history is getting in the way of humanity. You and these gangsters, who are the sons of mothers perhaps like yours and mine, have been brought here to this moment by history. And some very bad choices.

Although you share a predilection for bad choices with Ugly, Uglier, and Beatles, you find it hard to sympathize with them for they seem to be howling with laughter, judging from the movements

of their mouths and their facial expressions, the way the pirates howled as they approached your boat. I had forgotten about that, or at least I have tried not to think about it. Sympathy is my talent, not memory. I even feel sympathy for these gangsters who are placing bets on which bullet will do us in. But memory must be your talent. You have not forgotten. Your life is always waiting for YOU and ME, your memories always loaded and ready to be fired into my brain. Most of the time, the barrel is empty in this game of demonic mnemonics. Most of the time.

*Click!*

YOU did it again! YOU pulled the trigger! Now I am getting a little nervous. About as nervous as when we all realized that at last, at last, another boat had stopped for us on the open sea, but alas, alas, they were pirates. We were still dazed from surviving the storm of the day before when the pirates clambered aboard, reeking of stale sweat, bad booze, and worse intentions, wielding knives, pipes, chains, axes, and a few AK-47s to seal the deal. You are sure that there are many kind and decent Thai people, but this is the unfortunate sampling we met. The women on the boat screamed as the pirates stripped them and everyone of anything worth anything. Then the women braced themselves to be stripped by the pirates, who were distant cousins, in a way, of these gangsters surrounding you, poking and prodding, asking you something you cannot hear, and when you do not respond, slapping you, once, twice, three times. Oh, I'm so glad I'm not YOU!

Of course, things didn't turn out so bad on the boat. For us, anyway. Or for the women. Who knew these pirates were of the most peculiar kind? Everybody had heard stories of the kidnapping and raping of girls and women on these refugee boats. But no one had heard of *this*, a crew of unwashed pirates bypassing the young and nubile females, shivering in their thin blouses, doing

their best to shrink and appear unattractive. I won't let you take my sister! cried the noble young man next to you. You'll have to kill me first! Oh, how those pirates laughed! Oh, how those pirates fell all over themselves, slapping each other on the backs! Oh, how they bellowed at all of us in their own language, which none of us could understand! But the meaning suddenly became clear when the skinniest of the pirates sauntered up to our young man and, ignoring his teenage sister altogether, ran his grotesque finger over the young man's chapped lips and then seized him by the hair and dragged *him* and not his sister to the other boat.

Confusion! Pandemonium! Chaos! No one could quite believe what they were seeing, as the leering pirates grabbed a few more of the slimmest, most hairless young men and boys. What were those monsters doing? Were they taking the young men and boys to be pirate apprentices? Were they kidnapping them to be sold as slave labor? Could they possibly—could they—no—

# CLICK!

You—*stop*! Right now. Stop crying and for God's sake stop pulling that trigger! You're hysterical! I am not doing too well, either, I must admit. Who cares if Beatles is screaming at you and slapping you? You have to stop being the hysteric of history! So what about your mother and father, about your birth, about being a bastard, about your subterranean life as a spy, about the war, about the reeducation camp, about the faceless man, about the refugee boat, about being so ugly that the pirate captain took one look at you and said, in the broken English he must have picked up from the American soldiers who came to his country on vacation from your war, seeking some highly affordable number one boom-boom, You look like shit!

Well, he was not wrong, was he? Of course YOU looked like shit, after having been digested through the circuitous intestines of Hell. What do you think I looked like? You once said that your liver was the most abused part of your body. Correction: I am the most abused part! Even if, technically speaking, as your conscience and your conscious, I am not part of your body. But where your body ends and your mind or my mind begins, who knows? What I know is: Get over it! Move on! Forget! The past is past and the future lasts forever and the present is always here and yet gone. So I need you to feel sympathy with me, which is to say, YOU—

# CLICK!

NO! Are you crazy? Wait, I take that back. Yes, you *are* crazy! With good reason, perhaps, but that's no excuse. That's four tries and two more chambers. We are pushing our luck. Let me be the voice of reason here. I encourage you to give them what they want. They just want to know where the Boss is. Just by giving up the Boss doesn't mean you're giving up Bon—

# CLICK!

Jesus Christ! Holy shit! Who told you to do that, you crazy bastard? Are you not listening to what I'm saying to you? I've got a stake in this, too, motherfucker!

Okay, all right, excuse the outburst, but now that we've clarified matters, the choice is quite obvious, one hundred percent obvious in fact, let's calm down, stop shaking, put that gun down, no matter what Sonny and the crapulent major are telling you right now about how this gun in your hand bears quite a resemblance to the one that Bon used to kill the crapulent major, they are by definition

179

highly biased individuals in that they would love to see you dead, so don't listen to them, YOU have to realize that even though you've been through hell, and you're crazy, and you look like shit, that doesn't mean that you can't have a good life, you're still young, barely middle-aged if we assume we will live to a ripe old age, and why not, the future looks bright, you just got to get through this rough patch here, Bon can take care of himself. Stop laughing! Why are you laughing? This is not a joke! Don't—

# CLICK!

# HẾT

# FIN

# THE
# END

# Part Three

*I*

# CHAPTER 11

I was finished.

Or was I?

I was done.

But was I?

It was over.

Then again, maybe not . . .

Who was laughing?

It wasn't me.

It was YOU!

Wasn't it?

YOU couldn't be laughing *with* ME, since I wasn't laughing. That must mean YOU were laughing at ME, and why not? What a sight I was. I looked at myself holding the gun in my hand and wondered how it had gotten there since YOU were the one holding it. Everything was shaking so much I could not tell if my hand was trembling or if my eyeballs were rattling in my skull. *We will live!* That was the punch line of the joke, wasn't it? The joke was always on us, because God was a bastard. It must have been a very funny joke because the initially befuddled gangsters were laughing, the Mona Lisa having

magically produced the sixth bullet, the one with my name on it, VO
DANH. But I had dodged that bullet not because he had removed it
from the revolver before the game, or never even inserted the bullet
into its chamber in the first place. I had dodged that bullet because
he did not know that VO DANH simply meant "nameless." A man
with no name could not be killed by a bullet with his name on it!
The joke was on him, not me!

Why's he laughing? Ugly said.

He's one crazy bastard, Beatles said.

How long you been practicing that trick? Uglier asked.

Ever since I watched that Vietnam War movie, said the Mona
Lisa, wiping tears from his eyes as he got up. I got to take a leak.
Over his shoulder, before he went up the stairs, he said to me, I like
that look of agony on your face. Because I know it's true.

Let's do that again, said Ugly.

Do *you* want to do it again? said Beatles.

It doesn't matter, I—or we—said, laughing. We will live!

What? said Beatles.

We will live, we—or I—said.

You crazy bastard! Who is Le Chinois?

I laughed again, for now I understood that the sobriquet was
not an insult after all. No, no, no! It was a *joke*. Me! I said. *I* am Le
Chinois.

*You?*

Yes, me! We are all Le Chinois!

Ugly, Uglier, and Beatles looked at one another dubiously.

Each and every one of us! The guy at the pan-Asian deli making
you Asian food that no Asian will eat; the girl to whom you say *ni
hao!* and whom you will then curse for being so unfriendly as not to
say *ni hao!* back even though she is not actually Chinese; the ones
whose names you cannot remember or pronounce or spell correctly

no matter how many times you see or hear them; the ones whose origins you cannot tell and whom you therefore call—

You are one annoying—

—Le Chinois! I am the infamous criminal you call by that name and I am the famous cop you also call by that name; I am the one whom you do not want for a neighbor, but if you had to have a neighbor who is not white—not that you notice such a thing, since you are color-blind—then I am the one you want; I am the one you consult when you want to learn anything about my culture; I am the one who is not willing to give up my culture; I am the one whom you are always asking where I am from, no, where I am really from, even if that question should be asked of everyone, and the only answer that should matter is that I, like you, am from my mother, but if you must insist on asking where I am truly from, even if we are all supposed to be the same, even if we are all supposed to be French, even if some of my ancestors died fighting in your wars for your armies, even if my parents were born here, even if my grandparents were born here, even if the answer is that I am from here, or, in my unique case, that I am from Hell—

What's that crazy bastard saying—

—then I am from the one and only original Le Chinois—

Whatever I was going to say next, and in what language, I have forgotten, for I had just realized that I had given my speech in a mixture of French and Vietnamese and English when the door to the stairway slammed open and Le Cao Boi slid down the handrail by the seat of his pants, sunglasses shielding his eyes, toothpick in his mouth, automatic pistols in both hands—*bang! bang! bang!*— and behind him was the Ronin in a shiny green double-breasted suit with the collar of his silk shirt open to the sternum and with a pump-action shotgun—*bang! bang! bang!*—and following him was Bon, crouching at the top of the stairs and bracing a submachine gun

on his knee to provide cover fire—*bang! bang! bang!*—and it was awfully loud in the cellar, the screaming and shouting and cursing not helping matters, and I reached over and picked up the barely lit cigarette in the ashtray that Beatles had been smoking—*bang! bang! bang!*—and it felt so good after having been deprived of my addiction, the pleasure not ruined even when Beatles was knocked back onto the coffee table by the impact of several bullets, the gelatinous mush of his brains looking like all the brains I had ever seen because we are all human, and why couldn't we just get along—*bang! bang! bang!*—and I looked down at his lifeless eyes, the half-empty cup of his shattered head resting on the edge of the coffee table near my knee, and I wept for him because if I had been him, born in his place, living his life, I might have done the same heinous things he had done, even to me—*bang! bang! bang!*—and Ugly and Uglier were gushing blood, too, and their blood was not white or yellow or black or brown but red, deep red, even purple, and no matter what we looked like on the outside we all looked the same when turned inside out, and somewhere soon their mothers would worry when they did not come home and their worrying would never cease, it would remain with them, as they would forever feel the laconic presence of their ghostly sons, whom they would at last meet on the other side after the bittersweet moment of their own deaths, the ones they feared and longed for, as death would be the only ticket to a reunion with their loved ones—*bang! bang! bang!*—and if Ugly and Uglier were not yet dead they were dead now, after the Ronin took out a revolver from underneath his jacket and gave each one the final blessing of the coup de grâce. *Bang! Bang! Bang!*

That was fun, the Ronin said with great satisfaction, in French, and this time I did not find the French charming at all.

Goddamn, Camus, you look like shit, said Le Cao Boi.

I've heard that before, I muttered.

Looks like we got here just in time, said the Ronin.

I'm sorry, said Bon. We almost got you killed.

He slung his submachine gun around his neck and lifted me off the sofa. I was still naked, and the Ronin looked at me with admiration and said, You're pretty big for an Asian, but I guess that's thanks to your French father, and Le Cao Boi said, I've seen bigger, like mine, and Bon said, Shut the fuck up, you two almost got him killed, and I said, Where's the fourth guy? and they all looked at one another and said, Shit!

They didn't find the Mona Lisa, and neither would the trio of dwarfs coming down the stairs as the cleanup crew, Sony Walkman headphones on their ears, lugging garbage bags, jars of bleach, and what I thought were handsaws but later learned—to be technically correct—were bone saws. The bathroom was on the ground floor, and the Mona Lisa must have hidden there when he heard the gunfire, then run out after the dwarfs had rushed past. He had disappeared among the warehouses, where no one was present at that hour of the night. Bon helped me get dressed and slid me into the back seat of the Ronin's Aryan automobile, where the thick, textured, luxurious hide of a once sentient animal cradled me. While Bon sat with me, Le Cao Boi fiddled with the radio and the Ronin drove. Give him the good stuff, the Ronin said. The really good stuff.

The really good stuff was in the glove compartment, a bottle of cognac so refined that I felt guilty drinking it straight from the bottle, but since guilt had never halted me before, I drank it. The feel of the bottle against my bruised lips, willingly opened to receive this benediction, recalled for me the many moments over the last few hours, or days, or years, or however long the gangsters had me in their grasp, when they had inserted a funnel into my unwilling

mouth and poured water into it, teaching me that the difference between the stuff of life and the stuff of death was simply a matter of degree. Being tortured was, in that sense, like going to church. After a while, neither taught anything new. The ritual and the repetition simply reinforced knowledge already known but in danger of being forgotten, which was why torturers plied their trade not just with pliers but with the conviction of priests like my father, who tortured me in his own subtle way. The warm glow of sunrise lit up my dark interior, the same warm glow of sunrise that Jesus Christ must have seen every dawn that he survived hanging on his cross.

How did you find me? I asked.

I consulted a fortune teller, said the Ronin. I read your fate in the stars. I gutted a hyena and studied its innards. He looked at me in the rearview mirror and winked. Just kidding. I called up a pal, an old Indochina hand I knew back in the days when he was in military intelligence. He's still in intelligence. Hard to give up that game. Pry off the sole of your shoe and you'll find a magical little device that he gave me, a radio transmitting tracker the size of your thumbnail. The Japanese made it. Ingenious little fuckers.

You could have gotten here a little faster.

Last-minute rescues are more fun. At least for me.

You could have told me about the tracker.

I didn't want to give you false hope. What if it didn't work?

Would it really have been so bad to have had some hope, however false? I offered Bon the bottle but he shook his head, his hand gripping my knee and squeezing it. He felt terrible that he had let me down, I could feel it, but he could not find a way to articulate it beyond saying he was sorry, which he was better at than me. It had taken me years to finally say I was sorry to Sonny and the crapulent major. Was my apology half-hearted? Was it half-assed? At least it was a beginning. As for Bon, I could not find a way to acknowledge

his grief and regret except to say, Come on, you'll feel better, and he finally took the bottle and we drank ourselves into a brotherly stupor in the back seat, communicating wordlessly in the manner of men, or animals, or trees.

Our destination was Heaven, which had its own garage, where the disgusting mess that was me could be discreetly extracted and brought inside. Day was night and night was day in Heaven, and everyone was awake and having fun, judging from the laughter and shouting coming from the floor above, in the waiting room. Le Cao Boi went to the waiting room, while the Ronin and Bon led me down a hallway to the guest room where I had spent my week of convalescence. Sitting there was the Boss and a very chic, very tanned doctor of some quality, judging from his after-hours casual wear of slacks and a finely woven, custom-fitted shirt that looked more expensive than the nicest suit I had ever owned. He treated the Ronin and the Boss with familiarity and deference and regarded me and my condition without surprise. The Ronin and the Boss could have brought a cheaper doctor, the kind who worked in the grimy places usually reserved for people in Le Cao Boi's trade, where confidentiality mattered more than competence. But this doctor was the human version of the Aryan automobile, the best money could buy.

Did you talk? the Boss asked while the very chic, very tanned doctor examined my once again naked body. The Ronin and Bon stood while I lay on the bed where I had not experienced any pleasure, the Boss sitting in the only chair. Shorty was still staying there, the semi-lucky son of a bitch, and he had left used underwear and empty take-out cartons all over. The condition of the room was not helped when I looked up and saw not only Sonny and the crapulent major lying on the ceiling, smiling at me, but also Beatles, Ugly, and Uglier, scowling, glaring, and gesticulating at me, not used as

they were to being dead and suddenly capable of defying the laws of gravity and perception.

Does it look like I talked? I said. I told him about the Russian roulette. I pointed at the unloaded gun I had taken from Beatles's dead hand, the one souvenir from my time with the gangsters that I actually wanted.

Bon was holding the gun and said, I would have made their pain last for longer if I could have. What he did not say was that he had saved my life, not that he needed to. He didn't talk, said Bon. He was going to kill himself rather than give us up.

The Ronin whistled in admiration. So basically, he did kill himself. The intention was there. The follow-through was there. There just wasn't a bullet there.

The Boss took the unloaded gun from Bon, opened the chamber, spun it, listening to the clicks the way a safecracker listens for the fall of tumblers inside a safe. You're something special, he said, talking about me and not the gun. Many men have confronted death unwillingly. Many have died. Many have survived by luck. But only a few have willingly chosen death. And very, very few of those have ever survived. From now on, I will call you my brother. My little brother. The Boss turned to the doctor. How is he?

It is true that he looks like shit, the very chic, very tanned doctor said, which actually sounded charming in French. But he will live.

Thank you, Doctor. We will meet you at your car.

After the doctor left, the Boss said, So you will live. He seemed genuinely pleased as he stood up and looked down at me while I held the gun he had given to me. Then he turned to glower at Bon and the Ronin and said, So will that son of a bitch you two let escape.

Bon was impassive. The Ronin said, He got lucky.

Lucky? Amateurs are lucky. Or unlucky. I thought you two were professionals. You didn't cover the exits?

The dwarfs were waiting outside, the Ronin said.

So why didn't they get him?

The bathroom had a small window. He must have heard the shooting.

He was smart enough to go out the window, but you weren't smart enough to put someone outside that window.

We made a mistake, Bon said. We'll take care of it.

You better, said the Boss. Even so, it's too late. He's gone to find his friends. Now we have a witness. I hate witnesses.

Technically, he didn't see anything, the Ronin said. He was in the bathroom—

Shut the fuck up! the Boss screamed.

Mistakes happen, the Ronin said. You've never made a mistake? Never gotten unlucky? Don't answer. I know the answers.

I groaned softly despite myself, giving the Boss an excuse to turn away from the Ronin and look down on me. You are like me, he pronounced. And Bon. And Le Cao Boi. And the Ronin. All of us have chosen death and all of us have lived. Now you are one of us.

The shock wore off and I began to feel as bad as I looked. This time I did not stay in Heaven but was instead taken by the very chic, very tanned doctor to a private hospital, reserved only for those who still had considerable wealth even after French taxes and social charges, somewhere an hour outside of Paris. I was given my own comfortably furnished bedroom rather than a bed in a clinical hospital ward. My bathrobe was a cloud of fluffy white cotton, my television's reception was perfectly clear, my white nurses were polite and professional, my diet was monitored, my food was excellent, my walls were thick stone, and my view was of hayfields and the late autumn countryside. I could soak in the hot tub, sweat in the

sauna, and walk in the garden. I was the only nonwhite person in the sanitarium, which had once been a small chateau. I kept to myself. Every week or so the very chic, very tanned doctor would come by and check on my recovery. He brought me books and magazines, bottles of wine and cognac, and packets of hashish and vials of the remedy, which he did not approve of, but he had no choice in the matter: they were gifts from the Ronin, the kind you could not refuse. Besides the daily visits by the nurses and orderlies, and these occasional manifestations of the doctor, I was left alone. I ate my meals in my room, got around by myself, first with the aid of a walker, then a cane, then finally on my own two feet. Everything was so quiet that usually I only heard the singing of the birds. If I had already been to Heaven, then this was Paradise. In my enormous amounts of free time at the sanitarium, I applied myself wholly to refining my French by watching French television, listening to French music, reading the books and magazines that the doctor had brought at my request, and working my way through Fanon's *Black Skin, White Masks*. When I asked the doctor about the bill, he said, Your boss is taking care of that. I knew then that I had graduated, that I had hit bottom and bounced back up, emerging from the sewer looking like shit but gasping for breath. I was alive.

I understood now that when it came to death, we had nothing to fear. Was this not the lesson of the great religions? Or should this not be their lesson? Like Jesus Christ, I had died and been resurrected, and I had learned that fearing death was unnecessary, so long as one had lived a full, meaningful life. I had lived such a life, even if some would call it foolish and meaningless. Whether one's life has been worth living, however, is a question that can be answered only by oneself and God. And as He did not exist, that really left only oneself. I did not call on a god who did not exist before I went to sleep but instead repeated the last words of *Black*

*Skin, White Masks*: "My final prayer: O my body, make of me always a man who questions!"

The cognac, the hashish, and the remedy all helped my recovery. I applied them in a regimen that could be described thus: take what you want when you feel like it. And I felt like it a lot. As a whole, my regimen of nonmedical medications insulated my mind from my body and the pain it was experiencing, both physical and psychological. While the remedy slowed down my ability to read French, my verbal fluency and sociability both increased. Under the remedy's influence, I was eager to speak to the doctor, the nurses, and, on the few occasions I ran into them, the other patients, who tolerated me as their very own Le Chinois. I was now that guy or that girl, the lone Asian in a gathering of (white) people, the anxious little yellow splash on a white canvas that proved how liberal and tolerant everyone was, how they were sophisticated enough to wield chopsticks when eating rice. *Wasn't there always a Le Chinois, I wrote to my aunt, except when there was a La Chinoise?*

The weeks passed into winter. I read the newspapers each day, thankful to see no mention of a massacre in a warehouse. The dwarfs had disposed of the evidence and mopped up the scene. Even in our criminality, we Asians were discreet and polite. We took our shoes off when entering homes and we disposed of body parts quietly and cleanly. If only it was possible to get rid of the image of those body parts in one's conscience and one's memory! Nations, without exception, disposed of body parts all the time. How could we bear ourselves otherwise if not for the mass graves of our forgetting?

Eventually the very chic, very tanned doctor pronounced me cured, but my condition belied his diagnosis. It was true that I felt nothing,

inside and out, but was that not a problem? And when I was not numb, why did I feel the need for the remedy constantly? The answer must be that even if YOU had not fired a real bullet through my brain, YOU had fired an invisible bullet through my mind. For most people, the result would likely be disastrous. But I had survived far more than most people, and nothing, so far, had killed me. I was no longer a man, conventionally defined, but a superman. I was the Crazy Bastard. The invisible bullet passing through my head had not blown my head off but put it back together, more or less. You and I, me and myself, reunited at last. Or, to put it another way, me and myself were together the answer to that most important of all questions, that most universal of questions, that question that we all, at one time or another, have asked ourselves, or have asked of others, at least in our own minds:

# WHO

# THE FUCK

# DO YOU THINK YOU ARE?

The calm that descended on me in Paradise reminded me of the calm that had descended on the boat after we passed through the chaotic storm. All that could be heard was the lapping of the waves against the hull and the weeping of the survivors. Thank God! the priest said. Thank God! We have passed through the storm and we have lived! The worst is over! The priest was, of course, wrong. Tomorrow would bring the merry pirates.

Thinking of that priest and his delusions about the divine, I was disgusted with myself. What the fuck was wrong with me? Why had I done the remedy? I had a handful of clear plastic packets the

size of tea bags, each containing the white powder. Little tickets to the moon and, unfortunately, back. You could fool yourself that you were touching the face of God at the peak of the trip, when you were actually touching nothing. The remedy was a religion like every other, a man-made one, and I was an atheist. I would not be addicted like all the billions of zealots for whom religion was the opiate of the masses—or was it that opium was the religion of the masses?—so I ripped open the first of the packets and poured the powder into the toilet. Then I flushed.

I was done with the third packet and was about to open the fourth when suddenly I heard the voice of the hashish. *Are you out of your mind?* I paused. Well, yes, I possibly was out of my mind, at least one of them. *That's perfectly good shit you're flushing down the toilet!* True, but it was no good for me. *Do you know how much that's worth?* I had a pretty good idea. *More than its weight in gold!* Yes, but . . . *Think about it. Don't be rash. You never know when you might need it.* The two packets of white powder in my hand said nothing. Unlike the hashish, the remedy did not need to speak. Hashish might be the prophet, but the white powder was God.

It was the Boss's idea, or maybe it was the Ronin's. They came to visit me after the New Year, toward the end of my stay in Paradise, and brought up the subject of BFD. Despite the chill, we sat outside on a green bench in the garden, the Boss on one side of me and the Ronin on the other.

I hate the fucking bastard, the Ronin said. No offense. There are bastards and then there are bastards, and in your case you had no choice in the matter. This guy's a bastard by choice, or by upbringing, but regardless . . .

What's he got to do with your business? I said.

Blackmail's always good business, since there's so much to blackmail. But besides the financial profit, let's just say this is from the goodness of my heart. I also detest him because of his politics. And his socialist president as well. Not my president. The Soviets have taken Afghanistan and thousands of Soviet tanks are on the other side of the Fulda Gap. The communists are ready to invade Western Europe, and the French are stupid enough to elect a socialist? Somebody should have knocked him off when he was young, when it wouldn't have mattered. Maybe I can't touch the president now, but I can touch this bastard before he really matters. Especially as we have you so close to him.

I wouldn't say close.

Close enough. All you have to do is get him to Heaven.

What's in it for me?

You could buy a nice sports car with the cash. Take a trip around the world. Live in Heaven for a year or two.

I'll give you a down payment, the Boss added. A promotion from the restaurant, to my new bar.

You have a new bar?

It's called Opium, he said with a touch of pride. I came up with the name myself. What do you think?

It's incredible how much you've accomplished in such a relatively short time, I said, kissing his ass, licking his boot, and stroking his ego in the way that I knew so well, which is to say all at the same time. You have a real genius for business, Boss.

I've been investing through the Ronin for years. Had all the pieces set up here well before Saigon fell. Because you have to be ready for the contingencies.

*Claude would say the same,* I thought.

You'll love it. It's in one of the fancy parts of town, the Latin Quarter, where all the tourists like to go. Leather seats. Every kind

of liquor at every price. Sexy waitresses with water pipes for some serious smoking and hookahs for some exotic flavor. Private rooms modeled on opium dens. Just the hint of opium without the actual opium.

It's great, I said. It's . . . suggestive. But about BFD—what makes you think he's interested? In going to Heaven?

He likes women. Well, who doesn't? But he likes them a lot. Much more so than average. And he's willing to pay for them. Get him there and we'll take care of the rest.

What's the rest?

You'll see, said the Boss. There's something even better than Heaven.

# CHAPTER 12

The morning of the day that my aunt was going to retrieve me from the sanitarium, I took one last walk around the fields. How long had I been here? Almost two months? I had not known as restful a time as this for years. I had not burst into tears once, nor felt the pendulum of my mood swing too drastically. I had been almost . . . happy. Nothing could disturb me, not even the present that my aunt had given me on one of her visits. A new book from our old friend, she said. We're going to translate it. I almost recoiled at the sight of the name on the cover—Richard Hedd, the author of *Asian Communism and the Oriental Mode of Destruction*, the cipher we had used to send each other coded messages. His new book was titled, in English, *The Evil Empire's Oriental Origins*. The other name on the cover was of the man who endorsed it, Henry Kissinger, credited as "Winner of the Nobel Peace Prize," a punch line so funny it made me laugh. If I knifed somebody on the street, I was a murderer. But if I, like Kissinger, national security adviser to President Nixon, was agreeable to fleets of bombers dropping tons of bombs on thousands of innocent people, then I was

a statesman. And if I negotiated a deal to temporarily halt my war of pacification, then I could be lauded for bringing peace. If Hitler had triumphed, he might have won the Nobel Peace Prize, too, since nothing brought peace more effectively than exterminating as many of one's enemies as possible.

But I digress. Here is what Kissinger had to say about Hedd's newest work: "An illuminating and insightful exploration of the Soviet mind, which, as Hedd shows with devastating effect, is its own worst enemy." The thesis of the book was summarized in capital letters on the back cover:

THIS PENETRATING ANALYSIS BY A SEMINAL AUTHOR REVEALS HOW THE SOVIET UNION IS NOT TRULY EUROPEAN BUT RATHER *ORIENTAL*. LENDING NEW MEANING TO "ORIENTAL DESPOTISM," RICHARD HEDD SHOWS HOW EAST IS EAST AND WEST IS WEST WHEN IT COMES TO COMMUNISM VERSUS DEMOCRACY.

So communists were Orientals now? I was so flummoxed, being tainted by both communism and Orientalism, that I admit to not having yet read the book on that last day in Paradise. I much preferred spending my leisure time listening over and over to Johnny Hallyday songs in a futile attempt to understand his musical appeal, while also reading celebrity gossip in *Paris Match* (where I learned that the mayor of Paris and his wife had adopted a Vietnamese girl, a fate I envied). But I was carrying Hedd's book on that last walk, anticipating that I would need to show my aunt that I appreciated her gift.

I sat down on a bench under a gazebo and opened the book, flipping quickly to the end—512 pages!—and reading the first lines of the last page:

We must renew our commitment to democracy and victory, because democracy and victory are not inevitable. We have the advantage of a superior—indeed, exceptional—system of democratic thinking and belief, inherited from the Greeks and refined over millennia. They, however, have brute power. They do not hesitate to slaughter millions, even if those millions are their own. History has shown that sometimes the brutish win. The Soviets are attempting to demonstrate that sad, ugly truth once more in Afghanistan. We must be committed to ensuring that Afghanistan is their Vietnam.

"Their Vietnam"? What did that mean? Was that like saying, We'll always have Paris? Except that when people said "Paris" they meant flaky croissants, and the Eiffel Tower, and a cruise on the Seine like the one Cary Grant and Audrey Hepburn took in *Charade*, and a nice glass of Sancerre, and gazing on Notre-Dame while an accordion-playing mime in a beret and striped shirt entertained them, and so on and so on and so on. And, God help me—here I use "God" figuratively—I believed in this Paris, too! A Paris that existed as much as God existed. But when a man like Richard Hedd said "Vietnam," what he and most of his readers thought about were napalm, and burning girls, and bullets to the head, and crowds of faceless people under conical hats wearing basic black outfits that could have been the height of haute couture in Paris given the right circumstances. "Vietnam," in shorthand, was war, tragedy, and death, and so on and so on, and how, I begged to know, would it ever cease being that way?

By the time my aunt came to pick me up, I was still gnawing on the thighbone of that question. There were so many bones in the past, ready to be dug up, that I would never run out of things to chew on. I wanted to stop, truly, but someone as guilty as me had no

right to do so. Perhaps I had the right to forget the past only if I had been punished for my crime. The problem was that while I had been punished quite relentlessly in the reeducation camp, it had been for only one crime, watching the CIA-trained southern policemen rape the communist agent without trying to stop them. Meanwhile, all my other crimes were unpunished: betraying Bon, helping him kill the crapulent major, killing Sonny, and, most recently, being implicated in the demise of Beatles, Ugly, and Uglier. At least I had finally said that I was sorry to Sonny and the crapulent major. An apology was, at least, a beginning. But if this was the beginning, what was the ending?

My aunt pulled up to the entrance of Paradise in a charming Italian convertible borrowed from BFD. It's nice to have rich friends and benefactors, she said. I had told her that my care had been paid for by my very generous boss, who was concerned about my nervous breakdown, which was a lie that bordered on the truth. I was nervous, and I was broken down. How are you feeling now? she said as we pulled away from Paradise.

I turned to look at the stone farmhouse that had been converted decades ago into the main office of Paradise, and I sighed wistfully. Paradise was the nicest place that I had ever lived, and all I had to do to live there was to die. I'm feeling great, I said, but when she did not look like she believed me, I felt the urge to explain myself further: I've had seven weeks of doing nothing. Those seven weeks felt more like seven months—

Maybe you should move back in with me. I don't know if all this work you're doing at the restaurant is good for you. Or living with Bon. It can't be good for you if you had a nervous breakdown. You can sleep on my couch and you don't have to pay rent.

What about your commission on the hashish?

No, you're still going to keep paying me that as long as you're selling to my friends. But otherwise just go back to school and focus on your French. She glanced at the copy of *Black Skin, White Masks* on my lap. Did you actually read that in French?

I did, I said. My French is really good now, practically back to where it was when I left the lycée.

That was colonial schoolboy French. You cannot hope to be French unless your French is perfect, she said. Even in America, if you speak perfect English but look like you or I do, you aren't really American, are you?

I could hardly dispute her argument, but I said, You think you're totally French? And that white people think you're French?

Of course I'm French! We're not like the Americans, who are truly racist. Look at how they treat black people. Slavery! Lynching! Segregation! Rape! Perpetual second-class citizenship. My God, it must be awful to be a black person in America. You can never stop being black in America. What is the fashionable term now? "Afro-American"? Imagine always having to live with a hyphen dividing you! Here, anyone can be French. But you must want to be French. You must look in the mirror and see a French person, not an Asian person or some kind of color. Do you want to be French?

I hesitated. Part of me indeed longed to be French, the part of me that could not help but salivate before a tender slab of foie gras. I could have been French if my father had only recognized me as his son, but instead he disavowed me, a disavowal that differed little from the forgetfulness that was the most important ingredient for enjoying foie gras, for if we could see how it was made, with a farmer force-feeding the poor goose with enormous amounts of grain through a funnel until its liver was about to burst, then perhaps we would not have such a taste for the delicacy, which, like

many delicacies, was salted with misery. Even so, I wanted to say yes, truly, yes yes yes—

Do you want to be French? There they were, the hands of French culture and civilization being extended to me by my aunt, who was the living embodiment of what I could be, of what France promised. All I had to do was say—

No, I said. No.

Then that is where the problem lies.

I was the problem, of course. I was always the problem. When I looked in the mirror, I saw someone neither French nor American nor Vietnamese. No, I was not a nation. I was nobody, negation at best, bastard at worst. I took heart from Fanon, who wrote from the position of the Negro, who was also a kind of bastard, at least in the eyes of the Negrophobic. His dilemma was also my dilemma: "As I begin to recognize that the Negro is the symbol of sin, I catch myself hating the Negro. But then I recognize that I am a Negro. There are two ways out of this conflict. Either I ask others to pay no attention to my skin, or else I want them to be aware of it." For the Negro, there was no denying being a Negro, just as there was no way of me denying being a bastard. While people in general were alienated from themselves under capitalism, as Marx argued, so that even the middle class felt itself to be unhappy despite its wealth, people of color—and I counted myself as one—were doubly alienated because racism compounded their experiences under capitalism and its dancing partner, colonialism. There was only one solution to this alienation that was created not by the Negro or the bastard, but by the real bastards, the racists and colonizers who blamed the victim for the conditions that the victimizer created. And that solution was "to rise above this absurd drama that others have staged around me, to reject the two terms that are equally unacceptable, and, through one human being, to reach out for the universal."

Yes! I, too, was universal, and my universal identity was to be me and utterly me, even if I was completely fucked up, and isn't that what the French wanted? The French saw our shared past as a tragic happenstance of history, a romantic love story gone wrong, which was half correct, whereas I saw our past as a crime that they had committed, which was completely correct. And who are you going to believe? The rapist or the product of the rape? The civilized or the bastard?

I do hope you'll come and stay, my aunt went on. But I do have to warn you that someone is staying with me for a couple of nights right now.

Let me guess. Fifty-fifty chance. Our friend the Maoist PhD?

No.

BFD?

What did I say about you being depressingly conventional? I just sleep with them, I wouldn't actually let them stay more than a night. You'll meet her at the show.

My aunt was so full of surprises that somehow I was not even surprised.

We navigated through a quarter whose streets were narrower than the average French mind, finally finding parking around the corner from la Mutualité, where the Union's Tet culture show was taking place. Turning the corner of rue Saint-Victor on foot, we saw a noisy crowd gathered outside the hall, two or three dozen Vietnamese, from the looks of them, asserting their Frenchness or aspirational Frenchness by engaging in one of the most popular French national pastimes, protesting. Their signs said COMMUNISM IS EVIL, DOWN WITH COMMUNISM, HO CHI MINH IS A MURDERER, et cetera, ad nauseam. They shouted these and other slogans in Vietnamese,

while the people entering the hall spoke in muted French. The protesters exuded the je ne sais quoi of being recent refugees. Was it the men's pants bunching at the ankles, drawing attention to dusty shoes? Or the women's unfashionable haircuts with blunt bangs?

*Oh là là,* murmured my aunt, which I think meant that it was a little uncomfortable to have so many Vietnamese people in one place, not just gathering for some tasteful affirmation of their origins, like eating a meal or staging a culture show, but *making noise.* Making noise was not something the Vietnamese did in France. Making noise was something Vietnamese people in Vietnam or America did. The people of Vietnamese descent in France were quiet, discreet, charming, and, most of all, harmless. They were of a better class, or had been until now, imagining themselves as French (at their assimilatory best) and exiles (at their individualistic worst). But there was nothing assimilationist or individualistic about this crowd of tacky refugees.

*Communists!* a woman shouted, pointing at us. I wanted to say, I'm an ex-communist, if you please, but refrained. My aunt, on the other hand, aimed her finger right back and said, Communism unified and freed the country. People like you kept the country divided and now you're trying to divide us with your anticommunism.

You stupid *bitch*—

*You're* the stupid bitch, you fat cow—

One could not be both a bitch and a cow, but perhaps a bastard had no right to point that out. I pulled my aunt through the door, unsure whether she was suddenly being very Vietnamese or simply very Parisian, as rudeness was second nature to both cultures.

So embarrassing, my aunt muttered once we had passed the threshold. Those people!

Indeed, I murmured back as the Chairman of the Union emerged from the crowd attending the reception before the show.

He was in a considerable state of distress. My dear, he said to my aunt, for they were already acquainted, who *are* these people?

These people are our people, I wanted to say, but that was not entirely true. The protesters outside saw themselves as Vietnamese who happened to be in France, whereas the people inside saw themselves as French who happened to have a connection to Vietnam. Given these two choices, perhaps being a bastard was not so bad after all. I spotted Bon, who had always accepted my being a bastard, in the foyer. He loitered in a corner, wearing human camouflage: clean-shaven face, brushed hair, and a passable gray double-breasted suit with exaggerated shoulder pads, all of which, I assumed, could be credited to Loan. I had not seen him so presentable or so uncomfortable since before the fall of Saigon, when Linh made him dress like an adult.

You don't look like shit anymore, Bon said by way of greeting.

And you look like a normal human being, I replied.

Oh, yeah? Because I feel like shit. I should be outside with the Association.

The Association?

The Association for Free Vietnamese People. They've decided they're not going to let the communists of the Union speak for all Vietnamese people. I should be with them protesting these people, not inside pretending to be friends with these people.

I saw Loan approaching, and I said, You're doing it for Loan, not for yourself.

He grimaced and kept quiet as Loan came up, dressed in a silken red ao dai with silken yellow trousers, which were either the colors of the anticommunist flag (if looked at in one way) or the colors of the communist flag (if looked at the other way). Either way, the young woman wearing these colors resembled the willowy maidens who symbolized our country itself in the lacquer paintings and mother-of-pearl engravings found in nearly every home and

certainly every curio shop. Bon brightened and smiled tenderly, which was somewhat discomfiting since the Bon I knew and loved was a melancholic murderer. Darling, she said, and Darling, he said back, utterly bewildering me, for the world was a very confusing place if Bon could find love and I, someone wont to fall in love every few months, could not. Loan invited me to her apartment for dinner, insisting on it with great warmth. Her hospitality touched me, reminding me of humanity—not only hers, but mine.

I would be honored, I said.

You look wonderful, she said by way of parting, moving on to greet friends who had made it through the protest. Even though one part of me knew she was lying, the other part of me wanted to believe her. Perhaps I was actually on my way back to humanity, feeling my way blindly, aided by small kindnesses. Bon spoiled my mood when he whispered, Got something to show you, and took a photo from his blazer's inner pocket. A picture of the bastard.

At first I thought he meant me, but the picture was of someone else, a man wearing a brown fedora, a dark blue overcoat, and . . . a white mask. Unlike the masks of tragedy and comedy, crying and laughing, this mask was smooth, featureless, and expressionless, covering most of his face except for slots for his eyes and mouth. Behind him, a pedestrian had turned to look over her shoulder, concerned and puzzled by a man wearing a mask. At least she was not horrified and shocked by a man without a face.

You think it's him? I said, rubbing the photograph's edges.

I know it's him. He was coming out of the embassy. I sat at a café across the street for days and nights, waiting for a chance. I was going to follow him, but he got into a taxi and I couldn't find one. I think he lives in the embassy and hardly ever goes out. Let's go to the bathroom.

You go, I don't have to.

Let's go to the bathroom.

I followed him, pausing long enough to greet those bohemians of the Union who had become devotees of hashish and the remedy. Students, lawyers, dentists, doctors, and so on, all respectable people who also liked to expand their minds, discreetly.

You can't do this forever, Bon said in the bathroom. There's no future in it.

You're one to talk.

Once I kill the faceless man, I'm done, Bon said. I'll resign.

You don't resign from gangs, I said, hopelessly hoping to divert his attention. And the Boss wants you to kill the Mona Lisa.

Okay, he deserves to die after what he did to you. After I kill him, *then* I'll retire.

You think the Boss will let you go?

He knows I'll kill him if he doesn't.

You told him that?

Guys like him and me and the Ronin don't have to talk. We just have to see the look in the other's eyes. It's guys like you who have to talk. If you don't talk, you'd die. You wouldn't know what to do with yourself. At least you can do something meaningful by helping me kill the faceless man. Too bad he didn't come tonight.

I was secretly relieved, but I said, I didn't know you were expecting him.

The ambassador came.

Given that the faceless man doesn't have a face, I assume he's not very social. But you could always kill the ambassador.

Then I'd never get the chance to kill the faceless man.

If you kill the faceless man, you'll never get the chance to kill the ambassador.

You got me. Bon shrugged. So I want revenge, too. What's wrong with that?

Technically speaking, nothing. Also, technically speaking, how do you plan to get the faceless man when he hardly ever leaves the embassy?

I have a plan.

Another plan? My heart beat a little faster. When were you going to tell me what that plan is?

I'm telling you right now. He produced an envelope from his jacket pocket. Inside were two tickets to *Fantasia VIII: Live in Paris* next month, with the after party at Opium. When I unfolded the flyer in the envelope, the first thing I saw was *her*, the one woman I should not have fallen in love with, head tilted back, hair blowing about, red lips slightly parted to reveal just a hint of white teeth and maybe, just *maybe*, the tip of her tongue. My body still remembered the touch of that tongue. Lana. Two syllables, two taps of my tongue on my palate. *L-l-lah-nah!* Was that how I cried out her name when we had made love, or had sex, or fornicated, or copulated, or perhaps all of those things at the same time, so many years ago? Laaaannnnnaaaaaaaa!

Oh, I said.

Oh, indeed. You'll get a chance to meet your old love at Opium. Or maybe before, if she's willing to do something more private.

What's the plan?

Our faceless man has seen a lifetime of Tet celebrations. He didn't come to Paris to see another one. What he came here for, I don't know. But he'll see *Fantasia*.

Because he's a fun-loving guy?

Because he's Vietnamese. Every Vietnamese person in Paris is going to be at this show, even the ones who think they're French.

Even the communists?

They've been deprived of good entertainment for far too long. He smiled. Especially this communist. The commissar. There were rumors in the reeducation camp that this commissar was a little

215

corrupt. He liked Western music. Pop and rock. Ballads. The sick stuff, the yellow music.

I nodded. It was true. The sick stuff, the yellow music, was my vinyl collection, which I had given to Man before I left Saigon, with highlights from Elvis Presley, the Platters, Chuck Berry, and, of course, the Beatles and the Rolling Stones. Man had hauled my records to the reeducation camp, although I had never gotten to hear them there. But I did not mention my precious albums. Instead, I said, What's going to happen to you and Loan if you get caught? Loan may or may not be a communist, but she is at least surely a leftist. A sympathizer. Otherwise she wouldn't be in the same room with the ambassador. Doesn't this make you—

Don't worry about Loan, he snapped.

I had touched a nerve, not because I wanted to, but because so many nerves waited to be touched. Or had some part of me— myself, let's say—wanted to finger that nerve?

Like I said, I'm retiring. I'll finish off the faceless man and then I'll marry Loan.

I was so stunned I had nothing to say to yet another plan that he had been keeping from me. Bon smiled at the effect of his announcement on me, and to compound his pleasure he extracted a gun from underneath his blazer, hidden at the small of his back. It was not the gun he would later aim at me but the Mona Lisa's gun, the revolver with which I had killed myself. A little present for you, he said, handing it to me. Its grip was familiar, as was its heft. The revolver weighed about as much as a soul would, or five souls, or perhaps even three or four or six million souls. Why not? Dead souls, after all, could weigh almost nothing.

# CHAPTER 13

W
e went backstage and changed into our costumes for the first skit, where we played farmers. Such costumes, in real life, would be mud-and-sweat-soaked at best and patched rags at worst. But this was an official culture show, versus an unofficial one, so our brown shirts and black pants were neat, clean, and dry, as were our bare feet. I was thus attired and had taken my place on the side of the stage with the other dancers when the Chairman leaped to the stage. His remarks were twice as long as necessary, because they were bilingual, and I was dozing off when he at last finished, having recounted the Union's history, the importance of Vietnamese culture, and the gratitude of the Vietnamese to France, although he mentioned nothing about the Association protesting outside. Then he introduced the Vietnamese ambassador, and I almost screamed. The ambassador likewise proceeded to torture his audience with a bilingual soufflé of clichés, topped with the whipped cream of excessive compliments slathered onto French culture. Real talent was required to use so many words in two languages to say nothing.

By now my thighs were silently sobbing, just as the rest of me was, for all of us peasant farmers were squatting on our heels, a pose that goes back millennia but that I, Westernized, had not practiced for many years. Being a bastard, I was perhaps not genetically suited to squat like this, something my mother could do all day long, tending to the fire, cooking, or taking care of infants and young children to earn some money. I could sense the unease among the other farmers as well, who were urban French bourgeoisie who had most likely never even stepped on manure-decked land in either of their ancestral homelands. The faux farmers shifted from heel to heel and tried their best not to grimace, and as the ambassador finally finished, all of us got ready to spring to our feet. Then the Chairman returned to the podium and said, Now for our next speaker . . .

I groaned softly, as did the other farmers except for Bon, who merely grunted, unaffected by the squatting. The Chairman introduced the night's guest of honor, a "friend of Vietnam and the Vietnamese people" and a "revolutionary of May 1968." It was—who else?—BFD. My aunt had mentioned he would be here, delivering an undoubtedly canned speech that threatened to poison me with the botulism of botched ideas. He was the mayor of a different arrondissement, but his arrondissement, the 13th, was seeing more and more Vietnamese settlers, all communist-hating refugees, possibly including some of the protesters. To any one of those refugees, a socialist was just a communist in nicer threads, pink instead of red, a believer in the forced redistribution of wealth through taxes, social benefits, and the welfare state rather than through land reform, economic collectives, and the police state. BFD would get nowhere with those protesters, but he wanted to prove his support among Vietnamese people of a different ideological kind and of a better class, or so my aunt said.

A better class of people? I had said. Isn't that ironic for a social-ist to say?

The French are nothing if not ironic.

Well, were not all peoples ironic? Did any examples exist of nations that did not say one high-minded thing and then do something underhanded? BFD stepped onto the stage as a walking example of irony, a man of the people wearing a suit so expensive it could have fed a village. He was also an elected official courting an electorate not his own. Maybe he thought his speech would convince some in the audience to move to his arrondissement and vote for him. Or maybe he was following the example of Sartre, who, despite being a committed radical, had also joined in the call to help Vietnamese refugees fleeing from communism. Or maybe BFD, like every politician, could not resist that most basic political exercise of sweating under a spotlight.

My dear friends, he began. It's such a pleasure to be here tonight as you celebrate Vietnamese culture. We are two peoples, the French and the Vietnamese, with a long history that also deserves celebration. [*applause*] You have been a part of France for a long time now, and you remind us of the greatness of French culture and the greatness of Vietnamese culture, which the French have not always appreci-ated. When we came to Vietnam, we did not always behave the way we should have. Colonization was wrong, my friends. The French should never take away another country's independence. [*applause*] When the Vietnamese rose up against us, they taught us a lesson we sorely needed. But by 1968, many of us—including me—stood on the right side of history by supporting Ho Chi Minh. And France as a whole stood on the side of peace. I don't have to remind you that the peace accords that brought an end to American imperialism in Vietnam were signed here, in our glorious city! Let us hope that the American imperialists have learned their lesson from Vietnam, too.

If they have, they, too, will one day thank the courageous people of Vietnam! [*applause*] As regrettable as French colonization was, we never committed the horrors the Americans did. And we left behind *culture*. Because of this, I hope the Vietnamese people have forgiven the French. We came to Indochina with noble intentions. We brought liberty, equality, and fraternity. [*applause*] We built roads. We built canals and drained swamps. We built Saigon. We built lycées and universities so that everyone would have a chance to get an education and govern their country, not just the mandarins. We trained the artists who would paint the glorious paintings of Ho Chi Minh and his freedom fighters. And there would have been no Ho Chi Minh, or his allies, without France. We brought Vietnamese students to France and gave them the tools to fight their revolution—against us! In short, nothing is all good or all bad. And I have met many Vietnamese people who are happy here in France, where they feel at home. Of course they do! Because France is your home! You have come home! [*applause*] Your presence in France shows us that we can put the past behind us. Your presence tells us we are all French. Your presence in France proves the greatness of our French culture. Long live the Republic! Long live France! [*applause*]

Since I could still see any issue from both sides, despite the terrible cramps in my thighs, I could see that BFD was not totally wrong. He might even be almost right. And judging from the enthusiastic clapping of the audience, many evidently agreed with him. And why wouldn't they? Of course they felt at home here! It was likely the case that they, or their parents, or even their grandparents, would have been at home with France *when they were in Vietnam*! The Vietnamese who came to France and did not feel at home returned to Vietnam to fight for the revolution or were deported by the French who suspected them of not being French enough. These were the Vietnamese who believed so sincerely in liberty, equality, and fraternity that

they did not see the parentheses, which the French used in place of hyphens: "liberty, equality, and fraternity (but just not yet, at least for you)." Flabbergasted, these revolutionaries became the indigestible Vietnamese, the ones who could not swallow France and who could not be swallowed. As for the Vietnamese who stayed in France, French culture had chewed on them since they were in Vietnam. By the time they came to France, they were already, like certain species of cheese, quite soft and easily digestible, qualities inherited by their ideologically pasteurized children.

The culture show we put on—by the time we could finally get to our feet, wincing and with legs asleep—was meant for easy consumption. A hostile and critical culture show would have been quite interesting to someone as hostile and critical as myself, but my taste is rather outré. For most people, culture shows are dioramas featuring mutual hospitality, rather than the loving violence or violent love that characterized the show of power staged by the French in their colonies. In this case, the Chairman had scripted our extravaganza, which might have been vaguely autobiographical, or at least not wholly fantastical. His was a love story, proffered in misty retrospect by a prosperous, middle-aged doctor, about a young man from a poor, rural family who, by dint of hard work and the benevolent French educational system, wins a scholarship to France, where, by dint of hard work and the benevolent French culture, he becomes a doctor who, by dint of hard work and the benevolence of a French family, wins the love of a winsome French (white) girl who, by dint of hard work and the benevolence of French gustatory habits, maintains her slim French figure while birthing and raising two lovely French children, who have absolutely no problems in being French despite their mixed heritage. The end.

Oh, how I wanted that life! Who wouldn't? It was a much better life than my mother had experienced. Although she would

have been about the same age as the future doctor, she had seen a much different version of rural northern existence. As a girl, she had nearly died during the great famine that decimated the north, killing a million people when the population of the whole country was perhaps twenty million. A million! So many people, and yet such a paradoxically forgettable event. They died without the benefit of having their picture taken so that the world, or even just the Vietnamese, might remember what our Japanese occupiers did in the name of Greater East Asia Co-Prosperity and what the French who served the Japanese did perhaps for liberty, equality, and fraternity, or perhaps just for collaboration. Collaborating was the great twentieth-century sin of the French, who could only mumble the word, the pebbles of the syllables rolling in their mouths. The Algerians might disagree about collaboration being the greatest sin, weighed against the outright massacre of their people by the French colonizers we shared. But who cares what the Algerians have to say? For that matter, who cares what *we* have to say, especially if we say nothing, as the dead usually do?

I live among the dead, an invisible bullet having blown my mind. Even so, I have no way to see the dead. I can see only what my mother gave to me, the missing pictures that died with her, of dead people in lanes and fields, skeletons with skin, huddled in clothes too large for them by the time they died, neighbors, playmates, and babies. And who had saved her? My French father! He gave her rice, the same rice that our Japanese rulers had ordered their French flunkies to withhold as a reserve for the Japanese war effort. While my father the colonizing collaborator might have complained about getting rice instead of bread, for my mother that first bite of rice after weeks of starvation was simply the most wonderful meal of her life. My father fed her with spoonfuls of rice for a few days, getting her shriveled stomach used to having food, and then

bowlfuls of porridge after that. My poor little mother was a miracle, an orphan of twelve years of age, a survivor in a time of famine with no one to care for her. He saved me, she said. I couldn't help but fall in love with him even though he was a— She could not bring herself to say "priest" and substituted "man of the cloth," while she became his "maid." The fusion of two euphemisms created me two years later, seven pounds of high-explosive antipersonnel ordnance with a delayed fuse dropped from her bomb bay and waiting to go *BOOM!* I could see her face even now, forever gentle, forever youthful, having been younger than me when she died. I could remember my shock and then my rage when she told me the story about my father feeding her rice, my mother weeping as she held me close in a way no woman has before or since and said, Forgive him, my darling. I have forgiven him. Without him, I would not have you, whom I love more than my own life. Even if it is the last thing you do, forgive your father.

What are you crying for? Bon asked me when we stepped offstage.

Nothing, I said, wiping the tears from my eyes. Absolutely nothing.

After the show and after I had wiped the slime of my emotional sensitivity off my face, I retrieved the revolver from my duffel bag's rather crowded false bottom, where it nestled between my confession and the tattered, yellowing copy of Richard Hedd's *Asian Communism and the Oriental Mode of Destruction.* Then I squeezed the revolver into the back of my pants rather than the front, as I always worried about the gun going off and killing my future progeny, even if I never planned on begetting any. The hashish in my jacket pocket giggled and whispered in its usual way at my logic, but the revolver was the

masculine, silent type. It distracted me not by making noise, but by pressing against my spine and tailbone with its dark, handsome hardness. All guns want to be used. This one was no exception.

I toured the party with one part of me trying to figure out how to stop Bon and protect Man, while another part of me chatted with my clientele. I went outside to smoke some particularly potent cigarettes with a couple of them, a doctor and an import-export merchant. Through them and the rest of my clients, I sold my entire stock of goods and made appointments to sell more, although I was not happy about it. When I returned to the party, my aunt waved me over to introduce me to her new friend, whom I at first mistook for a man from a distance. She's a lawyer, my aunt said in Vietnamese. Just back from Cambodia.

The lawyer, dressed in a slim gray suit with a slim black tie, did not smile at me. I would soon learn not to take this personally, as she was so humorless that even perfunctory smiling was beyond her. She was very handsome, however, her face and short-cropped hair composed almost completely of straight lines, so that in the absence of a smile, the only curves on her face came from her eyes and eyebrows. Like me and my aunt, she existed somewhere along the East-West spectrum and most likely was of Vietnamese descent, given her decent command of our mother tongue.

Cambodia? Not the easiest place to visit, I suppose.

The handsome and humorless lawyer said, It wasn't for tourism.

No, I suppose not. So what was it for?

My aunt and the lawyer glanced at each other, and my aunt nodded. I was visiting Pol Pot, the lawyer said.

I played it cool. He must not be an easy man to visit.

He's a very difficult man to visit. The Vietnamese army isn't interested in letting anyone go through Cambodia to meet him,

so I had to go through Thailand. He's staying in a mountain camp near the border.

I'm sure the Vietnamese want to capture him and put him on trial.

They already put him on trial. In absentia. Guess the outcome. Guilty?

Do you know why they found him guilty?

Because he was guilty?

Because trials in absentia always end in a guilty verdict. The handsome and humorless lawyer, incapable of smiling at my naïveté, snorted. Has anyone ever been found *innocent* in absentia? Those trials aren't about justice. They're morality shows.

It seems just to convict someone responsible for the deaths of hundreds of thousands of his own people.

How do you know he was responsible for these deaths?

I admit to being flustered. I was used to being the most cynical person in the room, even if I hid my cynicism fairly well behind masks of genial bonhomie, tasteful servitude, or intellectual superiority, depending on my interlocutor's position. I was also unsettled by this very serious topic at such a pleasant event, especially as I was under the hypnosis of hashish.

How do you know? the lawyer repeated, as if I were a witness on the stand.

I thought about Madeleine weeping in the kitchen of Heaven and said, From the newspapers. And Cambodian friends.

Of course I'm not disputing that hundreds of thousands died. What I'm interested in is real justice, not the easy or fake justice most people want. He is a scapegoat. A demon whom we can point to and say, *He* did it.

But he did do it—

He says he didn't. He never saw those people dying. He says his Organization told him a different story.

And you believe him? And even if you do, that makes him innocent?

He deserves a real trial. The court of public opinion is not a real court. Take those protesters outside. They're challenging public opinion. In this case it's the reverse of Pol Pot. Everyone thinks Ho Chi Minh is a saint, except for the relatives of the people he killed, of whom I've met a few. I'm an anarchist, and I will tell you that Ho Chi Minh became a saint by murdering all his enemies to the left and to the right of him, including the anarchists.

I looked at my aunt. You have a picture of him.

She looked pained. I don't know if this is proven, either—

He wiped out all his Vietnamese competitors before he wiped out the French.

I tried to remember the occasional comments I had heard about Uncle Ho's political maneuverings. Purge, I said. He purged his competition.

Purged, the lawyer said. Like with a laxative. To purify oneself and the struggle of the anarchists like me, as well as the nationalists, the royalists, the Trotskyites, the insufficiently ideological anticolonialists. You know why? Too many sides. He needed to have only two sides, so that the people would understand—you were for or against the French. And those against had better agree that the only way was the communist way. None of the communists or socialists or leftists here will acknowledge that. They're interested in self-serving justice, like most people. They all romanticize the Vietnamese communists. They sanitize Ho Chi Minh so that they, too, will be clean. They talk about revolutionary justice, but that's not real justice. If you want real justice, you need real lawyers.

She's a really good lawyer, my aunt said admiringly. As an editor, she had very high standards about prose and ideas, which she conflated with her judgments of people. There aren't too many lawyers willing to defend Pol Pot.

Nor you, my ghost chorus said.

How do you bring yourself to defend someone like him? I said, my voice shrill. Even if you are an anarchist? And how can you be an anarchist lawyer, anyway?

She shrugged, doubtlessly having heard the question before. How do you defend what most people consider indefensible? she asked. It's actually quite easy. What the French did in Indochina, or in Algeria, was indefensible, but the French defend it all the time. Or simply forget about it. Same thing, based on the principle that what our enemies do is beyond comprehension, while what we do is totally justified. Defending what some people call the indefensible forces me to consider a question all lawyers and judges should think about—

How do you forgive the unforgivable? my aunt said.

And can you even forgive the unforgivable? the lawyer said, and the look she aimed at my aunt was so hot, and vice versa, that I got a little flushed. Nothing was sexier than sharing the same convictions in a world where few people did.

At that moment, BFD, the man with very flexible convictions, slid up. I stiffened, reminded that he knew my secret and only moderately reassured that he was unlikely to speak to Bon, whom he did not know. He irradiated us all with a smile, then said to the lawyer—in French—I've been reading about your newest client, my dear. The Cambodian!

Pol Pot.

He's giving the Vietnamese quite a problem, isn't he? BFD nodded in agreement with himself and put his finger on his chin as if he

were being photographed for an author portrait in the pose I most detested. It's ironic, isn't it? The Vietnamese stuck fighting a guerrilla war. Cambodia has become Vietnam's Vietnam, wouldn't you say?

I finally saw a waiter with a tray of Champagne and snatched a flute, which allowed me to sip rather than say something offensive, which is to say, truthful. Which was worse, my country reduced to a war or my country turned into a cliché?

You do like to court notoriety, BFD continued.

I do nothing of the sort. I simply enjoy a good trial.

And interesting defendants. BFD looked at me. You've heard about—

I've heard.

Did you also hear about her previous most notorious client? The Palestinian terrorist? Quite dashing in her keffiyeh!

Freedom fighter, the humorless and handsome lawyer said. States are the real terrorists. Who kills more people, a freedom fighter or a nation-state?

I stand corrected. There is something glamorous about hijacking an airplane.

Stay on my good side. You might need a lawyer yourself someday.

For someone so opposed to the state, it's odd that you believe so much in the law.

The law is only a means for justice. An imperfect means for an imperfect world.

So the repartee went on. I wrapped the bandanna of a meaningless smile on my face, which I hoped was as enigmatic as the *Mona Lisa*'s, which I had finally seen in person at the Louvre and from which I had wandered away bemused. That's it? How could one not be underwhelmed once confronted with the Western world's most famous painting? I studied it for as long as I could with the

crowds jostling me. A very good painting. But a portrait any better than a dozen others in the Louvre, some of which featured faces that seemed just as enigmatic? Or was enigmatic just the European equivalent of the Asiatic inscrutable? I was flummoxed by my inability to understand the fuss. Was I just uncouth? I could accept that. I focused on my uncouthness and readied myself for the end of the conversation, and when BFD at last began drifting away, I stepped next to him as he surveyed the crowd. He glanced at me, his meaningless smile also disguising his face, and I said, Have you heard of this place called Heaven?

His meaningless smile did not become any more meaningful as I summarized Heaven for him in English, sotto voce. I imagined myself as he saw me, and in order to do so, I had to imagine BFD, building him from details gleaned from my aunt and the newspapers. Someone in his family had participated in all the great historical events of the republic, always on the right side, which is to say the left, from storming the Bastille to manning the barricades with the communards. His grandfather had stood with Zola and staunchly defended Dreyfus. His father, a leader of the Communist Party, had criticized the colonization of Indochina and resisted the Nazis. BFD was ideologically diluted, a rosé socialist to his father's cabernet communism. He was less revolutionary than the Maoist PhD or the anarchist lawyer, but he had hurled cobblestones and been tear-gassed in May 1968, even though he was well past his college days at the Sorbonne. He had also chanted Ho Chi Minh's name and waved both the flag of the National Liberation Front and Mao's *Little Red Book*. In the 1970s, his revolutionary enthusiasm had aged into a pragmatic electoral leftism, his act cleaned up by marrying a young woman from a wealthy liberal family who had made its fortune in soap. He had it all, and what else could he see in me besides someone committed to the wrong side of history?

I was a little person who spoke an immigrant version of his language, the language of a country that basked in the best of both worlds: to have once been an imperial power that had mugged weaker countries at gunpoint, while no longer being an imperial power and having to deal with pesky things like mosquitoes and malaria or resentment and revolutions. My one advantage was that I spoke English, or more accurately, Americanese. Yippee! Yahoo! Yankees! Americanese was still an imperial language, and although BFD wholeheartedly opposed American imperialism, he was secretly nostalgic for French imperialism, as almost all the French were in their heart of hearts, their soul of souls, their Louvre of Louvres. While the best situation for an anti-imperialist was to live in an imperial country where one could benefit from imperialism while righteously opposed to it, as happened quite often in the United States, the French had the second-best situation: being anti-imperialist in a formerly imperialist country. Thus, for BFD, to hear me speak Americanese was to hear both the language of American imperialism and the dying echo of a lost French imperialism. He disliked me, but I was doing exactly what he expected of a nobody like me: appealing to his basest nature by luring him to Heaven. I had already been clued into what kind of man he was when my aunt had told me how he made passes at all her attractive friends. That's terrible, I had said, and she had replied, indifferently, He's a Frenchman. For all of my faults, I had never cheated on a lover or attempted to seduce her friends. I believed in commitment, even if the commitment never lasted more than a night. Commitment was a principle, and BFD had no such principle.

Interesting, he murmured as the crowd swirled around us at the party. Heaven, you say. Perhaps we'll take a drive sometime and visit this . . . interesting place.

Then he was gone, but the hook had been set and the Ronin was right. BFD would never buy the goods from me directly, but

his taste for another kind of goods drew him to the hot novelty of a beautiful stranger's nude youth. It was another kind of high, even if it didn't last as long, which meant that the taste for it could be indulged even more frequently. I confess to still being interested in such things myself, but not all of myself agreed with me. I told myself that it was hard to concentrate, what with the chorus of the dead whispering in my ear and the face of the communist agent staring over my shoulder when I looked in the mirror. The only solution was not to look.

That night, after we returned to my aunt's apartment, I lay on her sofa, disturbed by the sounds emanating from my aunt's bedroom. Even at two in the morning, my aunt and the lawyer made quite a bit of noise as I lay there in the dark, still wearing my pants and shirt. I pulled the blanket up to my chin and thought about Bon killing Man and me making love to Lana, all while listening with mild terror to the noises from behind my aunt's door. I had heard sounds coming from behind that door before, with BFD or the Maoist PhD, but those were muted and familiar. Mostly the sonic disturbance came from my aunt's bed groaning, a chorus that varied depending on the guest. BFD sprinted or galloped, getting to his destination as quickly as possible; the Maoist PhD was a flaneur, occasionally brisk but generally meandering. BFD finished with a guttural grunt, an exclamation point marking the end of History! The Maoist PhD concluded with a drawn-out, meditational sigh, an ellipsis indicating the unknown future yet to come . . . As for my aunt, she rarely made noise, except for some muted moaning and panting. Based on the audible evidence, she seemed to be a spectator at a sporting event, cheering occasionally at a good play. She must have been watching football, because once or twice I heard her cry out, GOOAAAAALLLLLL! or something

to that effect. At first the sounds she and the men made bothered me, but soon it was her silences that captured me. Once I even timed the gap between one noise she made and the next—four minutes thirty-two seconds, with her finally murmuring on the thirty-third. Why so quiet? What was she thinking? Or feeling? In those fertile absences of sound, a disturbing vine grew in my mind, its sinews suggesting that perhaps over my many encounters with women, there were silences that I had not heard . . . because all I could hear was myself.

Reluctantly listening to my aunt respond spontaneously to the humorless and handsome lawyer, I suddenly felt that nothing could be trusted anymore. Did the women really mean it when they said I was the best, that what had occurred was the best, or even simply that they enjoyed it? What was it that Lana had told me in our postcoital minute? *That was utterly amazing.* Had she been lying? Was I more akin to BFD and the Maoist PhD than I realized? I had thought that my aunt was one of those people who simply did not verbally express herself when making love. But no! Whatever was happening was drawing forth an onomatopoeia of pleasure from my aunt that made me deeply uncomfortable. Why was I not aroused? It was a terrific performance, the handsome and humorless lawyer playing my aunt expertly. I should be excited!

Even after the scoring had subsided and no more cries could be heard, a different set of noises continued. What mysterious activity was this? Could it be . . . *talking?* Although I could not hear what they said, the most amazing thing was that they talked at all. I could not recall more than a handful of times, postcoitus, when I had talked to the lovely beside me. Of course I had said a few polite words, some compliments for a job well done, but *conversations?* On *what?* What could two women be talking about so endlessly? For all that I strained to hear, I could not figure out this mystery. Unable to eavesdrop or sleep, I switched on the light and picked up the only available reading,

*The Evil Empire's Oriental Origins.* I calculated, correctly, that the book would divert me from the disturbing conversation I could not hear. First, the table of contents, with chapter titles like "America: A Force for Good," and "Fist of Power, Hand of Friendship," and "Freedom Will Not Abide Walls," and "Islam: A Committed Ally against Communism." Hedd's English accent resounded in my head from the one time we had met, the General dragging me along to meet Hedd in the hopes of enlisting him in the General's effort to take back our homeland. Hedd, great pundit. Hedd, international columnist. Hedd, friend of world leaders. Hedd, big fish in the scummy waters of a Washington think tank. Even Hedd the knight! For there was his title in his author's biography—*Sir* Richard Hedd!

I returned to the last page, for I liked to know how thrillers ended before I began, and his book was clearly of that much-maligned genre. The gripping story was the great conflict between communism and democracy, which was simply a code word for capitalism. Like many thrillers, it had no true suspense, since the good guys could never lose, even if a few got killed along the way. Then my eyes fell on the book's last words, and that concluding sentence struck my forehead with the force of a boomerang:

While life is valuable to the Oriental, life is *invaluable* to the Westerner.

Those were my words! I had spoken them to Hedd, along with a dozen witnesses, from the General to the Congressman and a clan of white men bedecked in suits and lies. How had these words ended up here? The fault lay, as it so often did, with cheap champagne, which was not even Champagne, as it came from California. Hedd had handed me a coupe of the déclassé American stuff and said, I hope you do not mind, young man, if I use your memorable turn

233

of phrase in my next book. Nothing could make me happier, I said. Of course I was lying, as many things could make me happier, but I was being either inscrutably Asian or simply polite. But regardless of what I was being, I had agreed on the assumption that if my words were to be used, they would be attributed to me. Instead, here they were, passed off as Sir Richard Hedd's own words, with myself erased. I was helpless with fury, which was my only excuse for turning once more to the remedy, which, if it did not make me feel much better, let me feel nothing at all.

I woke up with the sun backlighting the drapes and the meaty taste of an existential crisis in my mouth, salted with a liberal dose of panic. The moment I stepped foot onto the rug and tried to rise, I became one disoriented Asiatic, dizzy with vertigo. In the kitchen, the civet coffee was almost ready, while Françoise Hardy sang the wildly inappropriate "Tous les garçons et les filles" from my aunt's stereo (Hardy is, I admit, a clear sign of French civilization). While the lawyer was graced with the honorary robe granted to all my aunt's lovers, my aunt wore a turban and a silk dressing gown, lending her the appearance of a Persian courtesan as she lounged on the sofa, waiting for the lawyer to finish brewing coffee as black as the emptiness inside me.

Civet coffee? the lawyer said, reading the package.

My aunt, who had been using the coffee sparingly for "special occasions," said, It's made for someone like you.

The handsome and humorless lawyer wrinkled her nose, and a picture, unbidden, lit the heretofore darkened cinema of my mind, featuring my aunt and the lawyer, intertwined on her brass bed. We sat in the armchairs flanking the sofa where my aunt sat, and, over coffee and pastries, we discussed the last movies that they had seen,

the possibilities of communist renewal, and the Soviet struggles in Afghanistan. These two women clearly were in love with each other, or at least deeply infatuated. On the one hand, I was delighted that BFD and the Maoist PhD had not measured up to the handsome and humorless lawyer. On the other hand, they were men, I was a man, and if no place existed for men in this strange new love, then what place was there for me? But it would not do to bring that up. Instead, I mentioned Hedd.

"Penetrating analysis by a seminal author," my aunt said, quoting from the back cover. Oh my. *Seminal!*

When the lawyer laughed, I wondered what was so funny. My aunt must have glimpsed my expression, because she added, I would be more impressed if an author was described as "vaginal." How often has an author—almost always a man—described himself as giving birth to his book? If that's the case, "vaginal" is much more appropriate, no?

Wouldn't that rule out all the authors who don't—uh—you know, have vaginas?

But you don't have any problem with ruling out all the authors who don't produce semen, the lawyer said, with just a hint of courtroom menace.

I always thought "seminal" was just, you know, metaphorical. Or is that—I don't know—a simile? A seminal simile?

It's always nice when a figure of speech works in your favor, isn't it? my aunt asked.

Hot with embarrassment at all this "seminal" and "vaginal" conversation, I changed the subject. What do you think of this quote? I turned to the last page and read them the crucial line: "While life is valuable to the Oriental, life is *invaluable* to the Westerner."

My aunt groaned and the lawyer snorted. What's the American expression? the lawyer said. Oh, yes. He's a shithead.

We all laughed, me most of all, relieved that this was a joke that I could get. That was the judgment I was looking for! Except she was judging my words. I had meant those words ironically, but if a shithead quoted me, what did that make me?

All these men making proclamations about the world, said the lawyer. As if the only politics that matters has to do with states and armies and wars. Without even looking at his bibliography, I can guarantee you that he only cites men. Perhaps with one exception. Hannah Arendt.

I looked at the bibliography and, indeed, Arendt was there, for *On Revolution*. But a quick study of the rest of the entries did not show any other women's names. So whom should he be citing? I asked. I did not mean it as a challenge, but my aunt took it as such.

First, you exclude women from politics and governments and universities, and then you ask where are all the women, and which women should we be citing?

Well, I—

Frenchwomen couldn't even vote until 1945! *After* I was born. We've barely emerged from the Dark Ages! You men are absurd. You read Marx and Césaire and Fanon and talk endlessly about capitalism and colonialism and racism, but who was the last woman you read? When was the last time the word "sexism" or "patriarchy" or "phallus" ever came out of your mouth? Oh, why do I bother to even ask? It's not as if your confession is *l'écriture féminine*, is it? My God, Hélène Cixous would tear you apart. She stood up and went to a bookshelf, and I kept my mouth shut, which allowed me not to have to admit to having never heard of *l'écriture féminine* or Hélène Cixous. My aunt returned with a book and said, You at least have read Simone de Beauvoir, correct?

Of course! I lied, feigning indignance and quoting the only words I had heard attributed to Beauvoir: "Woman is made, not born!"

"One is not born, but rather becomes, a woman," my aunt said coldly. At least you came close. Now you should graduate to Julia Kristeva. That way you can say you've read two French feminists.

I looked at the book she thrust into my hand, *Pouvoirs de l'horreur: Essai sur l'abjection*. I opened it and scanned the table of contents:

Approaching Abjection
Something to Be Scared Of
From Filth to Defilement
Semiotics of Biblical Abomination
Suffering and Horror
Those Females Who Can Wreck the Infinite
In the Beginning and without End . . .
Powers of Horror

Trust me, my aunt said. It's perfect for you.

# CHAPTER 14

Later that evening, after the lawyer and my aunt had gone off to a dinner where they would continue talking to each other in my absence—did two women talking to each other without a man present actually make any sound?—BFD came to pick me up in his convertible. We greeted each other warily, and then the car took off at reckless speed. Maybe BFD always drove very fast, or maybe he did not want to be alone with me for long, or maybe he could not wait to get to Heaven. Or perhaps all of the above.

Steering with his left hand, he used his right to manipulate the stick shift, pop a cigarette into his mouth, and ignite it with the car's lighter. He had the movie star look I aspired to, the director in his case being Fellini, given his paisley ascot and Italian convertible, whose roof could not, unfortunately, be retracted in the middle of a chilly January. His pseudo-stardom almost offset the fact that anybody who wore an ascot deserved beheading, though that was just a personal opinion, albeit a very strong one. I was not short of opinions, and neither was BFD.

To avoid talking, we both smoked incessantly and listened to a greatest hits tape of Johnny Hallyday, the sonic equivalent of Ricard

Pastis, a taste the rest of the world could not acquire. We exchanged a few banalities, with the only matter of substance coming up when BFD said, casually, that he had not seen my aunt for a while. I suppose she must have found another man to keep her busy? he asked. Besides our dear friend, of course. He meant the Maoist PhD.

There's no other man in her life, I said. I did not mention the lawyer. Speaking of her and her astonishing feats seemed like a betrayal of the mystery that had happened behind that closed door, a secret to which I had no right, except in my imagination, which even the lawyer might agree was not responsible for its actions.

Maybe she needs a rest, BFD said as he turned onto the street that led to Heaven. Women are sensitive creatures.

I imagine you've known a lot of women, I said, flicking away my cigarette butt.

He parked the convertible with a satisfied smile. Haven't you?

*Yes,* I thought. *Literally countless women,* for I had long ago lost track. But I did not say this out loud. For once—for the first time—I was ashamed that I had known so many women, and the approval of BFD was not something that I craved. Indeed, his approval would mean that I would be like him—and I wasn't. Was I?

I'm Catholic, I said, opening my door, as if being Catholic explained everything, which it usually did.

BFD's smile veered from satisfaction to mild contempt. He was indifferent to religion, as were many of the French, which was one reason I found them charming. The delights and difficulties of women aren't for everybody, he said, following me to Heaven's entrance. They're a challenge, for those of us who like such things.

I suppressed the urge to punch him in the throat, which, both Claude and Bon had taught me, was the quickest way to take down a man, who would reflexively think that protecting his manhood would be a higher priority. Instead I smiled and rang the doorbell,

hard, and then a second time, pretending I was pushing his eyeball into its socket. The housekeeper ushered us in after I gave the password—*I'd like to go to Heaven*—which is what Jesus Christ must have whimpered as he faded on the cross. Nothing had changed since I left, Heaven being eternal, the housekeeper still ingratiating, the television still tuned to an intellectual talk show, the eschatological muscle still seated in his armchair with a thin volume on his lap. The only difference was that he did not have just one Band-Aid on his left cheek but another one on his right temple.

Even in this rather incongruous context, BFD gave off an air of casual brilliance and cosmopolitanism, with his pink trousers, white shirt unbuttoned to the sternum, lime-green sweater draped over his shoulders with its arms loosely tied over his chest, monogrammed handkerchief, gold Rolex, slightly worn espadrilles, and sockless white ankles. In this waiting room of average men, he was matched in his meticulous grooming only by the gentleman standing up as we came in. He bore the distinctive markings of one of France's threatened minorities: a capitalist, a kind of creature rarely seen in such splendor in the rougher neighborhoods of Paris in which I passed my time. This specimen flaunted the plumage of a tailored plaid suit, a tasteful tie in a fat Windsor knot, gleaming cuff links, polished wingtips, and a copy of *Le Figaro*, with the biggest bulge in his sleek profile not in the front of his pants but the back, where a thick wallet shielded his ass from being kicked. Only his heels showed signs of wear, having been used to grind down the hopes and dreams of the working class. While the American capitalist with his generously cut suit and expansive belly enjoyed gorging on the blood of the people, the slim and aristocratic French capitalist represented capitalism's charming and elegant side. On the one hand, the ugly American, who did not care what he ate so long as he ate too much of it, especially gigantic slabs of still-bleeding red meat.

On the other hand, the chic Frenchman, who preferred the refined cruelty of foie gras.

Now having run out of hands, one must then look down at one's feet to see the Chinese and Vietnamese varieties of capitalism, represented by the two-for-one Boss, who merged both as an ethnic Chinese from Vietnam. In contrast to American cowboy capitalism and French cosmopolitan capitalism, the Boss practiced gangster capitalism. Some see the gangster version as capitalism's lawless degeneration, except that gangsterism was actually capitalism's disavowed dog-eat-dog origin. Such an interesting English expression, the "dog-eat-dog world," since dogs don't really eat dogs (dogs do eat shit, but that's another story).

Darling! cried Crème Brûlée, the woman for whom our poor endangered capitalist had stood. She had emerged through a curtain of beads from a hallway, wearing her miniskirted kimono. Her gaze was fixed on the endangered capitalist, who had tossed his newspaper aside the way he probably tossed aside human lives. If she was beautiful and youthful, and he was plain and aged, that was what money and whiteness, multiplied together, could buy. My dear! she cooed. Did you miss little Crème Brûlée?

Like you wouldn't believe, he said. You're stunning, as always. I hope you didn't wait long.

Not long at all, except that your bodyguard insists on watching this awful show.

The eschatological muscle shrugged. If you listened, maybe you'd learn.

Don't mind him, Crème Brûlée purred. He's bored and he wants everyone bored.

She smiled and extended her arm. Her luminescent bare skin hypnotized the endangered capitalist, who walked to her slowly with his hand extended, one finger displaying the most meaningless

symbol in the world, a wedding ring. She backed through the beaded curtains, drawing him in, and even as I gestured to BFD to take the endangered capitalist's seat, the expressionist mistress emerged through the beads, smiling with such canned sincerity that I knew her smile was not for me.

My dear sir! She seized BFD's hand with her own. We've been expecting you!

My dear lady, he replied, giving a courtly bow. I am delighted to be here!

And with that, the expressionist mistress quickly ushered him through the curtain, fawning over him with sweet words that she had never used with me. She was escorting BFD toward the VIP lounge, for there was always a VIP lounge for people like BFD, which meant that the endangered capitalist was a lower-level capitalist if he had not been so privileged. Left in the waiting room with a few other non-VIP asses and the eschatological muscle, I asked him if he had hurt his head. In response, he raised Voltaire's *Candide* from his lap to cover his mouth and whispered, My head is fine.

Then why another Band-Aid? I asked, mystified. And the one on your cheek, too?

My cheek and my head may be fine, but the rest of me isn't.

What's wrong with you?

Exactly the question I want people to think when they see these Band-Aids. And everybody sees these Band-Aids.

It's a little noticeable, I said.

Band-Aids are meant to be invisible. But not on me.

The beads rustled again and parted to reveal Madeleine. She saw me and her professional smile remained affixed to her face, as enigmatic as the *Mona Lisa*'s. She nodded to me but sashayed to one of the asses on the sofa, an unshaven fellow dressed in a tracksuit, as

if going to a sporting event. As she led the lucky ass past me, toward the promising hallway hidden by the beads, I knew what I must do.

Can I see Madeleine? I asked the eschatological muscle.

He shrugged. Anyone can see Madeleine.

Over the next hour, as I wondered whether Madeleine or BFD would emerge from behind the curtains first, I spoke with the eschatological muscle about Césaire, Fanon, and my fear that in this tempest of a world, I was what Césaire considered Ariel. Was my reluctance to continue subscribing to Césaire and Fanon's vision of violence as being inevitable in the struggle against colonization a sign of theoretical revision on my part, based on my revolutionary experience? Or was it simply an excuse to justify my reluctance to commit in the way they saw commitment, as a demand for violent uprising?

Well, you're not black, you're not African, you are no longer colonized, and you're an intellectual, the eschatological muscle said. Does that answer your question?

Thanks, I muttered. And you? You choose to sit here and guard a brothel?

If revolutionaries can educate themselves in prisons, why not brothels? Can't prostitutes be as radical as prisoners?

So you are waiting for the right moment—

To come out of my hole? Yes. Or put it another way. You lived through what Gramsci called a war of maneuver. Violence, revolution, or at least confrontations in the streets. Me, I am in what Gramsci called a war of position. The war for ideas, for alliances, coalitions, new movements; the struggle for a new vision—

The beaded curtain parted and spared me from saying I had never heard of Gramsci. Madeleine stepped through, froze me with

her professional smile, and said—as she did to all the asses—Are you ready for a taste of Heaven? A few moments later my ass was back in her bedroom, the theater of so many humiliations, where I had unmanned myself with my self-sabotage. When Madeleine stepped forward and let the half-kimono fall, I raised my hand and said, Wait.

Wait? she said, as if she had never heard the word before from a man. But was I a man? Or just an ass with two cheeks, like all the others who demanded twenty or thirty minutes of her body? Two cheeks to match my two minds.

Sit, I said. Please.

In the litany of strange requests and demands she must have gotten during her career, this was innocuous. Madeleine kept smiling, shrugged, and sat on the edge of the bed, crossing her legs. What can I do for you? she asked.

Nothing. I want to do something for you.

I got on my knees before her.

Wait, she said, but I did not. I had knelt quite often in the reeducation camp. I had knelt all the time in church. But I had rarely knelt otherwise, unless one counts kneeling figuratively before that holiest of holies, secular French culture. Here I knelt voluntarily. This was not my normal behavior, but why the hell not? Why the hell could I not see what was there all along, until the handsome and humorless lawyer showed me, so to speak, from behind the closed door. I had hardly ever indulged in this behavior, it not being to my taste and not expected of me, given the generous women to whom I was attracted, who I now understood always gave me more than I gave them. But once I set myself a task I was nothing if not diligent, and I proceeded to please Madeleine as best as I could, lured on by her surprised murmurs and moans, learning as I went, split between focusing on the admittedly repetitive task at hand and being beaten

back in time by the saltwater tide of my thoughts, over the dark fields of this republic and the dark oceans separating it from home, to another occasion when I had knelt, my First Communion. The momentousness of this ritual at age seven matched in some way what I felt kneeling before Madeleine. First Communion initiated us into the community of willful believers who flanked our super-cute procession as we slowly marched toward the priest. The holy man was no less than my father, although I did not know it at the time. Behold the body of Christ, he said, holding before each of us a white moon the size of a coin. Then he placed it on our outstretched tongues. I quivered at the thought of Father's fingers touching my tongue, but I felt only the flat, dry wafer, and I wondered what part of Christ I had in my mouth—a slice of the intestine? a cross-section of an eyeball? a disk of bone? No time to ponder further, for the pious, holier-than-thou choirboy waited for me with the blood of Christ in a chalice. Even though I had seen the choirboy wipe the lip of the cup with a white cloth, I still trembled at the thought of all the mouths that had touched that cup. Then I applied my chapped lips to the edge of the cup and chased down my morsel of the body of Christ with a sip of His blood, making me both cannibal and vampire. This blood of Christ was a sweet syrup on a poor tongue unused to sweets, and it would lead me not toward greater devotion to God but rather, eventually, toward debauchery. If I love liquor too much, I blame God, or at least his minions. Sacramental wine was the first remedy this seven-year-old bastard enjoyed.

The last time I had tasted sacramental wine was when I attended Mass at the Cathedral of Notre-Dame in Saigon, a replica, on a reduced scale, of the Notre-Dame in Paris, suitable for us as minia-tures of our French masters. Now I had seen the real Notre-Dame, like my professor the Sponge before me, and the sight of it made me aware of how our colonized, tropical version was but a doll's house.

In this toy version of Notre-Dame, Man and I knelt in April 1975, both of us spies infiltrated into the southern army, he my superior giving me my mission: flee with the remnants of the southern army to America, and from there spy on their efforts to take their country back from our victorious communist revolution. While we knelt and shared our conspiracy in whispers, the old women who attended Mass every day chanted their prayers. I had always dreaded their droning as they counted their rosaries, their eyes fixed on the crucified Christ hanging above the altar. I preferred kneeling before Madeleine while I traced with my tongue the Vietnamese alphabet, which was not so different from the French alphabet. My father had taught me that alphabet, and now I spelled it on Madeleine, rehearsing every letter over and over again as she cried out in her mother tongue and as I added punctuation and accent marks for good measure, until I—at long, long last—was literate.

BFD was all smiles when he got into the convertible, and perhaps I was, too. Grant me my small triumph; let me for a moment be a sea anemone gently swaying in a current of happiness. I had not felt such exhilaration since my first encounter with a woman, in my freshman year at Occidental College, in that paradise known as Southern California, with a French major who liked to call me her *petit métis*. I would have been outraged by anyone except a beautiful blonde calling me by that name. A beautiful blonde could call me anything. So what if her hair turned out to be dyed? I forgave her that bit of camouflage, since I myself, in disguise as a harmless foreign student, was unlike how I appeared, not that any of us are exactly how we appear.

My apologies if I took a long time, BFD said, interrupting my reverie. He tapped the steering wheel to another song, having

switched cassettes to a greatest hits compilation of *yé-yé* music, a style I found quite charming. How could one not like "Les Sucettes," especially as sung by France Gall? I hummed along as BFD jockeyed his Italian steed past the various examples of Peugeot, Renault, and Citroën cars that few people except the French seemed interested in owning. I lost track of the time! BFD said, puffing on his cigarette enthusiastically. Very easy to do with Morning Peony and Beautiful Lotus. Young women know how to make a man feel like a man!

They did? Had I missed out by not consulting Morning Peony and Beautiful Lotus? I desperately needed to feel like a man! Or perhaps I just wanted to feel like a man. Not *needing* to be a man seemed ... liberating. Perhaps that was what I needed, to need fewer things. To need less. To want ... nothing?

But, I said, do you know how to make a woman feel like a woman?

He honked savagely at an offending German vehicle that had cut in front of him, the Bavarian beast reminding him of both his French weakness and that of his Italian convertible, which, like its country of origin, was both beautiful and underpowered. Ask any woman who has been with me, he growled. Their satisfaction is guaranteed! Of course—he glanced at me from the corner of his eye—some people doubt their ability to satisfy women. That has never been the case with me.

I suppressed the urge to gouge BFD in the eye, which, both Claude and Bon had told me, was the second-quickest way to take down a man. But we were traveling at a very fast speed through the dark and I did not want to die in a car crash like Camus, who had at least known fame before his sudden death. What had I accomplished? Nothing. And I had a mission to fulfill with BFD, one that required me not to antagonize him but to maximize one of my greatest talents, flattery. Still, I could not help but ask the most obvious

question: You don't think that the act of paying these young women might make it hard to determine whether they are truly satisfied?

I assume they were satisfied because I paid them, he said. Does capitalism debase them and me? Of course it does! Which is why I'm a socialist. If we had socialism, these young women would not *need* to be ladies of the night. They would *want* to be ladies of the night. And they would not need madams or pimps; they would own a share of the profits. They would be sexual stockholders rather than the sexual proletariat!

Something was wrong in BFD's self-satisfied, triumphant logic of erotic socialism, just as something felt wrong when I paid Madeleine, including when I did that most un-Vietnamese of things and tipped her. By that I mean a real tip, not the one dollar or five francs that most Vietnamese thought sufficed, regardless of the fare. By real tip I mean 10 percent, a sum that would horrify most Vietnamese people, especially Vietnamese men, especially in this case. They would argue that I had done all the work—work that no Vietnamese man would ever do or at least admit to doing—and gotten nothing in return. But I had wanted nothing in return.

Look, I said, changing the subject, if you enjoyed this little visit to Heaven, I know of a place even more heavenly than Heaven.

BFD grinned and squeezed my shoulder in a spontaneous show of affection, or perhaps a calculated one. If this place that is more heavenly than Heaven has more beauties like Morning Peony and Beautiful Lotus, I will be there, he said. Oh, the body of a twenty-five-year-old is extraordinary! And then when they are one of your kind—delicious! Your women—oh, my friend, you are so fortunate. They are unbelievable. So delicate, so intuitive, so hairless, so ageless, so *tireless*. The Asiatic woman knows men better than Western women do. She knows men better than we know ourselves. She is perfect!

And with that he brought his fingers to his lips and blew an appreciative kiss into the air, intended for this Asiatic woman whom I had never met, even though I had met thousands of Asiatic women. Was there an exclusive club of Asiatic women kept on reserve only for white men?

The only drawback to her, continued BFD, although it is also the source of her attraction, is that she is essentially unknowable.

Unknowable? I said.

Inscrutable. Like you.

Like me?

Yes. BFD turned to look at me even though the convertible was still hurtling at a terrific pace along the darkened periphery of central Paris. I can intuit a great deal from people. I am a politician, after all. But with you—it's impossible, I must admit. Your face is as imperturbable as . . . as the *Mona Lisa's*.

I don't know if I'm inscrutable. Perhaps unreadable.

What's the difference?

If I'm unreadable—if all these Asians you refer to are unreadable—perhaps we are only unreadable to those who do not know how to read.

Semantics—

And even if we are inscrutable, what does that make white people? Are white people ever referred to as inscrutable? No, you would say that a white person who is hard to read has a poker face, which has a positive connotation, a strategic one, suggesting a careful withholding of information, whereas we are just inscrutable because you white people believe that we always have something to hide—

There you go again, with your "white people" this and your "white person" that. He snorted and waved his finger in my face. You're nothing more than a communitarian.

You, of all people, accuse me of being a *communist*?

Communitarian, you idiot! Communitarian! A miserabilist! Someone who wallows in his misery, who cannot transcend the petty circumstances of his identity or his obsession with skin color, who cannot think outside of his little group, his *community*, and who can never *ever* just be *human*, much less *universal*!

Was I hearing right? A white man of the same culture as Victor Hugo—the man elevated to a saint by our Cao Dai religion—the man who had given the world *Les Misérables* (which I confess to not having yet read because, you know, it was a thousand pages long)— this man was accusing *me* of being a miserabilist, as if acknowledging misery was a bad thing? How terrible misery is, let's never wallow in it! Except, of course, when it came to acknowledging the misery of the working class or of the French, in which case such wallowing was not apparently miserabilism but *universalism*.

You! I shouted, as he was shouting, neither of us watching the road anymore. You—who are so upset that I called you and your fellow white people white—you are the one who calls me and my kind Asiatic!

I call you Asiatic because you call yourself Asiatic!

I have never called myself Asiatic! You are upset because I made you see yourself. You like to think of yourself as just a man, not a white man, unless you call yourself white, with a certain kind of self-aware irony. But for me to call *you* a white man is unacceptable, downright racist, even if you yourself and all white people routinely say of someone "an Asiatic woman" or "a black man," as if a black man were not just a man as you are just a man. So what if I noticed your whiteness—how unforgivable! I suppose the only thing ruder would be to notice your *penis*.

You stupid, vulgar bastard! You accuse me of racism yet again when all I have said is how much I love Asiatic women? What kind of—

Racist love is still racist! As for me not being universal—why? Because I'm yellow? Because I'm only half white? Because I'm a refugee? Because I'm from your former colony? Because I have the wrong accent? Because my looks are disdained? Because my food is offensive? If Jesus Christ, child of refugees, born poor in a stable, a colonized person, a hick from the backwaters, despised by his society's leaders and by the rulers of his leaders, a humble carpenter—if this Jesus Christ became universal—then so can I, motherfucker!

The convertible slammed to a stop before my aunt's address, so give BFD credit for delivering me to my destination rather than throwing me out onto the street. I flung open the door and jumped out onto the sidewalk, and thank the god I did not believe in that I did not step into a pile of shit, because if that had happened I probably would have murdered BFD right then and there for being a representative of a race, or a nation, or a people, or a culture, that bestowed more freedom and love and understanding on its dogs than its yellow people. But not having stepped into dog shit, I felt free, even though I had lost my cool and blown my cover as the inoffensive Asiatic, the friendly Vietnamese, the grateful colonial subject. I slammed the door shut, and only when I looked at BFD did I realize how much I had offended him, for he was, finally, at a loss for speech. Instead of spilling words from his mouth, he had pulled his eyes into slants with the tips of his index fingers, a pose he held for just a moment before taking his fingers from his eyes, sneering at me, and dashing away with a screech and a burst of hazy diesel fumes, leaving me stunned on the sidewalk. My heart was pumping terribly fast from the vileness of our exchange, and I stepped away from the door of my aunt's building to calm down. What a paradox, the people who professed never seeing race in fact seeing race fairly often!

Hiding in the shadows of the street, I inhaled deeply and closed my eyes. BFD would not ruin my evening. I would not let him

# CHAPTER 15

I returned to the Boss's restaurant in Paris the next afternoon, feeling a mix of guilt and shame, a concoction familiar to me as a reluctant Catholic, for I had been forced to drink it every day of my childhood. Did the people who did not see race even as they saw race actually have a point? Perhaps, for example, I had underestimated the worst Asian restaurant in Paris. It could be so much more than the worst *Asian* restaurant—it very well might be the worst restaurant in Paris, period. Why insult ourselves even in denigrating ourselves? If Michelin published a guide to the worst restaurants, ours would merit three stars! A perverse pride inflated me, but I deflated rapidly when Grumpy, mopping the floor when I walked in, pointed wordlessly toward the stairs leading down to the toilet.

*Merde?* I asked.

*Merde,* he confirmed.

*Merde!* The single most useful word in the French language, easy to pronounce and eloquently expressive of conditions from the literally fecal to the unpleasantly existential. I sighed and headed for the toilet, but Le Cao Boi stuck his head out from the kitchen

door and said, Come here, Camus. The Ronin and Bon were in the kitchen as well, along with a couple of the dwarfs preparing the flesh of an unknown dead animal that might eventually pass for a dinner entrée, whacking away with their cleavers as bridges of ash trembled at the tips of their cigarettes. The sight of Bon reminded me of what I had been longing for and dreading, the coming of *Fantasia* in two weeks, when I might see my beloved Lana again, if I was lucky, and Man, if I—and he—was unlucky. With our fatal rendezvous impending, I still had no idea how to save him, and I was happy to accept the comfort of a cigarette that Le Cao Boi offered me. Bon lit it, and the Ronin said, We found your shoes.

My shoes?

You remember we tracked you through your shoes? That tracker is state-of-the-art American surveillance technology and not a cheap device. I got a call from the old Indochina hand who lent it to me. I had to admit that I totally forgot about getting it back. Then it occurred to me the other night that when we found you, you were shoeless. Then it occurred to me that I hadn't noticed your shoes lying around in that cellar. Now, what if, I asked myself—

He walked off in my shoes.

The Ronin grinned and pointed at the industrial metal box on the counter next to him, its green cathode ray screen displaying a grid and one blinking dot, moving slowly. I've looked at this for a couple of days, the Ronin said. He's returned to the same spot two nights in a row and stayed there all night. I assume he's going back there tonight.

This is going to be fun, Le Cao Boi said with a laugh. He poured us each a shot of execrable Chinese liquor that looked like water and had no taste except for the rope burn that it left inside the esophagus. I gagged, tears in my eyes, but Bon seemed unaffected. My lack of manliness amused the Ronin, who chortled

as he poured himself a second shot and hummed with pleasure after downing it.

It's true, he said, smacking his lips. This will be so much fun!

We did not leave right away to find the Mona Lisa. First, I had to descend into the basement and unplug the victimized toilet's choked throat. Since we had so few customers at the restaurant, and since none of them ever finished a meal, the chances that the culprit was a customer were low. Meanwhile each of the restaurant staff regularly swore that it was not he who was responsible for the disaster but one of the others.

It does make you wistful, doesn't it, said Le Cao Boi, after I returned from the toilet trembling and blinking away tears, for the way we did it in the homeland, sitting over a stream or a pond, looking at the stars, listening to the cicadas? The benefit of fresh air! Never a clogged toilet or stinky bathroom. You just didn't want to be downstream. Here, have another, you'll feel better.

He poured me an additional shot of the abominable Chinese liquor, and the sting of it did, in fact, help me forget what I had just seen and smelled. To witness the interior of human beings was never, ever a pleasant experience.

We left in the early evening, setting forth in the van that the restaurant used for supplies, except that it had been repainted with the names of fictional electricians, LES FRÈRES CHIEN. Le Cao Boi drove badly, probably on purpose, for there were no other seats and Bon and I were stuck in the cavernous, grimy, windowless hold, sliding back and forth on the floor while Le Cao Boi chuckled. No one's going to wonder why an electrician's van might be parked on their street, the Ronin said from the passenger seat, where he sat with the tracking device in his lap, along with a map with the coordinates of where the

Mona Lisa had been staying. We rode for a half hour, from city streets to the periphery, all of us smoking while Le Cao Boi controlled the stereo and played a mix of pop and rock songs whose standout was "Seasons in the Sun," to which all four of us—and at least a couple of my ghosts—sang along with tears in our eyes:

> Goodbye my friend, it's hard to die
> When all the birds are singing in the sky
> Now that the spring is in the air
> Pretty girls are everywhere
> Think of me and I'll be there

The song had the appropriate mix of upbeat pop, downbeat melancholy, and accessible philosophy that perfectly expressed our Vietnamese sensibility. This included the honorary Vietnamese sensibility of the Ronin, who, like all white men who sought honorary Vietnamese status, found it easily given, for we were all bemused, amused, and honored that anybody not Vietnamese wanted to identify with us, which was, of course, just another sign of our country's small status and our collective mental colonization. The French and the Americans, as well as the Chinese and Japanese, simply took it for granted, as all imperialists did, that everybody wanted to be French or American or Chinese or Japanese.

> We had joy, we had fun
> We had seasons in the sun
> But the hills that we climbed
> Were just seasons out of time

So we entertained ourselves until Le Cao Boi parked the van outside the building where the Mona Lisa lived and said, Now we wait.

The Ronin tapped the screen of the tracking device and said, He's moving. A few kilometers away. He looked at me. You'll have to identify him.

We passed the next couple of hours with one person in the front and the other three in the back, smoking, playing cards, and gambling, which, after war and ahead of romantic love, has ruined more Vietnamese lives than any other cause. But we were gangsters! Ruining lives, including our own, was the stated intent and existential hazard of our profession. The only things we did not do to pass the time were drink alcohol and smoke hashish, for, as the Ronin proclaimed, we were working. I had lost all my money and was sitting in a corner of the van resentfully watching Le Cao Boi and Bon gamble with my cash when the Ronin said from the front seat, He's getting close. Bon and I slipped on long-haired brown wigs and woolen hats, followed by tinted glasses for Bon and my inauthentic aviator sunglasses for me. Then we took off our jackets and pants and put on another set of jackets and pants from a garbage bag of disguises, procured by the Ronin from who knows where. Le Cao Boi started the van and pulled out, and I squatted between his seat and the Ronin's. He studied the monitor of the tracking device and said, Left, right, right, straight, and so on as we drove to intercept the Mona Lisa, who was apparently moving slowly, probably on foot after having left the RER station. Through the windshield, I could see a dusty, dreary zone of lackluster apartment buildings, which, like their residents, had never been given a decent chance at life. If the metropolitan center of postcard Paris was an architectural feast of swoon-inducing traditions, this unappetizing colony of the *banlieue* was architectural fast food. Then we turned a corner and I saw the Mona Lisa only a few meters away, walking in *my* Bruno Magli shoes. He came toward us towing a grocery cart, one of the most charming aspects of life in Paris, where the residents walked to get their daily sustenance, which kept them reasonably

trim, unlike the average American of plush posterior who drove any distance longer than a block.

That's him, I said, ducking behind the Ronin's seat as if I were not in disguise. Gray overcoat. Le Cao Boi slammed on the brakes, and I bounced off the back of the Ronin's seat and landed on my side, with Bon cursing as he, too, was flung about, though he was wise enough to hold steady to the door handle. Regaining his footing, he flung open the sliding door, exposing me, and then jumped onto the street. I sat up and made eye contact with the uncomprehending Mona Lisa, who, as a professional gangster, should really have comprehended. Bon thrust his side against the Mona Lisa, bringing the two of them tightly together in seemingly brotherly or friendly contact, which allowed Bon to jam the muzzle of his P38 into the Mona Lisa's side without anyone seeing, and in the moment that the Mona Lisa froze, trying to decide whether to run, stay still, or do as Bon told him in French—*Allez! Dans le camion!*—I leaped out of the van and threw my arm around the Mona Lisa and jabbed my revolver, which had been his revolver, into his other side and propelled him toward the van. He began to yell, but the Ronin, who had slid into the back of the van, seized him by the lapel of his overcoat and pulled him in. Grab his cart, the Ronin said, and while Bon jumped back into the van, I turned around to do exactly that. As I did so, I saw a man in a beige raincoat emerging from a nearby doorway, old and bent over in the shape of a comma, shouting at me. My first instinct upon seeing him was to think, *Arab.* And what did he see, or whom? Surely not Asian or yellow, for I was disguised. No, what he saw was my universal identity, the burning light of my undisputed self that shone through the lampshade of my skin, embodied in the last word he uttered: *Stop, you bastard!*

\* \* \*

After a half hour's drive we came to another marginal gray world of warehouses, which was not the belly or even underbelly of Paris, nor its armpit or belly button, but rather the crack between the city's buttocks, the space that one hardly ever saw and almost never thought about. This damp, musty crack might have been the same soulless neighborhood where the Mona Lisa had kept me captive, but since I never saw that neighborhood in daylight I could not be certain.

Forget you know where this place is, Le Cao Boi said when he parked inside a gray warehouse with neither name nor personality, its exterior matching the pallor of the sky.

The Ronin said, Get him, pointing to the Mona Lisa, arms bound behind his back and a sack over his head.

Bon and I stripped off our disguises, stuffed them back into the garbage bag, and put on our own clothes. Then the four of us marched the Mona Lisa deeper into the recesses of the warehouse, past pallets towering with crates marked COFFEE, to where a couple of dwarfs were emerging from an office, wearing overalls, masks, and goggles.

What are they going to do? I asked.

Repaint the van, said Le Cao Boi. Les Frères Chien are history. They'll paint it yellow.

At the back of the office was a door that led to a storeroom, and at the back of the storeroom was another door leading to an empty, windowless, cavernous room, suitably chilly for wine and for torture. Shoved by Le Cao Boi, the Mona Lisa sprawled onto a cement floor lit by a single overhead light, a minimalist stage ready for an avant-garde drama by the likes of Samuel Beckett, who was already something of a sadist when it came to torturing his spectators. I had seen *Happy Days* and *Waiting for Godot* staged by the theater department of Occidental College, and I had been absolutely

flummoxed. What happened? Nothing happened! But if nothing happened, why could I not forget the plays, even now?

The Ronin turned to me, winked, and whispered, We'll soften him up for you. Then he said, loudly, Take off his hood.

Why was there always a hood, even if it was oftentimes only a sack? How many times had I seen prisoners with their heads cloaked, stumbling along blindly or, as now, shuddering on the ground? After the Mona Lisa was forced to strip, the Ronin and Le Cao Boi took turns with their fists and feet, as well as with chains, the Louisville Slugger, and the occasional bad poem by Le Cao Boi, pausing now and again for beer and snacks. Bon and I leaned against a far wall, squatted, sat on the floor, smoking cigarettes and watching.

You know what I'll regret? Bon asked.

What? I said.

That I won't get the chance to do this to the faceless man.

I, always the man with a plan, could not come up with a plan. I put on my Bruno Magli shoes and tried again to think of a plot that could save Man and keep my secret from Bon, but it was distracting to see and hear the Mona Lisa, who groaned, moaned, flopped, rolled, begged, screamed, and sobbed while the Ronin and Le Cao Boi cursed, jeered, laughed, joked, chortled, and snapped some Polaroids of their work. When at last the Mona Lisa was unconscious and I could finally hear myself think, Le Cao Boi wiped the sweat from his brow and the blood from his knuckles and said, All right, your turn.

For what? I said, although I knew for what.

You crazy bastard, he said with a laugh, punching my arm. You could be a little more enthusiastic. You get to have him all to yourself for a little while. A nice little gift from the Boss, huh? He figured you'd want some sweet revenge.

I tried to be a little more enthusiastic, but I didn't like sweets and was also not keen on torture, more commonly known as interrogation, less commonly known as fun. Let's have some fun! This is what Claude would say whenever a new prisoner was brought to us. And because I was very good at my job, both as interrogator and spy, I would pretend to have fun, even if my game back then was precarious: attempting to extract as many secrets as possible while inflicting the minimal amount of pain on the prisoner. I thought I had succeeded, until I came face-to-face with the communist agent, as naked then as the Mona Lisa was now. The interrogation room where she had experienced so much fun at the hands and extremities of the three panting policemen, what they called the "movie theater," was as brightly and badly lit as this room. Was it beyond hope that interrogators might understand the value of mood lighting?

The Boss said you're a professional, Le Cao Boi said. Like we're not.

You're not a professional like he is, Bon said. He was a secret policeman. A master interrogator for the Special Branch! In his tone was pride, in our friendship, in my competence, in our mission to eliminate the threat of communism, which had somehow become entangled in this other project of gangsterism. Still, if Bon was proud of me, it might only be because I had never told him about the interrogation of the communist agent and, of course, had never told him that I myself was, or had been, the one thing he could never forgive: a communist. But did one ever cease being communist, any more than one ever ceased being Catholic?

I'm a professional, I said. Like a doctor.

If you're a doctor, what's your specialty? said Le Cao Boi.

Proctology, I said, which made Le Cao Boi, the Ronin, and Bon grimace a little, further evidence that as an interrogator, I always knew where to put my fingers, this time pressing a rhetorical thumb

between their nether cheeks. That means I like doing my work in privacy, I added.

Take your time. The Ronin inspected a chipped fingernail. We're in no rush. But it would be best to get your revenge before the Boss gets here.

When's that?

Le Cao Boi shrugged. Whenever he feels like it.

What do you want from him? Bon said, nodding at the Mona Lisa.

Anything. And everything. He killed one of ours.

Which meant, as everyone knew, that the Mona Lisa must eventually die.

I was left alone with the Mona Lisa, except for one of the dwarfs coming an hour later with the interrogation materials that I requested: a carton of cigarettes, a bottle of whiskey, two bottles of water (one sparkling and one still), and the Mona Lisa's grocery cart. This dwarf was named Biggie, for he was the tallest of the seven, which was not saying much. Do you know how far I had to go to get you a bottle of whiskey? he said. What's a professional doing with a bottle of whiskey, anyway?

You don't know anything about the work of professionals, I said, waving him away.

Assured of no further interruptions except from my ghosts, I turned to two of my favorite leisure activities, drinking (#3) and reading (#2). Since seeing the eschatological muscle with his copy of *Candide*, I had picked up a pocket version of my own. I had read it at the lycée and enjoyed its human comedy greatly back then and even more so now. My sponge of a professor had actually dripped some lukewarm wisdom on my brow, for what he had once proclaimed to

our class was true, that books meant something different when we returned to them later, leavened by life. Take this mordant passage, for example, which left me both cringing and chuckling:

> "I should like to know which is worse: to be ravished a hundred times by Negro pirates, and have a buttock cut off, and run the gauntlet of the Bulgarians, and be flogged and hanged in an auto-da-fé, and be dissected, and have to row in a galley—in short, to undergo all the miseries we have each of us suffered—or simply to sit here and do nothing?"
>
> "That," said Candide, "is a big question."

Big indeed! And even bigger than Voltaire's question—but not as big as, presumably, the inexhaustible Negro pirates in his imagination—was the problem I sometimes had in hating the French. They were colonizing bastards, but they had given us words like this, even if these words might not be intended for a colonized bastard like me, only half French and half Vietnamese, a simple math problem that added up to inhuman, all too inhuman.

The Mona Lisa groaned. He was at last conscious, if groggy, lying on the floor, shaking his head and drooling a little, a patient awakening from being etherized on a table. I hauled him to a corner and propped him up. He huddled there, slivers of white eyeballs moving behind his eyelids.

How about a drink? This question, when addressed to me, always made me a little more cheerful. I sat on the cold floor next to him and poured a glass of whiskey. How about two?

I don't drink, he muttered.

Men who did not drink always shocked me a little, but I tried not to be judgmental, even if he was missing out on one of humanity's greatest inventions. I offered him water instead, and this time

he agreed. I held his hand steady as he lifted the glass, and when I offered him a cigarette, he did not refuse. The water and the smoke restored him a little, and his eyelids opened a little wider.

Happy now? he muttered. You got me.

I haven't been happy for a long time. You see, I'm a man with two minds—

Shut up.

—and I know how you feel right now. It's my one talent—

Shut up.

—and I have literally been where you are, in case you've forgotten. But what you did to me was not the first time those things have been done to me. And I have done many things to many people, so I know what it feels like to be the one having fun.

Shut up.

Right now there are two of you. One is sitting here telling me to shut up. The other is somewhere up on the ceiling, watching our little play. You have to crack the egg to separate the white from the yolk, and you have been cracked. I am talking to the yolk. The white part of you is up there, a transparent ectoplasm, a substance with the slipperiness of semen—

Shut up.

You may not understand me, but you also do understand me. Don't you?

Why don't you just get it over and done with? he muttered.

Behind him my quintet of ghosts hummed, *Get it over with,* but I ignored them and him. I said, I'm not going to do to you what you did to me. As I spoke, I gazed at the Mona Lisa the same way, I am sure, the *Mona Lisa* in the Louvre looked at the world, with intense sympathy for the millions who thronged to see her. If I looked at someone long enough, if I listened to him long enough, I could slip his face onto one of mine and observe the world through his eyes.

The goal, when I was a spy, was to reap information, which cadres above me used to undermine the cause of my subject. When I was an interrogator, questioning prisoners who did know that I was secretly on their side, my purpose differed. If I could get my subject to speak, perhaps I could save him from the torturers. If I could get my subject to stop resisting, then I could save him from himself.

Are you just going to sit there looking at me? he muttered. Say something.

Instead I silently offered him more water and cigarettes, two of the building blocks of life. We drank a little water and we smoked a lot, which is the right proportion, before he said, You think you're so smart, don't you? Like some kind of Tintin? A do-gooder? Well, I don't give a fuck about Tintin. He was just another colonizer.

Had he just insulted Tintin, boy reporter, amateur detective, intrepid hero? As a fan ever since I was a lycéen, I was offended. But I contained my offense and spoke of the more serious issue: I am not a colonizer! I am colonized, just like you.

Were you for the French or against the French?

The Boss believed that I was for the French, so, caught as always in the devices of my own making, I said, For the French.

He laughed again. Of course. Your father was a Frenchman.

I hate my father, I said, and it felt good to say this one true sentence, as clean as a bone.

The Mona Lisa studied me the way a student examines a calculus textbook, with great reluctance and some distaste. You should never hate your father, he said at last. Even if he is an asshole. We come from the wombs of our mothers and the assholes of our fathers.

He had started to talk, which is what every real interrogator who is not simply a torturer wants from his subject. Hungry? I said.

His hunger won out over his pride, and he nodded. Digging into his grocery cart, I uncovered clues to his existence: Orangina, a jar of

Nutella, paper napkins, grated carrots, a carton of eggs, and a bag of factory-made croissants, which struck me as sad or criminal or both in this land. There were also soft, aging bananas, and I peeled one and handed it to him. But his hands, having been stomped on by the Ronin and Le Cao Boi, could not grasp the banana, so I held it for him. He ate slowly. One bite, two bites, then on the third, and with the banana half gone, a half-digested memory rose from my bottomless depths, one that I had not chewed on in years, perhaps decades, of my mother feeding me a banana for breakfast as I read, sitting on a stool with a book on my lap while the banana hovered by my cheek, held by her hand. My mother, who could not read except very slowly and out loud—this mother never once doubted that I should learn to read and to read all the time. You were born to read, she told me more than once. And so I read, and read, and read, and up until now, I had not admitted to myself what my mother had told me the one time I asked where those books came from—my father's personal library.

Finished with the creamy white flesh, the Mona Lisa leaned back, leaving me with the banana's leopard hide, yellow and spotted with black dots. I flung the slippery hide into a far corner, where I would make Biggie clean it up later. Do they grow bananas in Algeria? I asked. Keep the subject talking, make him feel comfortable, conversation being the best and most enduring form of seduction.

The Mona Lisa grunted and said, I don't know. I've only been to Algeria a couple of times, when I was young and my parents thought I should know something about it.

Having been born there, I said.

I wasn't born there! I was born here. I'm French . . . officially.

And unofficially?

In Algeria, they call me French. But here, sometimes people say I'm Algerian. Sometimes they say I'm Arab. When I'm really lucky, I'm a dirty Arab.

Hello, you dirty Arab. I'm the Crazy Bastard.

He smiled with benevolence. Actually, you're Le Chinois.

Oh, yeah? You're— I stopped. I was ashamed of not having known any Algerians or Arabs or Muslims or North Africans before coming to Paris. I'm sorry, I said with utter sincerity. But I don't know any racial slurs for you.

None? That's a first. Okay . . . try *bougnoule*.

What?

Come on. *Bougnoule!* Don't be shy.

*Bougnoule!*

Perfect!

A glow of success lit my insides, a warmth as comforting as that induced by a highly refined whiskey, vodka, brandy, or cognac. My French was getting better!

Now say *sale bougnoule*, but with more force. Put a little spit in it.

*Sale bougnoule!*

Even better! You sound just like a Frenchman. Or Frenchwoman. Or even a French child. Just don't ever call me an *arabe de service*. I'll kill you.

The Mona Lisa trembled with laughter, and a wave of tenderness for him washed over the cold sands of my heart. Have some of this, I said, plucking a dose of the remedy from my pocket. How the hell did it get there? Hadn't I flushed it all away? How did it just keep magically reappearing in my pockets? A small, plastic-wrapped white musket ball of powder. You'll feel better, I said. Or you'll feel nothing, which, in your situation, is the same thing.

He stared at the white powder for a while, hesitating, before he finally nodded. The remedy was as versatile as a character actor. It could be rubbed onto the skin or the gums, fired into the veins, or vacuumed through the nose. I poured four white stripes of the powder onto a box of crackers from his cart. Then I rolled a tube

from a ten-franc note and held it for him so he could inhale the first line. Then the second. Wow, I said. Then the third. When he snorted the fourth, I said, You're a natural.

What? He looked up, sniffing. You want some?

For a guy who doesn't drink, you sucked that right up.

What do the Americans say? Oh, yes. It's good shit. I can barely feel a thing.

My stash of the remedy exhausted, I settled for a hashish cigarette, of which the Mona Lisa also partook. How did a nice boy like you end up doing this? I said through the smoke commingling from our lungs, a question that made him laugh again.

Ask my brother, he said. The one whose place you stole.

It's not like he left a note saying he owned his network.

True. Saïd's crazy, just like you. Or just crazy in his own way.

So where is he? In an asylum?

Afghanistan. Afghanistan! I hadn't even heard of it before he decided to go. He got it in his head that he wanted to fight the Soviets. What does that have to do with us? Who cares about communism? You know what he said? It's not about communism. It's about Islam. The Soviets are killing our brothers. Brothers? I said. Fellow Muslims, he said. This is why he's crazy. He didn't care about Islam when we were growing up. He didn't care about Islam even three years ago. He was just like me and you, stealing things, selling drugs. Having fun! The least he could do was give me his network, but you know what he said? I don't want to encourage you.

How did you feel about that? I said.

I wanted to punch him in the face.

As someone whom many people wanted to punch in the face, or in both faces, I could sympathize with Saïd. Oh, that damned emotion again! Crazy Saïd. But what else should we call someone unfortunate enough as to believe in God? Or was it Allah? Or

Muhammad? I knew as much about Islam as I did about Arabs. But Islam was a religion like Catholicism was a religion, and all religions were built on quicksand. They needed people who needed to believe in something. I was one of those people, until I was forced to believe in nothing, which, come to think of it, is also what religion is about.

Maybe you should forgive him, I said.

Forgive him?

Just like I forgive you, I said, my intonation priestly.

*You* forgive *me*? He twitched. For what?

I, who was not easily shocked, was shocked. Torturing me, I said, sputtering. Forcing me to play Russian roulette! Did you forget?

He laughed and laughed. If laughter was the best medicine, then I must be a pretty good proctologist. You should have seen your face, he said. Hilarious! Then he stopped laughing and said, I don't need your forgiveness.

You don't need to ask for forgiveness for me to forgive you, I said.

I don't want your forgiveness! he shouted. Fuck you and your forgiveness!

You don't have to want my forgiveness. I am just giving it to you.

The Mona Lisa appeared confused, as did my ghosts, who were standing behind him. They expected an act of medieval revenge, which was actually not so medieval, given how often our oh-so-civilized colonizers had carried out centuries-old policies of punishment and torture on us until, I don't know, a few years ago, just as we self-righteously gutted our enemies while beating our breasts with patriotic pride. But if I had surprised the Mona Lisa and my ghosts, I had also surprised myself, which is always either the best or the worst kind of surprise. I had not intended to forgive him,

even if I had not been sure what I would do. I had just wanted to see him, man-to-man, face-to-face, crotch-to-crotch, to find out. The reason I can forgive you, I said, my voice soaring on the winds of my own self-importance, is because what you did to me, I have done to others. I am no better than you and possibly far, far worse.

I'm not sorry, the Mona Lisa said. Hell, I'd do it again, you bastard.

And I would forgive you again, I said.

At one time, which is to say for most of my life, I would have threatened eye-gouging and kneecapping on anyone who called me a bastard. Like God, who should not be called by His name, I should not be called "bastard." Every time I was called bastard, my face flushed, my heartrate accelerated, my fists clenched, my throat constricted, and the lymph nodes of rage flooded my bloodstream. But I was not upset at this moment. What had happened? I could see me from his point of view. Inhabiting his heart as well as his brain, being the sympathizer par excellence, I knew he spoke my true name, the serial number of my being engraved in every structure of my cell by whatever hand had made me. And yet he was a bastard, too, at least in the moral sense. We sat just a few feet from each other, with me recognizing our common humanity, or, perhaps more likely, inhumanity. And what was the difference? To say that we were all human was merely sentimental, but to say that we were all inhuman was truth. In what era have we humans never been bastards?

You're a strange bastard, he muttered.

I have to be if I want to forgive the unforgivable.

The Mona Lisa looked confused. That's impossible.

Revolutions are always about making the impossible possible, I said. And I am a revolutionary who has found his revolution.

You're an idiot who's crazy.

That could also be true.

# Part Four

*Vous*

# CHAPTER 16

You know what you know.
   You know what you do *not* know.
      But what do you *not* know that you *do not* know?
         And what do you *already* know that you *refuse* to know?

These were the principles and questions that Claude, the master, drilled into me, his willing apprentice, for months and years while I was a secret policeman for the Special Branch, stepchild of the Central Intelligence Agency, fostered in accordance with the most advanced, state-of-the-art policing methods of the United States of America, delivered to my country with many strings attached by the unlikely crew cut technocrats of the obscure Michigan State University. We did not know at the time that Michigan State University was the second-best university of a mid-tier state. The only American universities we might have heard of were Harvard and maybe Yale or Stanford, so we chalked up not having heard of Michigan State University to our ignorance. Before coming to the United States as a foreign student, the only thing I even knew about Michigan was that it was a favorite place to spend summers for the young Ernest

Hemingway, who, Claude said, would surely have gone to Vietnam during the war years to test his manhood and his writing skills, if he had not already given himself the final test with a shotgun.

Only a real goddamn man can die that way, Claude said when he gifted me a copy of *Men without Women* on my twenty-fifth birthday, my first birthday present ever, unless you count my birth, which was and always would be the greatest birthday gift ever, given to me by the only person who could give it, my mother. Your first birthday present ever? Claude said, astonished. I told him that I had never even had a birthday party, at least one I could remember, since my people—the Vietnamese ones, not the French—did not celebrate birthdays except for the first and the eightieth. Turning one was significant, given high child mortality rates, and attaining eighty was also a landmark, given the many colorful ways of dying in a poor, rural, chaotic, and unjust (but still beautiful) land like mine.

Live and let live, said Claude, giving me the present, wrapped in newspaper. This is my favorite Hemingway, he went on as I took a seat in his slightly sweltering apartment in the Eden, the CIA's Saigon residence of choice. Hemingway was called the greatest writer of the greatest country of the greatest century in human history, Claude said. Ergo the greatest writer of all.

He poured me two fingers of Jack Daniel's and I was grateful that his fingers were substantially thicker than mine.

Lesser men would just use a pistol with a short barrel, Claude said, raising his glass with the reverence of my father raising his chalice before his congregation. But Papa Hemingway chose a shotgun. *Blam!*

May we all be so brave in the end, Claude later told all of his students, of whom only I had even heard of Hemingway, and that was only because I had read *The Sun Also Rises* in Professor Hammer's class on the Jazz Age and the Lost Generation at Occidental

College. I wonder, Claude mused before our befuddled class, if Papa Hemingway knew himself. Truly knew himself. Because your job as interrogators is to know yourself so that you can persuade your subjects to know themselves. I'm speaking of true interrogators, boys. Not torturers. *You're not torturers.* Anybody can be a torturer, even though that is also a kind of art, the way pornography can be a kind of art.

Claude's use of literary criticism to illustrate interrogation techniques sometimes confused my fellow students, but he came from a rarefied line of red-blooded Americans who were both patriotic and patrician. Like me, he had gone to a boarding school, the super-elite Phillips Exeter Academy of New England. Here he read the classics, rowed crew, and prepped to become a shock trooper of American exceptionalism, which is how Americans delicately refer to "American imperialism," a phrase that one must never say to Americans, who sincerely believe, as all imperialists do, that they have taken over the world for its own good, as if imperialism were a kind of penicillin (for the natives), with power, profit, and pleasure merely being surprising side effects (for the doctors). Like me, Claude believed in the virtues of art and literature, and did not find it at all contradictory that a person of cultural refinement could also be a warrior. Like the Greeks, he said. The body and what you do with it is an art, too.

So I practiced the art I learned from Claude on the Mona Lisa's body—and mind—in the warehouse for the next two weeks, as did Bon, the Ronin, and Le Cao Boi, and it gradually became clear that for the Ronin and Le Cao Boi, this interrogation was art for art's sake. Bon regarded interrogation as exercise, something that may or may not be pleasant but that must be done efficiently and relatively quickly. But the Ronin and Le Cao Boi were not efficient, sauntering in once every day or two to enjoy themselves, in no rush to get to

their goal of finding out where the rest of the Mona Lisa's comrades were hiding so the Boss could liquidate his competition. As for the Boss, he visited just once to inspect the progress. He examined the Mona Lisa's huddled, naked, bruised body, which appeared to satisfy him, but he was not impressed by the information that I had extracted and recorded into a notebook, such as the hometown of the Mona Lisa's parents (Sour El-Ghozlane), his academic performance (mediocre), his preferred hobby (building model airplanes), his favorite food (doner kebabs), the fate of one of his uncles (heaved into the Seine by gendarmes along with a few dozen other Algerians, since pigs are pigs no matter their nationality), his political views (somewhere between apathy and anarchism), or his motivations for becoming a gangster. Like me, he had father issues. But I don't hate my father, the Mona Lisa said. If he beat me and my brothers, it was only because the French beat him first. Or maybe not only. Maybe he really is just an asshole and the French only made it worse. Who knows? One of my other uncles fought against the French in Algeria. The paratroopers took him away and my father—he was just a teenager then—had to go pick up what was left of his brother for burial. That will fuck you up. Then you fuck up your children and your children will fuck up their children and so on.

If you're so aware of being fucked up, I said, you could try to stop.

Try? I tried. I didn't do so bad in school. I knew how to put on a tie and go for a job interview. I can speak fluent French. I was born here. But I could hear how their voices over the phone changed or see the look on their faces when they said my name, if I got that far. Moussa. That's not a French name, they would say, like they gave me the interview just to tell me that to my face. All I had to do was change my name. I'll admit, I tried on some different names. Gaspard. Maxime. Charles. They didn't fit. Didn't feel right. And I

thought, *I went to your schools, which are my schools. I learned your language, which is my language. I don't feel Arab at all, except when people call me an Arab. And that's not enough? Now I have to change my name, which my parents gave me?* And I knew this would not be the end. They would never stop. They wouldn't be happy until I married a woman who looked like them, gave them children who looked more like them than like me, made friends only with them. They wanted my soul. I wasn't going to give it to them. Either I could be one hundred percent French or I could be just a dirty Arab, so instead I decided to be one hundred percent gangster.

I recorded this dialogue in the notebook, which the Boss skimmed before hurling it into my chest. Why am I paying you for this shit? His favorite television shows and musicians? His ideal woman? What he wants to do with his life? Are you writing his biography? *Who gives a fuck?*

He paused, glowering at me, and I submissively lowered my eyes as we both waited for the appropriate silence to pass in response to his rhetorical question.

Get this done by next Saturday, the Boss finally said. *Fantasia* is that evening and there will be a very special party the night before for BFD and many other VIPs. He enjoyed his visit to Heaven. A lot. He's already been back a couple of times. If he liked Heaven—

He's going to love what we've lined up for him, the Ronin said with a laugh.

What's lined up? I asked.

You'll see. You're part of the show. We need everyone we can get. Be there at six. Show starts at nine, the Boss said. He gave me an address on the deluxe avenue Hoche, not far from where one of my clients lived, a loquacious lawyer specializing in mergers and acquisitions. As for this guy, if you can't finish this job, then I'll finish it, said the Boss, kicking the Mona Lisa in the ribs. The Mona Lisa

screamed theatrically, knowing that if he did not make it look good, the Boss would kick him again, and harder. Then the Boss left with Bon, who said, by way of farewell, When are you coming over for dinner with Loan? I made an excuse, about how this interrogation of the Mona Lisa was taking up all my time, when the truth was that seeing Bon with another woman made me uncomfortable.

Maybe even jealous? my ghosts asked with a collective snicker.

Shut up, I said.

I didn't say anything, the Mona Lisa mumbled from the floor.

I was alone again in the cell with him, while outside in the warehouse two dwarfs guarded the coffee, which, unlike the hashish, did not whisper. It did not need to speak at all. The truly powerful let others speak for them.

What was your boss talking about? the Mona Lisa mumbled from the floor.

You have a week left, I said, which meant I also had a week left before Bon faced Man, if Man attended *Fantasia*, which he would, because *Fantasia* was oxygen for our people. Everyone needed oxygen, no matter his or her age, occupation, or belief. For one night we would put aside our differences, pro- or anticommunism, and unify in our deep love of song, dance, and lowbrow comedy, the lower the better. On the one hand, I could not wait to see Lana. On the other hand, I wanted to indefinitely postpone seeing Bon's gun in his hand, pointed at the faceless man haunting his dreams. Meanwhile I did not know how to extricate myself from this situation with the Mona Lisa, who had resisted all my entreaties and persuasions. Perhaps I had not exhausted all the tricks that Claude taught me and those I had invented on my own. Or perhaps I was tired of knowing and did not want to break the Mona Lisa because I did not want to know what he knew. Or perhaps I already knew the most important thing the Mona Lisa knew, this man who had

said, more than once, sometimes with resignation and sometimes with defiance, I'd rather die.

I knew that I had lived in Paris for too long and had become too assimilated when I arrived at the address on avenue Hoche at exactly six in the evening on Friday night. Punctuality is not a trait of my fun-loving people, who have a more flexible notion of time than the French. For my people, the elegant edifice that confronted me could be an hour from the Mona Lisa's apartment or three hours, depending on their mood. The marble-clad lobby with its brass-accented double doors, mirrored walls, and crystal chandelier suggested that any one of this property's inhabitants was likely worth more than the Mona Lisa's dwelling and all its tenants combined. I saw myself in the floor-to-ceiling mirror, and my reflection reminded me that I was now thirty-seven years old by the Western method. By Vietnamese custom, I was thirty-eight, taking into account my nine-month lease of my mother's womb. And why not take those months into account? I had been warm and fed in the best kind of sensory deprivation tank in the world, versus the worst kind, the aquaria depriving prisoners of all light, sound, and sensation, reducing them to quivering masses of jelly, which Man had made for me in the reeducation camp after having read the CIA handbook on interrogation. I looked vaguely yellow in the mirrored wall, dressed like what I was, a waiter from a cheap restaurant, in uninspiring black slacks and a white long-sleeved shirt that was no longer quite white. The most glamorous parts of me were my Bruno Magli shoes and my hair, slicked back in the manner of the 1930s or 1940s, when every man's hair was glossy and short, rather than long and unkempt in today's tasteless fashion. But besides the hair, which remained black, the rest of me was tired and old, the booster rocket of my youth long ago jettisoned on my way

to the orbit of middle age. I had most likely lived half my life, which wasn't too bad, given the endless gallons of whiskey I had loved, the countless cigarettes I had adored, and the dozens of women I had hopefully amused.

I was elevated to the fourth floor of this six-floor building, which did not seem like such an impressive location until I later realized the apartment had three floors. When the elevator doors opened, I emerged onto a hexagonal landing layered in a thick bright red carpet into which my soles sank. The handrails were a polished dark wood, which I suspected was extracted without anesthesia from a denuded colony. Nothing creaked or exuded mustiness, the charming condition of almost every other Parisian building I had visited. I stabbed the doorbell and a bell cried on the other side. The eschatological muscle opened the door, wearing only a white loincloth wrapped around his hips, an iron collar around his neck, and three Band-Aids: the old ones on his cheek and his temple, a new one at a diagonal on his left breast, three pale landing strips floating on his black skin.

What are you doing here?

Don't ask, he muttered.

What are you wearing, for God's sake?

Don't ask, he muttered again.

Not only was he nearly naked, he gleamed with the luster of a brand-new car, his oiled body shining under the light. From beyond the foyer rose a murmur of voices, the rattling of plates, and the clinking of glasses.

Your costume is in the servants' quarters, the eschatological muscle said, all the way at the top. When I started to step into the foyer, he shook his head and pointed. Behind you. Go up the back stairs.

Behind me, the main, wide stairs coiled around the glass-walled elevator shaft. On the other side of the shaft, a door led to another

set of stairs, narrower and darker. I looked at the stairs, looked at him, and said, So is this the war of maneuver or the war of position we find ourselves in?

He grimaced and closed the door in my face. Up I went to the fifth and sixth floors and then one final set of stairs to the very top, the garrets, guarded by one of the seven dwarfs—the one named Lousy, for reasons I never wanted to ask about. He was dressed in a turban, a red brocade vest over his bare chest, voluptuous white silken pants that bloomed around his knees and ankles, and purple embroidered slippers with curling toes. Don't you fucking ask, he muttered, opening the door and gesturing me inside. And you better forget what you just saw.

These rooms might be garrets, but unlike the apartment I had shared with Bon the paint was not peeling, the parquet floors were not dull, and the windows were not cracked. The first room revealed a rack of costumes and the Ronin standing in front of a mirror, tying a black tie. He nodded at the outfits.

Tonight you're in charge of giving out the goods, he said. You get to dress up in real Vietnamese garb.

The Ronin wore colonial casual: white linen suit, white linen shirt, and brown oxfords. My Vietnamese garb was a brown ao dai and black silk pants, topped by a black fedora, the duds of a Cholon gangster of the 1920s, a raffish look I actually liked.

It's going to be quite a show, baby, the Ronin said, winking and heading toward the next set of rooms. Come on.

Inside the rooms I counted thirteen girls, each 90 percent naked and 100 percent blasé, grooming themselves under the supervision of the expressionist mistress, who wore a shiny, formfitting pantsuit woven from some type of silver space suit fabric. Three black girls, three more who I was fairly sure were Arab or North African, and three girls whose whiteness was so white that they

literally looked white: a blonde, a brunette, and a redhead. The four others I already knew—Morning Peony, Beautiful Lotus, Crème Brûlée, and Madeleine. The girls glanced up when the Ronin and I walked in, then resumed transforming themselves from naturally attractive girls to female incendiary devices. Chatter and the roar of hair dryers filled the air. Crème Brûlée curled her lip at me but Madeleine winked. I was not at all surprised when my heart beat stronger and my breathing quickened at the sight of all the flawless, gleaming, mostly hairless flesh and the bare, buoyant breasts, the only nod to modesty being lace panties as insubstantial and alluring as television ads. What did surprise me was the roiling uneasiness in my gut, a diarrheic churning of disgust that spoiled all pleasure.

I know, whispered the Ronin, as if he could read at least one of my minds. *I know.*

By the time the first of the guests arrived, I was in costume. Along with the eschatological muscle, I greeted the guests at the vestibule, on the first level of the triplex apartment. Potted palms lined the room, an Oriental rug lay on the floor, resigned to be trod on by shoes—which would never happen in the actual Orient—and on the wall hung a Chinese painting, a landscape of mountains and mist with one tiny human being climbing a mountain trail, dwarfed by the majestic country around him and by the poem of Chinese characters that I could not read because the Chinese had not colonized my people quite well enough. Further ambiance was created by the slivers of incense burning in every room, as well as by the jazz quartet in the corner of the parlor. A drummer, a bass cellist, an alto saxophonist, a pianist, all in snazzy, shiny suits, a couple with porkpie hats, possessors of American passports and inheritors of the hippest, most authentic jazz pedigree: Chicago, New Orleans,

Harlem, Washington, DC. I had chatted with them before the guests
came and blew them away with my American English and my grasp
of the American idiom and culture, including jazz, a passion of my
mentor Professor Hammer, who had a predilection for the West
Coast style and bebop. Hence I could name-drop—Charlie Parker,
Thelonious Monk, Dizzy Gillespie, Ella Fitzgerald, Billie Holiday,
and more. The quartet's members had nodded at these fabled names.
Like me, they were refugees, in their case fleeing from the flabby
belly of uncouth white American racism, straight into the bosom
of self-satisfied, self-congratulatory Parisian racism. When I tried
my French on them, the quartet's leader had shaken his head and
whispered, No, man, we can't speak French. I mean, we *can* speak
French, but we don't speak it *here*. Or when we do, we got to speak it
badly, like *Americans*, get me? If we speak good French, they'll think
we're *Africans*. They treat us great when they think we're *Americans*,
but when they think we're *Africans*—

They treat us like *shit*, the other three said.

The quartet was playing Dexter Gordon when the guests began
arriving, all in a good mood, and why not? A genuine black Ameri-
can band was playing jazz, America's greatest cultural contribution
to the world, if by culture we mean something worthy of the greats,
rather than the other notable American cultural contributions of the
twentieth century that transformed the world: rock 'n' roll, fast food,
the airplane, and the atomic bomb. What else made these guests
happy? Why not a sullen, threatening, nearly naked African open-
ing the door, caught and transported from the heart of darkness,
and an Indochinese drug dealer taking their coats? Our Afro-Asian
duo of manservants offered just the right amount of danger and
excitement, handcuffed by servility and enlivened by mystery. No
wonder Bon declined this job, as the Ronin told me. Not to men-
tion the spectacle of the nearly naked girls, which would offend his

devout Catholicism. I would see him tomorrow night at *Fantasia*, and there I planned to agree, at last, to Loan's dinner invitation. I would help him move forward, to acknowledge that he could mourn his dead wife and son and yet also find new love. But tonight, I wanted to regress. As instructed by the Ronin, I bowed and spoke slightly broken French, good enough to be understood and bad enough to be disdained as I figuratively kissed the guests' asses, a gesture as important for someone like me as the French habit of kissing cheeks. The guests acknowledged my presence only by loading me with coats of the finest quality, befitting men who appeared quite wealthy and quite white, even in their hair. The darkest any of them got was to have brown hair, and there were only a few of those middle-aged types. One was clad in an unimaginative black tuxedo and bow tie, an outfit that promised sexual interaction no more exciting than what a missionary would offer. Another was dressed nostalgically, in a white linen suit like the Ronin's, but with the swank addition of a pith helmet. Potentially more exciting, or terrifying, was the man wearing a monocle and a purple velvet smoking jacket whose aura of cigar smoke masked any potential body odor. Then there was the big game hunter in a safari outfit, equipped with a hunting rifle with a scope and an invisible callus on his soul. Two more guests wore military uniforms that were overly tight on their aging, expanding bodies, one with general's stars and the other sporting the khakis and white kepi hat of the Foreign Legion. A couple had me very concerned with their varieties of Oriental robes and turbans with some kind of Middle Eastern or North African origin. One of them even had his face blackened with what appeared to be shoe polish, so that the whites of his eyes and the red of his lips were even more pronounced. I'm Aladdin, he said proudly to whoever inquired and also to those who did not inquire, me among them. This turbaned Aladdin grinned broadly when he introduced himself, waving his

blackened hands and wriggling his blackened fingers, and his white fingernails and white teeth shone even more brightly against the blackness of his skin, although given that he was supposed to be Arab—was Aladdin an Arab? suddenly I was unsure, but he certainly was an Oriental of some kind—perhaps his skin should be called brown, although Aladdin had used a black shoe polish and not a brown one, but since we were in the realm of fantasy, what did it matter whether this mystical rascal was black or brown, or what black or brown really was when discussing varieties of skin tone versus the actualities of shoe polish? The other one who really startled me was the oddball in a priest's black robes, the skirts down to the ankle, the collar bone white, the head adorned with a little skullcap, and the shoulders under a drape. The crucifix around his neck swung subtly and almost hypnotized me, as did his bottomless gray eyes. I mumbled something inarticulate—was it "Father"?—and when the priest carved the sign of the cross in the air above me, I sensed that he was not actually wearing a costume at all but was, in fact, a priest. Ten gentlemen altogether, the tenth being BFD, who smirked and pretended to accidentally drop his coat on the floor. He was attired like an asshole, which is to say that he wore the long black tails, gray slacks, and top hat of an English gentleman or a nineteenth-century European nobleman, their refined manners and exquisite fashions suiting them perfectly for overseeing genocidal empires that looted nonwhite countries, enslaving and/or massacring their inhabitants, and sanctifying the results with the name "civilization." If the word of a bastard is not persuasive, then perhaps the word of Sartre, writing on Fanon, is: "With us, to be a man is to be an accomplice of colonialism, since all of us without exception have profited by colonial exploitation." Or to put it in my own words: Whitewashing the blood-soaked profits of colonization was the only kind of laundering white men did with their own hands.

BFD leaned close as I rose from my ass-kissing position of picking up his garment and said—just loud enough for me and the eschatological muscle to hear—Fuck you.

Thank you, I said, perhaps the only thing that would shut him up—not what I intended, although it was a pleasant side effect to see him frown, grunt, and walk away without so much as a you're welcome. Perhaps he thought I was being sarcastic, but I was very, very sincere. I was grateful for BFD's honesty in saying out loud what colonizers always think about the colonized, at least when they come face-to-face with them. Under all the pomp and circumstance and rhetoric of *la mission civilisatrice*, the reality was that they hated us at worst and thought us inferior at best, with our only hopes for equality being to transform ourselves into imitations of them. I imitated BFD's walk as I followed him into the parlor where the gentlemen were mingling, served by three of the dwarfs, who trafficked back and forth from the kitchen with trays of manly drinks and ornate hors d'oeuvres that resembled miniature still lifes. These three wore the same ludicrous Oriental outfit as Lousy, except that now I noticed how each of them also had a curved knife tucked into the yellow sash around his waist, and I suspected that it was not just for decoration. Biggie, Angry, and Smelly would carry only real knives.

Our jovial people had a penchant for colorful and accurate nicknames, including calling me the Bastard or, even better, the Crazy Bastard. But who was crazier, me or the unknown owner of this fabulous apartment, a person of most peculiar taste who had hung, above his fireplace, a painting of a Japanese woman of a more classical time, naked and being ravished by . . . an octopus? The woman's eyes were squeezed shut and her head was flung back as the octopus probed her with his tentacles. Or was it her tentacles? The gender-ambiguous octopus's bulbous eyes peered from between the woman's legs, its head in a pose I remembered all too well.

Hokusai, the Ronin murmured, pausing in his social circuit.

I had already smoked quite a bit of hashish, and the colors of the painting and the rise and fall of the jazz stuck to my body and mind, now as sticky as the suckers on the octopus's tentacles.

Those Japanese are weird fuckers, aren't they? the Ronin mused. That's why I love them!

He moved on, assuming that I was trembling because of the perverse painting, when I was really trembling because my second-most erogenous zone, my memory, had been turned on by the recall of that unforgettable one-night stand with that most unlikely of partners, the gutted, defenseless, anonymous squid my mother saved for dinner.

I did my job of ferrying a teak tray with the goods: tobacco cigarettes, hashish cigarettes, and the remedy, its formless white body, as necessary as sugar, resting in a golden bowl. I offered a tiny porcelain spoon to any gentleman who wished to partake, and no one declined. The dwarfs came and went, and the Champagne flowed, and the quartet was hot, hot, hot, and the fusillades of French were fired too fast for me to fully comprehend. At last the Ronin stepped toward the fireplace, stood under the Hokusai painting, and called for attention. The quartet ceased playing, the dwarfs retreated to the alcoves, and everyone turned toward the Ronin.

Gentlemen, welcome! he called. Thank you for honoring us with your presence at this most delightful of parties. You are adventurers, gentlemen, as am I, a Frenchman born on Indochinese soil, as some of you have been born elsewhere—Algeria, Morocco, New Caledonia. We are united here in our love of the foreign and our taste for the exotic. Gentlemen, that taste will be stimulated and satiated in this one night of one thousand and one nights! Now let me introduce to you some of the most stunning girls in Paris, who have come here from the four corners of the world!

With a wave, the Ronin signaled the quartet to resume playing. In the corner of the parlor was a spiral staircase, and one by one, the girls descended. They were clothed now—some of them— and the gathered men murmured, mixing their appreciation with chortles, laughs, and jokes that I mostly did not understand. With each passing second, the sands of dread accumulated in my stomach, pouring down the hourglass of my body from my mind. For the second time in my life—the first time being the horror inflicted on the communist agent—I did not want to look. Not at Morning Peony wearing a floral skirt wrapped around her waist but nothing above it except for the lily tucked over her ear, inspired by Paul Gauguin's Tahiti, according to the Ronin (even if Morning Peony was Chinese Singaporean). Not at the white girl who appeared to be in her late teens, wearing a lace choker and a tattered white frock, hands bound with rope, introduced by the Ronin as a white slave rescued from barbaric slave traders on the Barbary Coast. Not at a black girl completely naked except for bracelets and a necklace of white beads and shells. Not at another girl whose face I could not see at all because her black veil and hood revealed only her brown eyes, a modesty that clashed with her black minidress and fishnet stockings. The jazz was loud, but even louder was the hubbub from the assorted men, nudging each other and calling out lasciviously. But nothing was louder than the rataplan of my heartbeat in my ears, so loud it could be heard even through the heavy blanket of guilt and shame that smothered any desire.

Gentlemen, said the Ronin, here they come into our garden of delights, in the tradition of the legendary Le Chabanais, which some of your fathers or grandfathers may have visited. Here are some of the finest girls from the whorehouses, fleshpots, and slave markets of the greater Orient and Africa! From Algeria, Morocco, Tunisia, and Senegal to the south, and Egypt and Indochina to the east! With

side trips to dangerous Palestine and the seductive Pacific paradise of Tahiti! Yes, it's all a fantastic voyage, gentlemen, but fantasy is better than reality, which has syphilis. [*The gentlemen roared with laughter.*] Take a look, gentlemen. Have as many lovelies as you can satisfy, like a Turkish pasha. Girls who will die for you, girls who wish to be saved by you—unless you kill yourself first out of mad love for them! You will return to the origins of the world—no, not the Congo or the Nile, but here, and here, and here, between the voluptuous thighs of Princess Tam-Tam, in the Golden Triangle of the Dragon Lady, in the hothouse of this forbidden harem. Here you are the sultan, the despot, the colon, the white man exploring the dark continent with a whip in your hand. There are mysterious ladies to be conquered, from this passionate Viet Cong guerrilla in her black pajamas, fresh from the jungle, to this Palestinian freedom fighter just returned from hijacking a plane. All you can see is her face, but what a face! A real femme fatale! Or how about this cowering Muslim girl wearing the greatest sexual aid ever invented, a veil! Who knows what lurks behind it? Keep it on or take it off, as you wish, but know you are safe even if you choose . . . Madame Butterfly. Take a ride on her magic carpet and don't worry that in nine months she might return with an unwelcome surprise. Enjoy the forbidden love of the white man and the Oriental woman without fear that there might be forbidden fruit, like him!

And here the Ronin pointed straight at me. I could see the whites of their eyes when everyone turned to look at me, standing between the eschatological muscle and a potted palm tree, holding my tray with the sugar in the golden bowl, unable to move with the accumulating weight of sand in my belly.

If you have enjoyed opium, gentlemen, you will love the remedy that our bastard offspring of East and West has for you. Boy! The Ronin snapped his fingers. *Boy! BOY!*

Through the muddle of my mind, or minds, I realized he was speaking to ME.

What are you doing just standing there, boy? Take the remedy around to the gentlemen!

As I made my rounds among the so-called gentlemen, who smirked at me as they partook of the sugar in the golden bowl, the Ronin said, Now, gentlemen, we begin! Ready to bid for your first choice? [*The gentlemen cheered in assent.*] Let's bring this delightful doll up before you—step right here, on the pedestal, my dear— the Dragon Lady herself, an exquisite Annamite angel wearing the traditional ao dai that so many of us remember so fondly. But, in this case, without the pants. Annamite girls are not at all like our women, gentlemen, and frankly, that's a good thing. [*The gentlemen laughed uproariously.*] They are becoming too much like men. [*The gentlemen harrumphed in agreement.*] Fortunately, these temptresses have never heard of "feminism," and if they did, they certainly do not care for it. So, we have this seductress of the Mekong Delta, who tempts you not only with her body but with great peril—the peril of falling in love with her! Gentlemen, who will be the lucky man that will savor this delectable tropical dragon fruit first? Will she be your Annamite angel or your Dragon Lady?

The men started calling out their bids, and I despised them for their ignorance. Madeleine was not even an Annamite or a Viet-namese. Oh, Madeleine! She smiled and, at the Ronin's command, slowly pivoted on one high-heeled shoe and rotated on the side table so that all the men could see her from every angle in her red ao dai with the golden dragon flaming across its torso. Someone groaned, and it was me.

Do you see what I see, gentlemen? the Ronin cried. The beauty! The beauty!

When the beauty completed her rotation, I saw once more her smile and her eyes, neither of which moved a millimeter. The men hooted and hollered like members of British Parliament in a contentious session, calling out their bids until finally I was embarrassed to be a part of the same species as they were, or at least the same gender. At last the winner leaped up—the white-haired legionnaire in a tropical summer uniform, with the option of shorts instead of trousers. He offered Madeleine his hand and she stepped down, eyes to the ground, and when she looked up she saw me staring. She beckoned, and when I came up to her, she whispered, I'll take some of what you have. When I hesitated, she glared at me and hissed, What are you waiting for? Give it to me! It's the only way I'm going to get through this night.

So I gave her the remedy, but was there ever going to be enough of the remedy to be a cure, for her or for me? Sartre said that "the European has only been able to become a man through creating slaves and monsters," and if so, what were these girls? What was I? Perhaps I was not just a righteous bastard, enraged at being cast by the European in this dehumanizing manner. Perhaps I was also a rotten bastard who took comfort in these roles, since they gave me the chance to deny that I, too, had become a man in that most reliable of ways, through populating my imagination with my very own slaves and monsters.

When the auction concluded and the lights dimmed, I wandered past the couples and trios settled into the candle-lit couches, divans, pillows, chaises, and beds scattered throughout the parlor, the library, the billiards room, the several bedrooms, and the terrace with its view of the city lights and the dark shape of the

erection-inspired Eiffel Tower. Over the course of the evening, which ran until dawn, the men and the girls consumed enough of the remedy to kill an adult African elephant, or at least render one unconscious. I did my best to help, sniffing a white line here and there when no one was looking, which was often, as the men were focused on being perverts while the girls were dutifully being perverted. The only time any of the men said anything to me was when the sheikh paused long enough for a few sniffs of the remedy and gave me a ferocious grin and a slap on the arm. Amazing stuff, my boy! I tried not to be disturbed by the necklace of human ears around his neck, which on closer inspection were dried peaches. Absolutely amazing! A man can live and die like this! Bunga bunga!

And so the hours crept past, for there was nothing more boring than to watch other people have fun, if the girls could be said to be having fun. I considered myself a worldly man who had seen a wide range of human sexual behavior, but I had never seen anything like this. Then again, I was just a colonized provincial, not ready for this level of civilization, which would not have made the Marquis de Sade even blush. Finally, sometime near dawn, I found myself in the master bedroom of the third level, where the big game hunter was sitting in an armchair in his safari garb, the pale tuber of his erection sticking out from his unzipped pants, while he aimed his hunting rifle at the brunette and the redhead on the emperor-sized bed, peering through the scope.

That's it, girls! he shouted, his forehead damp with sweat. That's *hot*!

The room was indeed groin temperature. I was so exhausted and overheated I felt dizzy, the vertigo forcing me to sit down in the corner. Was the remedy causing my wooziness? Or was the remedy the cure? To decide, I inhaled another white line, then one more. But before I could divine whether the remedy caused or cured,

the big game hunter spotted me. Get up, boy! Get up! He swiv-eled and aimed his weapon at me, the crosshairs of his scope fixed between my eyes, and I tried to rise. But I couldn't get up any more than I could get it up, so what the hell . . . who gave a fuck . . . it's just the same old shit . . . I give up . . . I sucked up another dose of the remedy, closed my eyes, and waited, sobbing, for the big game hunter to pull his trigger.

# CHAPTER 17

After the sun finally rose, its light revealed that the Eastern and Western Hemispheres of my divided brains remained joined in my head. The big game hunter had not actually loaded his gun, which hadn't prevented him from giggling and squeezing the trigger a few times. What fun! The Boss laughed a great deal when he showed me this scene in his observation post, located in the locked garret where he had remained ensconced the entire night. The garret was crowded with monitors and videotape machines, connected by braids of wires that disappeared into the walls and were connected to cameras hidden throughout the fabulous apartment.

Where did you get all this? I asked.

My friend, the old Indochina hand, the Ronin said. A real pal ever since '54, when I handed him the Laos-to-Saigon opium route.

While I stood in the doorway, the Ronin had flopped onto the only other free seat besides the pair occupied by the Boss and his luscious secretary, who looked, as always, bored, not to mention hot, in the figurative sense. Like the sun, she bothered everyone except herself with her hotness.

Where's the coffee? the Boss said, without looking away from the monitors.

The luscious secretary unfolded her legs in slow motion. Beauty and youth are transitory—it's what's inside that matters—it's character that truly counts and defines a person—but those smooth, gleaming legs and everything they led to blew up my platitudes and caused the little bubble of my remaining testosterone to rise in the thermometer of my body until it reached the bulb of my head and my eyes swelled in their sockets. The Ronin and I watched her leave, and the Ronin sighed and said, Even after this night, I'm still ready for some of that. No offense, Boss.

The Boss merely grunted and continued fast-forwarding through the videotape. Take a look at this, he said finally, hitting play.

The scene reeled forth in black and white, the black-robed priest sitting on an armchair with one of the white slave girls. Brilliant! the Ronin said. He was high enough to skydive, propelled to that altitude by repeatedly refilling his tank with the remedy. She's confessing! I love this guy. Don't you love this guy? Tell me you love this guy.

What are you going to do with these tapes? I said. It was a semi-rhetorical question, because the answer was obvious, but I wanted the details.

The Boss, after sneering at my seeming lack of comprehension, said, What these guys paid to be here makes us a nice small profit, but what they will pay—eventually—to keep these tapes from leaking is where the real money is.

Ah, capitalism! the Ronin said, just as the luscious secretary returned with the coffee. As it dripped ever so slowly, the Ronin stripped the luscious secretary with his eyes. The greatest coffee in the world! he proclaimed. This is one way we Vietnamese have bettered the French.

It was remarkable how much easier it was for the Ronin to become Vietnamese than for me to become French. But I did not say this out loud. No one wanted to hear from me anyway, because everybody was watching the priest.

He's disgusting, the luscious secretary said. Why did you invite a priest? He's not going to have any money.

Just because he's a priest doesn't mean he doesn't have money, I said.

The luscious secretary looked at me the way the young glance at the old, the way the rich regard the poor, the way incredibly attractive females dismiss males no longer competitive in the sexual hunt. She killed me with that look, a mix of pity diluted by amusement and spiked with contempt, and while the best thing for me to do would have been just to die, my lips kept moving.

He could come from a wealthy family, but probably more useful is his store of secrets, I said, my well-trained fingers immediately finding the pulse of a plot. Can you imagine what a priest hears in his confessional, especially if he ministers to the elites?

The Crazy Bastard's right, the Boss said. This guy hears the confessions of the wealthy and powerful. I want to hear the confessions of the wealthy and powerful. And since I'm sure he doesn't want anyone seeing this, he's going to tell me what those confessions are.

On the monitor, the priest was committing a most unholy act with his rosary beads. I had never prayed the rosary, and never again would I see a rosary in the same way after witnessing the priest diabolically desecrate the beads.

I can't look, said the luscious secretary, turning her eyes away.

That's only because you're Catholic, the Ronin said with a leer.

It's because I'm a woman.

Shut up, the Boss said. He ejected the tape and passed it to the luscious secretary, who labeled it PRIEST WITH WHITE SLAVE

GIRL. The new videotape that the Boss put in featured BFD with Madeleine.

This guy's nonstop, said the Ronin.

Very impressive, the Boss agreed. I have some respect for him after watching him tonight.

Yeah, but his thing looks like . . . like . . . a *mushroom*, said the luscious secretary.

No one said a word, for what cannot be spoken of must be passed over in silence.

What is that? I asked, squinting.

Foie gras, said the Ronin.

Oh my God, the luscious secretary groaned. I'm going to vomit. What a creep.

The Boss chuckled. Aren't we all? he said, stirring his coffee. Looks like we have what we need. This tape we'll let age like fine wine. It'll be worth much, much more if BFD is as talented in politics as he thinks he is.

Mayor of Paris one day? the Ronin said. A cabinet minister?

Molotov! the Boss said, raising his glass.

Molotov? asked the Ronin.

Isn't that what the Jews say for congratulations?

Mazel tov, the luscious secretary said. You mean mazel tov.

The Boss shrugged. I like Molotov better.

I secured the videotapes in a suitcase and carried them to the trunk of the Boss's car, waiting outside with Le Cao Boi behind the wheel. He drove with me in the passenger seat and the Ronin and the Boss in the back, and we headed toward the warehouse under a midmorning sun because, as the Boss said, I want to finish this fucking business before *Fantasia* tonight. Le Cao Boi popped in a

cassette that the Ronin gave him, which was how I was introduced to the songs of Jacques Dutronc, who was much better than Johnny Hallyday, although some of his lines initially made me pause.

*Sept cent millions de chinois*
*Et moi, et moi, et moi*

What did the Chinese have to do with anything? Well, *c'est la vie*, as Dutronc sang at the end of each stanza, after counting Indonesians, blacks, and even Vietnamese. *C'est la vie*. So French! So charming! The only thing missing was a stanza to bastards, which was odd, given that Dutronc sang about Soviets and Martians and the imperfect and the starving, if I heard correctly. Surely there must be tens of millions of bastards the world over, an alien diaspora enormous enough to be its own motley nation. But did I even need a nation? I myself was nobody if not a nation, and if so, I needed no nation but my imagination.

The problem was that sometimes I had not used my imagination enough. The most shocking videotape of all made this clear, even though it depicted no carnal acts. It simply showed two of the girls alone, which would normally be hydrogen-bomb hot, except that these two were just . . . talking? I had turned up the volume to hear what the brunette and the redhead were saying, the first bit of dialogue on the videotapes not involving fornication, copulation, or just plain intercourse.

PALESTINIAN FREEDOM FIGHTER
That idiot dressed up as a sheikh—his
was shaped like a broken finger.
VIET CONG GUERRILLA
Oh God. He made me eat one of those ears
around his neck.

PALESTINIAN FREEDOM FIGHTER

Sick bastard!

VIET CONG GUERRILLA

What about the general? I couldn't find his
past his belly.

PALESTINIAN FREEDOM FIGHTER

Well, I found it, darling. It looked
like raw hamburger.

When the guerrilla and freedom fighter burst into laughter, the
Boss said, Disgusting. The luscious secretary smirked, but before
she could say anything, the Boss said, Shut up.

VIET CONG GUERRILLA

Have some more of the remedy. It helps.

PALESTINIAN FREEDOM FIGHTER

So—good. Um, so good.

VIET CONG GUERRILLA

And at least it's free.

PALESTINIAN FREEDOM FIGHTER

Well, give me some more!

VIET CONG GUERRILLA

Just count the money in your head. That's
what I do.

Then Aladdin entered the frame and the Palestinian freedom fighter
and the Viet Cong guerrilla turned their faces to him with glowing
smiles. Their eyes automatically descended from his blackened face
to his exposed manhood, which was naturally, utterly, and com-
pletely white.

Oh my God! whispered the luscious secretary. It's shaped like an egg.

Somewhere between avenue Hoche and the warehouse, I fell asleep. The Ronin woke me by slapping me in the face—lightly—after the car was parked. You're the youngest here and you can't even stay awake, he said, leaning close and peering into my eyes. Just because you stayed up one night? All you did was walk around with the remedy and the hashish! I was banging girls all night long and that is not easy work, my weak-kneed friend. When I pointed out that I was only invited to serve as the Cholon drug dealer, the Ronin shrugged. That's because you hadn't earned the opportunity yet, my friend. We earn our opportunities. They're not given to us!

Let's go, the Boss said, standing outside my window, an overnight bag from the trunk in his hand. He wordlessly led the way to the warehouse, where the door was unlocked.

Goddammit, Le Cao Boi said.

We walked between the pallets of coffee to the back of the cold, echoing warehouse. In the office, Grumpy and Shorty sat in front of the television playing a video game, another marvel invented during my time in reeducation. The game made a series of *ping*s and *pong*s as a ball bounced back and forth between two blocks that guarded opposite goals.

The Boss sighed and said, What the fuck are you idiots doing?

Grumpy and Shorty jumped to their feet, and Grumpy said, Sorry, Boss, but that guy's asleep anyway.

The Boss motioned to the door at the back of the office and Grumpy unlocked it. Make us some coffee, the Boss snapped to Grumpy before we went through the storeroom and to the cell behind it with Shorty.

A naked Mona Lisa lay in a far corner, curled up with his back to us. Shorty headed toward the Mona Lisa, but the Boss waved for him to stop before unzipping the overnight bag. He pulled out a pair of blue mechanic's overalls and took off his jacket and pants, which he gave to Shorty to fold. Then he slipped on the overalls, zipped them up, and bent down to the bag one more time. When he stood, I saw what he had in his hand—his beloved hammer.

Now this shit's going to get real, Le Cao Boi said with satisfaction.

Get me a chair, the Boss said to Shorty. Then wake him up.

Shorty had no success in waking the Mona Lisa up with yelling or nudges of his foot, so he resorted to a bucket of water and ice while the Boss watched with his hammer in his lap and the Ronin whistled Beethoven's "Ode to Joy." The ice water landed and the Mona Lisa jerked upright, spluttering, just as Grumpy came in with a folding table and a tray with the same arrangement that the luscious secretary had carried, except with four glasses and four filters. Placing the folding table next to the Boss, Grumpy put the tray on top and joined Shorty in flanking the Mona Lisa, huddled against the wall, head bowed, arms clutched around knees drawn up to his chest. The Boss tapped the tray with his hammer and the glasses rattled. You have until the coffee finishes dripping, the Boss said. Then you tell us where to find your friends. If you don't, you die. Simple. Understand?

The Mona Lisa did nothing but shiver.

The Boss glanced at the dwarfs, and Grumpy attempted to kick the Mona Lisa in the ribs but struck his elbow instead when the Mona Lisa shifted his arm to defend himself. Do you understand? the Boss said.

The Mona Lisa groaned, clutched his elbow, and nodded.

The Boss glanced at the dwarfs again, and Shorty, from the Mona Lisa's other side, expertly landed his boot in the Mona Lisa's ribs, thus demonstrating his perfection of that most basic skill of

both gangsters and chief executive officers: kicking a man when he's down. The Boss didn't hear you! Shorty shouted.

The Mona Lisa winced, panted, and at last said, Yes, I understand.

We had now moved to what Claude called the "ultimatum stage." Unintelligent people, Claude had told his students, the kind who watch television and think it's real life, believe that if you give a subject the do-or-die test, the subject will do whatever you want or tell you what you want to know, because the subject will not want to die. So let me tell you, from real-world experience, having applied this do-or-die test to many Viet Cong, that a lot of those fuckers will choose to die, and before they die, if they give you any information, it's most likely bad information. So the only reason to really do the do-or-die test is if you want to kill or inflict a great deal of pain. Capisce?

Since none of us Vietnamese students knew Italian or had seen the relevant American gangster films where the tough guy says "Capisce?"—not that we could wrap our Vietnamese lips around "capisce"—we could not say that we understood. Only after my years of experience in the Special Branch could I say, based on empirical experience, that I understood. Watching the scene before me now, I could also say that the Boss neither understood nor cared. He was going to kill the Mona Lisa one way or the other, and the only question was whether the Mona Lisa intuited that. The room lapsed into silence as the coffee dripped at the rate of one drop a second, a silence that the Ronin could bear only a half minute before ordering Grumpy to fetch a radio. Grumpy came back with one of the gigantic stereos that I saw being shipped out of the Boss's import-export store to my homeland, fated to be sold on the black market. Before Grumpy could turn on the stereo, my ghosts started humming and then singing from somewhere behind me:

*Vingt-deux millions de bâtards*
*Et moi, et moi, et moi*

Twenty-two million was just a guess on their part. How many bastards walked the world? As for France, if race did not exist, bastards could not also exist, could they? I was perplexed by the conundrum of my existence, by my uneasy citizenship in a diaspora of unknowns. But were I and the millions of bastards like me known unknowns? Or unknown unknowns?

Ah, that's more like it! said the Ronin, tuning the station on the stereo. I can dance to this.

He started to cha-cha, my people's favorite dance. I, too, could cha-cha to almost anything, at least anything faster than a rosary and slower than the twist. But my feet did not feel like moving. The Boss also did not dance. Neither did the Mona Lisa, nor the dwarfs, nor any of my ghosts, who had edged up from behind me to flank me and invade my personal space. Fascinated, we all watched the Ronin blissfully smiling as he did the cha-cha gracefully with an invisible partner until the Boss said, Enough dancing. The coffee had finished dripping. He rose, hammer in hand, while the Mona Lisa braced his back against the wall.

The Ronin stopped dancing, smirked, and said to the Mona Lisa, You and your Algerian friends have the right idea. But we Corsicans have been doing this since before you were born. Opium is a better cash crop than rubber, I'll tell you that. What a wonderful time we had back then in Indochina! May we see the likes of it again, the time when the French government had the good sense to encourage opium. My God, we couldn't have financed the government without selling opium to the natives! Now that was an effective business model. Vertical integration and horizontal monopolization meant we had total market control. Imagine how

much better France would be now if the government was still in the opium business. Our socialist president would have all the money he needs for his fancy welfare programs. Let's see how long that lasts without enough money to go around. But is anybody going to listen to me? They should! I'm a patriot! Lady Opium was white. But this remedy is so white it's snow white. Have you enjoyed the remedy?

The Mona Lisa nodded.

Then you know what I mean, my friend.

You ready? the Boss said, looking at me rather than the Ronin.

I'm always ready, I said, although I had no idea what he was talking about.

He offered me the hammer, although "offered" was a euphemism, for this was not a gift I could decline. The shaft was smooth wood, no splinters, as long as my forearm, its iron head slightly scarred and scratched, just like mine. Its weight was balanced, unlike me. The hammer extended my body, my arm, my hand, and, ultimately, my mind, at least one of them. I remembered what Professor Hammer once told me about his name and the epigram universally attributed to Bertolt Brecht but really coined by the poet Vladimir Mayakovsky or maybe by Leon Trotsky, or so Professor Hammer said: "Art is not a mirror held up to the world but a hammer with which to shape it." Oh! I had practically orgasmed at hearing this for the first time! Slogans were my turn-on and my political convictions were my most erogenous zone. My name is my destiny, Professor Hammer had said then, raising his glass of sherry to me as I sat in his office for my weekly tutorial with sherry accompaniment, poured from a bottle kept in the professor's desk drawer, taken out only for his favorite students, who were always men. I could still taste the far-too-sweet sherry as I clutched the Boss's hammer. Could the professor have imagined that one day I would hold this in my hand and that it would not be a metaphor or

a simile but an actual thing with which to hammer an actual head, smash an actual skull, bludgeon an actual brain? I held the hammer with horror, although the horror did not concern the hammer. The hammer was just a tool. I was the weapon and I horrified myself. Everyone was looking at me: the Boss, the Ronin, Grumpy and Shorty, Sonny, the crapulent major, Beatles, Ugly and Uglier, and most especially the Mona Lisa.

Your interrogation didn't work, the Boss said. Enough with the words. They didn't do anything. Now it's time to do something. But make it last. That's very important. Pay attention to the details. Me, for example, I like to work up from the toes. How do you want to do it?

YOU—that is, ME—were once again being examined with the hardest question of all, supposedly posed by Lenin, although really it was the novelist Nikolay Chernyshevsky: WHAT IS TO BE DONE?

a) Break the Mona Lisa's kneecaps
b) Fracture the Mona Lisa's ribs
c) Destroy the Mona Lisa's nose
d) Pulverize the Mona Lisa's hands

Mayakovsky, Chernyshevsky, Lenin . . . what was wrong with these Russians? Was it Siberia? The steppe? The cheap and plentiful vodka, visually synonymous with water? Or was it that the Russians were essentially Oriental, as Sir Richard Hedd claimed? Did the sum of these things make the Russians prone to brutal behavior, unrealistic expectations, and very thick novels? And, at least by reputation, deadly roulette? The Boss stirred his coffee into a nice caramel blend over ice and, having taken his seat again, sipped it with a slight smile.

Well, the Boss said, crossing his ankles and relaxing. What are you waiting for?

The ghosts grinned, snapped their fingers, and sang:

*Trente-trois millions de bâtards*
*Et moi, et moi, et moi*

YOU—that is, ME—looked at the Mona Lisa, and even though he grimaced in pain and misery, you could tell he would still rather die from the defiant way he looked back at you. For a moment, you thought about begging God for help, though God would say nothing. No, the only one who had ever guided you unswervingly had been your mother, who always accepted you and who would accept you even if she knew you were a communist or a spy or whatever you were now. *You are not half of anything, you are twice of everything!*

The hammer was heavy, even heavier than the bloated foie gras of your guilty conscience, force-fed with all the crimes you had committed. WHAT IS TO BE DONE? Grumpy and Shorty regarded you skeptically, fingering the cleavers holstered under their arms. The Ronin resumed dancing to the next song on the radio. The Boss studied you as if you were a very bad movie and he was a cineast. You dog-paddled in the waters of your rising panic, seeing no way out of this room or this situation, and since the only thing you could buy was time, you said, Do you have a last request?

A last request? said Le Cao Boi.

Well, it's not a bad idea, said the Ronin, depending on what he asks.

The Boss sipped his coffee. Make it quick.

The Mona Lisa made it quick. Give me some more of the remedy.

Please, said the Boss.

Please give me some of the remedy.

A perfect last request! said the Ronin. Because this is going to hurt.

It's *really* going to hurt, said Le Cao Boi.

You know what I do sometimes? said Shorty. He reached into his brown leather jacket's inner pocket for a Sony Walkman, headphones attached. Slip these babies on, crank up the volume. It helps. Hearing a guy scream for hours and hours can affect you.

That reminds me, said Grumpy. He also reached into the inner pocket of his black leather jacket, but in his case removed goggles and a surgical mask. For the blood splatter.

Ugh, yeah, I remember once I even got a bit of brain—

Shut up, said the Boss. Give him the remedy.

You offered the Mona Lisa the remedy. A lot of it. Almost all you had left in your pockets because somehow you were still carrying several packets. You were the magician who kept throwing something away only to discover that it kept reappearing in your pockets, the remedy a white rabbit with a magic of its own. The Mona Lisa inhaled the remedy while the Ronin and Le Cao Boi chuckled, Grumpy and Shorty chortled, the Boss sipped his coffee, and you yourself took the opportunity to snort a white line you withheld from the Mona Lisa. WHAT IS TO BE DONE?

You know what this reminds me of? said the Ronin. The monk who burned himself to death in Saigon.

We're not going to burn him to death, said the Boss.

It's an idea, isn't it? Wouldn't that teach the Algerians a lesson? But that's not what I'm talking about. People all over the world cried over that brave, noble monk. He went out with a real splash, so to speak, even if he did have himself splashed with imported gasoline. The left-wing media did their job, put him all over the news, turned him into a legend. You saw the pictures, didn't you, my friend? The human torch!

The Mona Lisa nodded, eyes half hooded.

Everyone saw the pictures, the Ronin went on. How dramatic! Especially on television. But of course the left-wing media didn't

actually report on *the truth*. You know what really happened? The commies *drugged* that poor monk. The reason he was so calm while burning to death was that he was a *zombie*.

Bullshit! the Mona Lisa said, eyes now wide open. He was a hero!

He was a patsy in a communist plot.

All right, said the Boss, looking at his watch. He wore it with its face on the inside of his wrist, which was probably how Death wore his watch, too. Let's get this over with.

Not that you have to make it quick, said the Ronin.

But the remedy hasn't kicked in yet, you said.

I'm getting the feeling you don't want to do this, said the Boss.

The dwarfs stopped giggling. Your ghosts hummed, shuffled their feet, sang:

> *Quarante millions de bâtards*
> *Et moi, et moi, et moi*

And suddenly you knew the answer to the question WHAT IS TO BE DONE? The answer had stared you in the face this entire time, always there while you refused to understand it, possibly for your entire life, and at the very least ever since Claude lectured you about the ultimatum stage, the do-or-die test, which, you realized, was what the Boss was administering to you. Like many good answers, this answer was, in retrospect, completely obvious, like the round wheel or the number zero, both of which must have caused people to slap their foreheads and say, Why didn't I think of that? In your case you overlooked the answer, dismissed or ignored it because it was too terrifying, too straightforward, too simple in what it demanded of you. Now the answer was so deafening it was

as if God Himself had finally broken His silence and spoke from the mountaintops and the clouds:

GOD
What is to be done?

ALSO GOD
Nothing!

You started to laugh. You finally got it! You had waited so long for God to speak, and when He did, He said, Nothing! Oh my God, God, You're such a funny guy! The original man with two minds! The greatest stand-up comedian of all time! All the world was a comedy club, and you were the idiot in the front row who kept getting picked on to be the butt of God's ribbing. Nothing! You shook with sound but no fury, a belly laugh from the same pit where your soul was entombed. Nothing! Ha! Everyone was staring at you now. Was it because you were electrified, every single hair on your body standing and saluting, even the filigrees in your nostrils? Oh my God, God, please, stop! Enough! What a riot! What a scream! And even after slapping yourself on both sides of your face, and with your cheeks stinging, you could hear yourself continuing to laugh hysterically, although it might also be possible that you were just laughing historically.

The joke, after all, was timeless.

## CHAPTER 18

What was the difference between history and hysteria, anyway? If you were a woman, you could have a hysterectomy to solve the histrionics of your hysteria, but since you were a man, or so you have been told, the only solution would be a historectomy. The Boss had a much simpler fix. He slapped you in the face, hard and sharp, the way Frenchmen liked to smack their women, the way Vietnamese men enjoyed slapping their women, too. Get a grip on yourself, the Boss said, and though he meant it figuratively, you stopped laughing and clutched yourself, left hand on right biceps, right hand still holding the hammer.

Get it over with, the Boss said.

You looked at the Mona Lisa and saw again the face of the communist agent on the examination table in the movie theater, surrounded by the three policemen. Her face had beseeched you and you had done nothing when you should have done something. But now the situation was reversed, and it was, in fact, time to get it over with.

You offered the Boss his hammer and said, No.

No? your chorus of ghosts gasped. You have stopped at nothing!

Le Cao Boi whistled. Oh boy, he said. You're in a world of shit now.

What do you mean, no? the Boss said.

Nothing to be done, you said, paraphrasing, or interpreting, God. I refuse.

You don't get to say no, the Boss said. This is not a country club. You can't just quit your membership and walk away.

You know too much, the Ronin said regretfully.

And yet you did not know enough. You did not know whether Marilyn Monroe really committed suicide. You did not know if John F. Kennedy was in fact killed by just one gunman. You did not know if Uncle Ho had possessed a secret wife, as the rumors said. You did not know why Johnny Hallyday was so popular among the French, although you were fairly certain that historians would eventually see that Brigitte Bardot singing *Je t'aime . . . moi non plus* was the peak of French civilization. You did not know where your mother was now, but by doing nothing you would soon find out.

Do you know what I'm saying? the Boss demanded.

I know what you're saying, you said, mouth completely dry, the bile of fear slathered on your tongue. But do you know what I'm getting at? I have chosen to do . . . nothing.

And at this you could not help yourself even though you desperately needed to help yourself—you burst out laughing, again, at this gag by a god who did not exist. God had never asked anything to be done, since He had ever and only said nothing—what a howler! What was really a screamer, though, was how so many massacred millions could have been saved if everybody who killed them had just done . . . nothing. If enough people had stood up,

or laid down as the case may be, and simply said no, even at the price of their lives, through a mundane act of heroism within everybody's grasp—

Don't you get it? you cried to the Boss, whose lack of a sense of humor would always prevent him from getting the joke. Wasn't the lack of a sense of humor the greatest lack of all? If only everyone possessed a sense of the absurd, then the world would not be such an absurd place! To the Boss, you said, Don't you see how much harder it is to do nothing rather than something? But if everybody just did nothing, then nothing would happen!

Give me that, you crazy bastard, the Boss said, snatching the hammer from your hand. He waved it slowly in front of your face and you almost got cross-eyed following its cobra motion. First, I'm going to show you how to do something. Then I'm going to do something to you.

The Boss pressed the metallic head of the hammer into your forehead.

No question about it, Beatles said. This hammer's hard enough to crush your skull.

Too bad, Ugly added. It's going to be messy.

Very messy, Uglier agreed. That's why we're going to love watching this!

Bon's not going to like it, said the Ronin.

All we do is tell him the Arab got loose and killed his friend.

You couldn't disagree with the Boss. In his shoes, you would have written the exact same plot. The only positive twist in the tale you could see was that the Boss would have to kill you quickly, one blow to the head, two max, since the Mona Lisa would not realistically have the chance to crush every bone in your body. As the Boss tapped his hammer in his hand and walked toward the Mona Lisa, you rubbed the spot where the Boss had pressed the hammer

against your head and probably left a red mark to guide his hand on his return. The taiko drum of your heart pounded, foreshadowing the pounding your head would get as soon as the Boss finished off the Mona Lisa, who was trembling with cold and fear but who did not close his eyes as he looked squarely at his fate. You could not help but admire him. He was, as he had claimed, 100 percent gangster.

I was wrong about you, said Sonny in an emotional voice.

Not so fast! protested the crapulent major. He's not dead yet.

The trick, of course, was knowing when to do something and when to do nothing. Or rather, to put it more accurately, since what one *should* do was in many cases quite clear, the trick was *actually* doing something or doing nothing. Doing nothing would cost you your life, but then again, what was your life actually worth?

The Boss paused before the Mona Lisa. Any last words?

Let me think, the Mona Lisa said. Oh, yeah. Fuck you.

The Boss snorted, raised the hammer above his head, and you turned your head away, unlike Le Cao Boi and the Ronin and Grumpy and Shorty, all gleeful with anticipation, and this was why you were the only one to see the door kicked open with a *bang!* and a man in a black balaclava storm through, dressed all in black, an AK-47 in his hands, the sight of which made you dive to the floor in a cowardly reflex that was second nature to you—*bang! bang! bang!*—and from this shameless position with your cheek against the ground you saw a second man in a black balaclava, also dressed all in black, follow the first, an identical AK-47 in his hands—*bang! bang! bang!*—and you clapped your hands over your ears to protect them from the staccato of automatic rifle fire that you knew all too well from years of war, the unmistakable jackhammer of an AK-47 that was loud anywhere but was deafening in the close confines of the interrogation room

that had become an echo chamber bouncing back and forth the
yells of astonishment and the screams of dying men:

> What
>> the
>>> fuck?!
>>>> Jesus
>>>>> fucking
>>>>>> Christ!
>>>>>>> Goddammit
>>>>>>>> to Hell!
>>>>>>>>> Holy
>>>>>>>>>> shit!

Those, unfortunately, were the not-very-articulate last words of
Grumpy and Shorty, their cleavers useless against the onslaught
of 7.62mm bullets fired at the maximum rate of 600 rounds per
minute or 10 rounds per second, as you learned during your appren-
ticeship with Claude. *Bang! Bang! Bang!* The first gunman fired in
short, precise bursts, the second one in long, undisciplined spasms,
which meant that the second one had to pause in the middle of
the slaughter and reload with a new thirty-round magazine, while
the first one still had enough rounds left to walk up to the Ronin,
sprawled on his back and bleeding from wounds to his abdomen, his
hand clawing for the gun in his waistband, and fire a bullet into the
Ronin's forehead, an act that the gunman carried out with dispas-
sion while his companion was still trying to insert the new magazine
with trembling hands, which he finally accomplished as the calm
and cool gunman swiveled and took the last few paces to the Mona
Lisa and the Boss, both sitting against the wall, the Mona Lisa in a
state of shock, judging from the expression on his face, and the Boss

looking—for the first and only time you had seen him—terrified, agonized at the riddle of how someone like him could be riddled, dark blood seeping through his overalls as the second gunman, the amateur, squeezed a long burst into the spine of Le Cao Boi, who was crawling pointlessly toward a corner after having been shot in the legs and hip, and who died at the outstretched feet of the Boss, who had dropped his hammer by his side, and who was holding his guts with both hands to keep them from falling out, and who was screaming in such pain that you almost wept, and whose screams abruptly stopped when the calm and cool gunman shot him in the mouth and blew his memories against the wall.

Then all was silent in the echo chamber except for the panting of the Mona Lisa and the blood in your head, whose waves you could hear because one of your ears was pressed against the cement floor, and when the gunmen turned from the carnage in your direction, you closed your eyes and played dead. Their booted feet thudded on the cement closer and closer, and one of them said, No, let me do it, and then something hard and hot pressed against your temple and you flinched and opened your eyes.

Ha! said the amateur gunman, his barrel aimed at your face. I knew you were still alive. He pulled off his balaclava and it was Rolling Stones. Hey there, you crazy bastard. Remember me?

How could you forget?

The calm and cool gunman pulled off his balaclava, too, and you saw the resemblance right away, the visual rhyme with the Mona Lisa in the elbow-like cheekbones, the enigmatic gaze, the black eyebrows as thick as cocoons, the teen idol lips.

Saïd, you said.

The cocoons twitched. So you've heard about me, he said. I've heard about you, too.

He knelt down to look more closely at you, and though he was here to kill you, you could not help but think, *This is one good-looking son of a bitch.*

You took my place, took what wasn't yours, Saïd went on, his finger tapping your forehead exactly where the Boss had pressed the hammer. Now you will pay the price.

Rolling Stones raised the AK-47 to his shoulder, and you turned from Saïd's calm eyes to the barrel of the gun aimed between your own eyes. Mao said that political power grows out of the barrel of a gun, but you could not imagine anything growing from this kind of barrel. All you could see was the power of horror in the barrel's black hole, its center of gravity being a 7.62mm slug with no name on it but yours, and you told yourself to keep your mouth shut and not to provoke Rolling Stones or Saïd, who did not seem, like the Boss, to be hung up on prolonging the agony of his victims. So many people had tried to fire a bullet into your head and you just wanted to make this quick. You had already killed yourself once, and this bullet would be the exclamation point on the last sentence of your life, a demise either truly unfortunate or very desirable, depending on one's point of view, and since you were a man of two minds, you were both horrified and ready to celebrate.

Any last requests? said Rolling Stones, and you experienced a moment of déjà vu.

Could I have a bit of the remedy, please, Ahmed?

Your use of his real name irked Rolling Stones with its little reminder of your shared, heartwarming (in)humanity, and he said, I'm just going to kill you, and your eyes locked on to his trigger finger, which had just started to move, when Saïd said, You asked him a question and he gave you an answer. Now be a man of your word.

Oh, for fuck's sake! Rolling Stones lowered his gun. All right, asshole. Where do I find some of this remedy?

You took a guess and said, The pockets of the dwarfs, which turned out to be right. As Rolling Stones returned with small packets of the remedy, one part of you thought about how nice it might be to die, while the other part of you that still clung stubbornly to life said to Saïd, Perhaps you'd like to know where you can find more of the remedy?

Saïd was kneeling by his brother and helping him pull his pants back on. He looked at you and said, You think that's going to save your life?

You anesthetized yourself quickly, inhaling first one dose of the remedy and then another. While the remedy's magic lay in giving its users a heightened sense of euphoria and megalomania, mixed with the numbing of various parts of the body and mind and a paradoxical increase of erogenous sensitivity, it made no claims to increasing intelligence. Thus, feeling a little better but no smarter, you were perplexed by the puzzle of the question given to you by Saïd, a problem the Mona Lisa solved for you.

Don't kill him, the Mona Lisa said.

What? Rolling Stones cried.

*What?* you thought, although you were intelligent enough not to say this out loud.

I've been looking forward to killing this *niakoué*! Rolling Stones said, and you finally, finally got what he was saying. You burst out laughing once again and Rolling Stones said, Now what, you crazy bastard?

Nhà quê! You're trying to say nhà quê!

That's what I said.

It means "peasant." "Hick." "Stupid." I suppose it's justice that you French took an insult we used against country people and turned it against us.

I don't give a fuck how you say it in your language, Rolling Stones hissed. *Niakoué! Niakoué! Niakoué!*

He saved my life, the Mona Lisa said.

He didn't save your life, said Saïd. *We* saved your life.

It's true, they were going to kill me. But this crazy bastard refused to kill me, and they were going to kill him right after me. The Mona Lisa finished buttoning his shirt and slowly stood up with the help of Saïd. He spared me, and I'm asking you to spare him.

Fuck no, Rolling Stones said, aiming his AK-47 at me once more.

Stop, Saïd said, and Rolling Stones, cursing, lowered his gun again. Saïd regarded me with those calm and collected eyes, his mind processing what his brother had told him. Then he said, My brother's word is good enough for me.

Saïd! Rolling Stones said.

Ahmed, stop thinking like the little gangster that you are. Saïd loomed over you now, and from your perspective on the floor, he appeared gigantic. Become a man of your word. You kill when necessary and you show mercy when necessary, but you always do what you say, so that no one will doubt who you are and what you stand for.

Sure, great, fantastic, Rolling Stones said. Let me start after I kill him.

Ahmed, show some commitment.

I am committed! I'm committed to killing this bastard!

You must learn to believe in something greater than yourself and your little schemes, Saïd said, staring down at you. Just because he's a thief and a drug dealer and a criminal like you—like I was at one time—doesn't mean you must behave like him. He's not a man, Ahmed, and neither are you. And do you know why?

I'm not a man? Rolling Stones said. Fuck you, Saïd!

You have to understand that Ahmed comes from a long line of sailors, although some called them pirates, Saïd said to you. He's still got the pirate blood in him from Annaba, but it's diluted now. Easy

to understand, given how his parents fled the War of Independence to come here. Mine, too. But the FLN had it right. We shouldn't be killing ourselves with crimes and drugs and violence. We should be *djounoud*, liberating ourselves with violence.

I don't want to hear another lecture, Rolling Stones said.

You wouldn't have to hear a lecture if you did the reading like I told you, Saïd said. If you had, you would know Fanon said that "violence detoxifies."

It "frees the colonized from his inferiority complex and from his despair and inaction," you said. Saïd locked eyes with you in a moment of mutual recognition and you both said, Violence "makes him fearless and restores his self-respect."

You see why I kind of maybe like this guy? the Mona Lisa said to Saïd.

Reading Fanon is still just reading, Saïd said. Better than nothing. But you have to *do* something. And you need the right kind of violence, the kind that makes you a man, not the kind that makes you a thief. Ahmed, do you know why you and this thief who stole from me are not men?

Rolling Stones sighed. Because we're not committed?

Exactly, Saïd said.

His gaze on you was a variation of the luscious secretary's, a stinging blend of pity, contempt, and understanding. You wanted to protest and say that while you may not be much of a man (anymore), you have been deeply, deeply committed, and look where it's gotten you. But you muted yourself so you could live again to talk another day, which was the right response.

You can go, Saïd said. Now.

Motherfucker, Rolling Stones muttered.

You lurched to your feet before Saïd changed his mind or Rolling Stones accidentally shot you. Questions loomed—how did Saïd

hear about his brother, and how had he gotten to Paris so fast? And how had he tracked down the Mona Lisa? But prolonging your time in front of Saïd and Rolling Stones meant risking your life to satisfy your curiosity, and these were not the kind of questions to die for. Instead you bowed and clasped your hands together in a vaguely Oriental form of submission, which might have been more Indian than Vietnamese, but who cared? You were all Orientals here.

Thank you both for your generosity, you said, and threw in a few more abject expressions of groveling gratitude, for you were nothing if not a master of abjection. Then you added, Just as a way of saying thank you, let me suggest that you look a little deeper into all those crates of coffee in the warehouse, at which Saïd raised a thick eyebrow. Then you said, You've already done a great deal for me, but could I ask you for just one more small thing? Maybe two?

As your ex-boss the General once observed, Those who do you favors are inclined to do you more in the right circumstances, which was why the General relentlessly curried favor with those above him by asking for favors, while steadfastly refusing to grant favors in almost all cases to those below him. Saïd had already granted you, in his royal way, the courtesy of not killing you, and now, sensing the magnitude of his own nobility, he might do you one more good turn. And indeed, instead of killing you or having you killed, Saïd sighed and said, What do you want?

What you wanted were Le Cao Boi's authentic aviator sunglasses, which he was wearing when he died, since he always wore them, and which he no longer needed. They were, you said, a memento to commemorate Le Cao Boi, your best friend, or so you told Saïd, a sentiment that you figured a man of honor like him would understand. The aviators fit perfectly and did their job of helping

you drive through the sunlit streets of Paris for the first time. Doing so while anesthetized by the remedy was akin to steering a pinball through a pinball machine, or so you thought, or so you remembered thinking by the time you inserted the key into the lock of the Boss's apartment. This key was what you really wanted, although you told Saïd you needed the Boss's car to get yourself home. You were betting on Saïd having his own transportation, although it might not be as fashionable as the Boss's Bavarian phenomenon. Rolling Stones was quite aware of this as he protested the favor, but you had already set up an implicit trade with Saïd concerning the treasure trove of which he was now the master. On the way out of the warehouse you passed the stacks of crates full of snow-white remedy masked as intestinally processed black coffee, and you hoped you were done with this trade, but you suspected you were not as you passed the rope-bound body of Biggie near the exit, eyes open, mouth gagged, and throat slit, a clue to how Saïd and Rolling Stones found the warehouse. During the orgy, Biggie had left to tend Delights of Asia by himself, and Saïd and Rolling Stones must have found him there.

The Boss's apartment was silent and clean. If you were not in a rush, you would take your time, pour yourself five inches of some of the Boss's expensive scotch or cognac, put your feet up, and admire the distant Eiffel Tower, huge in reality but only an inch or so long from here, but it was past noon and you had to be at Opium for *Fantasia*'s preshow party in a few hours, so you began looking for where the Boss kept his valuables. You dug through his kitchen cabinets, under his sofa cushions, in his closet, behind his television and stereo equipment, and were about to head toward his bedroom when a soft feminine voice said,

WHAT THE FUCK DO YOU THINK YOU'RE DOING?

which was another profoundly philosophical question you had occasionally asked yourself, although not at this moment. You began to turn around, and the voice that you recognized as belonging to the luscious secretary said, Raise your hands and move slow or I'll shoot. By the time you finished your slow pirouette, you were braced for the Luger-like pistol that was quite large in her tiny, steady hand. She was wearing a see-through nightgown and her long, lustrous black hair was tousled and in need of combing, which only made her more luscious.

The Boss will kill you, she said.

You were wearing the sunglasses, but you still felt it would be better to use every muscle in your body to keep your eyes fixed on hers, which made it hard for you to swallow the fear and desire that flooded your mouth. You managed to say, The Boss is dead.

The luscious secretary stared at you for five seconds—you counted—and said, You'd never have the balls to kill the Boss.

True. You explained to her as calmly as you could what had happened. A film passed over her eyes—not grief, not relief, but something else—uncertainty? She expressed neither shock nor surprise but instead said, How do I know you're not lying?

Do you think I could have gotten this key if the Boss were alive?

Take off those sunglasses, she said, keeping her gun pointed at you.

You had lost track of the number of times a gun had been aimed at you. You were also not quite certain how many times their triggers had been pulled, and how many of your lives had been blown away, for you to reach this point where the touch of air on your skin made you shiver with something bordering on the state of pleasure, which was always next to the state of pain.

So what are you doing here? she said.

The pinball you rode carried you forward with a plan you did not have until this moment, not knowing the luscious secretary would be here, which you should have known if you were thinking properly. I'm sure the Boss keeps cash here, you said, looking at the clock, above the television, that was carved in the shape of your country. The General had the same nostalgic clock in his Los Angeles restaurant, its open secret revealing how, for refugees, time only moved in circles. But the Boss's clock revealed another open secret, how, for refugees, time sometimes stopped completely.

I assume he keeps the money in a safe, you said. And I know the combination. But I don't know where the safe is. I'm guessing you might.

You actually did not know if there was a safe and you did not know the combination, but your first hunch was proven correct when she said, How do you know the combination?

Show me the safe first, you said.

I get half of what's inside.

Put the gun down first.

I know you think I'm stupid, but I'm not.

I don't think—

I see the way you look at me.

The way she looked at you indicated that she thought you were the stupid one, and admitting to yourself that you had never thought about the luscious secretary's intelligence, you continued straining every muscle in your body to keep your eyes locked on hers, despite the temptations in your peripheral vision. You're right, you said, swallowing that familiar mix of guilt and shame for which you had long ago developed a taste. They went so well together, like gin and tonic, like civilization and colonization, like resistance and collaboration, like Hitler and Goebbels, like Nixon and Kissinger,

like Vietnam and Algeria, like France and the United States, that there should be a cocktail, or at least a minor Russian novel, or maybe just a teenage dance craze, called the Guilt and the Shame. I'm sorry. Truly sorry.

No, you're not. You're just a typical Vietnamese man. Or half-Vietnamese man. It doesn't matter. You're all the same. You take us for granted. You assume we'll cook your food, wash your dishes, launder your clothes, giggle at your dumb jokes, swoon at your poetry or love songs that you love to write until the day you marry us, when you'll never write us another poem or love song again, since you'll be writing them to your girlfriends. You think we'll always be there to make love to you, have your kids, raise them on our own, do the shopping, listen to your complaints, massage your egos, keep the accounts, work for extra money, tolerate your parents, serve your mothers, ignore your mistresses, mend your clothes, find your keys, agree with all your nonsense, walk at least five steps behind you, take care of you when you're old, and, finally—finally—*finally*—die after you, just to make sure someone will cry at your funeral, throw you a big wake, tend your shrine and visit your grave, remember you every day, and then, when we die and join you, do the whole goddamned thing all over again *forever*.

Even though her voice trembled with fury, the barrel of the Luger never wavered. As a Vietnamese man, or half-Vietnamese man, you knew, deep in your gut, all the way down to your balls, in a rare moment of honesty occasioned by how these balls were not rolling as they properly should, that she was right. You, as a representative of Vietnamese manhood, deserved her fury, for everything you had ever done to Vietnamese women every day of their lives. You're right, you said. And I'm sorry. Very sorry.

Do you think the Boss was ever going to marry me? the luscious secretary said.

Yes, absolutely, yes. He was in love with you—

Don't lie to me. I don't care about him loving me. Getting married would just mean that he carried out his part of the bargain. Now that's not going to happen. The least I deserve is his money. Don't you agree?

You nodded vigorously and made more affirmative noises. The luscious secretary took you to the Boss's bedroom, where she had been sleeping before you woke her up, and pointed at a bookshelf next to the walk-in closet. The Boss did not read French, and yet these shelves were fully stocked with French books. Scanning them quickly, you were happy to see that the French did not just read philosophy and fancy literature, the highbrow tomes that one could display along with top-shelf liquor. These books and these authors deserved to be accompanied by only beer and carafes of house wine. They were French originals or French translations of authors who wrote the kinds of trashy bestsellers found in airports and convenience stores, the pulp that was so lowbrow it simply slid down from the reader's forehead to rest as a mustache on the upper lip. No need to name names, however. Why bother, when the Boss had not read these authors, since he never read anything except his invoices and ledgers.

Pull on that shelf, the luscious secretary said, waving her gun.

Like human beings, guns had a nasty tendency to go off without warning, so you said, in your most polite voice, Maybe you could take your finger off the trigger?

She pointed the gun at you, keeping her finger on the trigger, and you pulled on the shelf, which rolled forward on invisible wheels hidden beneath its base. When you rolled the bookshelf to the side, the safe was revealed, a gray iron box the size of a small refrigerator, tucked into the wall in a space next to the walk-in closet. All right, smart guy, the luscious secretary said. Show me what you got.

You had only one idea, and now you made your second bet.

Ever notice the clocks in the Boss's office and here? you said. They never worked. He was too lazy to replace their batteries.

No, not too lazy, you said with a breezy confidence that would soon be revealed as either genius or folly. Clues. Reminders. Just in case he forgot the combination. You said this without gloating, because if you gloated, she would—judging from her expression—shoot you. Possibly not to kill, but certainly to maim you for life. Seven fifty-nine, you said, cracking your knuckles. Or seven-five-nine.

Prove it.

The lock of the safe was a tumbler that had to be spun clockwise and counterclockwise. You knelt down to be eye level with the mechanism and set to work, trying not to sweat as you dialed the tumbler back and forth. Seven to the right once, fifty to the left twice, nine to the right once. The handle of the safe did not budge. Your armpits started to sweat as you tried seven to the left, fifty to the right, nine to the left. The handle still did not budge. Now your head was sweating, and you were acutely aware of the luscious secretary sitting in an armchair to your left, legs crossed, her hand with the gun resting on a knee, her finger still on the trigger, her body still in a see-through nightgown that would have compelled the pope to look. Hell, God Himself must be gazing at this very moment on one of His most perfect creations as you tried every other combination of seven, five, fifty, and nine that you could think of over the next few minutes. At some point you lost track of the combinations and simply spun the dial randomly over and over, playing yet another version of roulette.

Hey, Einstein, said the luscious secretary. Why don't you try nineteen-fifty-nine?

Someone hit the stop button to the world and everything and everyone froze for a few moments. Inside your head the hour hand of the clock rotated a complete circle, from seven in the morning to

nineteen hundred hours at night. Then play resumed and you spun the dial to nineteen to the right once, fifty to the left twice, nine to the right once. The handle of the safe clicked and shifted easily when you pulled on it, and the door to the safe opened with a hush.

Heaven was quiet when you arrived two hours later. Everyone is exhausted, sir, said the obsequious housekeeper, and you wondered how she had been spared a role in the orgy. You slipped her a hundred francs to let you in and found the eschatological muscle sleeping on the couch in the waiting room, an open volume of *Journey to the End of the Night* rising and falling on his bare chest, the television tuned, as always, to an intellectual talk show. A pale slash cut diagonally across his biceps, a new Band-Aid that you had not seen the night before. Upstairs, Madeleine was sleeping, and you opened her door without knocking. She was under the covers of her queen-sized bed, hair fanned around her head, face clear of makeup or any other sign of the fantastic orgy of the night before, except for the bruises around her neck from the hands of BFD. You thought about waking her up, but this was not about you. Instead you left the Monoprix shopping bag that you took from the Boss's kitchen cabinet next to Madeleine. Inside was half the money the luscious secretary had let you take from the Boss's safe, which was not to say it was half the money in the safe. Both of you had stared at the bricks of francs in the safe, each wrapped in a paper band with the sum total value written in blue ink. There were also clear plastic sandwich bags packed with bundles of gold ounces and taels, each individually packaged in plastic, each package printed with the issuer's name. The number of ounces or taels was also written on each bag in thick, indelible black marker. As with the bricks of cash, this, too, was in the Boss's handwriting.

327

I think we're rich, you said, hoping that the luscious secretary would not double-cross you and blow your brains out with a shot to the temple. You'd been dead for so long that now you wanted to live. There'll be plenty even after we go fifty-fifty.

Did I say fifty-fifty? the luscious secretary said, coyly covering her mouth with the hand not holding a gun. Oops! Silly me. I meant seventy-thirty.

Seventy-thirty? You kept your cool and said, Without me, that safe wouldn't even be open. Let's say fifty-five, forty-five.

The luscious secretary cocked her cannon. Let's say seventy-five, twenty-five, and you walk out of here with your balls where they belong.

This was how you ended up giving Madeleine half of 25 percent of the Boss's cash savings. The gold was not included, as the luscious secretary went on to clarify before she made you count the money, which took quite a long time, considering there was so much of it, and even though you pointed out that the Boss had helpfully wrapped and priced all the bundles. I just want to make sure we get everything right, the luscious secretary said calmly, daring you to look as she uncrossed and recrossed her legs while you knelt by the safe counting the cash. Part of you was nostalgic for Saïd and his uncompromising commitment to his word, but part of you was thankful that 25 percent of a lot of money was still quite a bit. After you had finished counting the last of it, you said, Can I use the bathroom?

The luscious secretary rolled her eyes and escorted you to the toilet in the hallway. Like most French apartments you had seen, even the spacious ones, the Boss's had only one toilet, which was fine by Vietnamese standards but primitive even by middle-class American standards. Americans, smartly enough, believed in having a backup in case of backups. They had an anxiety about seeing

shit, but not about getting fat; for the French, it was the opposite. As for the Vietnamese, we could not get fat even if we tried, given how poor the country was, leaving us no choice but to be pleased with having even one toilet, given the condition of the country's sewage system. But what was the French excuse? They must simply relate differently to excrement, which was already proven by their laissez-faire treatment of canine crap. Shit was the secret of every society, and how a society treated its shit told a stranger a great deal, to which a skeptic such as the luscious secretary might say, What a crock of shit. But what she actually said when you tried to close the door behind you was: Keep it open.

But—

Keep it open. You won't show me anything I haven't already seen.

Yes, but I, you know, need to, uh—

Oh, for God's sake. The luscious secretary looked rightfully disgusted. I don't need to see that. Keep the door open a crack and don't try to lock it or I'll shoot you through the door.

You had no desire to die on the throne like Elvis, and your plan was not to escape from the windowless toilet anyway. Keeping the door mostly closed sufficed for your plan, which was to remove the apartment key from the key chain also holding the Boss's car key. Since the door was open a bit, however, allowing the luscious secretary to eavesdrop on your personal sordid drama, you unzipped your pants, lowered the seat, sat down, and pretended to go through the motions as you fumbled with the Boss's ring of keys. Unfortunately, or fortunately, depending on your point of view, going through the motions induced a real motion, or perhaps it was an emotion that moved you, surprising you as your emotions sometimes did, the force of it so sudden and so real—Oh my *God*, said the luscious secretary from outside the door—as you coincidentally

reminded yourself of Newton's Third Law of Motion, how every action generates an equal and opposite reaction, so that even as one orifice made its presence heard aft, another orifice erupted with a groan of pain mingled with relief and surprise, for you did not know you had it in you, this mortal coil slithering forth from your innards with no seeming end, a sediment most foul accumulated over years, its thickness, density, and noxiousness suggesting that this dead beast of the bowels was the stubborn stuff that your body found impossible to fully digest—Could you *stop*? the luscious secretary cried—the dark matter of your darkest interior, the biblical abomination hidden in the recesses of the crevices of the twists and turns of the long and winding guts that so many people have hated—I mean, *Jesus Christ*, said the luscious secretary—until at last it appeared that you had unscrewed this corkscrew, but while it curled cryptically beneath you, as unique as an industrially contaminated snowflake, as individual as your morally soiled self, no two manifestations of one's interior ever being exactly the same, the sudden vacuum left behind by the rapid departure of your intestinal inhabitant hurt nearly as much as the evacuation, leaving you whimpering as you flushed away your colonic calamity, only to hear the toilet gurgle instead of gulp, and when you saw how the poor, tortured Gallic toilet had gagged on your refuse, you quickly closed the lid in horror and humiliation, washed your hands of any trace of waste, fixed an apologetic smile on your face, and strolled out with the key to the apartment in your hand, which the disgusted but still luscious secretary directed you to leave on the stand by the door so she would not have to touch it herself.

Pausing in the doorway, you said, Do you think I could have a pair of the Boss's shoes? You were in your socks and explained how, as you were about to leave the warehouse, the Mona Lisa had said, I still like your shoes, and you had been forced to give him the

Bruno Magli footwear that could have paid for a month's rent. The luscious secretary said, Just take them and get out, and you, continuing to heroically not see through her see-through nightgown, flashed her your most dashing bad-boy grin and said, You know, we kind of make a great team, to which she replied, Remember what I said about your balls.

And this was how you ended up with the key to the Boss's car, which you had separated from his house key while in the bathroom, anticipating the luscious secretary's demand for it. You looked down one last time at Madeleine's face and saw her eyes twitching behind her eyelids, and you wondered whether she was seeing a dream or a nightmare. Before you closed the door behind you, you imprinted her sleeping face on the soft wax of your memory, hoping her face would mask the wide-awake visage of the communist agent. Whatever had happened to her, wherever she was, you knew that she could still see you.

# CHAPTER 19

Above the open door, **OPIUM** was spelled out in the red neon typeface that adorned Chinese take-out boxes, a font whose name might be chop suey, ching-chong, or ah-so-asshole. At least the Boss had shown some class and did not have a gigantic gong inside, ready to be struck by an artificially buck-toothed servant every time a guest entered. Instead you heard the same jazz quartet that had played at the orgy and was now swinging here, having had the opportunity, unlike you, to go home and rest. This was true for Lousy as well, who had ditched his harem guard costume for a more contemporary look, a mixture of Parisian bohemian and Nazi chic: basic black turtleneck, black slacks, black leather jacket, and black boots. The look perfectly suited the vibe of **OPIUM**, for what **OPIUM** represented was not the ancient or even just slightly older Orient of the nineteenth and earlier twentieth centuries, when French and British monopolists, the original global drug runners and pharmaceutical warlords, had forced the natives at gunpoint to buy their opium. Oh, no! This was the new and modern Orient, where opium was both cool and quaint, chic and cute, addictive and undemanding. Opium was the whole package

and the perfect lover. No wonder why some people, like you, pre-
ferred the remedy.

Where's the Boss? said Lousy, who was manning the velvet
rope and artificially creating suspense by lining up a long queue of
patrons. The females were quite a sight, all legs, and the males were
quite a smell, more heavily dipped in cologne than the women were
in perfume. As for you, you had gone back to your aunt's apart-
ment after leaving Heaven, and there you had changed into the only
decent outfit you owned, a slim-fitting, secondhand dark gray suit
with a three-button jacket that dated from the early 1960s, which
clashed with the pastel shirts and exaggerated silhouettes of both
the men and the women, their shoulders inflated with enormous
pads large enough for eagles to land on. The suit was a gift from
the now-too-rotund Maoist PhD, who had worn it in his university
days when he rocked out to Johnny Hallyday. Your aunt had not
been home, and you had taken advantage of her absence to wake
yourself up with a shower, which also washed the sweat, smoke,
fear, and taint of death from your body. Then you had drunk the
last of the civet coffee and left the suitcase with the Boss's money
and the videos of the orgy under the sofa where you slept, the tapes
worth much more than the cash. Even with the coffee, you felt light-
headed by the time you parked far enough from OPIUM so that
none of the dwarfs would see you arrive in the Boss's car.

Where's the Boss? Lousy shouted again.

How the fuck do I know? Last I saw him, he had just killed the
Algerian. Then I went home.

The excuse would buy you some time. All you wanted was
enough time to survive the evening, see Lana and kiss her hem,
then come face-to-face with the faceless man and somehow manage
to pull off a magic trick and save him from Bon's vengeance. You
entered OPIUM and the smell licked you, the languorous ceiling

fans stirring the pheromonal trails of cologne and perfume, the smoke from cigarettes, hookahs, and your own homeland's water pipes, and the haze of the incense burning in a censer carried around the club by a petite woman whose face was masked by a veil ripped from the pages of *The Arabian Nights*. You did not see Lana as you scanned the sexy crowd, but you did see a few women who had gotten into the spirit of OPIUM and draped their feminine faces with the silky black veils proffered by the incense bearer.

The mix of scents and your own light-headedness and exhaustion made you dizzy, and the only cure for that was a drink, which was the cure for most things. You passed the banana trees and birds of paradise, the rattan armchairs and red lanterns, the rice paper screens and framed calligraphy, and waited your turn at the bar among a crowd of giggling young things demanding drinks served in ceramic Buddhas and graced with tiny paper umbrellas that could provide shade for crickets or for the withered little worm of your morality. When it was finally your turn, you said, or croaked, I'd like the Guilt and the Shame, please.

The what?

*The Guilt and the Shame!* you bellowed, louder than you intended.

For a moment, everyone in your vicinity looked at you but, seeing that there was nothing to see, went back to their business of getting buzzed and trying to get laid without appearing to do so.

The bartender adjusted his turban and said, stiffly, I don't know what that is, his professionalism being called into question by his ignorance.

It's easy, you said. One part tequila, one part vodka, no ice, no garnish, no nothing. It should look like holy water and taste like Hell.

That sounds disgusting, said the bartender.

And, sipping the Guilt and the Shame for the first time, you admitted that it was disgusting, but how else should such a pairing taste? A few doses of the Guilt and the Shame and you wouldn't remember a thing the next day, your head a coconut with the top sliced off, so someone could insert a straw and drink the contents of your mind while blowing bubbles into it. With a double Guilt and Shame in your hand—you always got a double, being a man of two minds—you wandered through OPIUM looking for Lana, but all you saw were servers wearing sexy cheongsams that ended midthigh and walls decorated with framed prints of black-and-white photographs from the nineteenth century: an aristocrat with curled fingernails the length of knife blades, bare-breasted women in indigenous clothing, an old lady smoking a cigar the size of a corncob. Are those Africans or Asians? a giggling young thing next to you asked another giggling young thing. I dunno, the other one said, resting her chin on the head of her ceramic Buddha. But they're cool.

You looked over a mural that covered an entire wall. It was mesmerizing, a photorealistic black-and-white painting of your half-naked countrymen and -women kneeling on the earth in what appeared to be a rubber plantation, wiry and grimy, wearing only tattered pants and headbands to keep the sweat out of their eyes. Their backs were to the painter, or to the viewer, their concentration focused on the woman striding among them, wearing a close-fitting vermilion dress that hugged an incredible form. In contrast to the rest of the mural, she was in full, blazing color, and she appeared to be the most beautiful woman in France, otherwise known as Catherine Deneuve. Why she had been transposed to a rubber plantation, only the painter knew. The only non-photorealistic detail about the entire mural was that Catherine Deneuve did not have sweat stains in the armpits of her dress or on the sternum-sticking front of her dress, for even the most beautiful woman in France,

and therefore the world, must sweat like everybody else. What a spell she cast, Catherine Deneuve, and indeed La France herself, her spectacle hypnotizing you until you felt a tap on your shoulder. It was Bon. Standing next to him was a slim woman in a minimalist, micro-miniskirted affair that was to "dress" what "bikini" was to "bathing suit." Her slender form struck you even more than the form of Catherine Deneuve, hers being a shiv that wedged between your ribs and came extremely close to your lungs and heart. A black silk veil covered everything beneath her caramel-brown eyes. A hand with long, delicate fingers and manicured nails as polished as an adulterer's lies rose from her side to sweep the veil off her face. You stepped forward, saying her name, ready to bestow *bisous* on her cheeks. She, in turn, drew back her elegant hand and slapped you so hard across the face you saw hammers and sickles, your ears ringing so loud you could barely hear your ever-present ghosts laughing their incorporeal asses off.

You bastard, Lana said, with an emphasis on "bastard." I've waited a long time to do that.

The last time you saw Lana, in her apartment in Los Angeles, only a few hours before you killed Sonny, the two of you had swung along the electric dialectic between Hegel and Marx, Spirit and Being, Ideal and Material, Mind and Body, Making Love and Having Sex. She was like one of the forbidden red books that Man had shared with you clandestinely in your study group, beginning with *The Communist Manifesto* and Mao's *Little Red Book*. Books like those inflamed the mind, energized the body, burned the hands that opened them, holding secret knowledge that paradoxically could be shared with everyone. You know you want it, Lana had said. I know you want it. And so you opened her. Both of you faced

the mirrored doors of her bedroom closet, actors and spectators at once. You looked at each other's reflections and each other's gazes in the mirror, everything backward and yet still making sense. Seeing yourselves in this glassy scene, yourselves and yet not yourselves, made you hard as a mirror. When your mirror shattered, you lost not only your sense of sight but your sense of touch, every extremity numb, including your toes and fingertips. You collapsed, still conjoined, the remnants of your shattered self inside her, and with her eyes closed, language reinhabited her.

You bastard, she whispered, with an emphasis on "bastard." I knew you'd be good.

Did Lana not remember that night? Or did she remember it all too well? It was difficult to ask, not just because of Bon being present but also Loan, who was saving a table on the second floor of **OPIUM**.

Your cheeks are so red, Loan said on seeing you. You're as excited as I am to see Lana!

You mumbled something inarticulate that simply made you seem starstruck, although in this case the star, Lana, was not a superstar whom everyone would recognize, like Cher, or Olivia Newton-John, or Karen Carpenter, but a distant star in a galaxy that required an ethnic telescope to see. All the Vietnamese knew Lana, while anyone not Vietnamese had no idea who she was, although that did not stop the people in **OPIUM**—men and women—from looking, simply because she exuded a star's heat and light.

You were hot just sitting next to her, and this, along with your exhaustion and your light-headedness and the memory of the Boss and the Ronin and Le Cao Boi, their faces permanently painted on the walls of the cave of your mind, combined with the Boss's ill-gotten cash, led you to call over one of the waifish servers in her sexy scarlet cheongsam and order a bottle of the finest Champagne.

We have a lot to celebrate, you said, and then leaned over and whispered, I work for the Boss, I should get the employee discount, to which she smiled stiffly, adjusted the chopsticks in her hair, and said she would see what she could do.

What are we celebrating? Loan said. Besides being here with Lana?

You lit Lana's cigarette, which she had been holding in the air for a minute, waiting, and said, Yes, we are celebrating Lana arriving at last in Paris. We are also celebrating you two lovebirds.

Bon flushed with embarrassment but said nothing, preferring to tug at his tie while Loan squeezed his other hand.

Congratulations, Lana said, leaning forward to shine her light on them. You deserve it, Bon.

You could tell she remembered the last time she had been in a dimly lit situation with Bon, when you and he had seen her perform at Fantasia in Los Angeles. There he had confessed the loss of the loves of his life and had wept, the only time he had ever wept in the presence of an adult besides his wife and me.

Loan, Lana went on, you are a beautiful woman and I am so happy for the two of you.

Bon said, Uh—

Are you happy, Bon? Loan said.

Bon flushed even redder. Am I—am I— Emotion embarrassed him and made him stutter in a way that death and killing never did. Am I—uh—

You nudged him under the table with your foot, and when he looked at you, you gave the most imperceptible of nods, and he said, Yes—yes—happy—and, you know—uh—we all have to move on . . .

Yes, you must move on, Loan said, taking his hand. But that does not mean that you have to forget Linh and Duc. You never have

to forget Linh and Duc, not that you ever would. They are always a part of you and therefore always a part me, dear Bon!

This flash-bang grenade of emotional explicitness thrown into Bon's lap left him shell-shocked. As for you—you poor, dumb, crazy, ugly bastard—you suddenly and unexpectedly started to weep uncontrollably, making everyone uncomfortable. What the fuck was wrong with you? Your body shook as the tears gushed out and you sobbed, God, sorry, I don't know—what—ugh—

You stood up to make a dash to the bathroom, but Bon leaned across the table, grabbed you by the hem of your jacket, and muttered, Sit down, you sad bastard. We're all friends here.

Lana put her hand on your arm. It's okay, she said. Let it out.

Not that you could have stopped. Where were these tears and sobs coming from, except from some false bottom in your soul? Beneath the false bottom, in unfathomable darkness, deeper than the pit of Hell, dwelt not fire but water, the profound well of your feelings, especially for your mother, the only woman whom you ever truly loved, a woman whom you would have died for, but no one gave you the chance. There was no other woman for whom you could have said the same thing, unlike Bon. Seeing the scar in the palm of his hand that signified your blood brotherhood, you knew he would die for you but that he would also do the same for Loan, as he would have sacrificed himself for Linh and Duc, if given the chance. As for you, you would die for Bon, and you would die for Man, even now, even after all he had done to you, because you were still blood brothers. Your love for these men, a love that might one day kill you, also let you know you were worthy of life.

I love you, Bon, you said.

It was something you neither wanted nor planned to say, and his stricken look told you that you had spoken the unspeakable, but so what? You had uttered so many obscenities in your life and

committed so many sins that not even Bon's dis-ease or the mocking laughter of your ghosts made you regret saying out loud what should have been performed only as inarticulate acts of manly camaraderie.

All right, Bon said, patting your hand. It's all right.

The server came back at that moment with the Champagne and an ice bucket, and the next minute passed in awkward silence as she uncorked the bottle and poured four flutes of Champagne, all while you wept, sobbed, breathed deeply, huffed, snuffled, sniffed, and, finally, eased shut the trapdoor covering your soul's false bottom. Um, the server said, perhaps taking pity on you, I just wanted to say that you do get the employee discount. She handed you the cloth napkin she would have wrapped the bottle with and left you to wipe away tears and blow the snot out of your nose.

Well, said Loan.

Sorry, you said, or maybe whimpered. So sorry. Really, very sorry.

Bon picked up his flute. I guess we should toast.

I have a toast, Lana said.

You all turned to look at her expectantly. She raised her flute, and so did everyone else. Here's to you, she said to you, which surprised you and brought a hopeful smile to your face. Congratulations, you bastard. You're a father.

To your credit, you neither passed out nor ran for the nearest exit. You simply gawked at Lana, swiveled your head left and right to look at the expressions of astonishment on Loan's and Bon's frozen faces, then turned back to an unmoving Lana. *You're a Father* was the title of the most horrifying horror movie you could imagine, unless it was one of the sequels like *You're a Father Part 2, 3,* or *4,* or, if you were Catholic, *You're a Father 5, 6, 7, 8, 9, 10, 11,* or *12.*

You knew yourself, and you had no desire to continue the cycle of abuse otherwise known as life. Your greatest contribution to the propagation of the human species was not to propagate yourself, even if your mother badly wanted a grandchild. Imagine how wonderful it would be if you brought a child into the world! On every occasion she had said this, you had smiled, caressed her hand, and lied. Of course, yes, one day, surely! Now doomsday had at last arrived and all you could blurt out to restart time and space was: But I used a condom!

Lana sipped her Champagne and said, Maybe you bought a bad condom.

If the rubber in that condom came from a French rubber plantation, then the French had fucked you yet again. You opened your mouth and Lana said, Don't you dare ask if there might be another candidate. You're the only asshole there is.

You shut your mouth and looked to Bon for help, but he swallowed all of his Champagne and said, It's not the end of the world. Some of us want children.

Well, Loan said, smiling brightly. Boy or girl?

Girl.

A boy would have petrified you, because he would surely one day grow up to slay you, which you admittedly deserved, but a girl was not much better, perhaps worse, because you would have to do things like braid her hair, avoid discussing her menstruation, and contemplate her one day meeting someone exactly like you and marrying the rotten bastard. You breathed deeply to calm yourself down. What did normal people say in situations like this?

How—how old is she?

Three years old.

She's here?

She's in Los Angeles with my parents.

What's her name?

Ada.

Ada. A slightly unusual name that Westerners could pronounce, and a completely foreign name that Vietnamese people could still wrap their tongues around. *A-d-a.* A Morse code of a name. Long *A*, hard *d*, short *a*. Three letters. A palindrome. The same whether left to right or East to West. Ada, the grandchild whom your mother had always wanted and whom you had finally given to her, too late.

Do you have a picture?

Ada was a little girl with pure black hair that framed her face and ended at her chin. You hated children, which was not a prejudice but rather a logical reaction from years of childhood exposure to the little trolls, who were nothing but monstrous adults-in-grooming. But this girl—everything about her face was round, from her eyes to her cheeks to the tip of her nose. Her eyes were dark, her lips pink, and her skin fair. If she had been fully white, her skin color would just be called white. But since she descended from you, and you were half white, she was only one-quarter white. Her semi-whiteness was not what interested you, however. What was most striking about her to you, besides the chubby cuteness that even you could recognize, was whom she resembled.

Your mother.

Ada, you said. Ada.

That's her name, Lana said.

After the bottle of Champagne was finished, and after you had drained your third chalice of Guilt and Shame, and after Bon told Lana the short version of what had brought the two of you to the City of Light, and after Lana asked why you had gone to France and not the United States and you said because you wanted to visit

the land of your father, and after she asked why you had never let anyone know you were here and you had honestly said because you didn't think anyone cared whether you lived or died, which made her bite her lip and look away, you and Bon made a break for the men's room. Facing the urinals, you informed Bon of the recent deaths, which fazed him not at all. They weren't exactly the best people, he said, shaking off their fates and zipping his pants. But that's a mess we have to clean up.

Right, you said, although you had no intention of cleaning anything up, which actually just meant making things even messier by continuing the war with the Mona Lisa and Saïd.

But first, we have to take care of the faceless man. Tonight.

You looked in the mirror and the sight of your reflection somewhat surprised you. Half the time now, you expected to see no one there, that your body would be as invisible as your soul. What you also saw, besides yourself and Bon washing hands, were your grinning ghosts, standing behind you and drilled with holes, still dripping with the perpetual stuff of life. But you did not see the Boss, Le Cao Boi, or the Ronin, or your father, or the communist agent.

He'll be there, Bon said, wiping his hands. I know it.

I don't have a gun, you said, which was your only gambit to avoid killing Man.

Bon shrugged, put his foot on the edge of the sink, and pulled up the hem of his pants to reveal a small pistol strapped to his ankle. My backup, he said, giving it to you. You should always have a backup. Have I taught you nothing?

You drove the Boss's Bavarian behemoth to the theater, Bon and Loan in the back seat holding hands, Lana next to you. The Boss had a cassette tape of her songs, and as you drove, you listened to her

cover of the song that had compelled you, when you heard her sing it in the Fantasia of Los Angeles, to take the fateful steps that led to her and ultimately to Ada. "Bang Bang (My Baby Shot Me Down)."

Does she know I'm her . . . father? you said, finding it hard even to say the word.

I don't have so much as a picture of you, Lana said. But she has asked about you.

She has?

Just who and where her father is, why everyone else has a father but not her.

What do you say?

My parents have forbidden me to say your name to her.

Madame. And the General, who had stuffed the muddy sock of these words in your mouth just as you were about to board the plane for Thailand and the invasion: *How could you ever believe we would allow our daughter to be with someone of your kind? You are a fine young man, but you are also, in case you have not noticed, a bastard.*

So I've been erased from her life? you said, still able to taste the foulness.

I tell Ada that her father is a soldier who went to take his country back, who gave everything he had to liberate his people. And that maybe one day he'll come back to us and we will give him a hero's welcome. When I say that she smiles and I hold her close. And feel sorry for you. Not because of what might have happened to you, but because you would never know what it feels like to hold your little girl, to hold her when she was a baby, to cuddle her fat little body, to squeeze her and make her giggle, to have her kiss you whenever you ask for it, to hear her say, Daddy, I love you, like the way she says, Mommy, I love you.

"Bang Bang (My Baby Shot Me Down)."

You've missed all those things and you'll never get them back. But that doesn't mean you have to miss what she is like now, what she'll be like next year and the rest of her life.

You want me to—

Not for me, you bastard. For her. She deserves to know her father and make up her own mind about you. Otherwise she'll grow up hoping her heroic papa might come back one day. Or else she'll believe that he's in France and never bothered to let anybody know he was still alive and that he had abandoned her. Don't do that to her.

Bon coughed. I think we passed the theater a couple of blocks ago.

After you parked the car, you and Bon walked to the theater behind Lana and Loan, who had many questions about *Fantasia* and its stars. The two of you smoked a cigarette in brotherly silence, each preparing for meeting the faceless man. You had no other ideas, a lack you blamed on having consumed too much of the remedy or not having any of the remedy on hand. Checking your pockets, you discovered that there was still no remedy secretly waiting for you. You began to tremble from all of it, the Champagne, the Guilt and the Shame, the fear of what would happen, the terror of suddenly being a father, the killing of the Boss, and the lack of the remedy. At the theater's back door, you said goodbye to Lana, who said, Come see me after the show. We have more to talk about. I'm leaving tomorrow for Berlin.

Germany?

The Vietnamese there love us.

She is so nice, a starstruck Loan said as you walked to the front. You're so lucky. I can't believe that she—that you—not that she wouldn't with—well, you know what I mean.

You did indeed know what Loan meant and you took no offense, since you were so revolting that you revolted even yourself. The only ones more offensive than you that night were Angry and Smelly, lurking in the theater lobby.

Where's the Boss? said Angry.

And Le Cao Boi? added Smelly.

How the fuck do I know? you said. Last I saw him, he had just killed the Algerian. Then I went home.

Hey, said Angry. There's the Boss's secretary.

The luscious secretary had arrived for the VIP reception in the lobby, thankfully no longer wearing a see-through nightgown but instead an elegant midnight-blue evening gown with a dead animal draped on her shoulders. On closer inspection, the poor thing turned out to be just a fur.

Hey, said Smelly. Where's the Boss?

How should I know? said the luscious secretary. Then she looked at you, curled her lip, and hissed, You're *disgusting*, you filthy *bastard*!

Goddamn! said Angry, nudging you as the luscious secretary walked away. She must be having a hell of a period.

Or you did something to her that the Boss won't like, said Smelly.

Angry and Smelly contemplated you the way butchers inspected barbecued ducks hung by hooks from their anus. So, before matters got worse, you confessed to your fecal faux pas in the Boss's bathroom, leaving Angry and Smelly howling with laughter until tears squeezed out of their eyes. *Filthy* bastard, they said, chuckling. Filthy *bastard*!

What was that all about? Loan said when you joined her and Bon.

She handed you a flute of Champagne and you said, Nothing. How about a toast? To the two of you. And because it was Paris, because it was love, you said, *Levons nos verres à l'amour!*

Loan's smile faded even as you and Bon clinked your flutes.
Something wrong? Bon asked, his flute suspended in the air.

Yes, Loan said, pale. He just asked us to raise our glasses to
death.

*L'amour ou la mort?* Love or death? What was the difference? Some
say *tom-ay-toe*, some say *tom-ah-toe*. It was only a slip of the tongue,
or rather, it was your tongue unable, in conjunction with your lips,
to mold the crucial word properly. Damn the language of Molière!
Always putting words in your mouth that got stuck in your molars,
but then again, every language does that. Unfortunately, there was
no way to call the whole thing off. Not with Bon's backup tucked into
your waistband backing you up, not with Bon next to you scanning
the lobby for the faceless man as more and more excited patrons of
*Fantasia* arrived. Loan had wandered off to chat with friends after
the fatal switch you had committed, while you made small talk with
the bohemian youth of the Union, who greeted you heartily and
then whispered to inquire about the goods. You told them to call
you tomorrow, although you had no idea where you would be then,
except covered with earth and six feet closer to your mother if the
remaining dwarfs found out what happened or if Saïd changed his
mind. Meanwhile, you just wanted to enjoy, for a brief moment, the
rare sight of harmony in the lobby, as Vietnamese people of all kinds
mixed together in joyful anticipation of *Fantasia*: the liberal to left-
wing to outright communist members of the Union, who had been
in France two or three generations and tended to be middle class
to upper-middle class and above; the conservative to right-wing
to outright fascist members of the Association, who were recent
refugees and tended to be very poor to somewhat poor to work-
ing class; and everyone in between, those on the margins, or the

politically uninterested, wanting only to enjoy themselves, which made them the same as just about everybody else on the planet.

It's the ambassador, Bon said.

The ambassador had the shape of a bowling pin and looked fairly well fed, given that he was representing a starving country where people lived on rations, or so *Le Monde* and *Le Figaro* reported. He was with a woman in an ao dai, presumably his wife, and two teenaged children, a boy and a girl, the former in an ill-fitting suit, the latter in an ao dai like her mother. Members of the Union flocked to greet them but also to put a wall between them and the Association's members, who glared and muttered. I'll get him, too, Bon said, and you murmured encouragingly. Who were you to get in the way of a man's dreams and aspirations?

Then it was showtime, with no sign of the faceless man, and you followed Bon into the theater to join Loan.

Everything all right? she said to Bon, ignoring you.

Everything's fine, Bon said. We were just people-watching.

Programs rustled in people's laps as they murmured, chattered, and laughed. The curtains were still closed but anticipation was high, for your people had waited months for *Fantasia* to arrive. The only one disappointed was Bon, although you were relieved, if for the exact same reason: no faceless man. Both of you should have known better.

You had barely taken your seats when someone behind you said, Take a look at that guy, so you did as the man strode down the aisle to your right. He wore a nondescript dark blue suit, an average outfit for an officially underpaid civil servant from a poor country. His wispy hair revealed an underlying parchment of scarred scalp, partly covered by a black band around the back of the head. Bon inhaled sharply as the man paused before the row in which the ambassador sat. When he turned to his left so that he could enter the row, the

entire theater saw what the person behind you had glimpsed: not a face but a mask, held in place by the black band. A mask with eyebrows, cheeks, and a broad, but certainly not flat, nose. A mask with lips, as well as holes for eyes that might be ever-so-slightly angled, or tilted, but certainly not slanted. A mask with a face that might have been Asian in its inscrutable features, but that might also have been just human in its unreadable immobility. A mask that was utterly, completely, thoroughly, and indisputably white.

# CHAPTER 20

The lights dimmed, the audience cheered, and the curtains opened with the spotlight focused on the one woman onstage, Lana, whose skintight red leather catsuit revealed a body that bore no trace of having been invaded and occupied by a child. The microphone in her hand was a joystick with which she steered the audience, who was carried away by her voice. You recognized the song immediately—"For Your Eyes Only," from the James Bond movie of the same name, which had been shown for the benefit of the entire refugee camp one evening on Pulau Galang. For refugees who had barely escaped with their lives, a James Bond movie was the escapism they needed. But for you immigrants, refugees, and exiles of Paris, or for your French-born children, the song had a special meaning: *Fantasia* was for your eyes only. You were not just objects being looked at, you were the subjects looking, your collective gaze concentrated on Lana, whose body embodied everything Vietnamese as she translated the admittedly banal lyrics into your common language. Banal or not, the lyrics spoke a truth about love, both the initial match strike between lovers and the flickering, fluctuating flame of love your people had for each

other, complicated and difficult, as all real love was. In this flame you saw not only your beauty but your ugliness, and Lana saw you, all of you, even you in your middling seat, and when she shouted, Good evening, Paris! all of you roared in appreciation, and when she cried, Hello, my dear people! you cheered, whistled, clapped, and stomped your feet, submitting to *Fantasia's* greatest fantasy, which was that you had never fought a war against each other, one which you even now were continuing to fight, since the bitterest of wars were civil wars. For a moment, you forgot reality, which was that the people who most hated Vietnamese people were other Vietnamese people. A tragedy, sure, but set it aside, since tonight was for *Fantasia*, as the next singer sauntering onto the stage reminded you.

It's Elvis! Loan squealed, clapping her hands.

The wave of hair resembled Elvis Presley's pompadour, but this was not *that* Elvis. This figure in black leather pants and a purple velvet smoking jacket with a paisley pocket square and lavender-tinted glasses was *your* Elvis, named after the King of Rock, a stroke of genius that made all of you wonder why you had not thought of it. And why not take the King's name? You never allowed anything successful to pass without immediately copying it, whether that was songs, or books, or restaurants, or tyrants, or exploitative and murderous systems of domination, theft, and embezzlement, otherwise known as colonialism, which sounded better when dubbed *la mission civilisatrice*. Everything sounded better in French, including rape, murder, and pillage! Regardless of the thievery or the homage, this Elvis possessed a hell of a voice, on par with Lana's, his only fault being that he was a man and not much to look at, but about that nothing can be done. You lean back and their sexy version of his classic "Love You" rolls over you as they cha-cha across the stage. How wise those lyrics are—*love you because I hate sadness, love you because I'm sick of people, love you because I'm tired of life. Love you.*

*Love you. Love you.* You wish the world was always like a music concert. Mass political or religious gatherings were a crapshoot as to whether attendees left intent on helping strangers or murdering them, but when was the last time music fans had massacred other people at a show's end?

*Fantasia* only gets better as it rolls along, with the lights gradually revealing the musicians at the back of the stage. A dozen extremely fit dancers accompany a parade of singers, male and female, who showcase the two most common and delectable emotions in your popular culture, namely love and sadness, with their subtle variations of loss, absence, melancholy, regret, and yearning. The show so overwhelms you that you have actually forgotten about the faceless man when Bon grabs your arm and whispers, He's leaving. He is silhouetted against the lights of the stage as he makes his way through his row. Now's our chance, Bon whispers as the faceless man walks up the aisle, and you curse Man's timing. You and everyone else are utterly entranced by the newest performer onstage, the bewitching and perplexing Alexa, a blond white Québécoise who sings in perfect Vietnamese. You want to stay and figure out how a white woman has pulled off this magic trick, but Bon whispers something to Loan, then pushes you until you rise and the two of you stumble over the feet of the others in your row.

Outside the theater, you catch a glimpse of the back of the faceless man as he turns a corner in the lobby, passing by an astonished Angry, smoking a cigarette.

He's going to the bathroom, Bon says, striding by you, hand under his jacket, touching his gun.

You can feel Bon's backup in the small of your back as you follow, and the joy and happiness of your few minutes with *Fantasia* turn into smoke, leaving only a dread lump of coal in your gut.

Who the hell was that? says Angry. What are you guys doing?

Tell you later, says Bon.

The two of you turn the corner just in time to see the door to the men's room close, and Bon asks if you are ready without looking at you. The question is rhetorical. He assumes you must be ready and he does not care if you are not, for he is now a heat-seeking missile. You and he cover the ground to the door in a few seconds, and as you do, he slips out his gun, racks the slide, and uses his left hand to push open the door while he raises the gun with his right. He moves so quickly that when he stops abruptly, you run into him and knock him aside, revealing the faceless man, back against the wall, facing the door, hands by his side, mask still on his face.

What took you so long? the faceless man says. I've been waiting for you.

Delights of Asia is shuttered, but nobody on rue de Belleville notices even though it is prime time on a Saturday night, for no loyal customers exist to be disappointed. You drove Bon and the faceless man here, the two of them in the back seat with Bon aiming his gun at the faceless man. He had offered no resistance in the men's room or on the walk out of the theater past the still-smoking, still-perplexed Angry, who again said, Who the hell is this guy? You drove without musical accompaniment, the better to hear what the faceless man said, sentences that might earn you a bullet in the back of your head. But in the car, the faceless man did not reveal his name or who he really was. Nor did Bon ask, because Bon thought he knew who the faceless man was: the commissar, the political officer of the reeducation camp charged with administering your ideological laxative and purging you of all the remnants of colonization in your colon, followed by making you over as communists in the image of Marx, Lenin, and Ho Chi Minh (but not Mao, for your

triumphant revolutionary regime, having kicked out the French and the Americans with a little help from the Chinese, was now free to hate the Chinese once again). Even among the camp guards and the camp commandant, the commissar was only known as the commissar. So this is what Bon called him, Commissar, hissing out the word, which appeared to bother the faceless man not at all.

Why the mask, Commissar? were the first words Bon said once you were in the Boss's brute, the three of you having walked in silence from the theater. You watched the scene in the rearview mirror, Bon staring at the faceless man's mask, the faceless man orienting his gaze so that he could see both Bon, next to him, and you, in the driver's seat. The faceless man laughed, or made some sound approximating laughter, for whatever noises he made were slightly muffled by the mask and distorted by his scarred throat. You remembered from your interrogation sessions with the commissar in the camp that he no longer sounded like Man, which—along with his missing face—meant Bon did not recognize him.

Don't you like me better with a mask?

I don't like you at all, mask or no mask. Why are you here?

Paris is my reward for being a hero of the state, the faceless man said in his raspy voice. Funny, after having thrown out our colonizers, how we like to take vacations among them. I process visas in a back office, so no one has to see me. Very painless and easy, except for the boredom. But the real reason to be here are the excellent plastic surgeons. In this and other ways, the French have tried to be helpful in the postwar years.

Why would they do that?

Guilt? It's easier for the French to feel guilty now, because they can point to the Americans and say they did much worse. Also, you don't know how much the French enjoy hearing our diplomats celebrate defeating the Americans in perfect French! The faceless

man laughed, and it was a horrible sound. Hearing us speak fluent French makes them believe we boys have finally become men.

And the plastic surgeons?

They offered to do it for free. The faceless man laughed again even though nothing was funny. The French enslaved us, but of course not all the French are responsible. The same colonizing class that exploited us exploit the French people too. At least these surgeons are human like us.

Human? You're not human. You're a monster. Let's see your face then, or what's left of it. All that time in the camp, I never got a real close look at you.

Oh, not yet. The faceless man laughed. He was apparently having the time of his life. The light is not good here. A monster needs excellent light.

The light is also not good in front of Delights of Asia, and this may account for what Bon does not notice as he approaches the shutters with a key. You enter, and the stage is now set. The actors are in place, the plot moves through the maze to its inevitable end, the script already written. And who is the scriptwriter but you? Still, as the person penning this scenario, you are only partly in control, for you are not the producer of what is clearly a black comedy, even if calling a comedy black is kind of, sort of, maybe, perhaps, residually racist, although if you suggested that to a Frenchman, or even to an American, and most probably to a Vietnamese, he would indignantly denounce you as racist for seeing something racial in an innocent use of the word "black." Just a coincidence! Nothing to do with black markets, or blackface, or how the French, in a really wonderful turn of phrase, call ghostwriters *nègres*—niggers!—the sheer bravado of it taking your breath away when you heard it for the first time. But why take offense over a playful use of words, when it really was the

case that ghostwriters were just slaves, minus the whipping, rap-
ing, lynching, lifetime servitude, and free labor? Still—what the
hell?—if words are just words, then let's call it a white comedy,
shall we? It's just a joke, take it easy, a bad joke, sure, but so was
the Unholy Trinity of colonialism, slavery, and genocide, not to
mention the Dynamic Duo of capitalism and communism, both
of which white people invented and which were contagious, like
smallpox and syphilis. White people have gotten over those bad
jokes, haven't they? In any case, all wordplay aside, this really is
a white comedy, for the real producers are white, the colonizers
and the capitalists who long ago financed this epic production
of which your bit is not even on the main stage. Oh, no, to add
insult to injury—because insult is always added to injury—you
are off-off-off-off-off-Broadway, on a sideshow of a sideshow of
a sideshow, molesting Molière's horrified ghost, in an intimate
theater of the absurd so cutting edge, so avant-garde, so far ahead
of the masses that there are not even any spectators! Except for
you three watching yourselves, the CAST:

BLOOD BROTHER #1 (Man, a.k.a. the commissar, a.k.a. the
faceless man)
BLOOD BROTHER #2 (you, a.k.a. the captain, a.k.a. Vo
Danh)
BLOOD BROTHER #3 (Bon, who has no other name)

What happy days, these! Your theatrical debut in a piece of
performance theater, where all the restaurant's a stage. Everything
is improvisational, everything is unpredictable, except the most
predictable thing of all, the end that must be achieved, the mask
that must be taken off, the gun that must be fired. But before this
white comedy can proceed to its last act, we have

## THE PENULTIMATE
(*that means next-to-last*)
## ACT

*The door opens with a crash. Enter SMELLY and ANGRY, cleavers in hand.*

SMELLY   What the fuck's going on?

ANGRY   You fuckers have been acting weird.

SMELLY   (*points to the faceless man*) Who the fuck is this?

BLOOD BROTHER #2   That is a great philosophical question.

SMELLY   Shut the fuck up, you crazy bastard.

ANGRY   Where's the Boss? Where's Le Cao Boi? Why is the restaurant closed?

BLOOD BROTHER #3   Why are you here? You're supposed to be at the theater.

SMELLY   You don't get to ask questions. You didn't even pull duty at the orgy.

ANGRY   You think you're too good for that? Fuck you.

SMELLY   So who the fuck is this? And why's he wearing that mask?

BLOOD BROTHER #3   Take off your mask.

BLOOD BROTHER #1   Gladly, brother. I have been waiting a long time to take this off.

BLOOD BROTHER #3   I'm not your brother.

*BLOOD BROTHER #1 removes his mask.*

SMELLY  Ugh. I mean—Jesus, come on, that—

ANGRY  What the fuck happened to your face?

BLOOD BROTHER #1  (*chuckles*) You should have seen it before the surgeries.

SMELLY  You need new surgeons.

BLOOD BROTHER #1  I've already had a half dozen operations. But when you start with nothing, when your entire face has been burned off by napalm, rebuilding it takes a while. God made this world in seven days, but even the most talented, highly trained, highly paid human beings require quite a bit more time to create something so simple as a face. I'm only halfway there.

ANGRY  Answer the goddamn question: Who the fuck are you?

BLOOD BROTHER #1  That is a great philosophical question. You must remember that the birth of a being that must proceed from nothingness, absolute beginning, is an event historically absurd.

SMELLY  WHO THE FUCK ARE YOU?

BLOOD BROTHER #1  You don't recognize me?

ANGRY  Why would we recognize you?

BLOOD BROTHER #1  I was asking Bon. But you should recognize me, too.

SMELLY  We don't even know you, you weird fuck.

BLOOD BROTHER #1  Have you looked in the mirror recently?

ANGRY  Fuck you—

BLOOD BROTHER #1  Really looked?

SMELLY   I don't even give a fuck anymore if you answer the question.

ANGRY   Wait until the Boss gets a look at you.

SMELLY   Where's the Boss, you crazy bastard?

*BLOOD BROTHER #3 shoots SMELLY in the side of the head.*

ANGRY   What the—

*BLOOD BROTHER #3 shoots ANGRY between the eyes.*

BLOOD BROTHER #2   Holy shit!

*SMELLY and ANGRY are supine on the floor.*

BLOOD BROTHER #3   They weren't the best people.

*SMELLY and ANGRY appear to be dead.*

BLOOD BROTHER #1   What doesn't kill you makes you stronger.

*SMELLY and ANGRY are definitely dead.*

BLOOD BROTHER #2   Why . . .

BLOOD BROTHER #3   Why? Those crazy fucks would cut you up while you were still alive and laugh while they did it. It was either kill them now or kill them later, and if it was later, it would be a lot messier.

*SMELLY and ANGRY are still dead.*

BLOOD BROTHER #2     No one gives a shit.

BLOOD BROTHER #1     Probably true. Aren't you afraid someone's going to call the police?

BLOOD BROTHER #3     Walls are thick. Shutters are closed. Only two shots. I'll take my chances.

BLOOD BROTHER #1     You're as focused as ever.

BLOOD BROTHER #3     Ever? What do you know about ever?

BLOOD BROTHER #1     Oh, Bon. Do you still not recognize me?

BLOOD BROTHER #3     You're the commissar.

BLOOD BROTHER #1     I'm more than the commissar. And less.

BLOOD BROTHER #3     I don't care. You're here to die and I'm here to kill you.

BLOOD BROTHER #2     Everything happens for a reason.

BLOOD BROTHER #3     Jesus, can you shut up? Where's your gun?

BLOOD BROTHER #2     I don't give a fuck.

BLOOD BROTHER #3     Well, I do, you poor bastard. You may not want to kill this son of a bitch, although I don't know why, given what he did to you, but I am going to kill him and I'm going to enjoy every second of it.

BLOOD BROTHER #1     Bon.

BLOOD BROTHER #3     You're not getting out of this.

BLOOD BROTHER #1     I don't want to get out of this. All I ask is that you recognize me first. Don't you understand? I wanted you to find me. Why do you think I came to Paris? The Soviets have excellent plastic surgeons, too.

BLOOD BROTHER #3     I'm not surprised.

BLOOD BROTHER #1     I visited Moscow. Do you know Lenin's corpse is on exhibit? Amazing how the taxidermists preserved him. Kind of like plastic surgery. And these experts came and did the same to Ho Chi Minh. He looks like he's sleeping. The people travel from far and wide to see him in his mausoleum. Ho Chi Minh's corpse is now the most beautiful work of art in our country.

*Something is leaking from SMELLY and ANGRY.*

BLOOD BROTHER #3     What do you mean, you wanted us to find you?

BLOOD BROTHER #1     I knew our brother here would not return to the United States, having killed a man there and having helped you kill another. France was the next likely place. There are many of us here. And, of course, France is the land of his father. Where else would he go? And if he went here, where else but Paris? Then it was simply a matter of making my presence known. A man with a mask instead of a face can hardly walk around without getting noticed.

BLOOD BROTHER #3     But why find us?

BLOOD BROTHER #1     We have unfinished business. It's just not the business you think.

*Dark stains from SMELLY and ANGRY are slowly spreading across the floor.*

BLOOD BROTHER #2     Who the fuck do you think you are?

BLOOD BROTHER #3   Who are you talking to, you crazy bastard?

BLOOD BROTHER #2   Myself. But also to our brother here.

BLOOD BROTHER #3   He's not our brother!

BLOOD BROTHER #1   Shall I tell him or shall you?

BLOOD BROTHER #3   Tell me what?

BLOOD BROTHER #2   I'm sorry, Bon. I'm so sorry. Really, very sorry.

BLOOD BROTHER #3   Sorry about what?

BLOOD BROTHER #1   As am I.

BLOOD BROTHER #3   Sorry about what?

BLOOD BROTHER #2   I believed I was doing the right thing.

BLOOD BROTHER #3   What are you trying to tell me?

BLOOD BROTHER #1   Are you sure you don't recognize me?

BLOOD BROTHER #3   Stop playing your mind games.

*SMELLY and ANGRY stare blankly at the ceiling, contemplating the meaning of life, or death, or whatever this is.*

BLOOD BROTHER #1   Do you recognize this?

*He holds up his left hand. A long red scar cuts across the palm.*

BLOOD BROTHER #3   (*hesitates*) So what?

BLOOD BROTHER #1   It's the same scar as on your hand.

BLOOD BROTHER #3   (*to BLOOD BROTHER #2*) Did you tell him about our oath?

BLOOD BROTHER #2   He already knew about the oath.

BLOOD BROTHER #3   How?

BLOOD BROTHER #1   Because I'm your brother, Bon. I'm Man.

BLOOD BROTHER #3   Anybody can cut themselves. You got the story about our oath from the crazy bastard here. He would have told you anything when you tortured him.

BLOOD BROTHER #2   I didn't have to tell him. He knows, because he's Man.

BLOOD BROTHER #3   What did he do to you? What did you say to him? Tell me the truth.

BLOOD BROTHER #1   Yes, tell him the truth.

BLOOD BROTHER #2   You go first.

BLOOD BROTHER #1   He won't believe it from me. Maybe he will believe it from you.

*Lights dim, except for spotlights on the three of you. SMELLY and ANGRY rise from the floor and recede into the shadows to join the chorus of your ghosts, who rub their hands and nudge one another in anticipation.*

## THE LAST ACT

Bon and Man stare at you, waiting for you to speak. You do not know what to say, you say, except that when people do not know what to say, they oftentimes do know what to say but just do not want to say it. The first thing you do, however, is remove Bon's backup gun from behind your back and hand it to him. What are you giving me this for? he says, although he takes the gun, the first sign that he knows something is very wrong.

I want you to know I wouldn't use it on you, you say. Or Man.

He's not Man. Why do you—just stop it. He brainwashed you back in the camp, didn't he?

This all started long before the camp, Bon. I'm sorry. I'm so very sorry. I don't know where to begin. Except that you have to believe him. The faceless man is the commissar. And the commissar is our blood brother, Man. He didn't die defending Saigon. He was hit by a napalm strike that burned his face off, but he survived.

Bon looks back and forth between the two of you. I don't—I—

Just listen. Man and I—we're—we are—we were—we have been—

What? Bon says, and for the first time the muzzle of his gun shifts from Man to you.

Communists. I was already a communist when I went to America to study, when I joined the Special Branch and worked for the General. But I am no longer a communist. Maybe Man still is one.

I don't understand, Bon says, his muzzle moving back to Man.

You have to understand, Man says. We are your blood brothers.

No, you're not, not if this is true—

And why wouldn't it be true? Man says. We are the ones telling you.

You evil son of a bitch! Bon shouts. What did he do to you in that camp?

A great deal, you say. But we had already started long before. Even at the lycée, when we swore our oaths to each other. We were blood brothers, but we were already different. It wasn't much later that Man began talking to me about the terrible things the French did to us—

I know the terrible things the French have done to us, Bon says.

But you believed that the Americans were there to rescue us. You were already ready to fight with them, against the communists. But Man told me the truth—the Americans weren't there to help us. They were there to have us help them fight the communists, when the communists were actually trying to liberate us—

So he started brainwashing you even back then—

Not brainwashing—

So now you admit it, Man says. You recognize me after all, don't
you?

I don't recognize a damn thing! Bon shouts. Even if you were—
even if you might have been—you're insane now. Maybe you always
were, and I never saw it. Maybe your insanity rubbed off on this
poor bastard, who really is a crazy bastard if he believed in your—

I'm not here to argue politics, Bon, you say. I'm just trying to—

You're a fucking communist! And a liar!

Yes, all true—

You're a fucking traitor!

That is not true. We're no more traitors than you are a traitor.
The communists call you a traitor, but you are a patriot. So are we.
You did what you believed was right for the country, just as we did
what we believed was right—

Then you're idiots.

That may be true.

Oh my God, Bon says, and you realize he is crying. Oh my God.
Bon—

Is nothing sacred to you?

At first you think it is a rhetorical question, because the answer
can only be that of course some things are sacred to you. Your beliefs.
Your friendships. Your mother. Or, conversely, defiantly, the answer
is that, no, nothing is sacred! Everything can be transgressed! And
then there is the third answer, which you finally understood only
when the Boss demanded something and you refused, and so . . .

Yes, you say. Nothing is sacred.

You're such a bastard, Bon says, and he is not only crying, he is
sobbing, which you have not seen him do since his wife and child
died. A real bastard. You know that? Not because your mother was

Vietnamese and your father was French. You've used that as a crutch your whole life. No. You're a bastard because you're a traitor.

I don't accept that, Bon. You did what you thought was right—

I'm not talking about politics, you stupid bastard! I'm talking about how you and he—Man—if he's still Man—how you betrayed me. And not only betrayed me. You betrayed us. Everything we stood for—our friendship—our loyalty—our oath—

I kept my oath, Bon! I went with you to Thailand and Laos. I went with you to the reeducation camp. I did my best to keep you alive. I was willing to die for you and I'm still willing to die for you. I'm your blood brother.

No! Bon shouts. Neither of you are my brothers!

He holds up his left hand, the scar a livid red line dividing the palm. An adolescent oath you all swore. A teenage commitment to a life of loyalty and friendship. Idealism branded into the skin. A bond that would never, you said, be broken.

If I could, Bon says, I'd cut my hand off.

No need, Bon, Man says. The solution is so much simpler.

Solution?

Why do you hesitate, Bon? Why not do what you have always done?

What have I always done?

Kill communists.

The muzzle of Bon's gun drifts between the two of you. His breathing is ragged, his expression confused. He is slowly coming face-to-face with both the truth as well as the only solution to the plot devised by the two of you, which you began laying out so many years ago in your secret cell at the lycée, in those days when revolution was romantic, death was unreal, and contradiction was only the gap between the departing train of liberty, equality, and fraternity and the platform of the colony on which you stood, stranded. But

age always reveals one's own contradictions, as Bon has pointed out. Your contradiction is that you are a bastard because of how people perceive your face, but you are also a bastard because of what you have done. That is deep, so deep you cannot see the bottom, and now it is time to face that void.

Do it, Bon, you say.

Do it? Bon says, his voice strangled.

It's time to do what has to be done.

The three of you are teenagers again, blood slick on your palms, palms stinging from the cut of the blade. An orchestra of cicadas drones in the grove, and the moon is a yellow crescent, or, as you once called it as a child, a banana. All for one and one for all! Until death do us part! Then, vows finished, you each shake hands with the others, mingling your blood. The sharp pain in your hand is a sign that you are alive, and loved, and that you love these two boys, who will be your lifelong friends and blood brothers, the family you choose. You know that Bon remembers that moment as well, as does Man, the three of you at last reunited and triangulated as Bon aims at Man, then at you, back and forth, his eyes wide, face and knuckles blanched. The compass of his barrel finally settles on you, aiming squarely between your eyes. Your ghost chorus is so excited it sings in anticipation, a doo-wop band crooning, *Do it.*

Don't feel bad, Bon, you say. *Do it.* It has to be done. *Do it.*

And when Bon pulls the trigger, you can't quite believe he actually did it, the flash of lightning that blinds you being the crack in the door as Heaven opens and closes for a split second, the bullet piercing your brain before the bang reaches your ears, and somehow you can hear the voice of God one more time, breaking His silence to say, There's nothing to be afraid of.

# CHAPTER 21

Y ou are glad that you have Le Cao Boi's authentic aviator
sunglasses, because the whiteness is blinding. Heaven's all
white, and in all of its whiteness, Heaven, or the afterlife,
or eternity, or purgatory, or limbo, or the bardo, or wherever the
hell it is you find yourself, now that you are as dead as the French
empire, looks strangely like Paradise. Everyone's dressed in white,
except for the Maoist psychoanalyst, who wears brown tweed and
green corduroy. It was actually not the voice of God you heard, just
the baritone of the Maoist PhD, who has laid down this last sheet
you have written and said:

Now, perhaps, we are ready to begin?

Begin? *Begin?* How about we *stop*? The problem with having
holes in your head is that everything leaks out! The very chic, very
tanned doctor can fix a great many things, but he cannot find the
right plugs for these leaks. That is the job of the Maoist psychoana-
lyst, with his PhD, which is the required expertise, or so your aunt
says, and you agree, since your problem, in the end, is not medical,
physical, or even metaphysical, but *philosophical*. Here the Maoist
PhD is an expert, quoting, for example, Sartre, who said that "the

hole is the symbol of a mode of being . . . a nothingness . . . the empty image of myself. I have only to crawl into it in order to make myself exist." And that is what you have done, crawling into yourself as you have written this confession, aided by the Maoist PhD, who visits every two weeks to talk to you and review what you have written over these many days, or weeks, or months, or years, or decades, or centuries, in Paradise. You meet in your room, which you share with a kind old gentleman, his hair white from his head to his genitalia. One evening you peeked up his nostrils while he slept and the cotton ball tufts inside were white as well. After a career in the colonies, he is of moderate wealth, like you, and of surprising abilities, also like you. Not long after he moved in, as the very chic, very tanned doctor gave him a checkup, the kind old gentleman started speaking to him in a foreign language, and the doctor responded in kind.

What language is that? you asked.

Arabic, the kind old gentleman said.

How did you learn Arabic?

Algeria.

You looked at the kind old gentleman's feet, but they were not black. They were quite white. You looked at the doctor and said, Are you Algerian?

I am French, he said stiffly, but my parents come from Tunisia.

Oh, you said. I just thought you were very tanned.

You are a great believer in nothing, the Maoist PhD says, looking at his notes.

I believe there is no way to avoid the void.

You have gone from being a Marxist and a communist to being a nihilist.

No! Non! Nyet! Nein! Negative! you shout. The kind old gentleman laughs from his bed. Never! Have you understood *nothing*? I am

through with your Western philosophies and beliefs and ideas and systems! Your Catholicism! Your colonialism! Your capitalism! Your Marxism! Your communism! Your nihilism, too! I am not a nihilist, for I believe in *something*—I believe *nothing is sacred*! Life is full of meaning! And I am full of principles!

Interesting, says the Maoist, sliding his yellow pad into his satchel. I have been to **CHINA**, you know. All this talk about nothingness and the void is quite **ORIENTAL**.

Fuck you, you whisper, and out loud you say, Have you read Julia Kristeva?

Of course I've read Kristeva.

You pick up *Pouvoirs de l'horreur: Essai sur l'abjection*, which you swear could have been written about you when it describes "unnamable otherness." How did Kristeva understand so well the mind of a spy, a man with two faces, who is, of necessity, even before having holes drilled in his head, empty, full only of what she calls "the void"? How did Kristeva index you the way that she has, and is she correct when she says that "it is only after his death, eventually, that the writer of abjection will escape his condition"? Because you certainly are abject, but perhaps you are a writer, at least of your own confession, and here she gives you a nail of hope on which to cling, or to be pinned: "writing, which allows one to recover, is equal to a resurrection." You read all these passages to the Maoist PhD, and since he has such difficulty understanding nothing, you conclude with this declaration: "I am comfortable only in the presence of *the nothing-at-all, the void.*"

So you see, Le Chinois? It's not only Orientals who are fascinated by nothing!

Well, she does come from Bulgaria, which is practically the Orient, the Maoist psychoanalyst says with a smile. In any case, we are close but not done yet. Or rather, you are not done yet.

Not done yet? Look how much I've written! What more do you want from me?

Besides removing those sunglasses from your face? Nothing.

Very funny, you say, not taking off your sunglasses.

The Maoist psychoanalyst says farewell, see you in two weeks, and departs. He is helping you for free, a great favor, because all the Boss's money has gone to pay for your extended stay in Paradise, where your aunt has committed you, with your approval, because what are you if not deeply committed, even if it is to nothing? Your residence is the Memory Ward, a euphemism, since some of those committed here are not quite right in the head, or so you have been told, because you feel quite right in the head, no matter what other people think. Your problem is that your head won't stop leaking. It's all Bon's fault, but the good thing about all this blood is that it provides an unlimited supply of ink for volume two of your confessions. As if volume one hadn't been enough! You would have been quite happy if your misbegotten life had provided enough material for only one volume, but here you are with so much to confess! And in case you have forgotten, your aunt has brought you volume one, which she has kindly translated into French because, she says, there is something of value in it and so that the Maoist PhD can read it. You read out loud from this translation every day to the kind old gentleman, who nods appreciatively at your pronunciation, so good that the staff and patients of Paradise regularly say, **L'INDOCHINOIS** speaks excellent French! Progress, indeed, you mutter to yourself, for at least they know not to call you **LE CHINOIS**! Regardless of whether you are **LE CHINOIS** or **L'INDOCHINOIS**, the fact of the matter is you are dead, even if you are still walking around, for Bon, after all, has fired a bullet into your head! What happens now?

You join us, your chorus of ghosts say. You pretend to ignore them and return to the problem of the yellow pad in front of you.

The Maoist psychoanalyst has brought you many yellow pads, and your aunt types up all of what you have written and rewritten, and the handsome and humorless lawyer adds copious comments to the margins. Her comments, like Stalin's, are written in blue, while your original manuscript is written in blood. Or perhaps it's just ink. Ink or blood? What's the difference?

Oh, there's a big difference, says your ghost chorus. Trust us.

The only decoration on your side of the room is a picture you have taped to the wall above your bed, clipped from a newspaper article that your aunt and the handsome and humorless lawyer brought you during one of their visits. The occasion is a march against racism and for equality, dominated by those protesting against the maltreatment of Arabs and Africans, but this black-and-white picture shows a band of young people of Vietnamese descent, which you know because the sign above their heads says VIETNAMESE IN FRANCE. Below it, the sign says IDENTITY IN INTEGRATION. Oh, how these young people give you hope! More than a crucifix or a communist flag. You recognized some members of the Union among them, including some of your clients. As Ho Chi Minh understood sixty years ago, the oppressed must stand in solidarity with one another. But what of the French with Vietnamese ancestry, many of whom feel they are not oppressed? One answer is that there is no better way to demonstrate one's Frenchness than by demonstrating, especially on the side of the oppressed. The other, related answer is that people do not have to be oppressed to march against oppression, in solidarity, against all kinds of racism, including the racism that benefits them as French people who are not Arab, or African, or black, or Muslim, or immigrant. But as remarkable as this display

of solidarity is, what strikes you the most are the three young men wearing masks. White masks. Masks almost exactly like the

one worn by Man, who has left his mark in Paris among these inspired youth. What mark have *you* left? In the hopes of achieving this identity and integration demanded by these youth, you have, with the encouragement of the Maoist PhD, the handsome and humorless lawyer, and your aunt, made many marks in writing this confession. Is that enough? Can it ever be enough? Piece it all together, your aunt says. Put it in your own words. Maybe then you can make sense of everything that happened.

What she really means is maybe you can make sense of yourself, a dead man whom others seem to think is still alive. So, in the mornings, you write. In the afternoons, you push the wheelchair of the kind old gentleman around the grounds of Paradise and tell him what you have written for the day. Oh my, he might say. Oh dear.

Are you offended? you asked him once, since you know the French are easily offended.

He looked at you with his genetically recessive blue eyes, smiled, and said, Yes, rather.

You smiled back and said, Well, monsieur, to you and any other Frenchperson who might be offended in reading my fun, playful, jocular depictions of French culture and civilization, all I can say is, Fuck you. What else can the colonized say after having been fucked by the colonizer? I guess I should also say thank you. Does that make you happy?

Yes, rather.

Very well then:

Fuck you! Thank you! Fuck you! Thank you! Fuck you! Thank you! Fuck you! Thank you! Fuck you! Thank you! Fuck you! Thank you! Fuck you! Thank you! Fuck you! Thank you! Fuck you! Thank you! Fuck you! Thank you! Fuck you! Thank you! Fuck you! Thank you! Fuck you! Thank you! Fuck you! Thank you! Thank you! Fuck you! Thank you! Fuck you! Thank you! Fuck you! Thank you! Fuck you! Thank you! Fuck you! Thank you! Fuck you! Thank you! Fuck you! Thank you! Fuck you! Thank you! Fuck you! Thank you! Fuck you! Thank you! Fuck you! Thank you! Fuck you! Thank you! Fuck you! Thank you! Fuck you! Thank you! Fuck you! Thank you! Fuck you! Thank you! Fuck you! Thank you! Fuck you! Thank you! Fuck you! Thank you! Fuck you! Thank you! Fuck you! Thank you! Fuck you! Thank you! Fuck you! Thank you! Fuck you! Thank you! Fuck you! Thank you! Fuck you! Thank you! Fuck you! Thank you! Fuck you! Thank you! Fuck you! Thank you! Fuck you! Thank you! Fuck you! Thank you! Fuck you! Thank you! Fuck you! Thank you! Fuck you! Thank you! Fuck you! Thank you! Fuck you! Thank you! Fuck you! Thank you! Fuck you! Thank you! Fuck you! Thank you! Fuck you! Thank you! Fuck you! Thank you! Fuck you! Thank you! Fuck you! Thank you! Fuck you! Thank you! Fuck you! Thank you! Fuck you! Thank you! Fuck you! Thank you! Fuck you! Thank you! Fuck you! Thank you! Fuck you! Thank you! Fuck you! Thank you! Fuck you! Thank you! Fuck you! Thank you! Fuck you! Thank you! Fuck you! Thank you! Fuck you! Thank you! Fuck you! Thank you! Fuck you! Thank you! Fuck you! Thank you! Fuck you! Thank you! Fuck you! Thank you! Fuck you! Thank you! Fuck you! Thank you! Fuck you! Thank you! Fuck you! Thank you! Fuck you! Thank you! Fuck you! Thank you! Fuck you! Thank you! No, really, fuck you.

You at last ran out of fucks, your voice hoarse. You could have gone on like this forever otherwise, regardless of the way that the staff and the patients kept looking at you as you perambulated with the kind old gentleman around the grounds of Paradise, as if *you* were crazy. Poor them. So utterly average! They have only one mind and one face each. YOU—and let's not forget yourself—are a man of two minds, a man of two faces, a man with two holes in his head, a superman with twice as many fucks to give as any ordinary man! So fuck you, La France, for fucking me, and thank you, La France, for civilizing me! *C'est la vie!* Same old shit.

   You are not truly worried about offending the kind old gentle-man. He is one of the few people—perhaps the only one—who does not seem bothered by the perpetual presence of your sunglasses. You were so seduced by his kind old eyes and genuine curiosity about you that you had told him all about yourself. The question that triggered it all was when he asked, Where are you from? Normally this question would incense you, but the kind old gentleman's kind old eyes made you pause, hesitate, and then attempt to be sincere, as if you really did give a fuck. You told the kind old gentleman where you were from, and when he gave an understanding murmur, you told him about your poor, beautiful mother, and when he murmured again, you began to unspool the entire thread of your life to him, minus the various acts of immorality, obscenity, and fatality with which you have been involved. You spoke for an hour, prodded along by the understanding murmurs and warm blue eyes of the kind old gentleman, who radi-ated empathy for you and curiosity about you. For the first time, you felt truly understood, truly listened to, and by a total stranger! You could not stop yourself. Your entire life reeled forth in paraphrase, in summary, sometimes elliptically, you being in such a rush and there being so much to say, bits and pieces of your autobiography as haiku

and epigraph and fragment, and all the while the kind old gentleman murmured and sometimes said, *Ah, bon?* And finally, at the end of an hour, you were done and you looked at the kind old gentleman expectantly, waiting for him to respond, and the kind old gentleman smiled beatifically, like Jesus Christ, or the Buddha, or Santa Claus, or Stalin, or Mao, or Ho Chi Minh, and said, with gentleness and warmth, curiosity and empathy, compassion and goodwill:

Where did you say you were from again?

So you perambulate around Paradise, the odd yet perfect couple, you who cannot stop remembering, he who cannot stop forgetting. You can tell the kind old gentleman anything, knowing he will listen with utter concentration and forget with absolute precision. You fill in the blanks of your original paraphrase of your life, over and over, with all the immorality, obscenity, and fatality included, all your deeds and misdeeds, including your daughter, Ada. She is both one of your deeds and misdeeds, so you have gotten her off to a good start in life, born from your seed, which makes her one-quarter French, three-quarters Vietnamese, and 100 percent bastard, since she, too, was born out of wedlock. You wonder if you will ever meet her, the prospect filling you with dread, since you would be the kind of father of whom a daughter can write only the most scathing memoir. And, with these two volumes of your confession, you have given her plenty of evidence.

Evidence, says the lawyer on her next visit. She is interested in you, given her specialty in representing the unforgivable. Of your three readers, she is the most challenging. Your aunt the editor reads for style and story, character and theme, while the Maoist psychoanalyst pores over your anal and erotic fixations. Admittedly you do say "shit" and "fuck" a lot, but that's because those are two of the most basic human activities!

And what about your Oedipal complex? he once asked.

*Oedipal* complex? Please! Did your immortals teach you that at the École Normale Supérieure, you Normalien? Normal . . . alien . . . heh heh heh.

He coughed, frowned, made a note in his yellow pad, and said, And what about your reading of the Eiffel Tower as a—what do you call it—a "gigantic dick"?

First of all, that was what the Boss called it, and second of all, it *is* a gigantic dick! I didn't create the absurdity in this world! I just see it!

Evidence, says the handsome and humorless lawyer, flipping through your pages. She sits in a chair in your room, while you sit in the wheelchair of the kind old gentleman, who observes the both of you from the throne of pillows on his bed.

There's a lot of it, you say.

But you're still missing one crucial piece of evidence.

Aren't you supposed to be defending me?

In order to defend a client, I have to know what a client has actually done.

Or not done.

Exactly. In your case, we know what you have not done. Less about what you have done.

I have admitted to doing quite a lot!

To be clearer: the *consequences* of what you have done.

You look around your room for comfort, but since you entered Paradise you have not seen any sign of the remedy, or hashish, or any form of the most life-sustaining liquid after water, which is to say holy water, which is to say liquor. The problem is that the angels of Paradise, as well as the very chic, very tanned doctor, have forbidden almost every form of what they call "intoxicants." As a result, you are the healthiest you have ever been, and you hate it. The one vice granted to you is cigarettes, this being France after all, and for

this benevolence your lungs are deeply, deeply grateful. You stub out your cigarette in the disgustingly overstuffed ashtray and light another one, a Gauloise.

Let's return to the scene, the handsome and humorless lawyer says.

I'd rather not.

You can't forgive the unforgivable unless you confront it.

*Forgive?* Who is there to forgive me?

Only yourself.

Ha! Now that is truly absurd. But even if I could forgive myself, who am I to ask for forgiveness? And even more important, counselor, how does one forgive the unforgivable? It's not that such forgiveness is impossible. It's simply that it's *insane!*

Let's return to the scene.

No—

The restaurant. Delights of Asia.

No one wants to return there. The food is shit. Inedible! And that, coming from me, says a lot. My people can eat almost anything. I mean, we ate Chinese shit for a thousand years! And we still suffer indigestion from it!

The handsome and humorless lawyer exhales smoke and adjusts her tie clip. Don't you know that life is a piece of shit? You have to eat it in small pieces.

Oh, brilliant! Positively philosophical! And exactly how the Chinese eat shit!

It's actually a French saying, the kind old gentleman says.

Well, now that makes sense, you say.

My dear old mother used to say that to me all the time.

Let's return to the scene, the lawyer says.

No—

There's nothing to be afraid of.

That's God talking! Not me!

Come on. You know as well as I do that there's no God. Now, the three of you are in the restaurant, standing before the cash register. Smelly and Angry are dead. Both Man and you have confessed your shared secret to Bon. Bon has his gun in his hand and your gun as well. You tell Bon to "do it." Now what did you mean by that?

What do you think I meant?

For the record, please clarify. And also tell us what you meant when you said, "It's time to do what has to be done."

Isn't it obvious?

Not to me. I wasn't there to see this scene. I wasn't even there to see the aftermath. And this is not exactly a situation where I can come to the police and say that I am representing you, since no one knows you were involved. Or rather, they do, but they have the wrong name. Joseph N'Guyen, the last man seen with one of the victims, Bon, as reported by his bereaved fiancée and confirmed by Lana.

Leave it up to the French to fuck with my name, even if it is a fake name. Or half-fake name. N'Guyen! N'Guyen! The French police can't even take the trouble to spell Nguyen correctly, even though it is the name of kings!

Perhaps that's why the press simply prefer to call you L'INDOCHINOIS.

Bullshit, bullshit, and bullshit!

Then tell us what happened.

Yes, tell us what happened, the kind old gentleman says.

What did you want Bon to do?

You can still see the barrel of Bon's gun aimed at you. There is no light at the end of its short tunnel, just a bullet with your name on it, because Bon actually knows all your names, from your birth name to your baptismal name, Joseph. This is the name

you used with Loan, pairing it with a surname not your own, Nguyen—Nguyen! Nguyen! Nguyen! The name of literally millions of people, you French bastards! Get it right!—to make you Joseph Nguyen. Your cover would have fallen apart if Lana, once contacted by the French police, had told the truth and said what your real name was. But your cover held up because Lana, for whatever reason, had covered for you. Could it be—love? You shudder at such a blasphemy as someone loving you, just as you shudder at being named after the most famous cuckold in Christian history. Your baptismal name is apt, for God, if He exists, has fucked you over many times. This final rendezvous with your blood brothers is only further proof of His unholy delight as you hear Bon ask, in his strangled voice, Do it?

Don't feel bad, Bon, you say. *Do it.* It has to be done.

Yes, we know, says the lawyer. You wrote it in your confession.

You adjust your sunglasses and look above her at the picture of the trio pinned to the wall. Isn't it funny?

I don't see what's so funny about it.

Of course you don't. I mean, isn't it funny how they're wearing white masks?

I was there for that march. Those are *yellow* masks.

Yellow—You burst out laughing. *Yellow* masks! Who can tell, in a black-and-white photograph, whether something or somebody is yellow? Or rather, in a black-and-white photograph, yellow can only appear to be white. I want one of those yellow masks, you say. Man only left me with his white mask. I'll make you a deal. You bring me a mask, I'll take off these sunglasses.

The lawyer looks at the mask hung above your bed. I can arrange for a yellow mask, she says. But you keep dodging my question. Just like you dodged the bullet.

*Dodged the bullet?* Have you seen the holes in my head?

There are no holes in your head.

I can put my fingers right on them. See?

What did Bon do after you told him that something must be done?

Do you know my greatest talent?

To see any issue from both sides?

Yes! You *are* a close reader! Even there, in Delights of Asia, with my best friend and blood brother aiming his gun at me, I could see the issue from both sides, even though any normal person would see the issue from only the side of self-preservation. Any normal person would have begged for his life, pleading with Bon to remember our childhood, our blood brotherhood, our oath, sacrificing all dignity and self-consciousness, as if life were the most important thing of all. But life is not the most important thing. Principles are. Bon knew that very well, as do I. We are both men of unswerving principles! And so, when I told him to do it, I knew what I was telling him to do. To follow through. Now, to answer your question, I must do what I do best, which is to look right into his head and see from his point of view, which means to see me through his eyes, since he was looking at me as well as at Man. Man was watching the entire time in case you need an eyewitness, although I don't know why you would, given that I am perfectly capable of saying to myself, *J'accuse!* Accused, accursed, I stand before you, my handsome and humorless lawyer, as I stood before Bon, who saw me exactly as I was. What was I? Not his bête noire! There was nothing black about me! No, I was his bête blanche, a communist, a traitor! How he looked upon me with such horror! My appearance appalling, my true face hideous, I was no longer his friend—I was a monster!

Now came his greatest test, the one that happens for all of us, when our thesis and antithesis collide. Our actions then reveal us for who we truly are. On the one hand, his oath to me, his blood

brother. On the other hand, his oath to killing his enemies. And there I stood before him, both in one, blood brother and mortal enemy. How would he resolve this contradiction between love and hate, friendship and betrayal? I believed the answer was simple. I believed there was only one solution. How I misjudged! How I did not understand Bon! How I actually couldn't see the world through his eyes until now! Now I can feel the weight of the gun in his hand as well as the weight of his decision. I will kill him, he thought. I have to kill him, the son of a bitch, the motherfucker, the bastard! He's a communist! A traitor! I have killed so many, this one will be easy. He's standing five feet away and I cannot miss, especially given how big his head is, how high that forehead to which so many of our teachers pointed as a sign of his intelligence. I was always the stupid one. Smart enough to get a scholarship, but in Saigon I learned that the smartest village boy was still a bumpkin compared with a city boy. I left the academics and wordplay to them. I couldn't beat them when it came to books. Where I beat them was on the fields, with my body. I outran, outfought, outshot them. Leave it to the smart guys like him to beat the communists with words and ideas. I'll stick to killing communists.

Even before I came to the lycée, I'd already killed my first communist. He was the rat who betrayed my father to the communist infiltrators as the head of the village. The communists made my father kneel in the middle of the village, made my mother and me and all my brothers and sisters watch from the front row. We wept and cried, saying, Ba, Ba, Ba, over and over, begging the communists not to harm our father, all while Ba did not cry or scream or beg at all. He knew he was going to die, and he gave us the greatest gift he could. He showed us we must face everything with strength and dignity, even our own end. He showed us that principles matter more than life. His last words to me were, Con oi! Obey your

mother and take care of her, con oi! Don't make her life hard, which he said while they tied his hands behind his back and denounced him. They told him to confess and he said, Confess to whom? You're not my priest. So they hung a sign around his neck that said PUP-PET. And when they fired a bullet into his head, he fell, his strings cut. I screamed so loud I can hear it now, twenty-eight years later:

## BA OI!!!

## BA OI!!!

# BA OI!!!

But no matter how hard I screamed, no matter how much I shook him or hugged him, he would not get up. His eyes were open, but he saw nothing. His mouth was open, but he said nothing. His blood was on my face, my shirt, my hands. His brains were spilling out of his head and I can feel them even now, soft and slippery in my hands. Ba oi, Ba oi, Ba oi . . . I would never scream that way again until Linh and Duc died.

God! Why have You done this to me?

God! Why have You taken away those whom I loved with every part of myself?

God! Why have You made it so hard for me to believe in You?

God! Why have You turned my blood brother into the devil?

God! What do You want me to do that I haven't already done for You?

I try to understand, God. You tested my father, and he passed. He now sits at Your feet in Heaven, looking down on me, with Linh and Duc at his side. I try to understand, God, and perhaps what I understand is that I may never join my father, my wife, and

my son in Heaven. I have killed so many communists, and while they all deserved to die, and while my priests have absolved me, I understand that perhaps You may not, which is why You insist on punishing me eternally. But why punish me, God, when I love You, when You have given me this talent to kill so many of these godless communists who hate You? God, I sacrificed them for You!

I remember very well that first communist I killed. I planned for killing that rat from the moment my father died. That was why I saved the rope used to bind my father's hands. I was only ten. I had to wait and prepare myself. I ran until I was the fastest in the village. I worked the fields until I was the strongest among the boys, and I wrestled until no boy could beat me. And I wasn't going to be some common soldier, because common soldiers couldn't kill that many communists. So I studied hard to get out of the village and become an officer someday and command men and kill many, many communists. And the night before I left for Saigon and the lycée, I waited in hiding for the rat, whom I had been watching for four years. I knew his routine, his path from house to outhouse, and late one evening when he passed by, I sprang out of the thicket, wrapped the rope that bound my father around the rat's neck, and dragged him into the thicket. He didn't scream. Just gurgled, then died, and I dragged his body to the river and tied him to a sack of rocks with that rope and threw him in. And I regret nothing.

Can You forgive me for that, God?

And for what I must now do?

Why do I hesitate?

The barrel is aimed squarely between his eyes. I cannot miss. I have never missed at this range. But why am I more afraid than him? The crazy bastard looks happy, like he wants it. I can see every detail of his face, and I recognize every detail, unlike with Man,

whose half-human face I cannot recognize at all. I will kill him, too, as soon as I—

But I can see every detail . . .

And I can see beneath the details . . .

I see not only his face now but the face he once wore, when we were fourteen, just boys. And on that young boy's face, I see the future, although what I cannot see is his fate, and mine. What I see instead are hope, idealism, love, brotherhood, sincerity, and pain as he slices his palm and swears his oath. To us. I can still feel the stickiness and the slipperiness of his blood on my stinging palm, mingling with my blood as we grasp each other's hands and become one. Oh, God! My God . . . forgive me.

Those were the days when we were young, and innocent, and pure.

# EPILOGUE

## *Tu*

The bullet shattered Bon's head and blew pieces of it all over the restaurant, then ricocheted off a wall, bounced off the floor, and pierced your temple, or perhaps it was your crown, leaving this second hole that will now not stop leaking. You screamed, and some part of you has not stopped screaming since, even though you are dead. You ran to Bon, who had collapsed as his father must have, doing nothing to break his fall, shattered head smashing against the tiled floor with a sickening crack, which echoed something breaking inside of you. Oh my God, you cried, even though you don't believe in God.

You knelt before Bon with your hands hovering over him, not touching him, not wanting to hurt him, and not knowing how to help him. His eyes were open, his mouth open, and you could see right into his head. There was nothing you could do. There's nothing we can do, Man said, kneeling next to you, his knees in the blood spilling from Bon's head.

But there must be something, you said, or screamed. Call an ambulance!

Bon is dead.

387

When you told Bon that he had to do it, that he knew what had to be done, this was not what you meant. How could he not understand? Wasn't it *obvious* that he was supposed to kill *you*, not himself?

Bon is dead.

How can he be dead when you have written about him over so many pages, over two volumes of your confessions? You have read and reread your confessions, and in them Bon is alive, still alive, forever alive. He must live! This is how you have kept him away from the shade of death and in the light, until now.

Bon is dead.

Call an ambulance!

What will we do when the police show up? How do we explain this mess?

Mess? This is Bon!

Bon's dead. And there is nothing we can do to bring him back.

But are your confessions merely nothing? You have written more than seven hundred pages. Who knew your life warranted this many words, you, a nobody who believes in nothing? But then again, most people are nobodies. Most of these nobodies may believe in God, but they are not so different from you. They also believe in nothing, except that they refuse to admit it. Nothing is sacred, and nothing is everywhere, just like God, for whom nothing is only another name. Nothing can bring back the dead, who come from nothing and return to nothing. No, nothing can be done, except for this, the words you have written, your only remedy, the thing to which you are the most committed.

Now you are done. You have given the handsome and humorless lawyer what she wants, the final piece of evidence in the case for you or against you, depending on one's point of view. You have also

given the Maoist psychoanalyst with a PhD what he wants, not so much a case to defend or to prosecute, but a case study to analyze. Although this was not actually a confession, he said on his last visit.

Oh, no? What is it then?

A suicide note, he said with great satisfaction. The longest suicide note in history.

And you laughed and laughed and laughed. A suicide note! You didn't think he had such a great sense of humor! You have committed to many things, and you have committed many things, but you have not yet committed suicide. Could a dead man commit suicide? That would take some real commitment, but are you not among the most committed men who ever lived?

Adorno wrote that we should be wary of committed writers, the Maoist PhD said. They are always committed to power.

Adorno! You hadn't heard his name since Professor Hammer's seminar, where you read his and Horkheimer's *Dialectic of Enlightenment*, written in one of the most unenlightened places on earth, Los Angeles, where you, like them, had been exiled, in their case from Nazi Germany. As thinkers and writers, they likely believed that power indeed comes from the barrel of a pen, perhaps even more than the barrel of a gun. While the colonizers, the capitalists, and the communists have slaughtered millions with their guns, were they not ultimately, in the last instance, driven by words, by ideas that flowed in the ink of the great philosophers, or sometimes just the demonic demagogues? You press the barrel of your pen against your temple and you cannot count the number of pens that you have gone through in writing your confession, all those spent cartridges of your favorite color, black, as indelible as squid ink, as dark as your interior, and the kind old gentleman, who had been watching and listening as always, said with the greatest of kindness, I think you must be mad.

Mad? Me? Perhaps. And you laughed and laughed and laughed and said, But let's look on the bright side, shall we? If only the insane can forgive the unforgivable, then I can now forgive myself.

Even with this power, you cannot forgive yourself, because you are preoccupied with whether Bon will ever forgive you. You wait for Bon to join your chorus of ghosts, so that you can at least see him again, but he does not appear. What does this mystery mean?

As for Man, your aunt tells you that he has left the embassy and returned to the homeland. You have no information about the status of his face. Why aren't you crying? you had demanded of Man, tears gushing from your eyes. Where did your body store its incredible quantity of fluid? Was there an aquifer somewhere above your gut, connected by a siphon to the tear ducts? Or was your body just a sponge, absorbing sorrow, and grief, and melancholy, and regret over the years, drop by salty drop, until the hands of pain and loss gathered your body in their grip and squeezed?

Why aren't you crying?

Man looked at you with reddened eyes that had neither eyelashes nor eyebrows. I can't cry anymore. My tear ducts have been burned shut. He took out a small vial and applied drops of clear liquid to each eye. He kept applying the drops until his eyes flooded and tears of saline lubricant rolled down his cheeks. This is how I cry now.

You do not recall how long the two of you sat with Bon's body, but you assume it was hours before you stopped shaking and shuddering from being wrung nearly dry by the hands of pain and loss. The dust washed from your eyes, you see very clearly, but your body feels off-kilter, given that it has been squeezed so hard and so much liquid has been lost. You watch as Man removes all forms

of identification from the bodies of Smelly, Angry, and Bon, and you watch yourself as you clasp Bon's hands, rub his arms and shoulders, pat his chest and cheeks, close his eyes and mouth, lie down next to him in his blood and get as close to him as you can, and you can see yourself doing all of this even during those moments when your eyes are closed. You watch as Man lifts you from the ground and ushers you out of Delights of Asia, and you watch as you moan at the door, looking one last time at Bon, until Man says that it's three in the morning and time to leave. The street is deserted. Man takes you to the Boss's car, drives you to your aunt's, explains the situation tersely. You watch yourself point the way to the Boss's cash and request—no, *demand*—that they check you into Paradise. And here you are, safe in your asylum, one of the committed.

The question is: Committed to what? You have had two years in Paradise to ponder that question, to reflect on your life and the shattered bits of Bon's head, to confess to the crimes you have committed, to acknowledge that after everything you have been through, everything you have done, you are still committed to revolution, which must mean you're crazy, but no crazier than the first idealistic cavewoman who dreamed of conjuring fire from nothing, whose fate, after she discovered fire, was most likely being burned at the stake by the more cynical cavemen who knew that fire was really something, was power itself, so that even back then at the earliest moments of human civilization, the dialectic was moving back and forth between aspiration and exploitation, a movement that will never stop, for you agree with Mao that the dialectic is infinite, with one important exception, for unlike Mao and Stalin and Winston Churchill and King Leopold and a lot of American presidents and English kings and French emperors and Catholic popes and Oriental despots and countless millions of fathers, husbands,

boyfriends, lovers, and playboys, you do not believe that such a dialectic requires the sacrifice of millions in the name of communism or capitalism or Christianity or nationalism or fascism or racism or, indeed, sexism, of which you are guilty, guilty, abjectly guilty, and this conviction in an infinite dialectic that does not require enforcement by a Repressive State Apparatus, this article of faith that history's wheels need not be oiled by blood, this skepticism about Fanon's belief in the positive benefits of violence, justifiable given the brutality of French violence in Algeria, but nonetheless blind to the possibility that violence could make us feel like men yet behave like devils, whereas *non*violence could detoxify us and free us from our inferiority complexes, lift us from despair and fear, and restore the self-respect we need for action, and instead of making us mirror images of our colonizers, *non*violence could break the mirror altogether and liberate us from the need to see ourselves in the eyes of our oppressors, forcing us into the disturbing space of the negative, the nothing, the blank, the void, where we must create ourselves anew, each of us unique, each of us in solidarity with others in their uniqueness, a sincere but maybe stupid belief that makes you a man of either vision or hallucination, but one who insists that humanity already knows everything it needs to know to save itself without resorting to murder, beginning with what the most sympathetic Federico García Lorca, assassinated by the Spanish fascists, once said, "I will always be on the side of those who have nothing and who are not even allowed to enjoy the nothing they have in peace," an empathetic principle that, *if followed with action,* whether it is doing something or doing nothing, depending on the dialectical need of the situation, will never lead you in the wrong direction, even if that direction is death, since so many people are committed to the exact opposite principle, to side with those who already have something and want everything, and if you

were sane you would side with them, too, but revolution is always an act of insanity, because revolution is not a revolution unless it is committed to the impossible, although if this is too depressing and daunting one needs to remember that only a few thousand years ago it was beyond the human imagination that one could travel around the world in a day, an amazing feat that has brought the world together, so that today nowhere in the world is beyond the reach of tourists, investors, missionaries, and intercontinental ballistic missiles, meaning that the infinite dialectic still swings back and forth between the impossible and the possible, between salvation and annihilation, between nonviolence and violence, between our capacity to save ourselves and destroy ourselves, and the only real mystery is which part of us—our humanity or inhumanity—will triumph in the human species' perpetual game of Russian roulette with itself, and you yourself, human and inhuman, are demented enough to believe that if the human species does not self-destruct—an IF that should be capitalized, it is so big—then one day the nobodies of the world with nothing to lose will finally have enough of not having enough and realize that they have more in common with the nobodies on the other side of the world, or just the other side of the nearest border, than they do with the somebodies of their own kind who care nothing about them, and when these nobodies with nothing finally do unite, stand up, take to the streets, and claim their voices and their power, the only thing that the somebodies with something must do is nothing, realizing that their Ideological State Apparatus cannot stop all these people, because for all of its might their Repressive State Apparatus cannot kill them all. Can it?

Your head hurts from thinking about the answer to that question, which is made all the more difficult because of the two holes in your head. After reeducation at the hands of Man, you thought you had hit bottom, with nothing to lose, but you were so very wrong.

You had Bon to lose. And the last of your illusions. Not to mention your life. Now, fortunately, you have pulled yourself together, even though, unfortunately, you are dead. Now, perhaps, you are no longer full of self-pity, for you, a nobody, have no self left to pity! You truly have nothing to lose, except now you know that not only is nothing more important than independence and freedom—*nothing is sacred.* What a joke! But the only revolution you can commit to is the one that lets you laugh and laugh and laugh, because the downfall of every revolution is when it loses its sense of absurdity. This, too, is the dialectic, to take the revolution seriously but not to take the revolutionaries seriously, for when revolutionaries take themselves too seriously, they cock their guns at the crack of a joke. Once that happens, it's all over, the revolutionaries have become the state, the state has become repressive, and the bullets, once used against the oppressor in the name of the people, will be used against the people in their own name. That is why the people, if they wish to survive and to dodge those bullets, must be nameless.

As for you, nameless, stateless, and selfless, the bullet remains lodged in your head, stuck in the seal between your two minds, as stubbornly wedged as a morsel of gristle and meat between your molars. You wiggle the bullet with your thoughts, but you cannot dislodge it. This bullet with your name on it is embedded where no one can see either it or your name, a thing that would drive you crazy, except that you are apparently already crazy. You must be deranged to write this confession, or maybe you have only been seized by the same impulse that drove Rousseau to write his confession, to acknowledge how "I am not made like any that I have seen; I venture to believe that I was not made like any that exist." You have haunted yourself in writing these pages, but you

have also sensed a shadow of another steadily creeping over them, a sense of spookiness that makes you uneasy, as if you are being watched, and not just by yourself. And then, one morning—at last!—the spook knocks on the door.

Someone's knocking on the door, the kind old gentleman says from his bed.

You cannot get up from your bed because the headache induced by the bullet in your brain is too much to overcome. You neither get up nor say anything, but after a pause the knocking continues.

Excuse me, the kind old gentleman says. Someone's knocking on the door.

The knocking continues. And continues. And continues, until finally you muster what concentration you have left, given the bullet in your brain, and say, Come in.

The door opens and the morning light floods into your chamber, which has its blackout curtains tightly drawn. You squint, and in the dazzling haze you see *him* enter, a shadow encased in a glowing nimbus, backlit by a halo. You lurch up from your bed, raising a hand to ward off the light, the hand with the burning brand of your oath. Is it—could it be?—tentatively, you extend your other hand toward the shadow framed in the doorway—it is! It's *him*! *He* is here, at last!

Father? you say, a catch in your voice. *Father!*

The shadow comes into your chamber, carrying a bag in his hand. He throws it onto the foot of your bed with a heavy thump, and when he unzips it, you recognize your leather duffel. He slips his hand into its slit and takes out a pair of shoes—your beautiful, polished brown Bruno Magli oxfords! The shadow throws them onto the floor and inserts his hand into the slit again and removes, one by one, the videos of the orgy, which you recognize by the luscious secretary's handwriting on the labels. Then he digs into

the slit even deeper, all the way into the false bottom, and extracts the two volumes of your confession, rubber-banded and white, which he tosses onto your lap, more than seven hundred pages and approximately a quarter million words, which impress you with their weight, their solidity, their miraculous existence, generated from nothing. But he's not finished. Your duffel must be bottomless! He reaches in again and produces the most beautiful thing you have seen in your deprived time in Paradise: a gleaming bottle of Jack Daniel's whiskey! Come to Daddy, sweet baby! Finally, with the other hand, he brings forth an equally gleaming silver-plated revolver. For a moment you are hypnotized by the light reflecting from the gun. Then you look up. Your eyes have adjusted to the sun's morning glare, and the shadow's face is clear to you now. It is not your father after all, but the spookiest of all spooks, the man who knows exactly what you want, the old Indochina hand.

Didn't I tell you never to commit your thoughts to paper, you stupid bastard? Claude says, offering you the holy water with one hand while with the other he aims the gun at your beaten heart. Now take that goddamned mask off your face.

And you are so happy you don't know whether to laugh or to cry.

historically absurd"; Jean-Jacques Rousseau, *Confessions*; Jean-Paul Sartre, *Existentialism and Human Emotions*, and his introduction to Fanon's *The Wretched of the Earth*; and Voltaire, whose *Candide* I first read and was greatly amused by as a boy.

Among the texts that helped me imagine Paris of the early 1980s, oriented around the world of Vietnamese immigrants, refugees, and their French descendants, I am indebted to Gisele Bousquet's invaluable *Behind the Bamboo Hedge: The Impact of Homeland Politics in the Parisian Vietnamese Community*, as well as the images in *Le Paris Asie: 150 ans de présence asiatique dans la capitale*, edited by Pascal Blanchard and Éric Deroo. Also useful in understanding and visualizing France's relationship to its colonized populations were the essays and images in *Sexe, race & colonies: La domination des corps du XVe siècle à nos jours*, edited by Pascal Blanchard, Nicolas Bancel, Gilles Boetsch, Dominic Thomas, and Christelle Taraud. For the history of French and CIA involvement in the production and selling of Southeast Asian opium, I relied on Alfred McCoy's *The Politics of Heroin: CIA Complicity in the Global Drug Trade*.

Several people in Paris or with connections to France were generous with their time in talking to me, including Hoai Huong Aubert-Nguyen, Doan Bui, Myriam Dao, Anna Moï, Nguyen Nhat Cuong, Liem Binh Luong Nguyen, Abdellah Taïa, and Quoc Dang Tran. Duc Ha Duong helped secure permission from the Union Générale des Vietnamiens de France for my use of the photo of the three masked men. I am also grateful to Chiori Miyagawa, Jordan Elgrably, Huê-Tâm Webb Jamme, and Laila Lalami for having read the novel in draft form and responding to my questions about the novel and French life and attitudes. In the United States, a visit to an exotic Asian-themed restaurant with food critic Soleil Ho helped me to imagine the bar Opium. I am also appreciative of the work of my graduate research assistants, Rebekah Park and Jenny Hoang, as

well as my undergraduate assistants, Yvette Chua, Ivy Hong, Nina Ibrahim, Sunjay Lee, Morgan Milender, Christine Nguyen, Tommy Nguyen, and Jordan Trinh. They helped give me time to focus on the novel, while Nancy Tan's copyediting, and additional proofreads by Kait Astrella and Alicia Burns, helped me polish the manuscript. Any mistakes I have made in this book are of course my own.

The MacArthur and Guggenheim Foundations provided fellowships that helped greatly in the writing of this book, as did the research support of the University of Southern California and its Dornsife College. My agents Nat Sobel and Judith Weber have been stalwart advisors, and the staff at Sobel Weber Associates have made my life easier, including Kristen Pini and Adia Wright. I am also fortunate to be an author with Grove Atlantic, which has been an ideal home, particularly with Morgan Entrekin's leadership, Peter Blackstock's superlative editorial guidance, and the support of Deb Seager, John Mark Boling, Judy Hottensen, Elisabeth Schmitz, and Emily Burns.

Finally, as always, my deep love and commitment to Lan Duong and our children, Ellison and Simone.

Read on for an essay by Viet Thanh Nguyen
and a reading group guide by Keturah Jenkins.

A version of this essay first appeared in the
*Washington Post* on May 3, 2018.

# CANON FODDER

I n 1992, as a first-year PhD student at Berkeley, I told the English
department chairman, a famous Americanist, that I wanted to
write a dissertation on Vietnamese and Vietnamese American
literature. "You can't do that," he said, fretting over my ambition
to teach in a university English department. "You won't get a job."
Since even my Marxist mentor agreed with the chair, I took the
safer route and wrote a dissertation on Asian American literature,
a subject in which *some* people had gotten tenure-track professo-
rial positions.

Still, this was not an easy path, as a scholar of Chicano literature
told me with a note of anger in his voice: "We have to read their
literature, but they don't have to read ours." He meant that we, in
the minority, would always have to know the minds of the major-
ity, a favor the majority knew it did not have to return. Knowledge
of this kind meant survival for the minority. Ignorance of this kind
was an expression of privilege for the majority.

I've been thinking of those years again because, somehow, the
decades-long war over what to include in the literary canon rages

on. A few years ago, at Barnard College in New York City, some English majors wanted greater diversity in their curriculum. "After years of experience, I would say 'too bad' to those students," Anne Lake Prescott, a senior scholar and professor emerita of English, told the university newspaper. "In order to understand later literature you need to have read some Shakespeare, Milton, Tennyson. This is good background for an English major. The brutal part of my mind says, 'If you don't like it, don't major in English.' Many professors would feel that if you don't give the basics of the British literature supplemented by American literature, you simply can't understand some of the moderns."

This "brutal" thinking is ever more vocal in American culture. The rise of anti-immigrant and anti-refugee xenophobia on the right finds a parallel in attacks against "identity politics" on the left. The right blames newcomers, foreigners, and minorities for the cultural and economic decline of the country. The left blames the same groups for insisting too strongly on their identities, which allegedly alienates some white people, distracts from the need to focus on inequality and, in academia, threatens the canon. People like me and the Barnard students who want to read different kinds of literature are the barbarians at the gate, the supposed purveyors of these identity politics. These battles are no longer restricted to higher education. The "culture wars" of the 1980s and 1990s over the dangers of multiculturalism and "political correctness" to the American body politic have morphed and grown even more intense, extending to high school and grade school curricula. The new and supposedly mortal dangers to the unity of the United States: "critical race theory" and pernicious works like *Beloved*, which some parents advocate for removal from school libraries.

I arrived at the University of California at Berkeley in 1990, already suspecting that I was one of the barbarians threatening

Western culture. I had gone to an elite, mostly white high school in San Jose, where I was one of the few students of Asian descent. We knew we were different. Every day at lunch, we gathered in a corner of the campus and called ourselves "the Asian invasion." I was primed to become what I did at Berkeley—an Asian American. The term was coined in 1968 by activists Yuji Ichioka and Emma Gee. Before then, we were "Orientals" at best, the "yellow peril" at worst, excluded from the Western canon except when Western cannons were aimed at us. (To people to whom all Asians looked alike, it didn't matter that Asian Americans were not the same as Asians: We were all foreigners who didn't belong.)

I am a descendant of Caliban, the character who learned the master's language, including how to curse in it. Still, my love for English, and the Western canon, runs deep. In college, as an English major, I read many of the Greek classics, Chaucer, Shakespeare, a good number of the Romantics and the Victorians, plus a considerable amount of American literature. I never thought of becoming a scholar of English. (How could I go home to my Vietnamese refugee parents, who worked 12- to 14-hour days in their grocery store, and say that I wanted to study Jane Austen or Lord Byron?) But I could enjoy the study of literature until I had to go to law school and begin a life of quiet desperation.

For people of color, double consciousness is second nature, something we experience every day, something I am reminded of whenever I am the only nonwhite person in an academic or literary setting, which happens often. But too many white people are not used to two-ness, to seeing themselves as both an American (or a European) and a white person. This awareness of one's own privilege as part of the majority is completely absent from the traditional great books curriculum, and its themes would be unrecognizable to centuries of authors who emerged from the majority in their homelands.

Some white people accept their visibility and make room for other voices; they include the late Emory Elliott, an American-literature scholar whose edited volume "The Columbia History of the American Novel" covered "classic" authors as well as submerged, overlooked and forgotten ones who make up the vast complexity of American literature (and culture). But this kind of inclusion makes other whites feel themselves to be under attack—and under threat of erasure. It is these people to whom Trump spoke when he said, in his inaugural address, "You will never be ignored again." People who believe they are being forgotten in favor of minorities are not just English professors who say, "If you don't like it, don't major in English." They are also people who say, "Love America or leave it." Their version of defending the canon and expelling trouble-some writers expresses itself through building a border wall and deporting people. But it's too late to get rid of all of us. We are here because white people were there, invading—sorry, *civilizing*—our countries of origin. Americans descended from Vietnamese refu-gees, undocumented Nicaraguan immigrants and enslaved Africans cannot unlearn English. In my case, I love English and will not leave it, even if some people use it to say, "Go back to where you came from." (They can't say "Speak English," since I teach it.) I write books hoping that people like me will one day be part of the canon, even if its defenders would never welcome us. We are not destroying anything by demanding to be part of the canon or the curriculum or the country. Those building walls are the ones allowing their fear to destroy what they wish to preserve.

Here's what the brutal part of *my* mind says. The gunners of the Western canon have always declared that there is no requirement to read the Other, since there is no equivalence. We are just the natives, English our second language. The gunners would agree with Saul Bellow when he asked: "Who is the Tolstoy of the Zulus?

The Proust of the Papuans? I'd be glad to read him." Never mind that Bellow presents a false choice between culture and chaos, or that he confuses the matter by gesturing at oral cultures rather than literary ones. (And would it be so perilous to learn things from radically different cultures that do not value the same things we do?) Why *don't* we read Murasaki Shikibu's *The Tale of Genji*, Cao Xueqin's *The Dream of the Red Chamber* or Nguyen Du's *The Tale of Kieu*, all of which predate Tolstoy and Proust?

But Bellow also misses the point, which is that the cultures that produced the canonical greats also produced mass slavery and colonization that killed millions. Both Shakespeare and slaughter are part of the Enlightenment. Can we recognize both these faces of modernity? Not if we read only Shakespeare. We must read Shakespeare *and* authors who are women, Arab, Muslim, queer. Most of the world is neither white nor European, and the United States may be a majority-minority country by mid-century. White people will gain more by embracing this reality rather than fighting it. As for literature, the mind-set that turns the canon into a bunker in order to defend one dialect of English is the same mind-set that closes borders, enacts tariffs and declares trade wars to protect its precious commodities and its besieged whiteness. But literature, like the economy, withers when it closes itself off from the world. The world is coming anyway. It demands that we know ourselves and the Other.

**GROVE PRESS**

Y

**Reading Group Guide**

**by Keturah Jenkins**

# THE COMMITTED

## Viet Thanh Nguyen

## ABOUT THIS GUIDE

We hope that these discussion questions will enhance your reading group's exploration of Viet Thanh Nguyen's *The Committed*. They are meant to stimulate discussion, offer new viewpoints, and enrich your enjoyment of the book.

More reading group guides and additional information, including summaries, author tours, and author sites for other fine Grove Atlantic titles may be found on our website, groveatlantic.com.

## QUESTIONS FOR DISCUSSION

The novel opens with a quote from Rithy Panh, "Nothing's more real than nothing." Discuss how this belief shapes the characters. Share what the quote means to you.

———

Discuss the relevance of the title, *The Committed*. Which characters in the novel show commitment? Consider whether Nguyen answers the question "committed to what?"

———

*The Committed* begins with several refugees stranded at sea praying for rescue. How does the tone of the prologue set the stage for the rest of the novel? Discuss how the characters carry this early experience throughout the story.

———

The narrator is prone to bouts of weeping and refers to himself as "we." Does this duality, and existential despair, make him an unreliable narrator? Explain your answers.

———

*The Committed* offers an unflinching analysis of the aftermath of colonial conquest and the turmoil of the Vietnam War. How is the book like other novels you have read about war and the experiences of refugees, and how is it different? Share how much you knew about the displacement of the Vietnamese people before reading the novel. Did the author provide you with another perspective? Why? How so?

———

What is the importance of Bon? Analyze the effects that Bon's father's death, and then later that of his wife and son, have on who he becomes. Why do you think Bon opens up to Loan and tells her the truth about who he is?

—————————

Discuss the aunt and her left-wing friend's significance in the story? Examine the aunt's power over the narrator.

—————————

Sonny and the crapulent major are haunting the narrator and make several appearances in the novel. How does the presence of ghosts change the reading experience? What do the ghosts of the book represent to the characters? Are the readers meant to take the existence of spirits literally? Provide examples of how other characters are connected to the dead.

—————————

While in the reeducation camp, our narrator is asked this question in the final exam: "What is more precious than independence and freedom?" The correct response is "Nothing is more precious than independence and freedom" (p. 57). Later in the novel, he amends his answer with "*nothing is sacred*" (p. 365). Why does he say this? Consider what your answer would have been. Explain your reasons.

—————————

How have the blood brothers evolved since the events of *The Sympathizer*? What still connects them as brothers, and what sets them apart? How would you characterize the friendship between the narrator and Man?

—————————

The City of Light of the early 1980s and its iconic landmarks convey a sense of place as the characters try to assimilate to French culture. How does Paris also function as a character?

—————————

On page 15, the French Vietnamese aunt says, "Politics is always personal, my dear. That's what makes it deadly." Do you agree with her? Why or why not? Consider how politics is personal to you.

---

Discuss the importance of naming and why Nguyen chooses to use pseudonyms or no names for several of the main characters. By leaving the characters nameless, what do you think the author is saying about the refugee experience?

---

The Committed examines the rich complexities of friendship, loyalty, and betrayal. The novel asks the question, "How well do we know our friends?" Discuss the significance of this question.

---

On page 48, the aunt delivers a scathing indictment of America and capitalism: "The American Way of Life! Eat too much, work too much, buy too much, read too little, think even less, and die in poverty and insecurity." Discuss her views of America and compare them to your own.

---

Evaluate the ending of the book. Were you satisfied with what happened to the characters and how their stories ended? If you could change anything about the conclusion, what might you have done differently? Explain your answers.

---

## SUGGESTIONS FOR FURTHER READING

The Sympathizer by Viet Thanh Nguyen

On Earth We're Briefly Gorgeous by Ocean Vuong

The Land at the End of the World by António Lobo Antunes

*Human Acts* by Han Kang

*Interior Chinatown* by Charles Yu

*Catch-22* by Joseph Heller

*At Night All Blood Is Black* by David Diop

*Journey to the End of the Night* by Louis-Ferdinand Céline

*Tomorrow They Won't Dare to Murder Us* by Joseph Andras

*The Wretched of the Earth* and *Black Skin, White Masks* by Frantz Fanon

*The Elimination: A Survivor of the Khmer Rouge Confronts His Past and the Commandant of the Killing Fields* by Rithy Panh with Christophe Bataille